APEX

PREDATORS

By

Anthony Karrier

COPYRIGHT

DEDICATIONS

For Ron "Gus" Uguccioni

One of the finest men I've ever had the honor of working with.

And

For Barry "Big Bear" MacLagan.

A Brother who faced every battle life threw at him with strength, courage and a loyalty so fierce that no words- written or spoken- could ever do it justice.

ACKNOWLEDGMENTS

Firstly, to my agent, the amazing Marleah Stout— your dedication and influence throughout this entire process mean more than you know. I am so grateful for every text, email, and phone call. Your guidance has been a lighthouse in this journey.

To my premier and most trusted beta reader, Greta Dearing—you are the perfect combination of brilliance and ferocity. You always asked the right questions and helped me better articulate what I was trying to say. Your insight has been invaluable, and your passion for the story fueled my own.

To the most unlikely ally and self-proclaimed High Priestess, my editor Kara McCaughen— your input and ability to take the chaos I send you and turn it into something coherent is nothing short of amazing. I am eternally grateful for the thousands of discussions, even the ones that resulted in heated debates with neither of us willing to back down. You are one of my first go-to's for questions and advice, and though I don't always take your suggestions, I always listen. Thank you for all your help in shaping this story.

And most importantly, to my wife, Mitch—you have been my biggest cheerleader, soundboard, and brainstorming partner. Your unwavering support, especially when I needed it most, has been the foundation of this journey. I could not have done this without you by my side.

Each of you, in your own way, contributed to transforming the twisted idea in my head into the novel it is today. I am forever grateful for the support, insight, and love you have poured into this project.

Thank you. A-K.

Chapter 1

Friday, December 23rd, 2022, 9:28 pm. Toronto, Ontario

The outside temperature was showing -15 Celsius. The fierce wind made it feel a lot colder. A man in a black Brooks Brothers peacoat fought to stop the glass door from flying open in the wind. He staggered, trying to hold his coat closed at the collar while holding shopping bags in one hand and fighting the windblown door with the other.

A tall man, he stood six foot three and weighed two hundred and twenty pounds. He was twenty-eight years old and had the smugness that only came from third generation money. His name was Roland Friedman.

Roland was a direct heir to Friedman Family Jewelers, the same company that polluted the television and radio airwaves in Toronto for over forty years. It was a family-owned business with three large jewelry stores strategically placed throughout the Greater Toronto area. The family outwardly bragged about selling the finest jewelry in Canada, custom- made from their state-of-the-art jewelry making facilities in their stores.

They also owned a dozen smaller jewelry stores/pawnshops under a different cooperate name in the poorer neighborhoods of Toronto. They were the type of places that lowballed desperate single mothers and knowingly bought stolen merchandise from crackheads and street hoods. This is where the real money was. Buy the stolen jewelry at the pawnshops without filling out the mandatory police forms, melt it down in the shops, and resell it to the white upper class at a 5000% mark up.

Roland was quite a sight. You would never guess he was currently on bail for eleven counts of aggravated sexual assault. Roland was awaiting trial for knowingly infecting eleven girls, one as young as sixteen years old, with HIV.

"Fuck!" he cursed as the wind caught the heavy glass door blowing it out of his grip. The Christmas bells his sister Loni had hung on the doors jingled both from the wind and the impact of the doors flying open.

The Friedmans were a Jewish family. They came to Canada in 1971 from South Africa and quickly opened the first of the three Friedmans Fine Jewelry stores. Mel Friedman, the patriarch of the family, knew how to pander to his customers. Race, religion-- it didn't matter to Mel. He only saw dollars and cents. Pick a religious holiday and Mel had a sale for it.

He was also the kind of slimeball that was only concerned with how the charges against his son would hurt the family business.

When Roland was first arrested, Mel hired a private investigator to uncover every piece of dirt he could on the victims. When he discovered that this would not be admissible in court, he took to social media, flooding Facebook, Twitter, Instagram and Snapchat with every deplorable rumor he could find about the victims. When Mel couldn't find enough dirt on the youngest victim, sixteen-year-old Krista Taylor, he did not hesitate to make some up. His defamation spread like wildfire and ultimately resulted in Krista, devastated and shunned, taking her own life.

Roland rushed out and grabbed the door handle, still fighting the wind. The city was enduring a severe weather warning. Blowing snow and high winds were making the city a nightmare to drive through. He managed to push the door closed, slid his key in to lock it, and pulled it twice to make sure, the door was secure. Turning into the wind, he headed towards a 2019 Audi Q-8; his winter car.

The parking lot was a disaster. Snow had come in quick. The plaza's maintenance contractors had struggled to clear the accumulating snow and throw salt down. As soon as the salt would melt the ice, the wind would refreeze it almost immediately, making the entire parking lot a mess of ice-covered brown slush.

Fumbling with the bags in his hands and slipping on the ice, Roland cursed at the relentless wind that whipped without mercy, a steady blistering cold. In the short thirty-foot walk to his car, his forehead had been so cold it was causing physical pain. He reached his hand out for the passenger side door handle when he felt a hard THUMP on his back, as if someone had punched him between the shoulder blades, knocking the wind out of him. At the same moment, the passenger side window of his luxury SUV exploded inward. Confused, Roland looked down and noticed a small black rod about 3/8 of an inch in diameter, with what appeared to be a small silver three-bladed head, protruding about six inches from his chest.

Unaware of what had happened, his fight or flight instincts kicked in. He knew something was wrong and that he needed to get away.

He turned to run back to the family store, but his left leg wasn't cooperating. A failed attempt to run resulted in him collapsing on his left side in the slush next to his car.   A set of black leather work boots stepped out from the side of the building; thin leather, with what were once white foam rubber flat wedge soles. Soles that over time been walked so smooth, they leave no distinguished pattern. Ironworker boots.

"A decent pair will fit like house slippers when broken in properly", was how the salesmen described them. Roland lay in the slush, the cold of the asphalt under him soaked through his clothing, as he fought for breath that was becoming harder to draw in.

The killer emerged. A mountain of a man, he stood at six feet-five inches and tipped the scales at two hundred and fifty-five. pounds. Large and physically imposing, he had wide shoulders, and a thick chest, the obvious traits of some French-Canadian lumberjack in his family bloodline. He was dressed in. camouflage patterns: dark green pants, a brown and green. coat, and a dark skin mask. A black silhouette was easier to spot at night, so the killer opted for earthy colours to blend in.

The killer walked over to Roland, crouched in front of him, and with a thin pair of tactical gloves on his hands, unscrewed. The silver head of the broad head arrow that was sticking out of Roland's chest. He placed the tip back into a hard black plastic case, careful not to get any of Roland's. blood on himself. Roland gasped for air, eyes wide, and reached out, almost as if he was asking for help. The killer brushed Roland's hand away and rolled him face down. Without any warning, he wrapped his hand around the plastic. vanes on the back of the bolt, an arrow from a crossbow, and pulled it out of Roland's back with one vicious yank.

The killer pushed Roland back onto his side. Blood started to fill and dribble out of his mouth.

"I aimed just left of your spine. Tried not to clip the greater aorta," the killer explained in a calm voice as he opened. Roland's coat and used it to the clean the blood off the bolt.

"Pretty sure I nicked your heart and took out a lung. You're going to die." he continued, taking Rolland's wallet, emptying it of the cash. "You're bleeding into your lung. You'll either bleed to death or drown in your own blood. Personally, I think either one is too good for you, but I'm pressed for time."

The killer placed the arrow back into a quiver that was attached to his belt and strapped to his right thigh. He stood up straight, and took a good look around, making sure there were no witnesses. He stared at the security camera, satisfied it he wasn't in the view of the lens, and calmly walked away. Roland made one last attempt to get his phone out of his pocket. He could no longer feel his left side. He saw the faint light colouring on the soles of the killer's boots as he disappeared around the corner. His vision darkened, and he was gone.

Chapter 2
Saturday, December 24th, 2022, 7:03 am.
Toronto, Ontario

"Jesus Fucking Christ! Why are we doing this?" shouted Jim as the cold wind coming off the water cut right through his winter work clothing as if he wasn't wearing any at all.

Two men in a blue eighty-foot telescoping man-lift with the word "Genie" in white decal down the side of the boom arm started their accent to the main connection points of a new structure being erected.

"Because we're fucking idiots." said Mike, the larger of the two.

Jim and Mike. The only guys dumb enough to agree to come in on Christmas Eve, even if it was only for the morning. Jim was celebrating four years clean and sober today. 2018's horrific Christmas Eve had been fueled with cocaine, beer, and whisky, all of which had resulted in a Christmas morning spent in a holding cell, followed by an aggravated assault charge against his children's stepfather. The charge was later pleaded down and resulted in two years' probation along with mandatory participation in a substance abuse program arranged through his union.

Mike worried about Jim, especially this time of year. Jim had picked up the broken pieces and moved on. He'd found himself a new girlfriend who was also a "12-stepper" as Jim called it. But Mike knew that Christmas Eve and Christmas morning were exceptionally hard on Jim, a stark reminder of the two children that still, four years later, would not return his phone calls or text messages.

The two men agreed to come in for the morning and had just started their shift. Both men were steel erectors, or ironworkers. They were working on a large airport hangar at Pearson International Airport; a new addition for warehousing that all the major parcel shipping companies were now having built in attempts handle the nonstop bombardment of packages that accompanied the new wave of online shopping.

On this bitterly cold Christmas Eve morning, the men were tasked with bolting up and impacting all the roof connections on the west end of the structure. The trade practice has always been to get the mobile cranes offsite as fast as possible. Put up the iron, toss a few bolts into each connection and send the next piece of iron. After the iron is up and the crane is broken down and moved to the next location, then the bolt up gang comes in.

The bolt up gang does just that, plugs the holes with bolts. Generally, an anti-climactic job, especially now with new safety standards and company policies having taken all the fun out of being an ironworker, what used to be referred to as "Walking the Iron" has turned into two guys standing in a telescoping man lift working out of a basket.

Both men had their tool belts with them in the lift. Jim was wearing his, whereas Mike's winter clothing was too bulky which prevented him from being able to buckle it. Instead, his belt was buckled over the top rail of the manlift.

An Ironworker's tool belt carried a number of trade-specific tools you didn't see elsewhere, and all told could weigh as much as up to twenty-five pounds without loaded bolt bags. Two full bolt bags could easily put the tool belt over the thirty-five-pound mark. Jim would periodically tug his toolbelt back up over his hip as they quietly worked.

Along with both men and their tools, the basket also held half a keg of bolts and a one-inch pneumatic airline. Between the tools, equipment, and Mike's large frame, Jim was worried they were overloading the Manlift's five hundred pound weight limit.

Often the connection holes didn't line up on the iron beams. The tip of a two-inch diameter metal spike known as a bull pin would be placed into a bolt hole and the ironworker would bash the shit out of the pin, pulling the holes in line. Walk by any steel erecting site no matter how big or small and you'll hear the sound of sledgehammers smashing iron into place and the steady banging of the bolt-up gang pinning holes.

These adjustments were constant due to the expansion and contraction of iron with the weather. Steel or iron will usually grow or shrink around three quarters of an inch over a one-hundred-foot span depending on the outside temperature. On cold days like in late December, the iron would shrink, and the crew would spend all day fighting to line up iron that was too short. On hot summer days, the iron expanded, and they conversely spent all day fighting with iron that was too big. The phrase "65 and sunny" was commonly uttered when erecting, referring to 65 degrees Fahrenheit and sunny as the optimal conditions in which to work.

The task was simple: get up to the top of the structure, bolt up the connections, and then impact the bolts. The men needed to complete the west end of the structure as soon as possible as there was a shipment of decking, a type of corrugated steel roofing, being delivered on Thursday. The structure needed to be completed before the extra weight from the bundles of decking was added to the roof, and with Christmas holidays falling on Sunday and Monday the next two days were statutory holidays.

Anybody who has worked outdoors in a Canadian winter will tell you, the only thing worse than being cold is being cold and wet. The damp air in Southern Ontario, which was perfectly situated in the middle of three of the Great Lakes, made working outdoors in the winter miserable and slow-going.

The two guys made it to the first connection. Standing in a basket fifteen meters in the air made it feel even colder, with wind whipping at them and nowhere to hide. Mike, wearing layers, struggled to move around his smaller partner.

Taking the pin out of his belt, Mike placed it in a hole and began smashing the mushroomed end. After a dozen good solid whacks, Jim was ready. He popped a bolt into the hole above the bull pin and slapped the washer and nut onto it. They continued the process more times until all eight bolts were installed. Jim lifted the pneumatic impact gun, slid the socket over the nut and pulled the trigger. The air that shot out of the bottom of the gun was blisteringly cold and wet. A steady high-speed mist of water, air, and air tool oil blasted at Mike.

"Hold it, hold it, hold it!" Mike yelled. "'Fuck sakes dude that's blowing right in my face."

"Alright, fuck it. It's too fucking cold for this shit." conceded Jim as he made the executive decision that enough was enough. He lowered them back to the ground. They shut down the big air compressor trailer, wrapped up the air line, put their tools and tool belts back in the shipping container, locked it up, and walked back to the lunch trailer.

Stomping up the aluminum stairs and knocking the snow and mud off their boots, they walked into the trailer and were greeted with a thick cloud of cigarette smoke. David, the job's foreman, sat inside. He was a large First Nations man with the type of build that comes from physically demanding work coupled with a terrible diet of red meat and beer. He was fat, but he had a solid layer of hardened muscle under that fat. At fifty-three years old, he could still run circles around guys twenty-five years younger, both at work and in a bar fight. He was sitting in the trailer smoking cigarettes again.

"What's the problem?" he bellowed from behind the partition separating the lunchroom from his office.

"It's too fucking cold out there!" hollered Jim.

They heard the sounds of David's chair scratching across the floor as he got up from his desk. The noise from a Netflix movie he had been watching at his desk stopped as he hit pause and stomped over to the doorway.

"Fuck do you mean, too cold?" he asked, frustrated, and annoyed.

"I mean it's too fucking cold out there to be up in the air!" Jim snapped back.

Mike had always been amused by ironworkers or construction trades in general. He often thought this was the only job in the world where you could argue, swear at, and even have a fist fight with your superior on a regular basis and still have a job the following morning. Ironworkers especially were a rare breed. Their world was very different. Most of them learned a number of life lessons quickly, like just because you're the foreman on today's job doesn't mean you won't be working for the guy you just fired on tomorrow's job. There was no seniority, often it seemed as if there was no rhyme or reason to how things worked. Most of the workers showed loyalty to each other and to their union halls. Very few cared about what companies' logo happened to be on their paycheck that week.

"Well fuck, we have the decking coming Thursday morning. I need that area done" David protested.

"So, what's stopping you?" Jim asked with a snarky tone.

Mike could tell that David was becoming increasingly more frustrated with Jim's attitude. Mike had known David since Mike was an apprentice or a "punk" as they were called at work. In most workplaces calling someone a punk would get you fired. In this world, the apprentice was a punk, that's how it was. If someone didn't like it, they were told to go flip burgers instead. Almost every ironworker apprentice was bullied and tormented throughout their apprenticeship, especially if they happened to be the boss's kid. A foreman loved or hated, that brought their kid onto a job site had to warn them in advance. "These guys will be on you like a pack of wolves on a three-legged cat!"

When Mike started, the journeymen would have betting pools on how long it would take to make an apprentice quit. By 2022 standards it was considered a toxic work environment, a lifestyle where only the strong or the stupid survived. There was something to be said about continuously returning to a job that at times had you three hundred feet in the air on a four-inch-wide I-beam.

Mike always figured a person had to be at least half insane to be and ironworker in the first place. He also believed that through an unseen force, these people were all drawn to each other. There seemed to be an almost primal instinct that made them seek each other out and align themselves together. For over a century, ironworking had rated in the top five most dangerous jobs in North America. Workers often found themselves trusting their lives to one another and, much like in the military, firefighting, or law enforcement, they did not want people who couldn't handle the stress of the job. It was a brotherhood, and each member earned their way in. Mike also knew David well enough to know he wasn't someone who's cage you wanted to rattle.

Mike interjected, "It's pretty bad out there. It's cold as shit and the wind is terrible. It's blowing us all over the place in the basket. I know we need this done, but it won't work today".

Ironworkers also learn early in their careers that the word "can't" is seriously frowned upon at work. When a job or task is not able to be completed properly the term most often used it "It won't work".

David stood in the doorway, twisting his lit cigarette by the filter. "How about Wednesday? Can we get it done then?"

"For double time? Sure!" replied Jim.

"Hey! Shut up," Mike glared at Jim. Turning to David he confirmed, "Yeah, we can try to come in on Wednesday if the weather cooperates. Sorry brother, but its nasty up there today"

David understood and nodded. It wasn't long ago that he had been the guy in the basket, and after this hanger addition he could very well find himself in the basket again. "Alright," he relented. "Go home."

Mike was already stripping off his outer layers. "You're not supposed to be smoking in the trailer," he teased his foreman.

David, turning away to shut down his laptop and pack up his belongings to head home, called back, "I don't see anybody here big enough to stop me."

Mike and Jim finished taking off their winter layers, grabbed their lunch pails, and headed for Mike's truck. They hopped in and fired it up, waiting for the heater to clear the fog off the inside of the windshield. Fortunately, the truck had not been sitting long, and within a few minutes the windshield was clear and they were driving away.

"Hey, you want to stop fucking with Dave, please? I put my name out for him to hire you and you've been acting like a dick since day one." Mike scolded.

Jim looked at Mike like a dear caught in the headlights and innocently asked, "What do you mean?"

"I mean you're acting like an asshole. Cut it out."

"What are you talking about? I haven't said anything," Jim defended.

The truck slowly rolled up to the security gate, Jim passed his work ID over to Mike. Rolling down his window, Mike tapped both work IDs on the electronic scanner and waited for the gate to open.

"Maybe that's the problem; you not realizing when you're an asshole. The 'So what's stopping you', and 'For double time' comments. He's already not happy. You're antagonizing him." Mike elaborated.

Jim sighed loudly. "I was just kidding".

"Well, he's about this close," Mike held the tip of his index finger and thumb apart about a millimeter, "to laying you off, and likely throwing in a beating when he does. So cut it out 'cause I'm not standing in his way if he thumps you." said Mike.

Jim knew exactly what Mike was talking about. Deep down, Jim still harbored a lot of resentment. He was angry that for four years he had been working on redeeming himself, but all his coworkers saw was the fall-down drunk he used to be. He felt like no matter how hard he worked or how well he did, people will always associate him with who he was and not who he is now. It seemed like Mike was the only guy that didn't kick him while he was down. And this was why Mike and Jim were friends. When Jim was at his worst, Mike was always there.

That loyalty didn't come easy though. Mike would help Jim when he needed it. Mike was the one who drove Jim six hours away for rehab after his Christmas Eve from hell. But Mike had always made it clear to Jim that he had a breaking point, and on more than one occasion Jim had tap-danced near the edge of it.

When Jim finished his rehab sentence, as he called it, Mike was there to meet him. As they drove home, Jim mentioned he had no idea where his tools were. When they got close to Jim's place, Mike pulled off the highway and hit a local store frequented by all the ironworkers in the area. Mike bought Jim a new belt and the tools to go on it. Next stop was for boots, and work clothes. When they got back in the truck Mike, with the key in the ignition, stopped for a few seconds staring straight ahead and told Jim, "This is the only time I'll do this for you. Next time you're on your own," and Jim knew Mike meant it.

The two had been friends for almost ten years. They met on a job site and hit it off right away. Jim was a short, stocky guy with long hair. He was scruffy looking and was always sporting a t-shirt with some obscure heavy metal band on it. He looked like Charles Manson and Bob Dylan had a love child, and he acted like it too. He was a talented musician who got into trades because it was an income and he needed to work until his music career took off.

Jim came from the type of childhood that would make people uncomfortable hearing about. Both parents died of drug overdoses when he was young, so he was raised by an abusive aunt and uncle who saw him as nothing more than a monthly cheque from the government. At fifteen he left home, although he figured the likelihood of the Children's Aid Society having been informed of that was pretty low. He had struggled with dependency his entire life and was currently living happily in his longest bout of sobriety to date.

Mike was the opposite. He was a hulking man. Tall and broad- shouldered with a large chest he had a face that showed scars from growing up in a boxing ring. He was raised in a home with both parents until he was thirteen, but it was not a functional home by any means. When Mike was six, he was bouncing around the house. Suddenly he was blindsided by the back of his Dad's hand. It sent him skidding across the ground until he hit the wall. Angry at his dad, Mike stood up, looked at the old man square in the eye and said, "That hurt your hand more than my head". Thankfully his mom was there to grab him up and rush him away from his dad. Eventually His mother had enough of his Dad's abuse, took the kids and left. But Mike returned to his dad three months later.

Mike grew up in a border town with a cop for a father and schoolteacher for a mother. They lived in a neighborhood where you had two choices after high school: a badge and a gun or hardhat and a hammer, and it really didn't matter which path you chose because on Saturday nights you were all fighting in the same alley behind the bar anyway.

This unlikely friendship between Mike and Jim was able to exist because for all of Jim's struggles and problems, he was smart, well-read, and self-educated. He had a quick wit and a very dark, almost disturbing sense of humor that Mike found highly entertaining, Mike had always thought Jim missed his calling as a comedy writer instead of a musician. Jim worked hard, recognized his faults, and even at his worst was always willing to help Mike when needed.

The two men drove in silence, Jim not quite sulking but not thrilled that Mike had given him shit over his comments in the lunch trailer. They got on the 427 South from Pearson heading towards the water and the Queen Elizabeth Parkway (or QEW as the locals called it) to head back home. Both men were working in Toronto but lived in Hamilton, Ontario.

As they got on the QEW, Mike pulled off to find coffee. Not a fan of drive thru's, especially at 8:30 am, he parked and hopped out, walking through the slippery mess that was continuing to accumulate in the parking lot. The coffee shop was still bustling even though it was Christmas eve. Mike held the door for a younger mother with two small children and made his way inside.

He stood in line listening to the Mariah Carey Christmas song that seemed to run on a nonstop loop in stores from November 1st to January 1st every year. He placed his order; a medium black coffee with ice cubes in it, a large double double for Jim, and two sausage breakfast sandwiches. His order came, he navigated his way through the mess of people and made it back outside.

Mike jumped in the truck and handed Jim his double double. He placed his own coffee in the cup holder, took one sandwich out of the bag, and tossed the bag containing the second sandwich onto Jim's lap.

"Here, peace offering." he said as he shifted the truck into reverse to pull out of the parking spot. Jim pulled his sandwich out and unwrapped it without a thank you.

"Hey, that Friedman guy got clipped last night." Jim stated.

"Who?" asked Mike.

"That Rolly Friedman guy. The rich kid. Him and his dad have those annoying commercials... The fucking guy that gave all those girls AIDS" Jim mumbled the last sentence through a mouthful of breakfast sandwich.

"Oh, no shit, What happened?"

Jim took another bite. "Didn't say. Just said someone killed him at the jewelry store on Islington on Saturday."

"Like a robbery or something?"

Jim shoved another bite of his sandwich in his mouth, took a sip of his steaming hot coffee, and mumbled out some noise that sounded like "I'unno" which emphasized his ignorance.

As they merged back onto the highway, Jim, completely unasked, said, "I've seen some of them girls he infected, they were HOT."

"Jesus," Mike groaned, knowing that Jim was about to say something incredibly messed up.

Jim elaborated, "Imagine. That guy taking all that fine pussy off the market. It's not good to anybody anymore."

"Yeah, I know. Selfish right?" Mike said sarcastically.

"Don't get me wrong, I feel bad for them girls. But I'm just saying is them were some fine-ass women. Now they're damaged goods."

"Are you angry that he got to destroy them before you did?"

"Hey! I break them on the inside, nothing seven or eight years of intensive therapy can't fix. Therapy don't cure AIDS." defended Jim.

"You're a dangerous man Jimmy. A very dangerous man."

They drove on. Mike, eating with one hand, flipped through the preloaded stations on the radio with the other. He landed on a local station specializing in "70's 80's 90's and today". It seemed to be the only station not running nonstop Christmas music. I Shot the Sheriff by Eric Clapton was playing, which Mike appreciated. It was impossible in Toronto, the most multicultural city in the world, to scroll through the radio stations in December without hearing at least a dozen Christmas songs.

Jim started telling Mike some unimportant unknown fact about Eric Clapton arguing with another artist backstage in 1970 and Mike wondered why Jim knew and, more importantly, why he decided to share this story. As the song wrapped up, the jingle from Mariah Carey's song started and Mike, grumbling switched the station.

Jim protested, "Hey, what are you doing? She's hot!"

Mike, looking at Jim from the side of his eye, commented, "It's on the radio dumbass, you can't see her."

"Yeah, but when I hear her, I think about her."

"Suffering Christ man, what's wrong with you?" Mike chuckled in a joking tone.

Mike scrolled through the stations, unable to find anything but Christmas music, so he opted to flip the radio off and drive in silence.

The roads weren't busy. It was pushing 8:30 am on Christmas Eve morning. The QEW highway was the main corridor from Toronto to Niagara Falls, with a pit stop in Hamilton and a few other cities and towns along the way. This stretch of road usually accommodated over 300,000 vehicles a day, but it was still early, and the bad weather that had carried over from the night before had most holiday travelers reluctant to get on the road to visit grandma for Christmas dinner.

Most of the vehicles on the road were work related: shop trucks, cube vans for various plumbers or electricians on emergency calls. Scattered in were in a few eighteen-wheelers and the odd salt-caked minivan with Quebec license plates on their way to visit family for the holidays.

The passing landscape could only be described as commercial with the odd patch of industrial. Car dealerships, big box stores, plazas, a large Ford Motor Company assembly plant, and fast-food stations all passed by while the two men drove on in silence. They neared the Brant Street exit with the major cut off. They could stay to the right, where the QEW becomes Highway 403 Westbound and takes you through Hamilton and beyond to Highway 401, about seventy-eight kilometers ahead.

Mike stayed right heading into Hamilton and noted the digital clock display showed it was 8:54 am. The drive home had been a slow one. The traffic was light but the roads were slick. Mike flipped the radio back on hoping to catch the 8:55 am news report as they sped up to match the traffic on the 403, which was mostly just semis and work vehicles seeing as most of the family travelers had stayed on the QEW to the Falls. Mike heard the familiar chime that signified the traffic report and the news that would directly follow.

"It's currently slow moving on all major highways. Expect volume on the 401 East between Yonge St. and the 404," the voice droned on. Jim took this time to start telling Mike another one of his weird stories.

"Remember Princess Jasmine from Aladdin?" Jim began.

"Hey. Shut up, I want to hear this" Mike snapped back.

Jim continued "I remember being in kindergarten and wanting to..."

"Shut up!" Mike yelled.

Jim stared at Mike, a little shocked. In the ten years they'd known each other Mike had never yelled, at least not at Jim.

The traffic report ended, and the two-minute news brief started. Mike listened as the familiar voice began.

"Police in Toronto's west end are investigating the city's latest suspicious death after Rolland Ariel Friedman was found dead outside the family's west end jewelry store. Police have not released any details, however, did say they're treating it as a homicide. Rolland Friedman was awaiting trial on 11 counts of aggravated sexual assault for allegedly infecting multiple sexual partners with HIV after testing positive himself in 2014. In Christmas news, Pearson Airport has reported Santa's sleigh was spotted over the Atlantic Ocean making its way to..." Mike flipped the radio off again.

Jim, without missing a beat, continued, "So, back to princess Jasmine," as they rolled into Hamilton.

The city of Hamilton was founded by George Hamilton after the war of 1812. It is a densely populated city on the Western tip of Lake Ontario. In the early 1900s, Hamilton found its footing as a steel making city. The city was best known for having two of the largest steel mills in Canada situated right beside each other on the waterfront. With that came the usual rowdiness that accompanied an industrial city. Local bars and taverns were usually packed with working class people who, for several generations, were known to get up from dinner for a good fist fight.

On top of the steel industry that fueled the working class in Hamilton, the city was also home to McMaster University, a school world-renowned for its medical science programs and responsible for producing some of the top doctors in North America. The two faces of the city were always an interesting concept to Mike. Doctors and lawyers lived next door to plumbers and mechanics.

Another interesting feature of this city was the escarpment. The city was established on the banks of Lake Ontario, but inland about six kilometers is an eleven kilometer long, ninety-meter-high sheer rock cliff that separates the lower half of Hamilton from the upper area referred to as "The Mountain". It was this upper area, made up mostly of war time houses, bungalows and raised ranches, that Jim called home.

Jim's was a wartime house where he lived with his current girlfriend Tara, a registered massage therapist. She was a short brunette with a lulu-bob hair style made popular by Uma Thurman in Pulp Fiction. She was a thick girl with the kind of body that matched her arms, which were muscular from constant usage at work. Jim had joked that Tara had Popeye forearms, although he never did so in front of her.

Mike's truck crunched through the recently refrozen slush on the street outside Jim's house. The wind had still not let up, the sky was grey and miserable, and the digital thermometer on the ceiling of the truck showed -13 Celsius, but Mike guessed with the wind and dampness it probably felt closer to -25.

"Coming in?" invited Jim.

"Naw, I gotta get going." declined Mike.

"Well, if you don't. Tara will cut you. No joke, she showed me the knife." Jim warned.

Mike threw the truck in park and shut it off. "Fine. But only because I'm not entirely convinced you're joking."

The two men walked up the driveway to the side door. It was one of those neighborhoods where everybody had a front porch, usually covered with an aluminum awning installed sometime in the 1970's. Mostly brown brick homes with white trim, they all had a front door, but everybody used the side doors instead.

Jim opened the side door and a blast of heat hit both men, instantly fogging over the glass on the storm door. The warmth of the house was accompanied by the smell baking cookies.

Inside the door was a small landing that curved 90 degrees at the stairs. Upstairs brought you directly into the kitchen. A left turn led you down a set of stairs to the basement, which was now taken over by Jim as his man-cave. The basement had the usual man-cave furnishings: a large TV, a big couch, a set of mismatched recliners, and an assortment of hockey and football memorabilia hung up over the ancient smoke-stained wood paneling. There was a wet bar in the far corner, but the alcohol had long since been removed. Instead, there were mini-Stanley cups from a long-ago beer selling campaign, and an assortment of vinyl record covers from bands Mike had never heard of.

A small brown-and-white dog stood at the top of the stairs yapping at them.

"Shaddap!" Jim yelled at the dog.

"You shut up; she lived here first!" a voice hollered back from the kitchen. "And what are you doing home?" Tara asked.

"Too fucking cold out to work in that shit." Jim yelled back.

"So, Mike dragged your ass into Toronto only to turn around and come back?" she asked, sarcasm creeping into her voice.

"Pretty much." replied Jim.

"What an asshole." Tara commented, not aware the Mike was within earshot.

"And a very Merry Christmas to you too!" Mike yelled up as he took his boots off.

He heard Tara laughing in the kitchen as he came up the stairs. He entered the kitchen to find Tara cleaning up after making a couple batches of Christmas cookies for a family gathering later that day. Like Jim, Tara was a recovering alcoholic and drug abuser. She was well into her ninth year of sobriety and kept herself occupied by cleaning the house constantly. She had a sharp tongue that made her an ideal companion for Jim, mainly because Mike could not think of another woman on the planet that would be able to put up with him. She was also very open and not the least bit shy.

Tara stood in the kitchen in loose-fitting ratty pajama pants that were patterned with the faded face of the Grinch Who Stole Christmas. She also wore a light blue t-shirt that did nothing to hide her breasts, with nothing underneath. She was an attractive girl in an unconventional way. She didn't fit into the standard mold for beauty. She was short, around Five foot two, and a little chunky. She had thick arms and legs, but they were thick with muscle from years of giving massages and squatting in her garden from April until November. Her hair style was outdated, but she said she wore it that way because it was easy to manage. At first glance she looked average. But a closer look revealed she had big light brown eyes and a big smile. She had been through hell in her late teens and twenties and as a result found every day to be a blessing. She was sarcastic and very quick-witted, but also very welcoming with a soothing effect on people. Drying her hands off with Christmas towel she walked to Mike and gave him a hug with a kiss on the cheek.

"Merry Christmas, asshole." she quipped as she pulled him in.

"Yeah, thanks," he said as he hugged her back. "Smells good in here. Whatcha making?" he asked.

"Nothing for you," she smirked as she walked over and kissed Jim hello.

"Shitty." Mike said wistfully, then asked. "Where are the kids?"

Tara had two kids, both teenagers now. Her daughter Elyse was Eighteen and her son Cedrick was thirteen. The fridge door was plastered with photos of them growing up throughout the years, except for the three years when she was at her worst and had no contact with them.

"Gone to their dad's." She replied maneuvering herself around the large man in her small kitchen. "They'll meet me at my mom's for dinner tonight. Are you staying? Can I make you a coffee?"

"No, thank you," Mike answered. "I just popped into say hi and hit the bathroom. I'm gonna head out."

"Well, what are you doing for Christmas? We have extra room at my mom's," she offered.

"I'm good hun, visiting family later today. Thank you though." Mike called out over his shoulder as he made his way down the hallway.

Tara and Jim lived in a small, cramped house, but Tara worked hard to make it a home for her and her children. Tara had a standing rule that bedroom doors stayed open during the day, not to spy on her kids but because the house was so small that the closed doors made it feel dark and cramped. As Mike passed by Tara, she looked at Jim and mouthed the words "He has family?". Jim shrugged as if to say, "Who knew?".

Mike passed Elyse's open bedroom door, behind which was a small eight by nine-foot room. The bed was made, and everything was in its place. The walls were plastered with posters of her favorite bands, again people Mike had never heard of, and some mythical decorations: dragons and fire, wizards, and fairies.

Mike knew Elyse from the frequent visits. She was a sweet kid. Physically she was heavy set and not conventionally attractive. When Tara and Jim first started dating, she was fifteen and had incredibly low self-esteem. Jim, for all his twisted humor, bonded with her quickly. At sixteen she began dating a boy who was seven years older. Both Tara and Jim expressed their concerns, but knew if they pushed the matter, it would drive her away. Instead, they went for the old reverse psychology trick, and tried to be welcoming. That didn't work either. One night after working a ten-hour shift together Mike stopped in at Jim's and met the boyfriend. Mike instantly disliked him. The next morning on their way to work he asked Jim what the deal was. When Jim explained the situation Mike decided he would deal with the boy himself. By that weekend Elyse was crying over the boy ghosting her. By the following weekend she was back to usual self and the boy never bothered them again.

Mike continued down the hallway until he got to the bathroom. It was a small room with what he figured were the original fixtures: a toilet, small sink, and bathtub/shower with sliding frosted plastic doors. He used the toilet, flushed, washed his hands, and went back to the kitchen.

Jim was looking in the fridge as Tara sat at the table looking at her phone.

"I saw that Friedman guy got killed on Saturday," she said looking down.

"Yeah, heard it on the news in the truck." Jim replied, pulling out some ham, mustard, and a loaf of bread. "Probably the father of one of the girls infected."

Mike slipped through the small kitchen past them both to the top of the stairs.

"Alright I'm out guys. Merry Christmas! Jim, I'll call you about Wednesday," he advised as he slipped his boots back on and let himself out.

Mike walked down the driveway thinking about Jim and Tara. He liked Tara the instant he met her. He thought she was good for Jim. She gave him a reason to stay sober and wouldn't tolerate him falling off the wagon.

Mike made it to his truck, climbed in, fired it up, and cranked the heat on full. He put the truck into drive and eased away from the curb, heading home. He turned the radio on and scrolled through the stations. As he neared the corner, he heard a voice mention the name "Friedman". He stopped and listened to the tail end of a news report.

"Police aren't saying much, only that this is the city's seventy-first homicide of the year, and that the Friedman family is expected to hold a press conference later today".

The voice on the radio trailed off talking about the current state of the healthcare system in Ontario, and Mike smiled to himself. He flipped the station and caught the end of the song Take On Me by A-Ha and wondered whatever happened to them. He pulled away from the stop sign and heard the jingle that started Mariah Carey's song again.

"Ugh, I oughtta kill that bitch next." he said.

Chapter 3
Saturday December 24th, 2022, 10:00, am
Hamilton, Ontario

Steve woke up in his room, his head splitting, his mouth dry and disgusting. He got out of bed and stumbled to the bathroom. He pissed, splashed water into his face, and made his way into the kitchen. Steve lived in a small one-bedroom apartment, a start over apartment, he called it.

Standing around six foot one, two hundred and twenty pounds, he was a large man; muscular, with long brown hair usually kept in a greasy ponytail, and with a shaggy unkept beard. He was starting to develop a dad-bod though, and occasionally considered working on it. The steady diet of fast food, hard liquor, and an average of twelve beers a night ensured that it wasn't going away anytime soon.

Steve was forty-four years old, in his nineteenth year as an Ontario Provincial Police officer, and in his fifth year working undercover, currently in narcotics. He was separated from his third wife. Six months ago he had been added to a task force for Operation Shooting Star, a joint operation between several police jurisdictions including the Royal Canadian Mounted Police, the Ontario Provincial Police, and several local police departments including Hamilton, Niagara Falls, Toronto, Ottawa and even as far away as Edmonton. Operation Shooting Star was charged with taking down a ring of fentanyl dealers suspected to be importing from Niagara Falls and distributing across Canada.

Steve didn't mind undercover work. It gave him freedom to do things like drink at work and meet loose women. The fact that he was able to do the occasional (or not so occasional) line of coke was an added bonus.

When Steve first got into undercover work, he had asked his superiors, "What do I do if they want me to get high?"

His supervisor plugged his ears and closed his eyes and said, "La la la la, I'm not listening, la la la la," like a kid on a playground.

Fair enough, Steve thought. He had read a few books from various undercover authors including Jay Dobyns, who claimed he'd earned a full patch with the Hell Angels while working undercover in the ATF. In the book, Dobyns claimed he won their trust by tricking them into thinking he both used meth and had killed a rival club member. Steve immediately called bullshit. In his five years working undercover, the one thing he knew was if you were going to fake using drugs, be it meth, coke, or even weed, the guys you're trying to fool would know.

When he first started working undercover, Steve simply said he didn't get high. When that wasn't an acceptable answer, he started using and left it out of his reports. He would smoke weed to fit in, and used cocaine regularly, but stayed away from meth and crack. When in doubt, he would do what all cops do: he lied.

Steve made a coffee, sat down at the table, and stared out the window. It was Christmas Eve morning, and he was stuck in Hamilton. He reached for his phone that was plugged in and saw he had several notifications. He typed in his PIN and saw two missed phone calls, one from "Mom", the other from "Dad", and three text messages with no names attached.

The first text message showed only two texts, one out going from Steve that said "looking" at 7:54 pm, with a reply coming in at 8:35 pm saying "no".

The other two messages were similar; nobody could help him score on a Sunday that just happened to be right before Christmas. Not that he was really looking, but it would help his cover.

The "Dad" phone call was his superintendent within the Ontario Provincial Police, or OPP. Steve had checked in three days ago but hadn't delivered anything worthwhile in weeks.

The "Mom" call was from the task force lead with the Royal Canadian Mounted Police, or RCMP. An older woman, she had introduced herself at the start of the of the investigation, but for the life of him, Steve couldn't remember her name. He wanted to put her in his phone as "Bitch on Wheels", but seeing as the phone was monitored 24-7 and all incoming and outgoing calls and messages were automatically retained as evidence, "Mom" it was.

Technology today was amazing, Steve thought. He could be anywhere and some guy in a room in Toronto would know exactly where he was, could access the camera on Steve's phone, and could see, hear, and more importantly record everything being said in real time. Whenever possible, Steve tried to leave his phone, keys, and wallet on the table or on the bar, but that was becoming more difficult as people became increasingly less trusting of electronics. Steve pulled up the call list went to "Dad" and hit dial.

His task force superintendent answered on the third ring. "Good morning Marcus!"

"I'm alone." Steve said right away.

The voice on the other end dropped the false cheer. "Anything?"

"Not yet. Might have something in a few days. Everyone is busy for the next few days." Steve replied, fighting off the feeling of nausea the was creeping in.

"OK, keep me posted." The voice said before asking, "Did you call your mother?"

"No, I have nothing yet" Steve repeated.

"I meant your actual mother." The voice explained, unimpressed. "At least call her tomorrow and wish her a Merry Christmas."

"Oh, right, guess I should." They both hung up. Steve finished his coffee, put the dirty mug in the sink, and took a shower.

Steve was born Stephen Matthew Parent in a small Saskatchewan town called Weyburn, situated about an hour Southeast of Regina. He grew up playing hockey and working on his family's wheat farm. During the summer between grade eleven and twelve, at seventeen years old, he joined the army reserves, mainly for the weapons training. After high school he immediately enrolled in Police Studies at Campion College in Regina. His goal initially was to join the RCMP.

After college he sent out his resumes to every police force he could think of: Municipal, Provincial, Federal, even some First Nations communities, hoping to get some experience. He was shocked when he got a phone call from the Ontario Provincial Police.

He was taken through the pre-screening process and given an application number. He was told to make his way to Aylmer Ontario, a small town about two hours southwest of Toronto, where he was put through a rigorous physical exam. A month later he was asked to come back for an in-person interview. He was sent for a psychological assessment, a medical assessment, and had a security and background check that investigated everything. They even questioned him about the time his next-door neighbor in Regina called the police on him for a noise complaint in his first year of college. They looked at his financials, conducted interviews with his teachers, hockey coaches and even the Subway manager where Steve worked in high school. A year later he got the call: he was hired.

His first detachment was in a small-town northwest of Sault Saint Marie, Ontario called Wawa. Being from rural Saskatchewan he was amazed with the green forest that surrounded the small town known mostly for its giant goose statue. After five years of absolute boredom, he transferred east to small community outside Timmins Ontario, where his job consisted mostly of notifying family members of a deceased relative after an automobile accident or breaking up bar fights every Friday and Saturday night.

After nine years in Timmins, Steve applied to an internal job posting that saw him transferred to Toronto and filling a "boots on the ground" role in several task forces over the years. His most recent major accomplishment was a multi-jurisdictional investigation partnering with the RCMP tackling child pornography and human trafficking starting in Windsor Ontario and branching out across Canada. Steve had worked undercover as a pimp and a drug dealer. His intel broke open a case involving several strip clubs and several small, privately owned motels across Canada that worked as stopping points to keep young girls in the sex trade against their will.

That case took a major toll on Steve's mental health. He witnessed things that still turned his stomach, and when reporting back to his superiors he was told to continue investigating instead of putting a stop to horrors he was seeing. The investigation ended after a multi-provincial set of raids that resulted in doors being broken down in eighteen locations across eight cities Canada-wide at precisely the same time. A picture of Steve in blue jeans and a red flannel button up shirt escorting a young First Nations girl out of a motel room with his OPP jacket draped over her barely-clothed body had circulated through all the newspapers. Steve took a few months off and eventually returned to task force work but asked to focus on the explosion of fentanyl plaguing Canada. His request was granted and now, three months later, he was sitting in an empty one-bedroom apartment, hung over, by himself on Christmas Eve morning.

Chapter 4

Thursday July 5th, 2007, 8:30pm.
Windsor Ontario:

It was a hot summer evening. The sun was still up at 8:30 pm. It was 26 degrees and oppressively humid outside. Inside the small, cramped boxing club, the song Holla if Ya Hear Me By 2pac filled the walls. The odor of moldy equipment and the dull smell of sweat and testosterone that filled every boxing club on the planet was heavy in the air. A small club both in numbers and footprint, Slater Street Boxing Club was unremarkable at first glance.

The building itself was a small block structure. Its exterior was only forty-eight feet wide by twenty feet deep, and it stood fifteen feet tall. It was painted battleship grey inside and out. One of the coaches had joked that they place gets painted grey every ten years whether it needs it or not.

The interior consisted of two rooms, both eighteen by eighteen, with a ten-foot-long hallway separating them. The front door opened to the center of the hallway with a small office across the hall. There were trophy cases on each side, some awards dating back to the 1950s.

A left turn would find you in a room with a sixteen-by-sixteen-foot ring. Turn right and you were in the bag room, consisting of a few heavy bags, a speed bag, some weights, and a chin up bar. All the equipment had been either donated or brought in by members for communal use. The back left corner of the bag room had a doorless opening that entered the toilet and shower areas tucked away behind the office.

It was a hole-in-the-wall of a club. It was not flashy; this was a club people joined to find out how tough they were not. The club owner and three coaches worked as gatekeepers, stopping the crime that plagued the streets from entering.

A seventeen-year-old Mike worked a heavy bag while his dad, Ed, held the stopwatch. Ed had been running him through a particularly grueling workout and they were coming into the last round on the heavy bag. Mike began going to the club with his dad on Saturday mornings when he was six years old. As a kid, he used to bring in colouring books or GI Joes to entertain himself while he watched his old man train the fighters.

Ed was a Windsor Police Sergeant forced into an early retirement after being rear-ended on his police motorcycle by a drunk driver. He was a short stocky powerhouse of a man. He had a physical resemblance to a fire hydrant: compact with a cement head and lead in his hands. He was well known across Windsor as one of the meanest bastards to ever wear a Windsor Police uniform.

Ed became a cop in the mid 1970's, a time when the police department was ripe with corruption and police brutality allegations. The department was full of the type of cops that happily accommodated when presented with the offer to drop the badge and gun and see how tough they really were.

What Ed lacked in height he made up for in toughness. Most Windsor police officers were happy to see him pull up when they needed help. He didn't have their backs, because he was usually right in the middle of whatever chaos was going on.

He was a gruff man, the kind that dropped racial slurs at home like he was paid royalties for saying them. But he had a reputation, especially with the young black community, as a decent man. He acted as a surrogate father to many people in the west end of Windsor who otherwise had no one to go to. However, to Mike it seemed like Ed could only point out what he was doing wrong. Unless Mike was hurting someone, If Mike knocked an opponent through the ropes or better yet dropped them in the center of the ring, then Ed was happy. At fourteen Mike started playing football. His size and power landed him a position as a linebacker. On Mikes first play He found an opening in the offensive line; He smashed his way through and sacked the opposing quarterback hard enough the boy was carried off the field on a stretcher. When Mike took a knee while the medics worked on the Quarterback, he noticed Ed cheering him on.

On this night in the gym, Ed had Mike doing thirty second intervals on the heavy bag. Holding the bag for a three-minute round, he had Mike hit a fast 1-2, 1-2, 1-2. After thirty seconds he had Mike switch to power shots: four and five punch combinations with heavy hooks and upper cuts. After thirty seconds it was back to speed, then power, and so on for the full three minutes.

Mike, standing six foot three and weighing in at two hundred and five pounds, was long and lean. Showing naturally heavy hands even as a young boy, Cecil the club's owner and Ed developed a set of hand speed drills that seven years later Mike still used religiously.

Mike often looked on, jealous of the attention his dad gave the other students. Kids who could barely string three or four punches together were congratulated and praised. Mike was folding the heavy bag with lighting fast speed and was only told where he was leaving himself open.

As the timer chimed loudly through the gym signifying the last thirty seconds of the round, Ed shouted his final "POWER!", and Mike took to throwing heavy power shots into the bag. THUMP THUMP THUMP. Turning at the waist and pivoting on his toes he drove all his hatred and jealousy into every punch, grunting, flinging sweat off his body. "Come on, Harder!" Ed yelled, holding the bag steady. Mike, a lefty, drove what would be a rib-shattering hook into the bag at body height, torquing his body back and forth and following up another shot at head level, hitting hard enough to knock Ed off balance with each shot.

"TIME!" Ed yelled as the timer went off. Mike was standing in front of the bag, soaking wet with sweat and panting. He noticed the four remaining guys had stopped and were watching him. The music still blaring but nothing being said. Without another word, Ed walked away from the bag.

Mike walked over to Wallace. The two came up together in the boxing club, joining around the same time. Wallace was of Jamaican descent, although he was born in Detroit. He was a year older than Mike, but substantially smaller. Standing around five foot ten and one hundred and eighty pounds, he was a tough kid, and one of Ed's rescues. Mike wasn't sure of all the details, but he knew that Ed had arrested Wallace's father after a domestic violence call. Rumors had circulated through the club that Wallace's father had beaten his mother so bad that she developed a speech problem, but then again it was the west end, where "If you haven't heard a rumor by noon, feel free to make one up" was an unwritten rule. What Mike did know was that shortly after Wallace's father was arrested, Ed was called to a local grade school where Wallace was fighting and stealing. Instead of slapping cuffs on him to scare him straight, Ed sat with the boy and talked with him. That night was Wallace's first visit to the club, and he'd been a staple there ever since. Eight years later, Wallace's dad was still nowhere to be seen. As Mike got closer, he saw Wallace was grinning.

"One day you're gonna snap that chain." Wallace commented, referring to the seven-foot-long chain holding up the heavy bag.

Mike raised his eyebrows in a "yeah whatever" response. Mike held his right hand out, and without saying a word, Wallace undid the Velcro strap and pulled off Mike's right glove. With his now free hand, undid the left glove and dropped it at his feet. His hands still wrapped, he grabbed his water bottle. Pulling his mouth guard out, he took a big pull on the bottle and grabbed his towel to wipe himself down.

Mike always used his mouth guard when training. When he was a kid, he noticed some of his dad's students would get fatigued in the second or third round of a match. One of the first clues to their weariness was when they would start breathing with their mouths open. After watching the crowd go crazy cheering on two eleven-year-old boys at local boxing event, Mike asked his dad if he could be a fighter. He was nine years old at the time. The following Monday he started training, and from that day on he trained with his mouthguard in. He was a believer that you had to get use to breathing with it in.

Mike finished wiping his face down, caught his breath, and unwrapped his hands. The first weekend in July was the Sunflower Boxing Tournament in Barberton Ohio. Every year the Slater Street Boxing Club loaded up their top boxers, crossed the border, and drove the four-hour trek to go put on a show. The fact that Mike's godfather, Ken Steinhoff, lived in the area was just an added bonus. Ken was Ed's best friend and a retired Cleveland PD SWAT Sergeant. Ohio had a bad reputation in the boxing world for being notoriously corrupt. If you fought a local and left it to the judges to decide a winner, you were guaranteed to lose. But the Slater Street Club went every year anyway. It was good experience, and the networking with other clubs was priceless.

Ed popped his head back into the bag room. "I'm leaving. Lock up when you're done."

Wallace nodded. "You got it coach."

Ed started walking away but suddenly stopped dead in his tracks. He looked back in at the students in the room. Making eye contact with each of the five fighters, he said, "No Sparing!".

Every club was different, and in this little club, Murphy's Law ruled everything. For that reason, the club had a strict No Contact policy when fighters had matches coming up. Both Ed and Cecil were always pointing out that the last two weeks before a match is when a fighter always got hurt training. From flash knock outs to a broken wrist, or just some poor unlucky asshole rolling his ankle getting out of the ring, the weeks leading up to the fight were always ripe with injury. So sparing was out. The last two weeks before a competition, fighters worked on technique and conditioning. There was bag work, focus mitts, shadow boxing, and a lot of running. But no contact.

"You got it coach!", came the reply for all the fighters. Ed walked out of the gym, the heavy steel door slamming shut behind him.

The five guys ranged in age from fifteen to eighteen, and varied in size from five foot four, one hundred and thirty-five pounds to six foot three, two hundred and five pounds. They all stared at each other with shit-eating grins, waiting to hear Ed drive away. After they heard the faint crunch of gravel from the van leaving the parking lot, the five of them all rushed into ring room pushing, shoving and tripping each other, all trying to be the first ones in, giggling like little kids the whole time.

Mike, with his large frame, was not as fast as the smaller guys. A young Lebanese kid nicknamed Lil Mo slid under the bottom rope like a professional wrestler entering the ring. Next up was a young tough-as-nails fighter who had recently relocated from Winnipeg. The youngest of five sons (all fighters), Darcy was a welcome addition to the team. When he first joined the club, he easily ran through most of the fighters the team had. With him came a ferocity reminiscent of the early Mike Tyson. Taking part in his first shark tank, a ritual in many clubs where the new guy gets in the ring and fights two minutes against each team member, Darcy had dropped two of the regulars. Afterwards Ed asked Darcy's dad in a joking manner "Jesus Christ, What the hell did you do to those boys?"

Darcy's dad replied with a straight face, "I had five boys and I only set four place settings at the dinner table."

Watching Darcy make easy work of his well-trained fighters, Ed wasn't sure if he was kidding or not.

The five guys had decided on a game of King of the Hill: two guys start boxing and the winner of the round stays in and keeps going until he loses. A terrible idea for any combat sport, it was an especially stupid idea for an unsupervised group of hotheaded teenage boys. Wallace started the timer and right away Mo and Darcy charged towards each other. Darcy, the larger of the two, had only two settings: on and off. He was not capable of sparing at fifty percent. Mo, although smaller, was substantially faster with his hands and his feet. Where Darcy would charge in, Mo would slip and move.

Boxing is a sport of inches; an inch here or there can be the difference between winning and losing. To the untrained eye, boxers are two brutes trading punches until one can no longer stand. But to boxers, it's a different story; a ballet. Boxing is an art form. It's the art of touching your opponent without being touched. Muhammad Ali was a master of the sport. In his prime, he could be seen slipping and dodging punches with what seemed like superhuman reflexes. Ali was to grace and timing what George Forman was to power and what Joe Frasier was to speed. Any boxing historian will tell you the three combined put on some of the greatest displays ever witnessed.

Darcy, becoming frustrated with Mo's speed and accuracy, found an opening. As he moved in, Mo attempted to tie him up. Darcy stepped in using the peekaboo style of boxing, with both hands out in front and his stance square. As Mo attempted to grab on, Darcy shoved him into the corner with all his might. Knowing Mo would try to slip out, Darcy closed the gap, immediately shutting down any escape Mo would have had, and started throwing what the guys called "hurt bombs".

Darcy's peekaboo style was a tough one to master, but one that allowed a fighter to unload power shots with either hand. Darcy launched several heavy shots on the smaller opponent. Mo, young but a seasoned amateur, had enough sense to know he'd been had, and before he had the chance to absorb too much punishment he covered up and dropped to one knee, signifying the end of the round.

Darcy stepped back to the sound of his teammates laughing and hooting at how quickly things changed. He helped Mo back up, the two hugged, and Wallace hopped into the ring.

Much like Mo, Wallace was faster than Darcy, but closer to Darcy's size. On multiple occasions over the last six months the two would spar, and the entire club would come to a standstill to watch them. They were fairly evenly matched by way of size and power. Darcy hit harder, but Wallace hit faster. Their sparing sessions usually went to who landed first and could keep pressure on his opponent. Wallace was better than Darcy in his ability to keep his head on. Darcy was fast and mean but would stop thinking when he got flustered, and one of two things would happen: he would lose his temper and start swinging for the fences, abandoning all defenses and training, or he would freeze and not know how to react. And on this day the former happened.

As the two came out, Wallace threw a quick one-two combination. Darcy raised his glove slightly to pop the shots and deflect the punches. Wallace stepped to the outside of Darcy's left foot. Before Darcy realized what was happening, Wallace threw several fast punches to Darcy's head and ribs. Darcy froze for a second, but that was all the time Wallace needed. Darcy went into survival mode, swinging haymakers, trying to end it with one shot. Unfortunately for Darcy, wild punches are telegraphed: the shoulder drops and the arm draws back before punching, like in an old John Wayne movie, except in real life the opponent doesn't stand still and count the seconds as punches are thrown. Every time Darcy would load up and draw back, Wallace would connect. Darcy, off balance, would throw a wild punch that Wallace saw coming. Wallace would slip back, Darcy would get nothing but air, and Wallace would counter with two or three punches of his own, each one finding their mark. After three minutes of Cat and Mouse. Wallace was declared the winner and Mike stepped in.

Mike was the largest of the group, and arguably the best of the bunch. A big guy with fast hands and a chin made of steel, he was intimidating both in and out of the ring. When it came to sparring, he had good self-control. By age seventeen he'd already been training for eight years and fighting competitively for six. Most of the fighters in the club liked working with him. Drop your guard and you'd get a bloody nose or a black eye, but in training he seldom threw punches with bad intentions.

Mike and Wallace started their round. He couldn't put an exact number on the number of times they had shared the ring, but if Mike had to guess he would say it was easily in the hundreds over the last seven years. They had sparred so often that they didn't feel they really benefitted from it anymore; they both knew exactly what the other guy was going to do before he did it, which is why what happened next was so bizarre.

As Mike used his jab with his longer reach to set the distance, Wallace slipped under and threw a looping right hand. Mike, reacting on instinct and his fast reflexes, threw a right to counter and pivoted on his lead foot, circling away from Wallace. Mike miscalculated the arc of Wallace's swing and spun off balance as he tried to step out to create more distance. Both fighters' hands collided almost palm to palm. Mike took the blunt of the impact on heel of his glove where there was no padding. Instantly he felt a white-hot pain shoot through his hand and up his arm. Immediately he knew there was something wrong.

"FUCK!" he yelled, turning away, holding his hand close to his abdomen. He dropped to his knees and spit his mouth guard out on the mat. "Fuck!" he yelled again.

A small chorus of "Ooooh" and "Oh shit" came from the other guys.

Wallace shook the pain off in his own hand. "Shit, sorry dude."

Mo, on the side of the ring, piped up, "What happened?"

"I broke my fucking hand, that's what happened!" explained Mike, through clenched teeth.

"You sure?" asked Mo.

Mike bit at the Velcro on his wrist and stripped the glove off. Looking at his unwrapped hand he knew right away he was in deep shit.

"Yeah, I'm sure. Dammit!" he growled, standing up as Wallace was striding over.

"Sorry Dude. I'm really sorry," he said through his mouthguard. "Lemme see."

Mike held his right hand out thumb pointing up hand open. It was shaking a bit, almost twitching from the pain. It was already starting to swell, and Wallace used both hands to gently examine the damage. As he did so he shifted the metacarpal bone.

"Ow! Shit. Don't do that" Mike barked, pulling his hand away.

Patrick, the fifth member of their group came up. "Oh, damn dude. That's broken," he observed.

"Thank you, doctor." Mike snapped.

"Don't get shitty with me I didn't do it." Patrick drawled. "I broke that same spot last year."

Before joining the club, Patrick had considered himself a local tough guy. Mike noticed he was more of a sucker-punch artist who was tough when he was going after someone that either wouldn't fight back or didn't see him coming. A white kid claiming to be of Irish decent, although both sides of his family had been in the Windsor area for over a hundred years, and Mike knew that Patrick's mom was a Ducharme; a French family. Patrick was a similar size to Wallace, five foot ten, one hundred and eighty pounds. He started coming to the club after a house party seven months before where he tried to pick a fight with little Mo and ended up getting two teeth punched out and a concussion for his efforts. All street beefs ended the second you walked in the door at Slater Street, so Patrick and Mo squashed their issues, and once Patrick received a healthy serving of humble pie, he was actually a fun guy to hang out with. The five boys stood in the ring, Mike holding his wrist trying to steady his hand.

"What's your pops going to say?" asked Darcy, and the other four looked at him realizing they were all now in deep shit.

Chapter 5
Friday July 6th, 2007, 8:30 am.
Windsor Ontario

The Next Morning Mike came down the stairs with his travel bags packed. His boxing bag, an old hockey bag repurposed for his fight gear, was already loaded and sitting at the back door. Ed was sitting at the table smoking a cigarette, having a coffee and reading the latest Tom Clancy hardcover. Mike, now certain he had broken something in his hand last night, was dealing with the pain, but was far more scared to tell his dad.

He walked to the fruit basket and grabbed a banana. The plan was to leave at 9:00 am and meet the other guys at the club shortly thereafter. They would all pile into Ed's van, a dark Green GMC conversion van that comfortably fit seven people. It was like a smaller version of camper. Without thinking, Mike fumbled with the banana, not realizing he needed both hands to open it.

"What happened to your hand?" Ed asked without looking up.

"Huh?" Mike replied.

Ed hated responses like that. After twenty-one years on the police force, there was nothing he hated more than "over there answers" as he called them. After pulling someone over and getting their information, one question he would ask is "Where are you going?" or "Where do you live?" and nothing got under his skin worse than someone trying to bide their time and avoid the question by answering, "Over there," and pointing in a general direction, thinking it was an acceptable answer.

"What. The fuck. Did you do to your hand?" Ed demanded.

Mike knew he was in trouble. Even at his age and size, he was still terrified of his father.

"I, I don't know. I woke up this morning and it was hurting. I think I rolled it on the bag last night maybe." Mike stammered.

Without a warning, Ed threw the heavy hardcovered book at Mike. Mike dodged out of the way, but before he could regroup Ed had gotten up out of his seat, grabbed Mike by his face, and slammed his head into the wall. Holding Mike's head with one hand, Ed grabbed Mike's broken hand with the other. The pain was excruciating. Ed, although a short man standing around five foot nine, had unusually large hands for a man his size. Hands that almost completely masked a beer can when he held it.

"What did I tell you!" Ed roared at Mike. "I said no fucking sparing, didn't I?" He relaxed the pressure on Mike face allowing his head to come off the wall about five inches, "DIDN'T I!" He screamed as he slammed Mikes head a second time.

Mike said nothing. After seventeen years in a house with this angry beast, he knew it was best to shut up.

Ed let go of Mike and stormed off toward the front of the house.

"Get your shit ready. We're leaving!" he yelled, as he stomped away, cursing to himself.

Mike grabbed his bag. He wasn't hungry anymore and had to make weight later that day anyway. He loaded his fight bag and backpack into the back of the van, closed the heavy doors and sat in the front seat waiting for Ed. His dad finally emerged from the house five minutes later carrying a small stainless-steel bucket, one usually used as a spit bucket between rounds. Ed rounded the front of the van, glaring at his son with what Mike thought of as pure hatred. Mike could hear Ed muttering angrily. Ed opened the driver's door and threw the bucket at Mike without a word. Mike placed it between his feet, feeling weak and ashamed despite all his accomplishments in the ring. A big kid, he felt small and insignificant to his dad. He said nothing as Ed started the van.

They drove the few short blocks to the Slater Street Club. The four other fighters and Cecil were all sharing a laugh in the parking lot as Ed pulled in and parked the van. Mike undid his belt and opened the door.

"Take your fucking bucket," Ed growled at him again.

Mike grabbed the bucket, hopped out of the front seat, opened the side door of the van, and climbed into the far back bench seat. Ed got out of the van, and it was as if someone had flipped a switch. He had gone from radiating hatred towards his son, to showing his big broad smile and joking with the guys in the parking lot. Ed was a master at changing faces. Mike remembered many occasions growing up where his dad would be screaming at him, his sister or their mother; almost foaming at the mouth. The next instant he would pick up a ringing telephone and be laughing with whoever was on the other end of the line.

The version of Ed in the parking lot right now was happy and excited for the drive. He collected everyone's passports, had them load their gear into the van, and even cracked a few jokes with the boys. As everyone piled into the van, Wallace met Mikes eye. Wallace knew right away that it was bad side of Ed that had greeted Mike that morning.

The van, now loaded with the fighters in the back and the two coaches up front, pulled out of the club's parking lot. They turned right and drove the hundred yards to the first quiet intersection, made a left turn, and drove two blocks before another left onto the busier road. From there they drove the two kilometers to the bridge that would bring them to the US border. The boys in the back flipped through the DVD cases looking for something to throw on. Ed and Cecil were discussing where they were staying, while Cecil looked over the lineup for the first matches. Mike stared out the window, not engaging with anyone. He had no idea why his dad made him come, or why he was holding the stupid bucket.

The entrance to the Ambassador Bridge was about a five-minute drive from Slater Street. Originally built in the 1920's and opening in 1929, the suspension bridge crossed over the narrowest part of the Detroit River linking sister cities Windsor Ontario with Detroit Michigan. Over the last few years, the bridge had been a major topic of debate as it was falling apart and seemingly only held together by its multiple layers of lead paint. The bridge was privately owned by a man that had more money than God, but he refused to sell.

When the Provincial and State governments got together and decided to build a new crossing, the bridge's owner bought all the real estate in the area and tried to drown the courts on both side of the border with lawsuits and frivolous paperwork. The bridge itself, for all its problems, was a beautiful site despite the crumbling infrastructure. Chunks of concrete from the underside often broke off and came crashing to the ground fifteen meters below, causing major throughways that passed under it in both cities to routinely be closed down for safety concerns, snarling traffic on both sides of the busiest border crossing in the world.

When he was younger, it seemed like Mike and his family crossed the border a couple times a week. If traffic wasn't bad, he could get from his front door to the main gate at the old Tiger Stadium for a baseball game in less than twenty minutes. Ed, being a cop, would pull up at customs and show his driver's license that he coincidentally and conveniently kept securely right next to his Windsor Police badge. In the pre-9/11 days, that was enough for customs to wave him through without so much as a question. In 2007 there were questions, but the shiny piece of tin, coupled with the fact that Ed drank with a number of customs officers on both sides of the border, usually meant the van would clear customs in a matter of seconds. Wallace had joked last year that Ed spent more time shooting the shit with the guy in the booth then they spent waiting in line.

By 9:15 am the van was pulling onto I-75 heading south out of Detroit. They would follow 75 to Toledo Ohio, link up with the Ohio Turnpike, and head east towards Cleveland. Once they cleared the southwest end of Detroit, Ed pulled over at the first truck stop. Pulling up at a gas pump, he handed Cecil his credit card and asked him to top up the van. Looking back at Mike he said, "Let's go. Grab your bucket".

The four other fighters all looked back at Mike, who hadn't said a word to anybody since they got in. Mike crawled to the side door. Little Mo, who was sitting next to it, opened the door and hopped out to give Mike room to get out.

While none of the guys had personally witnessed Ed lose his temper with Mike, they were all aware that it happened often. They all saw the way Ed snaped and growled at Mike. They witnessed how Ed belittled him in front of the others. And they had all seen bruises on Mike that weren't from boxing. It was understood why Mike was quiet that morning.

Mike followed Ed into the truck stop. Ed grabbed a big bag of ice from the freezer and tossed it to Mike. He grabbed a case of water bottles and made his way to the cashier. He paid for the water and ice, along with two packs of Salem Menthol cigarettes, and walked out. Mike, carrying the bucket and the ice, figured his job for the weekend would be to hold water and help corner the fighters, and that Ed was just making a show of degrading him to punish him. Once they got outside Ed stopped and instructed, "Fill up the bucket about halfway with ice." Mike did as he was told, and Ed poured a couple bottles of water in. "Let me see your hand," Ed demanded. Mike was scared but knew better than to say no.

Ed took Mikes hand. Having been involved with boxing since he himself was twelve and having been involved with countless street brawls over the years, Ed was no stranger to dealing with broken hands. Mike gave Ed his hand and was surprised when Ed was incredibly gentle.

"What happened?" Ed asked calmly "And don't lie. The damage is done. I need to know what we're dealing with".

Mike told Ed about how he and Wallace collided hands the night before. He told Ed where it hurt and how it felt. Ed examined his hand and said "Okay, you broke your metacarpal, that's this bone here," and used his own hand to show where the bone behind the thumb ran towards the wrist. Continuing calmly, he added, "This is why I said no sparing."

Mike was listening to his dad, fighting back the urge to let the tears stream down his face. The shame and guilt coupled with his need for acceptance from his dad had his brain downing in emotions he couldn't understand.

"Ok. It's too late to pull you out. You have weight at 4:00 pm and your first fight at 7:00 pm." Ed advised, handing Mike his stopwatch. "Twenty minutes in the ice, twenty minutes out until we get to the hotel," he instructed. "I'll call Steinhoff and see what he can do," referring to his best friend and Mike's godfather.

They made their way back to the van. Mike hopped back in, crawled his way to the back seat, and started the timer. He dunked his hand in the cold icy water and was met with a pain he had never felt before.

Ed climbed back in the front seat. He turned and faced the group. "When I say no sparing, I mean no fucking sparing. I don't tell you guys this stuff to be an asshole. It's for your own benefit. Mike has a long weekend ahead of him with a broken hand. If he loses its because of you guys. You failed him. You failed your coaches. You failed each other as a team."

He turned back around, facing forwards, and started the van. Cecil over his shoulder gave the guys a look that told them he agreed with Ed.

Without yelling, finger pointing, or losing his temper, Ed had hit each of the guys right in the heart. They knew they fucked up, and in doing so had disappointed the two men they didn't want to disappoint.

The drive was uneventful. Darcy, Mo, Patrick and Wallace watched Diggstown, a corny boxing movie from 1992 staring James Woods. Mike was staring out the window watching the highway blow past. It was July 5th and it was hot outside. Ed kept the digital thermometer gauge in the van set to Fahrenheit and it was showing 86 degrees at 10:00 am. It was going to be a hot humid day, but the AC in the big van worked and it was blowing cold.

Mike was following his dad's twenty-minute icing instructions. By the fourth dip in, his hand was completely numb and bright red. He worried if he was going to give himself frost bite. They made the transition to the Ohio turnpike and coasted along at seventy miles an hour.

At 1:15 pm they pulled into the parking lot of a small family-owned motel called The Knotty Pine. Ed eased the van up in front of the office and shut the engine down. Cecil hopped out of the front passenger side, Mo popped the side door open, and the five fighters all climbed out and stood around stretching. Ed and Cecil made their way into the office to get the room keys. Mike dumped the now mostly water filled bucket. A few small ice cubes mixed in with the water melted almost immediately when they contacted the hot asphalt.

Wallace, letting out a loud groaning stretch, asked Mike "How's the paw?"

Mike, in a better mood now, answered honestly, "Sore as fuck."

As he looked at it, he saw that the ice had worked. The swelling was almost gone. His hand was red and numb, and he could barely move it. The skin felt tight, but the pain for the most part was gone.

After a few minutes Ed and Cecil reappeared holding plastic key cards, which they handed out to the boys. Ed and Cecil would share a room, Mike and Wallace would be in another. Patrick, Darcy, and Mo would share the third room since they were the smallest of the group.

The boys had travelled together many times, and unlike hockey and baseball tournaments, Ed didn't worry about the boys sneaking out at night or showing up hungover in the morning. The boys on this team were there because they wanted to compete, not party. Ed and Cecil made sure the boys on the team understood this and had gone as far as having a sign made up that hung in the bag room: a black and white picture taken of Ed and Cecil cornering a fighter long ago with the caption that said "You can play baseball, you can play hockey, you can play basketball. You DON'T play boxing."

The boys walked over to their rooms while Ed and Cecil drove the van over. The air was hot, stifling almost, each breath thick and heavy with humidity. The boys opened the doors to their rooms, and like a well-rehearsed dance, knew what to do.

Mike always took the bed farthest from the door. He walked in, tossed his bags on his bed, and went to the A/C unit to crank it up. Wallace opened the curtains and flipped on the TV. Wallace always scrolled through the stations twice, seeing if anything caught his eye.

It was now 1:30 pm. The boys had just enough time to riffle through their bags, find their running shoes, shorts, and tank tops with the Slater Street Boxing Club logo on the front. By 1:35 pm all five boys were to meet at the van. Weigh-ins were at 4:00 pm; that gave them time for a six-mile run to get the blood flowing and shed those last two or three pounds, shower, get to the venue, register, and get on the scale.

Mike and Wallace were both slated to fight tonight. Mo, Patrick, and Darcy were looking at 8:00, 8:30 and 9:00 am matches respectively the next morning. Mike knew the route to run. He had spent four or five weeks in Barberton every summer growing up. Ken Steinhoff, his godfather lived here, and this is where he came to help his uncle on the farm.

Chapter 6
Friday July 6th, 2007, 1:35 pm.
Barberton, Ohio:

Ken was a huge man, standing six-foot six clocking in at well over three hundred pounds in his younger years. He was a retired Cleveland Ohio police sergeant, finishing his career on the SWAT team. He was terrifying man who, before joining the Cleveland Police department, had served several tours in both Korea and Vietnam as UDT which later became navy SEALs.

Ken was a blatantly racist skinhead of a man, proud of his German heritage. Every year he openly celebrated Adolf Hitlers birthday. He was also a gun nut, having completed a gunsmith's course in Colorado after retiring from the police department. He supplemented his income between his police and military pensions by working as a gunsmith for most of the local residents as well as local police and sheriff's departments.

The year before, out of curiosity Mike did and internet search of Uncle Ken's name and found several troubling articles from the Cleveland News-Herald going back to the early 1970's. At Mike's count, Uncle Ken had been brought up on police brutality charges on eleven separate occasions, and each time the witnesses either recanted or went missing.

He had openly bragged over drinks about how he carried throw away guns and had no issue placing them in the hands of someone he had just shot. Life was not valuable to Uncle Ken, not his or anyone else. He thought he had celebrated his 69th birthday in May. But wasn't sure what year he was born in, and still lived on a steady diet of crockpot chili, bean soup, Miller Genuine Draft, and Marlboro cigarettes. Since selling his farm, he spent most nights at a local bar in town drinking until 2:00 am then walking home.

For all his faults, he was also a very smart man, and very funny. When Mike was five on a camping trip, Uncle Ken taught him how to make a delayed fuse with an M-100, showing the young Mike a large firecracker and a lit cigarette.

"Think…" Uncle Ken instructed and sent Mike off into the woods.

When Ed looked around and asked, "Where's Mikey?" Ken told him about large firecracker.

Ed, panicking at first asked, "Does he have matches or a lighter?"

Ken replied "No."

Ed relaxed a bit until Ken said, "I gave him a lit cigarette."

"Jesus Christ Ken! He's going to kill himself!"

Ken, in his usual deep and nonchalant voice replied, "No he won't. He might blow a hand off, but he'll live."

As Ed got up from the table to go find Mike, they heard a thunderous boom and saw an old tree sixty yards away fall over. Ed, still healing from his motorcycle accident, took off running to find Mike. As he got closer to the tree line, Mike came walking out as if nothing happened. Ed dropped to his knees looking at Mike, checking his hands, looking for any damage. Worriedly, he asked Mike "What Happened?"

Mike, in a similar tone used by his Uncle Ken replied, "The tree fell.".

Later in life Mike had questioned why his parents, his dad especially, thought it was a good idea to send him to live with what could only be described as a homicidal sociopath for a month every summer. Mike always had fun at Uncle Ken's, but it was no place for a child. At the time, Ken owned a large piece of farmland between Cleveland and Barberton Ohio. It was on this farm that Mike learned some valuable skills.

First, he learned the value of an honest day's work for an honest day's pay. Uncle Ken worked Mike hard, but he paid him well for his labor.

Second, he taught Mike how to shoot and, more to the point, how to kill. After the chores on the farm came the shooting range. Here, Mike practiced target shooting, complete with explanations on how different rounds impacted a body. Ken also taught Mike what a kill shot was, how to shoot to wound, and where to shoot someone and still keep him alive. Mike learned how to shoot up close with pistols and how to pick targets off at a distance with riffles. Ken taught Mike how to breath while looking down a scope, and how to not flinch when squeezing the trigger.

In addition to guns, Ken taught Mike how to use compound bows, crossbows, knives, and hand to hand combat. He taught Mike how to make explosives with items under the kitchen sink, and how to make various forms of now outdated but still effective detonators, as well as how to lay (and more importantly spot) trip lines and booby traps. Mike learned how to move quietly through not only the woods, but in urban areas as well. It was Uncle Ken who taught Mike to wear earth colours and showed him firsthand how easy it is in an urban setting to spot someone trying to hide in black.

The four boys met in front of Ed's van at 1:35 pm. Four of the five knew the route. It would be a 3.1 mile run to the local Dairy Mart, a popular chain of convenience stores in Ohio, followed by a five-minute water break, then the same route back to the motel. The boys finished their stretching and set off jogging at a medium pace.

The sun was blistering, and before the end of the first city block, all five boys were drenched with sweat, the steady rhythm of their shoe soles slapping down on the cement. Their footsteps fell in line almost as if they were a small military unit marching together. There was seldom any conversation during these runs. Mike often drifted away, almost meditating, mentally preparing himself for the upcoming fights. He didn't daydream or work out a game plan in his head. He just used the run to clear his mind, get the anxiety under control, and get ready for war.

The five boys made it to the Dairy Mart in a little over twenty-nine minutes, not sprinting, but at a good solid therapeutic jog. As they crossed the busy street and made it into the parking lot, they all slowed to a nice walking pace. Mike used the bottom of his tank top wipe the sweat off his face. Now breathing heavy, little Mo's eyes locked on the front door.

"Water...I need water," he gasped, as if he'd just returned from days in the desert.

The four other boys made their way to the big glass-doored fridge, and each grabbed a small bottle of cold water. Mike, following another of Uncle Ken's early life lessons, grabbed a warm bottle off the shelf. His teammates always thought he was weird for not drinking cold water. Mike seemed to cramp up drinking it cold, so always took it room temperature or warmer. They made their way back up to the counter and placed the bottles at the till. The man behind the counter rang in the five bottles. Mike pulled out his debit card, covered the $3.90, and they stepped back out into the heat.

Cracking open their bottles, Mike downed his in one draw, crushed the bottle, and tossed it in the trash bin. This was where the five-minute break would help. Mike would down the bottle, let his stomach settle, then they would jog back to the motel. The five boys milled around the side of the store and were taking in what little shade was available when they heard another round of shoes hitting the ground coming from parking lot. Mike and Wallace looked over and counted eight more guys around the same age, now walking through the parking lot on the same mission. An older black man, Mike guessed in his early 50's, saw them and smiled.

"Y'all them boys from Canada?" he asked, a big-toothed smile showing one gold bicuspid up front.

"Yes sir," Mike replied.

Four of his students went inside to get water and the other four stayed outside with their coach. If this was a corny 1980's Hollywood movie, there would have been an intense stare down, but Hollywood was out of touch with reality and sportsmanship.

"When y'all get in today?" asked the coach.

"'Bout an hour ago," answered Mike, slowly walking over to the group. He stuck his hand out in a fist bump and introduced himself, "Mike Wolly."

The two groups had a small introduction in the parking lot. The other team was from Philadelphia. Mostly black, there was one Latino guy in the group who had broken away from the other three and had gone inside the store. The coach looked at the group and spotted little Mo.

"Are you Muhammad?" he asked.

"Yes Sir," Mo replied as they shook hands.

"You're up against my boy tomorrow morning," he said nodding towards the young Latino boy in the store. Mo eyed the boy and saw he was a small guy with a naturally hard look; a face that showed the reminder of multiple fights both in and out of the ring.

Unsure of what to say, Mo nodded his response to the coach.

The group exchanged small talk. Mike recognized one of the boys as Daryll Williams. Mike had faced his older brother Bobby in a brutal back and forth the year before.

By this time their four remaining teammates had returned with water. Their coach made a quick group introduction, ending on Jose Ramirez. He introduced Jose to Mo. They shook hands and wished each other luck in tomorrow's match. This was an amateur tournament; there was no money on the line. There was no animosity between competitors. More often than not, fighters had never met or known anything about each other going into a bout, but they came out as friends. They were matched up according to weight, and the class they fell into: A, B, or C. Their class was determined solely by the number of matches they'd had. Facing someone and putting on a good match up often resulted in invites to each other's clubs.

Mike looked back at his team and asked, "We good?"

They all nodded. They exchanged nods with the other team, wished each other luck, and set off running back to the motel.

Thirty minutes later they slowed to a walk, huffing and puffing as they made their way through the motel's blacktop parking lot. Now close to 2:45 pm, the temperature outside was pushing 95^0 degrees and the humidity added another ten degrees. The five boys walked back towards their rooms when Mike heard his Uncle Ken's booming voice coming from Ed's door.

"Miiiiiiichhhhaaaeeeel!"

Mike stopped and saw his uncle. Ken stood there in his typical attire; a pair of brown Carhart work pants, faded and torn from years of work in the field or his machine shop, likely washed a thousand times over. He also wore a bright pink t-shirt with white lettering that said, "I Beat Anorexia" and his favourite black tactical style combat boots. Mike walked over to say hello while Wallace went ahead to the room for a shower.

Ed was standing behind Ken in the doorway.

"Come here," Ed demanded.

Mike walked in. Cecil removed himself from the room saying he was going to check on the other boys and make sure they would be ready by 3:15 pm. Ed motioned for Mike to sit down. There was a third man in the room that Mike had never met before. Without a word being said, the stranger approached Mike carrying a little black bag.

"Which hand?" he asked without an introduction.

Mike held out his right hand. The stranger took it, not gently but not hurting him either. He examined it quickly, asking Mike "Does this hurt?" while applying pressure in various areas. Mike grimaced in response.

"What happened?" the man asked still checking it over, squeezing in different spots.

Mike told him about his hand colliding with Wallace's the night before.

The man turned to Ed and confirmed what they already knew. "He broke the metacarpal." Ed nodded. Without anything else being said, the man opened his little black bag and removed a syringe and a small glass vial.

"This is Lidocaine," the man explained to Ed. "A nerve blocker. I'll give him one injection. It'll start working now, and usually last between thirty minutes to three hours. If he breaks out in hives or starts having chest pains, bring him to a hospital right away."

Mike started to worry.

"He has a fight at 7:00 pm," Ed advised.

"It could wear off before then," admitted the man.

"Can't you just give him more now?" Ed asked, concerned that the effects of injection would be gone before Mike's match.

"No," the man replied very matter-of-factly. "Too much will speed up his heart rate." He wiped Mikes palm with an alcohol swab.

Not understanding fully what was happening, Mike looked at his dad.

"What's going on?" Mike finally spoke up, clearly nervous.

"Shut up." Ed replied.

The stranger filled the syringe, gently squeezed Mike's hand, and injected the clear liquid into the fleshy part under Mike's thumb. A second injection went into the back of Mike's hand between the thumb and index finger, followed by a final shot along his metacarpal, about halfway between the base of his thumb and his wrist. Mike felt a hot sensation at first, but it quickly faded out, leaving his hand feeling cold and tingly. The man stood up, put the cap back on the syringe, and placed it on the motel dresser. He returned the rest of his equipment to the black bag and turned to leave.

Uncle Ken's gigantic frame blocked the door. "And, what about tonight?"

The man explained, "Well, that may wear off before 7:00 pm."

Ed and Ken both stared at the man. The stranger engaged in a game of who-will-blink-first against two men with which he had no hopes of winning. The man, clearly uncomfortable and starting to get nervous, fumbled in his black bag and produced a small glass vial and sterile packaged syringe.

"Here," he offered. "Inject it into the palm and outside edge here and here." He indicated the thick part on the heel of his palm and the outside area between the thumb and index finger. "Around five to seven milliliters. Do NOT give more than ten milliliters. He really should get an x-ray on that hand," he added while handing the vial and syringe to Ed.

The two men ended the staring contest and Ken moved away from the door. The man hurried to leave and just as he stepped outside, Ken in his deep gruff voice beckoned.

"Ohhh Doctor?"

The man stopped and looked back.

"We'll be requiring your services tomorrow as well," Ken added, with an upward inflection at the end, over exaggerating his politeness.

The man looked defeated but nodded. Ed mumbled something to Ken, and Ken in the same tone said to the man "Possibly Sunday too".

And with that, the man disappeared into the bright sunlight. Ed turned to Mike and said, "Go get ready."

Mike jumped up from his chair and headed towards the door. He walked with his head down, embarrassed by the whole event. As he passed by, Uncle Ken nudged him. "Hey kid."

"Hi," Mike murmured sheepishly.

Ken, showing a big, white-toothed smile full of dentures, grabbed Mike playfully by the back of the neck. Mike thought the man could probably choke him from behind with one hand. Mike was big, but Uncle Ken was huge and was shaking Mike around.

"How ya feeling? Ready to put on a show?" Ken asked.

"I'll try sir" Mike replied, smiling a bit.

Ken gave him a big, hefty pat on the back, almost knocking him off balance. "Looking forward to it".

"Aye, sir" Mike said walking out.

Mike was not a flashy, arrogant fighter. He was taught a lesson in sportsmanship and humility in one very embarrassing moment by Ed when he was eleven. Mike had just competed in and won his first ever match. When his hand was raised, he threw the other hand up and let out a "Whoo!" that had been building inside him for two years, He'd dreamed of this day for what felt like forever and had finally proven to his dad that he was a real boxer. In the midst of his celebration, Ed subtly slapped him in the back of the head. Confused, Mike looked at Ed, who quietly leaned down and through clenched teeth said, "That boy beside you just fought his fucking heart out, you show him some goddamn respect!"

Mike got his emotions in check. He understood what his dad was telling him, but he hated that in his first victory his dad could only point out what he did wrong.

Chapter 7

Friday July 6th, 2007, 2:55 pm.
Barberton, Ohio:

Mike hustled back to his room to find the door left open a crack. Wallace, having showered, was sitting on the bed in his red nylon work out pants with a two-inch white strip down the sides. The warmup pants were part of a suit with a zip-up jacket that had a big maple leaf and the word "Canada" across the top, but the afternoon was much too hot for the jacket to be worn today. Instead, Wallace wore his White t-shirt with the Slater Street logo in red on the front. Mike hurried into the room stripping off his sweat-soaked tank top and kicking off his shoes at the same time.

He hopped on one foot then the other, taking off his socks, and proceeded to drop his shorts outside the bathroom door. It was 2:58 pm and the van left at 3:15 pm on the dot. Mike turned on the cold tap, ignoring the hot completely. It didn't matter; it wasn't like the cold water went through a cooling system before spitting out of the shower head in a high-powered mist, and the water wasn't much cooler than the ambient temperature. Mike stepped into the shower letting it rinse the salt and heat off him.

He stood in the water for about thirty seconds, but it felt longer. He reached with his right hand for the small travel-sized shampoo bottle the motel had left in the shower and realized he couldn't feel his hand at all. No pain, nothing. It was like he was trying to grab the small bottle while already wearing a boxing glove. It didn't feel like that tingling feeling he got when he had slept on it funny. It felt like nothing was there at all.

Mike finished washing up, cut the water off, grabbed a towel, and pulled the shower curtain open. Wallace had left a pair of underwear on the bathroom countertop for Mike. The two boys had been through this same scenario so many times they knew what the other needed. He dried off, pulled on the boxer, and walked out into the motel room.

Mike immediately noticed his fight bag was packed and his warmup pants and matching Slater Street t-shirt were laid out on his bed. Throwing both on, he sat down and clumsily put on his socks and shoes. With his numb right hand, he tried to pick up his bag, dropping it immediately. Switching hands, he picked it back up and stepped out into the sunlight where at 3:07 pm everybody was standing at the van in the same matching outfits, ready to go.

The van made the five-minute drive to the venue, a small local sports complex built in the early 1960s and never updated. The local high school football and baseball teams played their home games here, but in early July the field was brown and yellow with patches of dirt showing throughout. The building stood about twenty feet high with a boxy looking red brick exterior with the odd dark brown brick seemingly thrown in at random. Inside it looked like every other US government funded building ever built. The main entrance contained three sets of double glass doors with only the center ones unlocked.

As the group entered, they were greeted by two overweight Midwest women. The first had a hairstyle that went out of style in the late 1980s. She wore a pink t-shirt with a cat on it, acid washed jeans, and white Reebok sneakers. She was seated with another women whose style predated her partner by about a decade, but who compensated with big, red-rimmed glasses on a costume jewelry chain to complete the ensemble. Both women had a pile of snacks and oversized fountain Diet Cokes bought from the Dairy Mart on their way to the venue an hour earlier. As the team walked through the door the cat lady hollered, "Register over here!".

Ed walked over and handed the lady five completed forms for the fighters, two separate forms for the coaches, and $375 USD in cash. This would cover the coaches' fees of $25 dollars a year to work a fighter's corner in Ohio. It also covered the $35 dollar annual registration fee for each fighter and the $30 dollar striking fee. Every time you wanted to fight in a tournament in Ohio, you had to give the state $30 for the privilege of getting beat up.

Cat lady skimmed over the seven documents and marked each one with her "Approved" stamp. She pulled out two business card-sized pieces of paper, wrote Ed and Cecil's information on them and ran them through the already-hot laminator beside her. She cut the freshly laminated cards out, handed them to Ed and Cecil and advised, "Don't lose these, they're good for the year".

She reached into a box beside her, pulled out five small black lanyards with three-inch by five-inch plastic sleeves on the end, each one containing a picture of the current fight poster with the word "Fighter" written on the back in black sharpie. "Don't lose these," she cautioned in a very curt manner. "You lose it, you can't get back in."

She passed them to Cecil who gave one to each boy. "Medicals are down the hall. Follow the signs. Get your papers stamped before weigh ins." She handed Ed back the paperwork he had just given her. The whole process took about three minutes.

Mike looked around and saw a few of the other club's coaches and fighters filling out the same forms that Ed had shown up with already completed.

By 3:45 pm the five boys were outside the medical room. Two doctors and two nurses were seeing the fighters in groups of four and administering quick medical exams in order to clear the fighters to compete. Mike was sitting on the chair in the hallway closest to the door, with Wallace beside him. Ed sat next to Cecil. Mo was sitting on the floor with his back against the wall. Darcy was across the hallway leaning against the cinder blocks while Patrick, feeling nervous, was pacing back and forth, lightly shadow boxing.

"The fuck is taking so long?" Patrick complained impatiently, throwing loose uppercuts as he completed his twentieth loop of the ten-foot-long hallway, in front of the others.

"Relax, it's part of the fun." Mike sighed, leaning forward, elbows on his knees, staring straight ahead.

Patrick made another turn and came back "I'm hungry though." he whined.

Mike ignored him. He'd been through this too many times to count. It was part of the process, like waiting at the airport for a flight; they'll call you in when they're damn good and ready. Patrick, growing increasingly more impatient, asked again. "What's taking so long?" to nobody in particular.

Mike snapped. "Hey. Shut up. You're getting on my nerves. It takes time. Go outside or sit down and shut up. You're trying my fucking patience right now."

Cecil interjected right away. "Calm down. Both of you."

Patrick stood frozen staring at Mike, then walked and sat next to little Mo. Mo had his ear buds in and was listening to a mixed CD on a Discman. Without a word he popped the right ear bud out and handed it to Patrick, who placed into his left ear.

At 3:51 pm Mike, Patrick, Darcy and Wallace were called into the exam rooms. Mike sat in a chair while a young nurse in her mid-twenties administered his tests. She was a pretty girl; small, physically fit, and wore light blue scrubs that accented her shoulder-length auburn hair that she had pulled back into a ponytail. She slapped a blood pressure cuff on him and started pumping the bulb.

"Where are you from?" she asked, showing a pretty and calming smile.

"Windsor," Mike replied, "Uh, Ontario. We're Canadian."

She was looking at the dial on the cuff, then shifted her eyes up and smiled.

"Nice," she said "I'm from Detroit. When's your first match?"

"Tonight at 7:00," he replied.

She took the cuff off, shined a pocket light into each eye, held her finger in front of his nose and said, "Follow my finger please." She moved her finger side to side, then up and down. She jotted something down on his form and asked, "Any injuries, illnesses?"

"No," Mike lied. She had him stand up as she stood in front of him, only coming up to his shoulders.

"Turn your head, sided to side." She requested. He did as he was asked.

"Good. Okay, arms straight out, bring them together over your head like this," she demonstrated.

Mike, thought of belting out "Y.M.C.A." but was sure she had already heard it a dozen times today and would hear it at least a dozen more.

She said, "Bend over and touch your toes?"

He did.

She took both his hands. Looking at his right palm, she asked "What's wrong with your hand?" Mike had been anticipating this question, and without stuttering replied, "I'm a boxer," and gave her a blank stare as if to say, "What you've never seen damaged hands before?"

"Any pain in it?" She squeezed on the word "it".

"No, none." Mike answered truthfully. "I rolled it on a heavy bag about a month ago. It's fine now."

She gave him a suspicious look, then smiled after a few seconds. Stamping his form, she said, "Good luck."

Mike walked out into the hallway and waited for the rest of his team. Little Mo had been called in as Mike was walking out, so it wouldn't be a long wait.

By 4:05 the group had entered the gymnasium. It looked like a stereotypical high school gym. It was a large, bright room with a high ceiling and no windows. Basketball and badminton court markings divided up the worn hardwood floor, and the wooden collapsible bleachers had been pulled out.

Scattered in the bleachers and throughout the room were about a hundred people; some sitting, some huddled in small groups. Several of the coaches were making the rounds, stopping to greet familiar faces, shake hands, or occasionally give big back-slapping one-armed hugs to each other. The odd camera flashed as coaches from different clubs or fighters that had faced each other in the past posed for pictures together.

Ed and Cecil, although both very social, were both "on the clock" as Cecil put it, and did not stray from their own group. Their rule was always to go get weighed in first, then go play with your friends.

The seven of them made their way to the weight station. There were four scales set up, each with a small lineup. The process was simple and moved like an assembly line. Unlike professional competitive boxing or MMA weigh ins, which are extravagant events used to promote ticket sales, weigh ins for this level of competition were done to keep fighters honest.

Handing over his registration papers and medical form, Mike stepped up to the scale. He had stripped down to just his underwear and realized the pair Wallace had placed in his room where bright yellow satin Boxer shorts with a giant happy face printed on both the front and back.

A tired looking official asked, "Name?"

"Mike Wolly."

"Date of Birth?"

"February 2nd, 1990."

The official directed Mike to the scale and he stepped on. The digital numbers, backlit in green, jumbled around and then came to a stop on the screen.

"Wolly, 205.1 pounds" The official said to the lady behind him who added the information to a document she was working on. No posing, no camera flash, no face off with the opponent.

Mike stepped off the scale, grabbed his clothes and threw them back on.

"Nice drawers." Darcy snickered.

"You like them?" Mike joked, feeling embarrassed.

Mike did a quick scan of the room, looking for anybody he might know, but with the number of people, the noise buzzing around, and the pre-fight anxiety, he couldn't concentrate. Mike found Ed talking to a short old man that Mike guessed had to be pushing ninety years old. As Mike approached them, Ed looked over at him and tilted his chin up. It was his way of asking "All good?"

Mike nodded as he got closer. He stepped up to Ed and was introduced to the old man.

"This is my son Mike. He's up at 7:00 pm tonight." with no introduction or explanation to Mike of who the old man was.

The old man nodded a hello.

Mike said to Ed, "Can we eat? I'm starving."

Ed nodded and said, "Grab the others. I'll meet you outside," and went back to his conversation with the old man.

Chapter 8

Friday July 6th, 2007, 6:35 pm.
Barberton, Ohio:

Mike sat backwards in a chair with his right hand extended all the way out in front of him, the forearm resting on the back of another chair. He stared off into space, trying to keep his nerves in line.

Sitting in front of Mike was Ed. Ed wore an oversized white silk shirt with black trim around the sleeves and collar, and the Slater Street Boxing Club logo embroidered on the back. "ED" was stitched in bold red letters over the left breast and "Coach" stitched in one-inch-high letters on each sleeve. Black cotton dress pants and black shoes finished off his look: this was his coaching uniform.

Ed, under the watchful eye of the Ohio State Athletic commission, was taping Mike's hands. This was a process that typically took about ten minutes per hand when done properly. The state was very strict in their rules for taping hands. The coaches had been handed a pamphlet explaining the rules when they arrived. Ed threw his in the garbage. He had been taping hands for over forty years he didn't need a piece of paper telling him how to do it.

The gaming official was an older black man; Mike guessed him to be in his mid-sixties to early seventies. He was around six feet tall with a slim build, still carrying some muscle definition on his aging body. His dark skin contrasted against the light ring of white hairs, and Mike thought he looked like someone had glued a ring of cotton balls around his head. His eyes were blood shot and watery but ever vigilant. He stood by closely, watching Ed tape up, inspecting the tape and gauze before Ed was allowed to apply it.

Ed finished taping Mikes right hand, and without being prompted or looking up, Mike adjusted in the seat and held his hand out for the gaming official to inspect it. This was the moment of truth. The gaming official would take Mikes hand, and while inspecting the wrapping to ensure it was done according to Ohio State regulations, he would also inadvertently be checking the hand for injury. If Mike flinched from pain, his fight would be cancelled. Ed had given Mike his second dose of Lidocaine, a full ten milligrams, twenty minutes ago and while he could tell his hand was being moved around while the official inspected it, he could not feel the hand at all.

The official approved the tape job, and with a thick black magic marker he scribbled what was allegedly his initials on the tape. Immediately Ed slid Mike's gloves on, tied them tight, and taped the wrist with multiple layers of the same white hospital tape. The official added the same scribble, and just like that Mike was cleared to fight.

Ed stood up, walked over to the opened fight bag on the bench and dug out a pair of focus mitts. This was the time Mike looked forward to: just him and his dad, alone in the dressing room. Ed donned the leather mitts, a gift from a fight promoter many years ago. They were big and bulky, the dark red leather turning almost brown with time, the words "Rough House" scrawled on the back of the Velcro strap where other mitts usually said "EVERLAST". The palms looked paper thin from years of use.

Ed walked back over to Mike who was now standing, bouncing slightly on the balls of his feet. Ed raised the pads and called, "One, two." Instantly the sound of two loud snaps filled the small room. "One, one, two" Ed barked, and Mike threw two stiff right jabs followed by a powerful straight left. "Double slip, two, three, two". Ed, with mitted hands, threw two punches at Mike who responded by moving his head side to side with cat-like speed to slip both punches and counter with a straight left, a right hook, and another straight left. This dance continued for another fifteen minutes until 6:55 pm. Ed called time and Mike took a drink of water.

Mike kept moving, shadow boxing and bouncing, watching the minutes tick by while waiting for the official to tell him his match was starting. The muffled sound of the crowd cheering was sporadically interrupted by music every three minutes, lasting for exactly one minute, then it was back to the crowd's cheers. The third round of the ongoing match was ending, and Mike kept looking at the clock. With one minute left, there was a bang on the door. Ed opened it. Cecil, Wallace, Darcy, Mo, and Patrick all walked in.

Mike was fighting out of the blue corner; the "Away" team. The small team utilized a strategy favoured by many clubs. Both Ed and Cecil would be in the Mike's corner, while the four teammates would position themselves spaced out on all sides of the ring. No matter where Mike was, he would be able to hear his teammates. With the door open they heard the match end, and that was it: showtime. Right on time, the official stepped into the hallway outside the changing room and yelled "Wolly! You're up!"

Mike stood in a dark hallway with his eyes closed as the song "Burn" by the Cure started to play. A song off the soundtrack from the 1994 Brandon Lee movie, The Crow, it was dark and sinister but had high energy. Mike waited until the song was well a minute in before opening his eyes. He started bouncing on the balls of his feet.

At the two-minute mark he walked into the gymnasium. Lead by Cecil, Mike followed with his dad bringing up the tail. He walked at a slow but steady pace; this was his warmup and he needed it.

At three minutes he made it to the ringside where the Ohio Athletic Commission official waited patiently. Placing Mike's blue headgear on his head and fastening it tight, he asked Mike to smile and show his mouth guard. Mike complied, then turned to face Ed who applied Vaseline to Mike's eyebrows, cheeks, and the bridge of his nose. This was done to prevent the leather from tearing the skin open. Mike stared at the steps to the ring. The fear in his gut felt like a fire.

At the three minute and thirty-five second mark, Mike jumped up on to the apron. Stepping through the top and middle rope, he swung his upper half in and out, three times before finally entering the ring. Many people have incorrectly called this action showboating. It is in fact a tradition done for luck, like hockey players who don't shave during playoffs. At the three minute forty-three second mark of the song, just as it hit its instrumental apex, Mike climbed through the ropes fully.

Mike, now in his own little world, bounced sideways around the inside of the ring, taking it all in. After a full lap, his music cut out and "Hit 'Em Up" by 2Pac started playing. Mike's opponent was an eighteen-year-old black man from Syracuse, New York. Similar in size to Mike, he was an inch shorter at six foot two, and at two hundred and six pounds he was also a lean fighter.

His opponent entered the ring at the red corner. Mike was on the opposite side, facing his own corner. As soon as he felt his opponent enter the ring, he turned and faced him. In Mike's world, this is where he switched on. All the noise, all the cheering, music, talking-- everything faded out. As he did on the first day he set foot in a boxing ring, Mike had the same thought in his head about his opponent: you're in my yard.

Mike stared directly into his competitor's eyes. From this moment until the fight started, Mike would not take his eyes off Red. Mike was scared, but a good scared. He knew this was his domain; all the training, all the early morning runs, late evenings workouts, sweat, blood, tears, sore muscles, broken bones, swollen black eyes, bloody noses, fat lips, all the white flashes when he zigged instead of zagged and was caught with a heavy shot sparing-- all of it was for this moment. He was ready. He trained, and he trained hard. Harder than his opponents did - he was sure of it. This was the type of scared that sharpened his senses and made his reflexes faster.

Both fighters and their coaches were called to the center of the ring. They were given the standard pep talk by the ref, asked if they had any questions, touched gloves, and without turning around Mike danced backwards to his corner, still keeping his eyes on Red.

"Hey, HEY!" Ed yelled.

Mike nodded not taking his eyes off his opponent.

"Take it to him, you hear me? Get your retaliation in first!" Ed barked. "What did I say?" he asked, shaking Mike's shoulder.

"Go kill that motherfucker!" Mike replied.

Ed hopped off the apron, looked back up at his son, and yelled "Take it to him Mike!"

The referee stood in the middle of the ring. He was a large man, about thirty years old, with styled brown hair, a blue dress shirt with a black bowtie, black slacks, and black boxing shoes. He looked in Mike's direction. "Blue corner, are you ready?"

Mike nodded raising one glove, while bouncing on his feet.

"Red corner, ready?" Red's eyes flashed from Mike to the ref and back before he nodded.

And in that split second Mike said to himself, "Got him."

"Okay gentlemen, BOX!"

The bell rang. Mike smashed his blue gloves together and bounced out of his corner. Mike wasn't really a fast or a slow starter, where he excelled was in taking people out of their comfort zones. If his opponent was the type to rush out of their corner, Mike would hang back and limit engagement, frustrating them. If they were a slow or nervous starter, he would work side to side, advancing and putting pressure on them. He was also the type of guy that would cut off the ring and position himself between his opponent and their corner as soon as possible; a subtle way of saying "You can't go home now."

The two fighters moved around each other. Mike used his long jab to set his distance and get a feel for his opponent. He noticed two small holes in his opponent's game: one, he drew back his left hand before he would jab, and two, after he jabbed, he would leave his hand out for a half a second too long.

Okay, Mike thought. Watch for the jab and be ready with a right hook over top. Don't think just throw.

Mike, a lefty, lowered his right hand just a bit to bait his opponent, and slid his lead right foot forward and like a train that's always on time. His opponent's left hand twitched back and then darted straight out. Willing to take one in order to give one, Mike let the jab hit him in the nose while simultaneously torquing his body at the hips and shoulders, throwing a powerful right hook that collided with his opponent's forehead, followed by a left hand straight down the middle. He followed up with another right hand that had no target to hit because when the left hand connected, Red's feet slipped out from under him and before he realized what happened he had landed on his butt. Surprised, but not hurt, he bounced right back up. The ref appeared immediately to talk to him.

"Are you Okay?" asked the ref, brushing Reds gloves off on his shirt.

"Yeah, yeah I'm good" Red insisted.

The ref issued a standing eight count, looked back at Mike, and then yelled, "Fight."

Like a shark smelling blood in the water, Mike bounced forward and thought to himself, okay, he doesn't like getting hit.

Nobody really enjoys getting hit, but some people could eat your best shots and it wouldn't slow them down. Mike had faced a more than a few of them over the years. Others would get hit and the instant you connected; you broke them. It took their heart and killed their spirit. Drop someone in the first minute of a fight, they'll spend the rest of the fight trying not to get hit again.

Mike came forward and threw two jabs in quick succession. Red, anticipating a hard left behind, it raised his hands to cover up. And Mike saw it. On the right side of Red's torso, Mike threw a left to the body and landed a crushing blow to Red's liver followed by another right hook to the head. Both connected, though the left hook behind it missed. Red backed away from the onslaught, but like most well-placed liver punches there was a delayed reaction. Taking a step back, Red felt the pain raise up through his core. First a dull ache, rapidly expanding and resulting in his legs getting weak. The pain continuing to spread like a bomb going off in his abdomen. Three seconds after taking the brutal shot he turned away and dropped to one knee and collapsed on his side, spitting out his mouth guard in the process. The ref looking from Red, to Mike to Red again, waved off the fight.

And just like that, Mike clicked back into reality. The sound came rushing back into his ears and he heard his dad and Cecil yelling, the crowd cheering. He turned and calmly walked back to his corner. He leaned back into the blue pad, draping his arms over the ropes, and waited for the ref to call him back to the center for the official announcement.

The entire bout took just one minute and twelve seconds. Finding well-matched opponents for Mike, especially in the US, was becoming harder to do, and Mike had started noticing the talent pool for his division was become shallower. Mike was called back to the center of the ring where his hand was raised. He hugged his opponent, showed the proper respect to Red's coaches, and made his way back to the dressing room where he was greeted by the occasional compliment from someone in the crowd. "Damn good fight son," or "Nice hit."

Mike thanked everyone that took the time to acknowledge him, but he had to get moving. Wallace had a match coming up soon with a very tough guy from somewhere in Pennsylvania. Over the years Mike had understood the celebrations would happen later, and if Wallace lost tonight, possibly not at all. Your team is only going to be as happy as the least happy person in the vehicle on the way home at the end of the night. Mike entered the change room to a brief round of applause from his teammates. Wallace gave him a hug "That was nasty, why you try and kill that boy like that?"

Mike smiled "'Cause he'd have done it to me if I wasn't first".

Cecil walked by and slapped Mike on the back. "Nicely done young man. Nicely done."

"Thank you, Coach," Mike replied.

"Okay boys, don't start sucking each other's dicks yet!" Ed barked. "Darcy, can you please go find someone and tell them I want to tape Wallace's hands right away." Darcy nodded and booked it out of the room. Ed continued "Wallace, start moving around. Mike, help him if you can".

And the celebration for Mike was over. Wallace quickly threw on his fight gear and his cup, a big stuffing filled piece of equipment. It resembles a medieval knight's codpiece, covering the family jewels, with a four-inch-thick padded strap that wrapped around the lower abdomen and tied up around the back. Another strap on the bottom on the cup area came up between the wearers leg and tied into the back. Mike sinched up Wallace's cup.

Next came the blue trunks which were the same as Mike's, followed by a blue mesh tank top with the Slater Street logo on the front. It was too big on Wallace. Mike looked at his dad and said "Tape," holding up his left hand. Without looking up, Ed tossed a roll of silver duct tape into Mike's left hand. Mike pulled out a length about eighteen inches long, tore it off with his teeth, and pinched the back of Wallace's tank top tight, taking the slack out of the front. He wrapped the tape around the bunched-up material. Wallace sat on the bench, slipped his runners off and put on his boxing boots. They were thin leather with a hard flat one quarter inch sole. Mike remembered his first pair and thought they looked like something a professional wrestler would wear. Wallace quickly laced them up, popped up from the bench tucked his shirt into his trunks, and was ready to go.

Wallace didn't need to be told but Ed said, "Start moving," anyway, instructing him to start warming up. Mike and Wallace faced each other and stared bouncing around like they were fighting, hands up but no punches being thrown. The two were playing a game where Mike had to try and trap Wallace in a corner, and using only his foot speed, Wallace had to find a way out of danger. Mike, the aggressor, would fake and juke side to side trying to back Wallace up.

Darcy reappeared in the door with the same official that oversaw Mike's taping. Ed whistled. The boys stopped their dance. Ed looked at Wallace, and walking over with a freezer bag said, "Sit," nodding toward the three chairs that made up the hand wrapping station.

Mike wished Wallace luck and ducked out of the room. He found the other three guys in the hallway, and they made their way to the gymnasium, positioning themselves on every side of the ring, ready for Wallace's match. Mike made it ringside where Uncle Ken was sitting with a pile of empty plastic cups at his feet that had recently held beer. He had a full cup in his left hand and half-full cup in his right, which he drained in one gulp, adding it to the growing stack of empty cups. Mike sat down beside Uncle Ken, who looked over and praised, "Good job kid."

"Thank you, sir," Mike replied.

Uncle Ken patted him on the leg and leaned in. "Hey, kid?"

Mike looked over and met Uncle Kens eyes., "I mean it," Ken continued, "I'm really proud of you."

"Thank you"

"I know your dad is too."

Mike stared ahead. Uncle Ken patted him twice on the thigh, sat back, and looked around.

"Where the fuck is that beer lady?" he asked loudly. "I'm almost out." Mike looked at the full cup and smiled.

Chapter 9
Friday July 6th, 2007, 8:30 pm.
Barberton, Ohio:

Wallace won his match, a hard-earned victory over a very tough opponent. It had been a long day on everybody, both physically and mentally, and the muggy heat didn't help.

Back in the room, Wallace showered first while Mike walked down to the corner to find a pay phone. He used a $20 calling card he'd purchased at a convenience store earlier in the week and called his mother. After four rings the answering machine picked up. Mike left a message, just five words: "I won. First round stoppage." and hung up.

Next, he called his girlfriend, Tamika. The two had been dating since November the previous year. She was sixteen and tall for her age, around five foot ten, with an athletic build that came from years of track and field. She was a biracial girl with a white mother, and presumably a black father. In the almost eight months they had been dating, Mike had never met her father and couldn't recall any pictures of him at her house.

Tamika had approached Mike when she saw him at a friend's party. She remembered watching him the weekend before at an amateur event in which her older brother, Will, also took part. Mike and Will had known each other but not well.

They shared a few mutual friends, but before he started dating Tamika, Mike couldn't remember ever seeing Will in any context that wasn't related to boxing. Mike was a member of the Slater Street Boxing Club, and Will was a long-standing member of one of the larger clubs in the city.

"Tell me some good news." Tamika demanded cheerfully, forgoing the usual salutations.

"I won," Mike offered, smiling.

"Of course you did! Tell me everything"

"Stopped him in the first round. Body shot." Mike explained.

"That's my man!" She exclaimed with a loud laugh.

Mike could hear someone talking in the background, and Tamika called out, "He won, first round!" Mike could hear Laurie, Tamika's mother, in the background yelling out her congratulations.

"You get hit at all?" Tamika asked, returning her attention to Mike.

"Nothing bad. Caught me solid in the nose, but it didn't bleed. I think I broke my hand on his head though." Mike lied. He figured he'd taken enough heat and abuse from Ed over his hand today. He didn't want to take it from Tamika too.

"Oh no. Are you done?" she asked, with genuine concern in her voice.

"No, I did the medical today. I think I can fight through it tomorrow. Besides, I don't want to pay for a doctor in the States, I'll get it looked at when I get home."

"Baby, you gotta take care of yourself." she chastised.

Mike's eyes were welling up with tears. He'd had a long day and didn't have the maturity to process everything that had happened. He was tired of everybody making him feel stupid.

"I'll be fine," he assured her, trying to remain calm "I've done it before, plus I'm not even sure if it's broken. I'll ice it before and after tomorrow's fight."

"Okay, baby," Tamika soothed, sensing the frustration in his voice. Tamika was the only person in whom Mike had ever confided about how Ed made him feel. Many people knew or could see it; it was obvious. But she was the only person to ever hear it from Mike's mouth.

"Who else fought tonight?" she asked in an attempt to change the subject.

"Wallace." Mike replied. "He went the distance, but he won. Good fight though, a lot of back and forth. Some guy from up near Pittsburg. We just got back to the room."

"Did you call your mom?" she inquired.

"Yeah, no answer." He paused then added, "I'm gonna head back to the room. It's been a rough day. I need to sleep. We have three fights in the morning and two in the afternoon."

"Sure thing, baby. What time are you fighting tomorrow?"

"2:00pm, I think? Wallace and I both fight tomorrow afternoon. If I win tomorrow, I'll be in the finals Sunday." The events of the day were hitting Mike like waves, making it hard to remember the schedule.

"Okay babe. Take care of yourself. Tell Wallace I said congrats and wish the other guys luck. Hold on," she instructed and answered her mother, yelling, "Either tomorrow or Sunday". He could hear Laurie muffled in the background again and Tamika's reply of, "I don't know," then "Ugh. Hold on," and Laurie got on the line.

"Hi Michael" Laurie's voice was full of warmth and cheer. Since day one she had called him by his full name.

"Hi," Mike replied.

"When do you get back?" she asked.

"If I lose tomorrow, we're coming home. But it won't be till late, like ten at night. If I win tomorrow, then I'll be fighting Sunday morning, so probably Sunday around dinner time?" he guessed.

"Okay, let us know, hun. I'll make dinner for you when you get back. Congratulations, sweetie."

"Thank you." he mumbled as Tamika came back on the line.

"Are you okay?" She asked again.

"Just tired" he repeated. "I'm gonna go wash up and get some sleep."

"Okay. I love you" she said.

"Me too." he replied and hung up.

Mike walked back the motel enjoying the quiet, he'd felt like he had been going nonstop since 8:00 am and could finally take a few minutes for himself. He replayed the night's bout in his head. He couldn't think of anything he needed to improve but was sure a later look at a video would reveal a few holes he could touch up on.

As he walked towards his room, the door to Ed's room opened. Ed was stepping outside for a cigarette. Cecil didn't smoke, and years ago the two had come to an agreement; Ed could smoke in the van with the window down but couldn't smoke in the room. He lit his smoke with the Zippo lighter Mike had gotten him for him last Christmas. It had a small reprint of a police officer sitting at a diner, talking to a little boy who was carrying a stick with a handkerchief holding his belongings while the fry cook smiled at them. It was an old Norman Rockwell painting that had hung in their home as long as Mike could remember. Mike was around five years old when he realized it was not a picture of him and Ed.

"What are you doing?" Ed asked in his gravelly voice.

"Nothing. Taking a walk. Wallace called dibs on the shower, and I needed to clear my head." Mike answered.

Ed gave him a suspicious look taking a long drag off his cigarette. "You saw the lazy jab, huh?"

Mike smiled. "Yeah, knew I could get it. Just needed to bait him a little bit."

Ed blew out a cloud of smoke and let out a small chuckle. "First combo was nice. He's lucky that second right didn't land. Likely to have taken his head clean off if it did. Next time swing where he's going to be."

"I will." Mike promised, As Ed critiqued his performance. Mike always felt like if he came home with a 96% on a match exam, Ed would ask about the missing 4%.

Ed took another drag and said "We'll work on it Monday." Ed blew out smoke and added, "We've got about eight months to go Mikey, that's all. We gotta keep you busy for the eight months, then you can go pro."

Mike just nodded.

Ed continued. "It's getting harder to find matches for you. When we get home, we'll talk about crossing to Detroit, see if Kronk can keep you moving around." Ed was referring to bringing Mike to spar at Kronk, a world-famous gym in Detroit that was home to some of the top fighters in the world like James Toney and Tommy Hearns.

Ed looked thoughtfully at his cigarette, the red glowing amber in the dark parking lot. "Next time swing where he's going to be."

Mike said nothing, just nodded. Finally, he said "I'm gonna head to bed"

As Mike walked away, Ed asked, "How's your hand?"

Mike opened and closed it a couple times and replied, "A little tight, but still pretty numb."

"Get a bucket of ice and take some Advil. It'll be on fire around midnight," Ed advised, then flicked his cigarette and went back inside.

Mike returned to his room. Wallace had left the door open a crack for him and was watching a football movie. Mike dug out the Advil from his bag and popped three right away. Grabbing a pair of shorts from his bag, he went for a shower. He yelled "If you get the urge to filled up the ice bucket for my hand, don't fight it," and shut the door.

Ed was wrong. Mike's hand didn't hurt at midnight. It was 2:05 am when Mike woke up with his hand feeling like it had been placed on a table and beaten with a hammer. He grabbed the ice bucket that was in the mini fridge, compliments of Wallace. Swallowing three more Advil, he dunked his hand in, watching the clock: twenty minutes in, twenty minutes out. After a trip to refill the bucket and taking it out for the third time, Mike saw it was now almost 4:00 am and tried to get back to sleep.

Chapter 10

Saturday July 7th, 2007, 6:30 am.
Barberton, Ohio:

At 6:30 am sharp Cecil pounded on the door. Mike and Wallace both hopped out of bed. Mike hand was throbbing. He could use it, but it was sore and bruised. They dressed, and by 6:40am they were all out at the van. Ed came out and looked at Mike. "How's your hand feeling?"

Mike tried to shrug it off like it was no big deal. "Woke up around 2:00am Soaked it in ice for a couple hours."

"You wanna come? Or stay" Ed asked.

"Let's go," Mike said, and they set off for the sports complex.

The fights were early today. Mo was first up at 8:00 am and was scheduled to face the young Latino boy they'd met the day before. Mo was quiet on the drive, mentally preparing for his match.

Mo was very well respected in their group. He was the smallest, standing at five foot four inches and one hundred and thirty-five pounds. He was fast, he hit hard, and had a solid chin. In the four years he had been training with them, seventeen-year-old Mo had earned a reputation as one of the toughest guys to ever train at Slater Street. Promoters or other clubs often asked for him by name when putting together fight cards because they knew that Mo would definitely put on a banger for the crowd.

Ed called back from the front seat, "We're going to get Mo ready," referring to himself and Cecil. "Mike, you take Patrick. Wallace you're with Darcy. We have fifteen minutes between each bout. Stacy will be there to tape hands. I want both you boys sweating by the time Mo's done, got it?"

A mix of "Yes, coach" and "Yes, sir" came from the five boys.

They pulled up at the venue and hightailed it inside. Walking in, Ed saw the first official and explained "Hand taping, right away. He's on deck at 8:00 am," pointing his thumb back at Mo. The official nodded his head and matched their quickening speed, heading to the makeshift changing room.

Mike addressed Patrick and Darcy, "Go get geared up. I'll find the girl." With Wallace behind them, the two headed straight for the other changing rooms.

Mike popped his head into the gymnasium and did a quick look around. He found Stacey, the wife of one of the local Cleveland club owners. Stacey was black and in her mid-fifties. She had short blonde hair gelled down and could easily pass for her early thirties. She had very soft features; big dark eyes and a huge open-mouthed smile. She was a little bottom heavy but wore her size well and always dressed in clothing that flattered every part of her.

Mike hurried over to Stacey and smiled. "Morning!"

Stacey, with her big smile, hugged Mike and gave him a kiss on the cheek "Morning, handsome!" she beamed. "Good show last night."

"Thank you," Mike replied and added, "Dad said you can tape for us?"

Her smile went away, strictly business now. "Yes sugar. How many?"

"Dad's doing Mo right now. We have two more on deck, going up right after."

Stacey turned to her husband, Buford. A large man, and former pro boxer turned head coach at their club, Buford saw Mike and smiled. He was wearing a Cleveland Browns ball cap, a black t-shirt with the Rock and Roll Hall of Fame logo on it, black jeans, and black and red Air Jordans. A thick gold chain hung around his almost nonexistent neck.

Pulling Mike in for a hug he said, "Whatshappin, baby?" Stacey cut in, "Ed needs his boys taped." Buford nodded. The three of them walked out of the gym and went straight towards the change rooms where Darcy and Patrick were warming up. Mike pointed at their door, "They're in there," then veered off to find Ed.

Mike Popped his head into the room while Ed taped Lil Mo.

"Excuse me?" He spoke. The Official looked "I need wraps for the guys." Ed nodded towards the gym bag. Mike grabbed four ziplock bags. Then to the official he said "Two more across the hall, ready for taping"

The official didn't take his eyes off Ed but keyed his mic. Mumbled something than said "Two minutes."

Twenty minutes later Mike was holding focus mitts for Patrick when they heard the music cut out and the ring announcer take over. In the cinder-block dressing room with the door closed they couldn't hear what was being said, but Mike recognized the familiar cadence; asking the small crowd how they were, asking them if they're ready, thanking the sponsors, thanking the officials, and announcing the referee for the first bout. Judges were announced with a small pause between each name for applause. A moment of silence followed, after which there was a ten count with the bell to pay respects to an old boxer or local war vet who recently passed away.

They could hear the familiar rhythm of another match starting, Mike looked at the clock. 8:02am Say what you wanted to about Boxing in Ohio but the events always ran smoothly. Mike tried prepping Patrick, but found himself staring at the clock, watching the seconds go by and wondering how Lil Mo was doing.

Patrick glanced at Mike while shadow boxing "I'm good man, go watch."

"No," Mike declined, determined. "I'm staying here".

The familiar noise continued Mike looked at the clock again 8:11am

"Fight must be over now" Mike muttered, and right on cue he heard the announcer say something followed by the crowd roaring again. Mike figured it was the announcer asking the crowd to give it up for both fighters. "Mo Musta have banged it out."

"When doesn't he?" Patrick replied. They both waited, trying to hear something through the closed door. Mike finally opened it just in time to hear the crowd start cheering again.

Mike tuned back to Patrick "Hey, keep moving".

Patrick started shadow boxing again. Mike stood in the doorway looking towards the gym. The music came back on. Any second now they'd be coming out.

Mike was surprised to see Mo and Jose come around the corner together, both soaked from sweat and looking like they had just been put through a meat grinder. Blood trickled from both their noses while bright red patches, abrasions called raspberries, bloomed on both their faces. The walked side by side, while Mo held his towel out to Jose, displaying the patches of bright red blood on it from where he used it to dab at his nose. Both guys were smiling and laughing, Ed and the man they met at the Dairy Mart the day before walked out side by side as well.

Mike nodded to Mo. "Well?"

Mo smiled and shrugged "Draw."

Mike stepped out of the room and shook Jose's hand. "You gotta be one tough motherfucker to draw with this guy," he said nodding towards Mo.

"Thank you." Jose said understanding the Mike wasn't being sarcastic.

Ed came up and asked, "Pat ready?"

Mike nodded "Shadow boxing. He's good. All set."

Ed and the other coach shook hands. He spoke to Jose while the other coach spoke to Mo, both congratulating the other fighter on an amazing performance. Then Ed went towards Patrick's dressing room.

"Hell of a way to start the show!" the other coach yelled as they walked away.

Mike looked over at Mo, "You good?"

Mo smiled, then his upper lip quivered a bit as tears welled in his eyes. Mike understood right away. Some fighters cried after a hard match. It wasn't pain, or happiness, it was simply that at the end of the day, these were sixteen- and seventeen-year-old boys. They were on emotional overload and had no idea what was going on or how to deal with it. Mike grabbed Mo, ushered him to his dressing room, held the door open, then waited outside. "Two minutes oughta do it," he called in as he stood guard.

An official came down the hallway. Without saying a word, Mike pointed at Patrick's door. The ref banged twice then hollered, "WALSH! You're up!" and stepped back out, waiting to escort Patrick to the ring. A few moments later, Ed stepped out first, followed by Patrick and Cecil. Ed gave Mike an inquisitive look.

"He's taking a minute," Mike explained. Ed nodded he completely understood.

Mike looked at Patrick and said, "As soon as Mo's good I'll be out there." Patrick, bouncing on the spot, mouth guard in, gloves on and taped up at the wrist, nodded. He put one hand out. Mike fist bumped him and said, "Show them who you are."

The official touched his earpiece, looked back and instructed, "Let's go". The four of them set off for the ring.

Mike waited another thirty seconds then pushed the door open "Good?"

Mo sniffed, coughed, and yelled back "Yeah. Go help Pat."

"You sure?" Mike asked again.

"Yeah, I'm good. I'll be out there in a minute." Mo replied.

Mike closed the door, then popped over across the hall to check on Darcy and Wallace. "You guys good?" he asked.

"Yeah," Wallace replied. "What happened?" Referring to Mo's bout.

"Draw." Mike answered. "Guess they went scorched earth though. They both come out looking like shit."

Wallace smiled. "No shit. We could hear it".

Mike nodded to the other changeroom. "He's next door. Give it five minutes then check on him. I'm going to see Patrick."

He hustled to get to the Gymnasium and was astounded when he stepped in. It wasn't even 8:30 am and the place was packed, standing room only already. Mike made his way around to the far side of the ring. Patrick was blue corner, so Mike wanted to get to the red corner in case Patrick needed to hear someone on his team. He heard the ref say "OK, Box!" While trying not to trip over anyone in the dimly lit seating area, he had taken his eyes off the ring for second and heard the crowd erupt. He looked back in time to see Patrick on the mats. Patrick stood up trying to say he was okay, to keep going. He staggered and lost his balance, stumbling a bit. That was all the ref needed and he waved off the fight. Shit, Mike thought. "What the hell happened?"

Mike back-tracked to the blue corner. Patrick was standing in the corner shaking his head, as if the ref made a bad call. He looked over at Mike and said "Bullshit, I slipped" with his mouth guard still in. Mike inched his way up to Ed and Cecil and asked. "What happened?"

Cecil replied, "He got caught."

"Clean? Or..." Mike asked Cecil, trying to confirm if it was a clean hit that got Patrick or if he slipped.

Cecil looked back at Mike. "Floored him, he was out."

Mike nodded. It's not uncommon for a fighter to get their bell rung, losing a few seconds in the process. They don't remember getting hit. Mike had been there himself. Most boxing or MMA fans over the years have witnessed a ref stop a fight, and the person on the receiving end of the punishment jumps up in protest, not understanding why the fight was just stopped. The reality often doesn't set in until they watch the fight video and see it for themselves. Mike had witnessed fighters arguing with their own coaches, adamant that they were not knocked out.

Ed jumped up on the apron and informed Patrick of what happened. Patrick still in denial, continued to shake his head and yelled out, "This is fucking Bullshit!" Ed grabbed him by the front of his shirt, catching him off guard, and yanked him close. Quietly and calmly, he explained, "I said you went down. We'll watch the tape later. But right now, you're representing our club, and you look like an asshole. So, get your fucking attitude in check or find your own fucking way home." He let go and Patrick got the message.

The two fighters were called to the center of the ring for the official announcement. Ed and Cecil went along. They all shook hands in the ring, Ed and Cecil congratulating the other fighter. They made their way back to the dressing room.

The dressing room is where you celebrated or where you had your temper tantrum afterwards; in the back, in private where no one could see. As they were walking back, a lady with a clip board stopped Ed. The rest of the team carried on walking.

When they got back to the locker room Patrick sat down on the bench and asked Cecil. "Was I really out?" Cecil nodded his head, and Patrick responded, "Fuck, I don't remember getting hit." They heard footsteps running down the hall.

Ed barged in out of breath. He didn't run anymore, so the short distance was hard on him. Patrick said, "I'm sorry Coach."

Ed, still huffing, waved Patrick off. Looking at Mike he said, "Gear up, you're fighting at 9:30!"

Not fully understanding Mike, looked at Ed, confused. "What?"

Ed repeated, "Get your gear on! NOW!"

Mike didn't ask anything more. He ran out to the van and grabbed his fight bag. He sprinted back in past the cat lady who didn't ask for his fighter I.D. So much for "Don't lose it", he thought as he hurried back. He rushed past the open gymnasium door, and saw Darcy make his entrance to the ring.

Chapter 11
Saturday July 7th, 2007, 8:55 am.
Barberton, Ohio:

Mike went into the room Mo was in earlier. Stacey was already sitting there with an official, with the three chairs positioned ready for him to get his hands tapped. He sat down and looked at Stacey.

"What's going on?"

"Both heavyweights slated for this morning pulled out," Stacey explained. "You're automatically advanced to the finals. They were supposed to have the first deciding match at 9:30 am today. They moved the finals up. Sit down, sugar."

Mike sat down and Stacey started on his right hand. With her first pass the pain swelled in his hand, Shit, he thought, and immediately started strategizing about how he could possibly fight with his broken hand. He started breathing heavy, almost grunting between breaths. Stacey paused and asked, "You okay, sug?"

"Yeah" he lied, "Just trying to get my breathing exercises in before my match," thinking this would maybe be a good act of subterfuge when the official examined his wraps. Stacey was a pro and flew through both hands in less than sixteen minutes. The official signed off and was gone.

Stacey placed the empty Ziplock in Ed's travel bag winked at Mike. "How's that breathing?"

She smiled, wished him luck and walked out. Wallace came in right at the same time with Mike's fight clothes. Mike was facing a local kid from Cleveland, so he'd be blue again. He stripped down to his underwear. Wallace helped him put on his cup; not only was Mike essentially one handed, but he was also taped up and needed help. Wallace laced him up and threw Mike his blue trunks.

Mike's head was spinning. Everything was happening so fast. He was about to face a hometown kid, for the finals, with one hand. By this point his right hand hurt so bad from holding the pads earlier that he didn't think he could use it for anything. Not to block, not to jab, nothing. He pulled his trunks on. Wallace was kneeling down.

"Boots!" barked Wallace. Mike sat down and Wallace slipped on and tied Mike's boots. Mike stood up, grabbed his tank top, and threw it on. It was still damp from the night before.

"Okay, think Mike, think... Okay, we can try a defensive stance," he said to himself. A fighting style used effectively by Floyd Mayweather Sr. The fighter stands with their lead shoulder facing the opponent, lead hand low, using the shoulder to block. When done effectively, each slip cocks the hammer on the gun, loading up the fighter up with a counter power punch. The downside to this strategy was that Mike knew the style but wasn't that great at it. Plus, it also relied on the jab.

Mike reasoned that if he entered the ring and lost because of his hand, his father would be pissed. He would rather throw power shots into the heavy bag all day then deal with that fallout. "Gloves?" Mike asked Wallace.

"No." Wallace replied.

"Gimme my gloves, man." Mike repeated.

"Your pops said not yet" Wallace countered.

As if on cue, Ed burst through the door. He dug through his bag and pulled out the syringe they had used yesterday, and a vial of Lidocaine. "Lemme see your hand" he demanded, rushing back over. Mike was again caught off guard.

"They're wrapped" he argued.

"We don't have time. Give me your hand!" Ed snapped.

Mike held his hand out. Ed filled the syringe with ten milliliters of the clear fluid. He found a patch of gauze without tape and used it to inject half of the Lidocaine into Mike's palm. He flipped Mikes hand over, found another spot without tape and injected the rest on the outer side of Mikes hand. Mike looked at where Ed had stuck the needles. Close enough, he thought.

Ed looked back at Wallace and said, "Gloves?" Wallace had them ready. He slipped them on Mikes hands and tied them up while Ed put the syringe and vial back in his bag. Ed walked over, opened the door, looked out and yelled down to an official in the hallway. "Ready for gloves." The official entered the room.

"Gloves off!" the official demanded as he entered.

Ed looked over at Wallace and said, "Come on, you know better," hoping to chalk it up to confusion on the kid's part. The official looked over Mike's wrapped hands. He checked and rechecked for any powder residue that might be a sign of Plaster of Paris. He looked closely at the signature the previous official signed and asked, "Why didn't you glove up then?"

Without missing a beat Mike answered, "Heavy weight finals were moved up to this morning. I just found out. I needed to skip and warm up".

Ed, now holding a glove, asked, "Are we good? I want to get some pad work in."

The official nodded and Wallace and Ed each slipped a glove on to Mikes hands. Ed started tying the right one and asked Wallace, "Can you go grab my pads please?" Wallace hurried out of the room. Ed tied the other glove, and wrapped the wrist in tape. The official signed off on them and left the room. Ed breathed a sigh of relief then looked at Mike and said, "Get busy."

Mike started shadow boxing until Wallace came back. While Ed was strapping on the focus mitts, Mike looked at the clock. 9:13 am. He had fifteen minutes to warm up and prepare for a championship bout. He looked at Ed and asked, "How did Darcy do?"

Ed, biting on the strap to pull it tight, answered, "He won. Unanimous decision".

Good, Mike thought and moved into his pad routine.

At 9:26 am, the official banged on the door. "Wolly! You're up," he yelled and stepped back out into the hall.

Ed opened the door and Mike stepped out. Cecil was already there. His four teammates were there as well. Mike stood behind the official and said, "I'll tell you when I'm ready". The official nodded, and Mike stood in the hallway and closed his eyes.

Finding his way into his own mind, he heard the crashing start of the song Soul-Crusher by White Zombie. A fast-paced heavy metal song, it rang through the Slater Street club on a regular basis. The song starts with a fast guitar riff, joined by a buildup of drums and bass, then exploding into a tempo change, with the drummer's feet matching the guitarists hand, before switching to a second tempo change of heavy distortion.

Mike listened to the song build through the three different tempos. When the vocals started, Mike snapped his eyes open. "Let's do this!"

The official nodded and, without looking back, started the walk to the ring. Mike jumped through the door into the gymnasium. Bouncing on the balls of his feet, keeping warm, he followed the beat of the song. He made it to the ring where the next official put on Mike's head gear and checked for his mouth guard and cup.

Mike turned to Ed who applied the Vaseline. He bounced up the stairs onto the apron. He swung his right leg in, bent at the waist and swung his upper half in and out three times for luck, then entered the ring ready to go. Following the same path as the night before, he bounced sideways around the ring once before returning to the blue corner as his music faded out.

A rap song by a local Cleveland artist started up. Mike had never heard the song before. He stood in his corner and shadow boxed, throwing crisp clean hooks, waiting for his opponent. As the red corner made his way to the ring, Mike stayed focused in his own mind. Red stopped outside the ring at his corner to have his head gear put on. Mike turned and faced his own corner again, breathing heavily.

Ed grabbed Mike by the shoulder. Leaning into Mike's ear, he cautioned, "Slow your heart down. Breathe." Ed waited a second and repeated, "Breathe."

Mike calmed himself down and waited. He felt the ring shake as Red entered, and Mike turned to face him. His eyes locked on his opponent and again he thought, you're in my yard.

The ring announcer went through the motions, notifying the crowd that this was now the heavyweight finals. He thanked the sponsors, introduced both fighters, and they were called to the center of the ring. The ref gave the same pep talk.

"Ok Gentlemen I want a good clean fight. We went over the rules before. Watch out for head butts and rabbit punches. Watch the low blows. When I say break, you break. Obey My commands at all times and protect yourselves at all times. If you want to touch gloves, do it now." Mike held one hand out and Red bumped it. The ref said, "Go back to your corners and come out fighting".

Mike again danced backwards not taking his eyes off Red. He backed into the blue padding and Ed instructed, "Take it to him Mike. Eleven minutes. You owe me Eleven minutes!" referring to the three, three-minute rounds with the two-minute breaks in between. Ed climbed off the apron.

The ref looked at Mike, "Blue corner, ready?"

Mike, still bouncing and still staring at Red, raised a hand and nodded. "Red corner, ready?" Red nodded "Okay, gentlemen, BOX!" announced the ref, and both fighters advanced out of their corners.

Mike, his hand now completely numb, stuck a fast jab out. He had a weird sensation; he could tell it made contact, but he couldn't feel it. He couldn't tell if it was grazing or landing solid. No time for that, Mike thought. If they're landing, they count. He stuck in another jab while circling away from Red's right hand and tried to cut him off from his corner.

Red had skills. He had fast body movement and could get in and out quickly. He also bobbed and weaved his head unpredictably, making it hard to time a shot, or aim where he might be. Mike, almost matching Reds movements, continued to circle away from Red's right hand. The two exchanged light quick exchanges, one fighter coming in with an attack and the other countering.

Mike heard Ed yell out from his corner, "Bad plan!" That was Ed's way of telling Mike that Red left his hands low when he backed out after an attack. It sounded cheesy but it was their way of communicating without showing their hand. Ed was telling Mike that Red had a bad exit plan.

Mike heard him.

He slid one step forward, then backed up two. Red took the bait and came forward for another attack. Mike knew he had to be careful here; Red had been coming in with four and five punch combinations on every exchange. He knew that timing would count. He'd still dodge and block, but as Red threw his third punch, Mike would need to start his counter.

Red came in with a left jab, a right straight, a left hook, and Mike assumed there would be another straight right hand behind it. "Jab, straight, hook, straight." A predictable combination in boxing because it's used often, but it's used often because, when executed properly, it's very effective.

As the first hook landed, Mike shifted his weight to his own right foot, moving slightly further away from Red's right hand. At the same time, he torqued his hips and shoulders and landed a solid right hook on Red's forehead; the same spot he landed on his opponent last night. With a slight shift, he sailed his left hand down the pipe and again connected clean. Not wanting to miss a follow up, and anticipating that Red would duck off to Mike's right side, Mike continued the counter offensive with a cross between a right hook and uppercut. The assumption paid off. As Red ducked to Mike's right, Mike's right glove crashed into Red's face, staggering him backwards a step. The entire six punches took maybe a little more than a second and a half, but the damage was done.

Mike, now in the driver's seat, came forward stuck his jab, glancing it off Red's head, looking to follow up. Red, now in hot water, grabbed on to Mike to tie him up. Mike tried to shake him off but had no luck. Red was holding on for dear life to weather the storm. The ref jumped in and yelled, "Break". Red wouldn't let go. Louder, the ref repeated, "BREAK!" Mike put his hands up to show he wasn't holding, and Red took the opportunity to throw a solid three punch combo. Mike was knocked to the mat. He heard Ed and Cecil yelling about the late hits. He looked up at the ref and to his surprise the ref was counting.

"Counting?" he thought. "Those were illegal hits!" Mike didn't waste any time complaining. He hopped back up, shook his head and said, "I'm good!" The ref brushed Mikes gloves on the front of his shirt asked, "Can you continue?"

Mike, not bouncing, not moving, looked at him and said, "Yes," putting his hands up.

The ref backed out, looked at Red and said, "Box!"

Red came rushing back in. Mike knew that he was going to try and end it now. He quickly bounced sideways away from Red's right hand. It was a simple strategy for lefties: move to the opponents left. The opponent will try to pivot and match. As soon as he drops the right hand even just a little, jolt back to the left and let it go down the pipe again. Mike did just that.

For the second time, Mike's heavy left hand found its home on Red's face. Mike followed with a right to the body and another left upstairs, but neither did any damage. He heard the wooden blocks clack; ten seconds left. He kept moving side to side, looking for an opening and using his long jab to keep Red back.

They both moved in for another exchange. Mike heard the bell ring. The Ref yelled "TIME", and again Mike was hit with three more solid punches. This time the crowd erupted into a rumble of boos and fans screaming at the ref to do his job. Mike, now a bit dazed, sat on the stool. Cecil put an ice pack on the back of Mike's neck while Ed took his mouth guard out. Mike felt something not right in his mouth and used his tongue to push it. He felt a sharp pinch and spit out his second to last molar on the bottom left side of his mouth. Ed looked in the bucket, saw the big white molar and asked, "Are you Okay?"

Getting his bearings, Mike spat, "What the fuck is going on out there?"

Ed poured water into Mike's mouth with one hand and applied a cold compress below his left eye with the other.

"It's fucking Ohio, that's what going on".

Ed dropped the water bottle quickly wiped more Vaseline on Mikes face. "You gotta put him away Mike. If you don't stop him, they're gonna to fuck you. Do you hear me?" Ed grabbed Mikes chin and shook his face lightly. "What did I just say?" he demanded.

Mike looked at him and repeated, "Stop him".

As Mike said that the ref came over and said, "Seconds out!", cueing the cornermen to get out of the ring. Mike stood up, shook the cobwebs out of his head, and reminded himself of who he was facing. He made his way back to the center of the ring. The ref looked between the two fighters and yelled, "Box!"

Not wanting to play this game, Mike thought to himself, you've taken his six best. You're still standing. You gotta take it to him now. Two steps forward one back, he's going to try and tie you up. Don't let him.

Mike circled again, looking for an opening. He kept using his jab with the occasional straight left behind it, but the more he touched Red, the less willing Red was to engage. Mike knew he'd hurt him in the first round. He also knew he was facing a dirty fighter who relied on cheap shots to win the fight either late in the second or in the third round. Mike had to hit first and hit hard.

Mike decided to try something taught to him by Ed, who was the only person Mike knew that was truly ambidextrous. Ed could fluently write and throw with both hands. Mike switched up his stance from southpaw to orthodox, shuffled his feet, and circled back to his left, going towards Red's power hand. Mike slid forward, closing the gap, and landed a solid left jab followed by a fast-looping left hook. He again followed up with a straight, only this time it was with his right. All three punches found their mark.

Red's head snapped back, to the left, then back again violently. Knocked off balance, his upper half went stiff, and he slumped into the ropes. Mike, thinking he'd just knocked Red out, raised his hands. Ed and Cecil both jumped up cheering. Then Mike felt the ref grabbing him telling him to go to a neutral corner.

Mike thought, Neutral corner? Why are you counting? He's out!

He heard both Ed and Cecil yelling at the ref, who pushed Mike towards the corner. Mike watched as the ref walked back to Red who was struggling to get up. The ref reached down and stood Red up. Ed jumped up on the apron yelling, "What the fuck are you doing?" The ref pointed at Ed and yelled for him to get down.

Mike stood in the corner, baffled. He looked at Ed and Cecil for direction as the ref walked over to Red, grabbed his gloves brushed them off on his shirt and then started the eight count. Mike thought to himself. "Do I really have to kill this guy today?"

The ref, looked back at Mike and said "Box!"

Mike looked at Ed, who was holding a stopwatch. Ed yelled "Forty-eight seconds". Mike put up his gloves and moved forward. Red, still wobbling from the last combination, refused to engage. He back pedaled and almost ran away anytime Mike got close. Mike looked at the ref with a hand out, as if to ask "What am I supposed to do here?", but the ref yelled at Mike "Get busy!"

They heard the wooden blocks clack. Ten seconds left. Red was still scrambling away from Mike, causing the crowd to boo. Mike saw one last opportunity, and relied on the foot work drills he had done with Wallace the night before. He cut Red off, backing him into a corner and trapping him. He started with a jab but heard the bell ding shortly thereafter. As he stopped, Red came up swinging and hit Mike twice again. This time Mike saw it coming and threw back one of his own. The ref grabbed Mike and pushed him backwards sticking his finger in Mikes face yelling "You do that again, you're disqualified!"

Mike was in complete disbelief, which quickly evolved into anger. He stormed over to his corner. Ed was on the apron. Mike kicked the stool over and pushed it under the rope with his foot. Ed asked, "What are you doing?" Mike turning back staring straight ahead at Red's corner said, "Get out!"

Ed tried to get his attention, but Mike shoved him off with his forearm and yelled "Get out!" through his blood-filled mouth guard.

Mike was past angry. He was outraged with the ref and livid at the cheap shots. He was resentful that his fight was moved ahead with little notice. He was furious that his fucking hand was broken. He was pissed that Ed slammed his head in the wall, and for all the times Ed hit him, or worse insulted him, He was infuriated that his mother didn't answer the phone. He was maddened that this fight was turning into a nine-minute version of his whole fucking life. No matter how hard he worked, no matter how good he did it was never fucking good enough.

The ref looked over at him. Not caring anymore Mike, yelled out clear enough to be heard by everyone around the ring "This is on you!", then raised his hands in his stance, pacing like a caged animal ready to go. The ref, looking back to Red said "Box!"

Mike shot out of his corner like a bullet from a gun, almost racing across the ring. Red barely had time to realize what was happening, let alone react. Mike didn't punch at first, he collided with Red, shoving him back into the corner, and started to unload on him with both hands. It was like when Ed yelled "Power" in the club on the heavy bags, and Mike was putting all his fury into every punch. Red tried to cover up, but Mike grabbed Red's glove with his right hand and lowered it, smashing his left fist into the side of Red's head. Mike followed with another right and another left.

Red's arms dropped completely he slumped over and started to fall, but Mike kept punching. At seven second into the third round, the ref stepped in and called off the fight, pushing Mike back. Mike backed up a couple steps. He looked down at the ref who was waving to the fight doctor at ringside. And like last night, the sound rushed back into Mike's ears.

He turned back to the blue corner. Ed and Cecil were both up on the apron, stoic and silent. Ed was holding the stainless-steel bucket. Mike spit his mouth guard into it, along with a mouth full of blood from the broken molar. He looked at Cecil and said "Water." Cecil gave him a mouthful, he swished it around, spit it out this pink mixture, then took another swig. He turned around and faced the opposite corner.

Red was coming around. He was sitting on the stool head down nodding as the doctors asked him questions. Mike looked over and saw the ref leaning out between the ropes talking to two of the three judges. They were engaged in what looked like a heated discussion. Time seemed to drag on. Unprompted, Ed undid Mike's headgear and slipped it off, poured some water over his head, and wiped his face off.

After what felt like an eternity, Red tried to stand and sat back down. The ring announcer was standing near a neutral corner. The ref handed him a card and stood in the center of the ring. He motioned for Mike to join him. Mike walked out with Ed and Cecil behind him.

The announcer said "At seven seconds of the third-round, referee Kyle Davis called a stop to this bout, declaring the winner. As a result of a disqualification…" The boos from the crowd were deafening.

Mike was enraged. He looked at the referee and took one step forward. Ed grabbed him and held him back. Mike, holding eye contact, spit a mouthful of blood on the mat at the ref's feet. With blood-stained teeth he cursed "Fuck you!" and stormed out of the ring to the growing sound of boos as the crowd began throwing cups and trash in the ring.

Chapter 12
Saturday July 7th, 2007, 6:10 pm.
Somewhere along the Ohio Turnpike

The ride home was somber. Wallace had won his second fight but there was no celebrating. They had decided to drive home Saturday evening. Mike was sitting in the back of the van hand in a bucket of ice, a piece of gauze taken from one of the hand wrap kits wadded up in his mouth as he bit down where his molar use to be.

Mo at the start of the drive had asked if a movie was okay. Everyone agreed, so he popped in HEAT, with Robert DeNiro and Al Pacino. A great movie that would have had them captivated on any other occasion, but today they were all silent as all five boys stared out the window.

Wallace would celebrate when he got home, Mike was sure of that. Wallace, Darcy, and Mo likely had plans to go out already. Patrick would go if he felt like it, but he hadn't said much since his loss. Between Mike and Wallace's second matches, Ed had found someone who had recorded Mike's fight. Ed counted twenty-six seconds the ref allowed Red to recover after the first knockdown. For over an hour in the dressing room he was ranting about how they were going to appeal the match. Mike didn't care.

At 8:30 pm they rolled into the Slater Street parking lot. Ed shut the engine off and everyone got out. Cecil said to Mo, Darcy, and Wallace "You guys can come back Monday but no contact this week." He then turned to Patrick "Doc says stay home this week. Come back next Monday." As a medical precaution, Patrick was forbidden to box after being knocked out. The guys all grabbed their fight bags and brought them inside.

On Monday Mike would go through the bags and take out what belonged to the club. Right now, they were all tired. It was 8:30 pm on a Saturday night in July. The sun was still up, it was hot, but it felt like weeks since the night Ed had said "No sparing". Mike threw his bag up on the apron in the ring room, unzipped it to let it breath, then went to the office, picked up the phone and called Tamika.

Laurie answered on the third ring "You're back early." The club's number must have shown up on caller ID.

Mike replied, "Yes ma'am. We just got back. Is Tamika home?"

"You just missed her, hun," Laurie explained. "She just left with Jessica. Try her cell. They're on foot - can't be far."

Mike thanked her, hung up, and called Tamika's cell. She answered on the second ring.

"Are you back?" she asked, excitedly.

"Yeah. Just at the club now." he replied. She noticed tension in his voice.

"Did you want to come over?" she offered.

"When will you be home?"

She thought for a minute. "We were walking down to see Rusty," Rusty was Jessica's boyfriend, and Jessica was Tamika's best friend since kindergarten. "But I'll go back home," she added.

Mike considered the offer and replied, "Take your time. I'll walk over," knowing it would take about thirty minutes to get there by foot.

Mike had a Motorcycle, a 1996 Yamaha FZ 750CC. It was mostly white with some red and black trim. Ed got it for him on his sixteenth birthday for two reasons: first, for at least half the year Mike wouldn't ask for him rides, and second, to put it in Ed's words, Mike was "too big to ride bitch" on the back of his bike now.

Mike had on more than one occasion pushed the bike to its limits. One Sunday afternoon on the 401, he had pushed the bike up to 206 kilometers per hour. He backed off when he felt the first little speed wobble. Mike enjoyed the freedom that came with being a bit reckless on his bike, but knew when to be responsible. One of the lessons Ed had taught him after getting his bike license was "you can be right and still be dead!" Ed himself had been injured when a drunk driver rear-ended him on his police bike. The experience left both Mike and Ed a little extra cautious when out on the open road.

Mike never felt any fear on his bike, but always exercised caution when he had Tamika with him. She was the only person he'd ever let ride on the back. When she rode with him, he remained extra vigilant, never speeding or tailgating. He paid closer attention at intersections and slowed down in case someone in a car decided to blow through a stop sign or run a red light.

With a broken hand and some swelling on his face, working the throttle or even putting on his helmet weren't happening for a few days. Mike walked out of the of club and found Ed in the parking lot.

"My gear is inside airing out. I'm going to go see Tamika".

Ed frowned. He didn't like Tamika and really didn't like Mike dating her, not just because of her race, although he never referred to her by name and often used racial slurs when referring to her, he also didn't like her because her brother trained at the other club.

Mike was tired and defeated and didn't have the energy to argue He was relieved when "Bring your keys," was all Ed said.

Mike and Ed lived only about a quarter of a kilometer from the club. It took Mike less than five minutes to get home. He went inside, took the stairs two at a time up to his room, changed his shirt and grabbed his MP3 player. It had been a gift from his mom last Christmas, still considered new technology at the time. His mom had shown him how to load it. It was one of the last times he had seen her.

He was leaving as Ed pulled in the driveway. They barely acknowledged each other as Mike left.

Mike popped in his ear buds in and set out for Tamika's. He hit the play button, then skip. It was on shuffle, and he had about five hundred songs on it. Wallace had called Mike's play list an emotional roller coaster. It had everything from gansta rap, heavy metal, old and new country, and even the Dirty Dancing soundtrack. Not really what anybody would expect a seventeen-year-old boxer to be listening to.

The first song that came on was "Yellow Ledbetter" by Pearl Jam. One night Mike and Wallace had looked up the lyrics. Laughing, Mike observed, "This is what English must sound like to people who don't speak English". But Mike also thought it was a song where even if you didn't understand the lyrics, you knew what the song meant through the sadness in Eddie Vedder's voice. Mike walked along listening to the slow song, humming to himself. Now knowing the lyrics, he choked up and fought back tears as Eddie Vedder's deep voice sang "I don't, I don't know whether I am the boxer or the bag, oh yeeeeah." Mike wiped away his tears and kept walking.

Shortly after 9:00 pm Mike walked up the front steps to Tamika's house. Tamika lived closer to downtown Windsor. The house looked bigger outside than it was. Looking like a two story with a pitched roof, the attic was unusable, it was like putting on a top hat and saying it made you seven feet tall: just a lot of wasted space. It was a brown brick home in a row of identical houses sitting in a row of identical city blocks. Tamika's house stood out as it was the only one on the block with a bricked-in front porch

Mike walked up the cement stairs and knocked on the glass storm door. Tamika answered right away, Her smile was bright but faded instantly when she saw his face. She took his face in her hands as soon as he walked in, the morning's swelling now settling into the early signs of bruising under his eyes. She could tell Mike had an emotional meltdown on the way over. She stared into his eyes as he struggled to find the words to explain the what he was feeling. He opted to just stay quiet, and she conceded to let him. She leaned in, hugged him and said, "They can't hurt you now," a saying she said to him often. It was a quote from the song "Because the Night". Tamika loved the Natalie Merchant version of the song and always told Mike it reminded her of him. She often used that quote after he'd had a fight or a hard training session.

She held on to Mike until he was ready to let go. After a few moments he stopped squeezing. "Come in", she invited. He slipped his shoes off. Laurie appeared in the doorway from the dining room.

"Hey sweetie, are you hungry?"

Laurie was in her early forties, around five foot nine, and a little heavy set. Mike had seen pictures of her when she was in her late teens and early twenties. She had a natural beauty then that hadn't diminished much with her age. She worked at Chrysler driving a forklift, and worked overtime when she could. The household and her kids came before her social life or a gym membership, but when she did dress up and put on her "war paint" as she called it, she was still turning heads. This evening however, she was already wearing her pajamas, had her hair up, and a green mask on her face.

"No thank you. I got a molar knocked out today," Mike declined.

Laurie stared at him for a few seconds making sure she heard him correctly. She shook her head and walked away saying "These boys".

Tamika led Mike through house and down to the basement. Jessica and Rusty were waiting for them on a big oversized sectional couch. They had queued up a movie and had it on pause. As the four of them settled in, Rusty hit play.

The next thing he remembered was Will coming down the stairs. Mike had no idea what time it was, but he guessed it was likely around 3:00 am. Will worked at a local pizzeria that closed at 2:00 am on Saturdays. Will quietly went to his room, careful not to disturb the household with his late hour entry.

Mike was half sitting up on the couch with his legs outstretched in front of him. Tamika was under his arm, Her head on his chest, feet stretched out the other way. Rusty and Jessica must have left, but Mike had no idea when. Laurie had a strict "no overnight" policy but He'd had a long few days and guessed he must have fallen asleep as soon as the movie started. He wasn't even sure what they had watched. Mike laid awake for a while, listening to Tamika's breathing, feeling her slight frame against his, letting it calm him. The pain in his hand was manageable now, but his jaw pulsed with every heartbeat. He eventually dozed off.

Mike spent Sunday at Tamika's place. Early in the morning they discussed what they wanted to do for the day. By 10:00 am the temperature was already at 32 degrees, so they opted to stay in the basement and hide from the sunlight. Around noon, Will woke up and came out of his room in a pair of shorts. Rubbing his eyes, he nodded at Mike.

"S'up. Heard ya got fucked."

Mike, a little shocked that Will had heard about it already, replied, "Yeah. Pretty much. How'd you hear?"

Will explained, "Wallace and them came by the shop last night. Said you 'bout killed that boy, but got a DQ".

Tamika, listening in, asked, "What happened?"

Mike told them both the story, Will, scratched his head, sucked his teeth and observed, "I dunno why you guys go down there, man. Ohio is fucked up, son."

Mike shrugged. It wasn't his decision to make.

Sunday evening Mike went home. He had a summer job rebuilding chimneys. He not only needed to be up early, but he was picked up at home. His boss, Claude, knew Ed and had worked with Mike's grandfather part time when Claude was a teenager. The hours were long, and the pay sucked, but Claude knew Mike was a boxer, and when Mike needed to be at the gym, Claude made sure he was there on time.

Claude was in his mid-forties, around six feet tall, and had the frame that comes from slugging bricks all day. He was a good-looking guy, at least Mike had noticed that women seemed drawn to him. Occasionally they would stop for a beer and a burger for lunch while traveling from site to site. Claude always seemed to have the waitress's full attention. He had dark hair with touches of grey, and big smile that seemed to cause woman to melt over him. The first time Claude dropped Mike off at Tamika's, Laurie was sitting on the porch having a coffee. She asked Mike who he was. When Mike told her, Laurie completely ignored his answer, fanned herself, and exclaimed, "Oh my Lord."

Chapter 13
Saturday July 21st 2007, 6:00 pm
Windsor, Ontario

Two weeks had passed since the fights in Ohio. Mike's hand was still sore, but it had healed enough that he was working and riding his motorcycle again. He was following a schedule: wake up, eat, go to work, finish around 5:00 pm. On Monday, Wednesday, and Friday he went to the boxing club. The days he didn't train, he would spend with Tamika. Saturday mornings he was at the club until noon, then relaxed until Monday when it would start all over again.

They were sitting on Tamika's front porch. The temperature was still hot and muggy, but the heat wave that had held them hostage for the last two weeks had broken. They planned on heading downtown, about a twenty-minute walk from Tamika's, to meet up with a group of friends and catch a movie. There had been much debate on what to see. They all agreed on Rush Hour 3 or the Simpsons Movie, and decided they would flip a coin at the theater.

At 7:00 pm Mike and Tamika left to head downtown. They walked through a park not far from her house. A few kids were playing on the jungle gym, with a few others chasing each other through the grass field.

Hanging on to Mike's arm, Tamika asked, "What do you want to do, you know, after school?"

Mike thought for a minute. "I dunno. I think I want to keep fighting. But that won't last forever." He was very much aware of how hard it would be for a white, Canadian boxer to earn a real living. He added, "Thought maybe I'd be a cop like my dad? Or firefighter?"

Mike's grandfather had been a firefighter but died eight years before Mike was born. Ed's younger brother, Rob, had followed in his footsteps and was still on the Windsor FD. "I don't think I could do Fords or Chryslers though. The same shit, same parts, same people every day? I'd kill myself".

Mike didn't feel like he was exaggerating either. He and Tamika both knew dozens of people whose parents worked on the assembly lines. It was mind-numbing work. Mike had read an article earlier that year mentioning that Windsor had more drug and alcohol rehab centers per capita than anywhere else in Canada. Seeing the zombies staggering in and out of the car plants, even at seventeen, he understood why that number was so high.

"What about you?" Mike inquired.

"For years I wanted to be a veterinarian," she confessed. "But for real, even the vet tech program has a five-year backlog. I was looking at other schools and what classes they have. I want to leave Windsor after high school."

Stopping, she looked up at Mike and asked, "Will you come with me?"

"Where?"

"Don't know yet. We can talk about it more later. I have two years of school left. But after high school, will you come with me if I go somewhere else? Get away from this..." She trailed off and looked around. "This place. Get away from Ed."

That idea hit Mike like a freight train. The reality that as happy as he was with Tamika, he was not allowed to bring her around Ed's house. That this sweet girl that calmed his angry soul, had the exact opposite effect on Ed. The mention of her name instantly put Ed in a bad mood. Mike thought for a second and wondered what life would be like without Ed in control.

"I hear Ottawa is beautiful" he commented, smiling at her. Mike's older sister had recently relocated to Ottawa for school.

Tamika smiled back, hugged onto his arm again, and they continued walking.

They made it to Ouellette Ave, the main drag through downtown Windsor. The street started at the waterfront and went south straight through the city. Even though Windsor had expanded over the years, most recently the east side pushing further east, Ouellette Ave was still considered the city's dividing line.

Walking along, they were talking about last year's high school football season. Mike played for Forster Secondary, a school in the west end. Tamika was a cheerleader for Catholic Central. Their schools occasionally played each other. Tamika joked that once the referees took the clubs, brass knuckles, and switch blades away from Forster, they didn't know how to play. Mike retorted that if the preppy wimps at Central didn't want to get stabbed, then they shouldn't be on the field.

They walked past a group of five guys around the same age, sitting on a concrete bus stop bench. As they passed one said hi to Tamika, and another asked Mike, "Got the time?"

Mike looked at his watch. "7:12"

The guy said, "8:30?" being a smart ass.

The first one hoped off the bench and leered at Tamika. "Where you going, girl?"

She stopped hugging Mike's arm but held his hand. "Let's go please," she urged as she started walking faster.

"Hey!" The first guy yelled after them. Mike looked back and all five of them were up and walking towards them. Four of them were black, one was white. Mike thought the white kid looked ridiculous; his clothing was so over the top urban that he could be the poster boy for "trying too hard".

Mike looked at Tamika. "You know them?"

Tamika explained, "The one talking is Dion, he goes to Catholic Central. He's an asshole".

Mike heard footsteps approaching faster and turned around, putting himself between the group and Tamika. "What?" Mike asked, not cowering but not aggressive.

Dion looked past him said to Tamika "Let me holla at you for a second."

Mike stepped in front of his gaze and said, "She don't wanna talk to you. What's up?"

As they got closer, the other four tried to fan out around them. Mike used the back of his left shoulder and nudged Tamika back.

"What you doing with this fool?" Dion asked Tamika.

"Dion, go away please." she pleaded.

Mike noticed one of the other guys mumbling something to one of his buddies, then saw him take a few steps over towards Mike's right. "This is it" Mike thought, "These fools are going to try to jump me." Dion stepped closer to them, and Mike stuck his right hand out to stop him from advancing.

Mike grew up in a rough neighborhood with a dad that was a cop; a cop in the same neighborhood he lived in. Throughout grade school it was not an uncommon occurrence for Ed to arrest somebody's dad on a Friday or Saturday night. On Monday morning, the guy's kids were waiting for Mike to get off the bus.

Right now, Mike could see the signs. He figured if Dion stepped forward, it was to try and get into range to sucker punch him. When Mike stuck his hand out, he was setting range on his terms. These guys had decided to jump him, it was going to happen. In their minds it was just a matter of when. Mike understood this was not Hollywood and knew he wasn't going to be able to fight them all off, but he'd damn sure hurt at least one of them in the process. Dion took another step forward and Mike had him figured out.

Dion was going to step into Mike's hand, look down at it give him a "You touched me!" look, and start swinging. Mike had witnessed this a thousand times in the street, at parties, and even at school growing up. It was as predictable as averting your focus behind someone and saying, "Oh shit," so they look away, then hitting them when they turn back to face you. Dion leaned forward and bumped his chest into Mike hand. Game on, Mike thought and when Dion looked down Mike threw a tooth-loosening left hand that busted open Dion's top and bottom lip knocking him to the ground.

The next closest opponent to Mike was the white kid. Without hesitating, Mike threw a right and left at him, connecting solid with the right but falling short of the left. That was about all the time it took for the other three to realize what was happening and spring into action. Mike was trying to line up a third shot on the white kid and keep a mental list of where the other three were. It turned out to be harder than he thought.

The first punch hit him on the left side of the head. He felt a heavy shot, probably a kick to the left side of his body, then a solid flash-inducing hit to the right side of the head. They were all around him now, a dog pile. Mike knew better then to waste energy on throwing punches that weren't going to do anything, so he covered up. Not sure how or when he got there, but he realized he was now on his knees. Another flash and he was on his side. Roll, roll, he told himself. Don't stay still. He could hear the thuds hitting his body but couldn't feel them yet. He could hear the grunting from the attackers, and in a brief moment of clarity he heard Tamika yelling for them to stop.

In an instant, it stopped. Watch for the last one, he thought and tightened up. Mike had seen a swarming like this before; a flurry of assault with the attackers fumbling over each other and not doing much damage, but when the attack stops, the victim lifts their head and is met with a solid kick to the face or head. It didn't come. Instead Tamika dropped beside him.

"Baby, baby are you okay?" she asked, crying. Mike uncovered his head and looked. Dion and his crew had backed off. Two cars had pulled over and a group of four men, all around twenty years old, were standing there, one holding a baseball bat. Another had come rushing over.

"You okay?" he asked Mike, reaching his hand out. Mike took it and stood up and did a quick inventory. He'd be sore tomorrow, but these guys were punks; wanna be tough guys. They didn't really know how to hit or where to hit him. Mike looked at Dion, looked at Tamika, and then back at Dion and started for him. Dion, mouth bleeding badly flinched. Mike was stopped by the one of the guys that pulled over to help. He heard Dion, trying to be tough, start laughing. The guy with the bat started toward him. Dion and his group took off running. They walked Mike over to a car and he sat on the hood. Tamika was crying.

"What happened"? asked one of the other guys.

Mike replied, "I dunno, they jumped me."

"Do you know them?"

"No." Mike explained, "We walked by them. They started mouthing off and bothering her," Mike nodded to Tamika. "I got in front of them, and they swarmed me."

One of the other guys looked closely at Mike's battered face and asked, "Mike?"

Mike looked over and recognized Randy Emery. Randy had been a member at the Slater Street club for years and was one of Ed's rescues.

"Hey Randy," Mike quipped. "Fancy meeting you here."

Randy immediately became more concerned. This wasn't just a random guy getting jumped. Randy had known Mike since he was six years old. He said something to his friend who nodded and jogged back to the other car, returning a few moments later with a small first aid kit. Randy asked, "Did you go out?"

"I don't know" Mike replied, honestly.

Randy looked to Tamika and asked, "Are you his girlfriend?" She nodded wiping away tears "Did he fall? or go down on his own?" Randy asked.

"I don't think he fell. Like, he didn't get hit and fall down," she tried to explain.

"Did you see if they kicked him in the head?" Randy probed.

"Yes. At least twice, He was trying to get away," she trailed, her tears starting again.

Randy looked at Mike. "We're going to take you to the hospital, make sure you're ok."

At that moment, out of the side of his eye Mike saw the flickering of red and blue light followed by the 'woop woop' of a police vehicle pulling up. The front-facing lights shut down. The rear facing continued to flicker, warning traffic. A large man stepped out the Windsor Police SUV.

Mike replied to Randy, "No, I'm good."

Randy wasn't hearing it. "You're going. I'll call your dad."

Mike was still sitting on the hood of the car with his head down, Tamika standing beside him, and Randy in front of him with his hand on Mike's shoulder. An older cop walked up and asked, "What happened?"

Mike looked up to answer. He recognized the cop but couldn't remember his name. Randy immediately took over. "We were stopped at the light back there". He pointed north down Ouellette Ave. The backs of the street signs in the distance reflected the red and blue lights. "I noticed a group running up on these two. By the time the light changed, they swarmed him."

Mike thought to himself, good. He left out the part where I hit Dion first.

The cop asked the usual questions: how many were there, which way did they go, what were they wearing. Randy answered as best he could and added "One of them was bleeding badly from the mouth. He's probably looking to get to an ER." He paused and added "It was bad." The cop looked back at the one holding the bat and Randy said, "We didn't touch him." He shook Mike's shoulder and said, "This is Mike Wolly, Ed's kid". The cop immediately recognized Mike. It was then his demeanor changed also.

"You okay Mikey?" he asked, putting his note pad away and leaning in to look at Mike.

"Yeah, I'm good" Mike replied, the shock wearing off and the body aches creeping their way in.

The cop, almost playfully, asked "You get one of them?"

Tamika still with tears running down her face let out a small laugh and corrected, "Two of them!"

The cop smirked and shook Mike's shoulder harder. "Good one." He keyed his radio and looked at Mike "Do you want an ambulance?" Mike Shook his head no, and Randy interjected, "I'll take him to the ER."

The cop nodded. "Do that now. I'd like to talk to your friends."

Randy nodded and grabbed Mike. "Come on, let's go."

The drive to the hospital only took a few minutes. It was about six blocks away. Finding somewhere to park took longer than the commute. Randy escorted Mike and Tamika in, sat them down and walked over to the counter. The emergency room was busy, which was typical for a Saturday night in downtown Windsor in July. Mike counted seventeen people in there, although a few were there to support the injured or sick. Mike and Tamika sat next to a middle-aged man in blood-stained light green golf shirt and khaki shorts, holding blood-soaked towel around his hand. "Full contact gardening" he explained to Mike, raising the towel.

Randy rushed over to the triage desk and the nurse looked up. Randy pointed towards Mike and told her why they were there. As soon as he mentioned Mike getting kicked in the head, they ushered him out of the waiting room into an exam room. Randy left his cell number with Tamika and made her promise to send him an update. Mike was sent to x-ray to look for fractures, a CT-scan to look at any possible brain injury, and an ultrasound to check for internal bleeding. The whole process took several hours. Mike was sitting in a room waiting to see the doctor before being released when a half drunk, fully angry Ed stormed in.

"What happened?" he snarled at Mike.

"I got jumped," Mike answered.

"By who, Mike?" Ed shouted angrily, almost accusing his son.

"I don't know them. I was walking down Ouellette with Tamika and some guys jumped me," Mike explained. He looked around the room. "Where is she?"

"She left." Ed spat.

"When?" Mike asked. Leaving seemed out of character for her.

"When I told her to," Ed retorted.

"What did you say to her?" Mike demanded, now worried.

Ed looked at him, like being asked the question was equal parts inconvenient and insulting. The doctor came shortly thereafter. He told Mike he was lucky, but he'd be sore for a few days. He cautioned that Mike might see blood in his urine, but all thing considered he was going to recover.

Mike hoped off the bed and started for the door.

Ed asked, "Where are you going?"

Mike called out over his shoulder, "To Tamika's," and picked up his pace.

Ed, stood in the hallway. He yelled after his son "Hey!" but Mike kept going.

Mike stopped outside the door of the emergency room and looked at his watch. The small digital screen was half grey half black. Busted, great, he thought. He looked back in at the big clock behind the triage desk, which read 12:32 am. He set off for Tamika's house.

Walking quickly, he started back up Ouellette Avenue. He got to the first traffic light and Ed pulled up in the van with his window down. "Get in!" he ordered. Mike ignored him as he waited at the red light. The light turned green, and Ed said "Fuck ya then!" and drove off.

Chapter 14
Sunday July 22nd, 2007, 12:50 am
Windsor, Ontario

Mike leaped up the steps at Tamika's and knocked on the door. Laurie answered right away, her face a mess of anger and tears. "Is Tamika home?" he asked. She hesitated for a second then let him in. He stood in the doorway.

"Are you okay?" Laurie asked, still angry, but showing concern.

"Yes ma'am." Mike replied, "Where is she?" he asked worried.

Laurie looked over her shoulder towards the dining room. Tamika wasn't at the table, so he figured she was either in her bedroom, or the bathroom. He walked towards the dining room and heard the bathroom door open. Tamika stepped out wearing the same clothes she'd had on earlier, her face freshly washed, her eyes red from an entire night of crying. She stood in the small hallway staring at him. "What did he say?" Mike asked. She held his gaze now looking more angry then sad.

"Tamika, what did he say?"

"You know already what he said," she replied staring at him.

Mike stood in the dining room, gripping the back of one of the chairs, squeezing it so hard Laurie thought he was going to break it. He took a deep breath, looked up at the ceiling and said, "I'm sorry."

Tamika looked at Mike. He was in dirty clothes splattered with blood, some of it his, some Dion's. His knees were raw and bloody, and bruising was starting to develop around his face. She was upset that he was in that condition, and angry that his dad had been so mean to her when she was trying to help. "Why does he hate me?" she asked.

Mike, still looking up, lowered his stare into hers and answered, "For the same reason he hates me."

Laurie had been trying to blend into her surroundings. Tamika was her baby, but she liked Michael. He treated her daughter right. Laurie chalked that up to Michael's mother. There was no way that animal he lived with now taught his children how to respect anybody. Trying to ease the tension she stepped into the dining room.

"Michael, honey, let's get you cleaned up." She asked Tamika to go grab some clothes from Will's room. Laurie placed her hand on Mike's shoulder and asked. "Do you have anywhere else to stay? An aunt and uncle? Grandparents? Siblings?" Mike thought for a few seconds trying to understand what she was asking him.

Laurie hesitated before suggesting "What about your mom?"

Mike's head snapped up and he shook it vigorously. "No. Not an option. I can't stay with my mom."

"But I'm sure she'd..."

"It's really not an option." Mike stated more firmly than he intended, indicating the topic was finished. More gently, he continued, "I, uh. I have an uncle on my mom's side. He lives in the east end."

"Maybe you should call him." She encouraged.

"Sit down, honey" she suggested in a way that indicated he didn't have much of a choice. Mike sat down. She pulled another chair out and sat in front of him, taking both his hands in hers.

"Michael, you can't stay with Ed anymore. It's not safe for you. Look at you, in the months you've been coming around here I have never seen you without a black eye, and those aren't all from boxing. You were attacked by a group of people in the street tonight, it took him four hours to show up. And he was more concerned with my daughter's skin colour then his own son's wellbeing."

She paused. Mike, still staring off focused on a picture by the doorway: Laurie, Will and Tamika standing on a rock in the wilderness somewhere with a waterfall behind them. All three of them smiling. A happy family, he thought. Mike sat staring at the picture unable to make eye contact.

"We love you here," Laurie continued. "I can't have my sixteen-year-old daughter's boyfriend move in, but I can't watch you live like this either." She stood up, placed her hand on the back of his head "You should stay here tonight, Call your uncle in the morning."

Tamika came back up from the basement with a pair of grey sweatpants and a faded blue t-shirt. Mike was still sitting in the same chair, elbows on his knees with his face in his hands. Tamika sat in front of him, placed her hands on either side of his face and lifted until his eyes met hers.

"I hear Ottawa is beautiful this time of year," she said.

The following morning Mike grabbed Laurie's cordless phone, stepped out on the front porch and called Nick, his mom's older brother. Nick answered right away. They chatted about school and Mike's boxing. Nick asked if Mike had called his grandfather recently, and after a few minutes of small talk, Mike mustered the courage and asked, "Uncle Nick, is there any chance you have room at your house for me?"

Nick, caught a little off guard, replied with a question of his own. "What's going on Mike?"

"Things aren't good with dad. He's um, he's been...It's just..." Mike fought back a lump in his throat. "It's hard to be around him," Mike explained as the tears started coming.

Nick sat silently for a few moments and asked, "It's that bad huh?"

Mike had broken down was unable to answer. Nick could hear him sniffle and wipe his face.

"Well, I was going to put a stripper pole in the living room. Guess that can wait a couple years though."

Mike laughed. Nick was good at breaking the tension.

"I have an extra bedroom here, but there are rules," Nick began. "No free rides. You're working, or you're in school. You'll make my life a lot easier come fall if you're doing both."

Mile replied, "I have a job. I'm laying bricks."

"Good. When do you want to come over?" Nick inquired.

"I need to go get my stuff from dad's," Mike hoped Nick could accommodate him sooner rather than later.

"Do you need me to come?" Nick offered.

"No. it's fine." Mike quickly replied, knowing Nicks presence would only anger Ed. "Thank you," he added and hung up.

Mike wiped his face off again, collected his thoughts, caught his breath, and went back in the house. He told Laurie he was going to stay with his uncle and needed to go to Ed's and grab his things. Laurie insisted on driving him. Ten minutes later they were in the driveway.

As Mike let himself in, the smell of cigarette smoke and stale beer filled his nose. Ed was home. Mike walked through the house towards the kitchen. Ed was reading a book and sipping at a coffee. He had a lit cigarette in front of him and a pile of empty beer bottles beside him on the counter. Ed looked up at Mike, held his stare and then looked back down. "How's the jungle bunny?" he asked smirking.

Mike had started to turn away and stopped. Nervously he said, "I'm leaving."

The smile on Ed's face dropped. He took a drag off his cigarette, stubbed it out, slowly stood up and walked towards Mike. "So, that's it huh? You're going to go live with that nigger and her family?"

"I'm not going to live there," Mike retorted, standing up straight. Before he could stop them, the words just jumped out of his mouth, "And the Only nigger I know is you!"

Without warning, Ed punched Mike in the face. Hard. Mike stumbled back a couple steps, eyes welling up with tears, blood coming out of his nose, feeling that horrible pressure behind the eyes that comes with a punch landed square in the nose. "When you can come back from one of those, then you can talk to me like that," Ed glowered.

Mike had reached his breaking point. Almost as a reflex, he wiped his nose on his arm, darted forward, and sent a left hand at Ed's face. Ed anticipated the retaliation and nodded downward, causing Mike to connect with the top of his head. Mike was certain that basic physics would not allow it, but he was almost positive that when he hit Ed, his hand stopped on contact like it was punching a brick wall. Ed swung back at Mike, hitting him in the face again, twice. He grabbed a hold of Mike, and using a hip toss, threw him to the ground.

Ed had been a fighter his whole life. For twenty-one of those years, he'd been fighting some of the meanest guys on the meanest streets in a very mean city. His seventeen-year-old son wasn't a fight. It was an appetizer for a very hungry man. Ed hit Mike several times while he was down, antagonizing him while he did it.

After a few solid hits, he stopped, got to his feet, and let Mike up. Mike, without a penny to his name and just the borrowed clothes on his back, picked himself up. His face bloodied, he held eye contact with Ed as he spat a mouthful of blood on the floor at Ed's feet. "Fuck you, Ed." And he walked out the door.

Laurie sat waiting in her car. She saw the screen door swing open and Mike step outside, his face a bloody mess. He peeled off the shirt he was wearing and used it to clean himself up. She flung open the driver's side door and jumped out of the car. "Michael! What happened?" she frantically asked.

"That went better than expected," he halfheartedly joked, pulling his shirt away from his nose. A thick line of blood reappeared immediately. "Can we go please?" he pleaded.

She slammed her door, staring at the house, trying to decide if she was going to go inside and tell Ed what she thought of him. Mike, almost sensing what she was thinking said, "It won't matter. He doesn't care," then wiped his nose again. Laurie stood there staring at Mike. Yes, he was big, but he was still just a boy. She could not understand how this sweet kid, who she knew had such a caring heart, could take so many beatings that he didn't deserve and keep standing. Tears rolled down her face and she conceded. "Okay, honey. Get in the car."

They pulled out of the driveway. Mike looked in the mirror and noticed Ed standing at the open front door before Laurie put the car in drive. Ed turned his back and walked back inside.

Laurie pulled up at a nearby 7-11. She went inside and grabbed a bottle of water and a handful of napkins from the counter. When she returned to the car Mike was leaning back with the shirt covering his nose and mouth. Laurie got in the car and started, "We should go to the hosp-..."

"I'm not going to the hospital!" Mike interrupted. "It's broken I don't need to sit in the ER for the next four hours to be told that." Laurie understood. Mike was, after all, a boxer. He'd had his first broken nose at twelve, a sparing mishap, and had probably broken it again six or seven times since. Sounding like a kid plugging his nose Mike requested, "Can we go to my uncle's please?" Laurie sighed and pulled out of the parking lot.

Mike's Uncle Nick lived on a small side street off Central Avenue and Tecumseh Road East in Windsor. It was a working-class neighborhood where both parents in most households worked, usually at one of the car plants. Nick owned a modest dark blue one-story house with white trim. As they pulled in the driveway Nick was waiting on the front porch.

Laurie put the car in park as Nick made his way down the driveway. Nick was a tall man at six foot four; this was where Mike got his height. But where Mike was broad, Nick was lean, built like a long-distance runner or swimmer. Nick was in his early 50's. He had short, cropped brown hair and golden-brown eyes hidden behind dark sunglasses that he wore all the time. Today he was also wearing a maroon t-shirt with a blue Canadian Airborne regiment logo on the front, black golf shorts, and pink bunny slippers. He made his way down towards them. Laurie, looking at the slippers mumbled "What the fuck?"

Mike calmly explained, "That's my uncle Nick," as he got out of the car.

Nick walked down the driveway. A lifelong bachelor, he was paying close attention to the pretty blond lady dropping Mike off. It wasn't until he got closer that he noticed Mike's face. "Jesus Christ Mikey, what happened?"

"I told dad I was leaving" Mike replied.

Nick, now looking closer, saw the blue marks that would soon be turning purple all over Mikes body and asked, "Did he beat you with a club or something?"

"No, that wasn't dad. I got jumped yesterday".

"By a troop of gorillas?" Nick laughed.

Laurie cleared her throat, not amused. Nick looked over and shifted his attention back to her. He stuck out his right hand and introduced himself. Then looked over to Mike and asked, "Where's your stuff, bud?

Mike looked down at Will's bloody clothes "I'm wearing it."

Sensing things were even worse than he thought after the morning phone call, Nick turned towards the house and suggested, "Come on, I'll give you the ten-cent tour," and started walking up the driveway.

Entering the house, Laurie was expecting a domestic disaster, but was surprised to find the house was in immaculate shape. Everything was clean and sparkling.

The front door entered the living room, a large room with hardwood floors and a burgundy Persian style rug in the center. It had leather sectional sofa, and a large black entertainment center with a large TV and stereo system. The décor was mostly a few old tin Harley Davidson signs, a framed picture of Marlon Brando on the Triumph Thunderbird from the movie "The Wild one". One wall was a floor to ceiling bookshelf filled with mostly true crime and nonfiction, but a few of the old classics as well. Nick had given Mike the collective works of Mark Twain on his thirteenth birthday and quizzed him for months after to make sure he was reading it.

Off the living room was a closed door that led to Nick's bedroom. As they made their way into the dining room Laurie noticed a framed picture on the wall showing who she recognized as Nick about ten years ago, standing with another man. Both wore maroon berets and matching maroon coats, and both men had large racks of medals on their chests. Laurie paused and asked, "Is this you?"

Nick following her gaze said "Yes ma'am. That was Remembrance Day in Ottawa, 1996".

She looked at the number of medals on his chest and asked, "What were you given those for?"

"For shooting at people."

"Oh, I see," she replied, her dislike for this man growing more pronounced every second.

Nick had served in the Canadian Armed Forces, joining right out of high school. Eventually he joined the airborne regiment and serving as a medic. He was wounded, although not seriously in 1993 during the Croatia Serbia conflict in Operation Medak Pocket, Canada's largest battle since the Korean war. A mission that few people were aware of.

Nick continued through the dining room into the kitchen. The light was off but large windows on both the right side and the back of the room allowed for ample sunlight. The appliances were new and black. There was a bathroom/laundry room combination off to the left, and another bedroom beside it.

"This is you." Nick said as he opened the door. It was a small room, about ten feet by ten feet. Against the far wall was a single bed with light blue sheets and pillowcases, with a dark blue comforter on top. A black nightstand with a small lamp, and a matching dresser with a fan on top made up the rest of the room. A large window faced directly into the neighbors back yard.

Following Mike's gaze, Nick pointed out the window. "Wendy lives next door. I don't want to hear about you being a peeping Tom. But if you see anything worth looking at, let me know right away."

Laurie was not amused. Not really attempting to hide her annoyance, she turned to Mike. "Michael, would you like to go get some clothes?"

Nick interjected, "It's fine. We'll take care of that."

"Okay, I guess I'm done here then." She gave Mike a hug and let herself out. Walking down the driveway she heard Nick say, "Excuse me, Laurie?"

She stopped and saw that he was walking down after her. When he got close, he said "Look, I'm sorry. I was trying to keep things lighthearted in there for Mike. I know what an asshole Ed can be. He was married to my sister." Laurie said nothing but relaxed a little bit. Nick added "My rules aren't many, but they'll be strictly enforced." She looked at him straight in the eyes, then down at his fuzzy bunny slippers. When she looked back up, he said, "Killer Bunnies."

She laughed, wiped a tear away from her eye and said, "Please take good care of him, He's just a boy."

"A big one." Nick agreed, thinking about how his grocery bill was about to triple.

Laurie added, "But still just a boy."

Nick nodded and walked her back to her car. He held the door open. "Thank you for bringing him here."

She smiled, closed the door, and drove off.

Chapter 15

Sunday September 30th, 2007, 2:30 pm
Windsor Ontario

By the end of September, Mike's life had some balance. He had settled in well to his life at Nick's. He didn't feel the anxiety in his stomach when he got home from school and saw Nick's truck in the driveway the same way he did was he used to see Ed's van.

Mike was training at the same club as Will, although since Ohio he hadn't feel much like competing. He hadn't heard from Ed since he'd left home, but he'd kept in touch with some of the guys from Slater Street. It was through talking to Wallace that Mike found out he was able to keep his motorcycle. Keeping his bike made staying enrolled at Forester easier, at least until the winter.

Nick became an ironworker after leaving the military, which had him working odd hours. He'd go a week of working Monday to Friday 7:00 am to 3:00 pm, then be on nights for twelve hours seven day a week, then be home on a Wednesday. Mike stopped trying to track his hours.

Knowing how Ed could be, Nick had gone out of his way to make sure Tamika felt welcome in their home. Laurie's initial hesitation with Nick had melted away after Tamika returned from her first visit with Mike in his new home. She'd come home smiling telling Laurie how amazing Nick was.

Mike's grandfather lived about forty minutes outside of Windsor in a small farming community. Every Sunday, weather permitting, Mike and Nick jumped on their motorcycles and rode out to visit for Sunday dinner.

Mike's Grandfather was a World War two veteran who worked at the Chrysler assembly plant after the war until he retired. After Mike's grandmother died, his grandfather had remarried to a woman around his own age with grown children, and the two families seemed to mesh well.

That morning Mike had breakfast at Tamika's with her family. They spent the day working on Mike's chemistry assignment which was due the following morning. At 2:30 pm they packed up his things and went out to his bike. Mike had promised to meet Nick before the three of them headed out to his grandfathers for dinner.

Mike and Tamika pulled into Nick's driveway. Nick had his motorcycle, a blue 2001 Harley Davidson Road Glide, warming up already. They parked. Mike went inside, used the bathroom, and the three of them set off for Sunday dinner.

As they made their way through the city, Mike was cognizant of Tamika on the back and made sure to take the corners a little more gently, easing off on the gas when he might have otherwise hit the throttle. Despite his extra cautions, Mike still enjoyed the ride. He loved having Tamika's arms wrapped around him as they rode through town.

Nick liked to take the long way out to his dad's. They would take Tecumseh Road to Walker Road, one of the main roadways. They would follow Walker out of town into the farming area and follow the open two-lane eighty kilometer an hour highway. It was nice and straight and mostly flat.

They left the city and were cruising along nicely. They passed some newer houses and rode through the industrial section of the city before the scenery opened into the patchwork landscape of the farms.

They were riding along, they approached a small hill with a solid yellow line. As they crested the mound, a bright blue Ford Expedition SUV appeared, coming straight at them. The driver, annoyed with someone doing only ten kms above the speed limit, had decided to pass on a solid line and a blind hill.

Approaching fast, both Mike and Nick had less than a second to react. Nick, on the right, veered off towards the shoulder. As his bike left the asphalt and hit the gravel, he was able to keep it upright but just barely. Mike wasn't so lucky. As he veered to follow Nicks route, the SUV clipped the back of his bike just behind Tamika's seat. Unable to control the bike, Mike felt himself slam against the driver side door of the SUV. There was a white flash, then it went dark.

"Mikey, Mikey!" Nick was yelling as Mike opened his eyes. Nick was kneeled beside him looking away.

"Check her!" Nick hollered, pointing to someone Mike couldn't see. He tried to sit up Nick looked back him and said, "Stay down Mike." His vision went dark again.

Mike had no sense of time or what was going on. It felt like a dream. He felt himself being moved around fresh air hit his face. He thought in scrambled questions: "Is my helmet off? Why can't I see anything. Okay, this isn't right. I feel like I'm in a dark hamster ball. I gotta get out of here."

"Stay down Mikey. Help is coming!"

Who said that? Was that Uncle Nick? Mike continued to ask silently. He felt like his body was numb. He was having a hard time breathing, like he'd had the wind knocked out of him but worse.

Mike came to again in the ambulance. It was chaos all around him: the stretcher was rocking, he was strapped down, and he could hear people speaking frantically. The sirens were too loud. A dark-haired girl reached over him. Where's Tamika, he thought and started to panic. He tried to talk but couldn't. He tried to sit up but couldn't. The medic noticed him struggling and announced, "He's awake!" Then to Mike she explained, "Mike, you were in an accident, we're taking you to Met right now" referring to Metropolitan Hospital in Windsor. He kept trying to talk but couldn't. Why can't I open my mouth, he thought. His vision faded out.

Mike felt the stretcher shake. He was moving. He heard a loud thump like a door slamming followed by more yelling.

What? Where am I? Bike! I was on the bike! What happened? I went down! Tamika! His thoughts came one after another, but he still couldn't talk or move What the hell is going on, he wondered.

He felt himself being moved around. He thought it got colder and realized he was naked now. What the hell happened to my clothes, he thought and tried to sit up, but something fell on him.

"Help over here!" he heard.

Help? Help who? With what, he tried again, and something even heavier held him down.

"Hurry up! He's a strong one!" he heard.

Who said that? What's happening? Then it was dark again.

Mike tried to open his eyes, the daylight coming in the window felt hot on his face. He had no idea where he was. He was sore. He opened his eyes but couldn't focus. His mouth was dry, and it hurt. He tried to speak, and his throat was on fire. He tried to move his mouth around and generate some saliva.

"Mike, honey, can you hear me?" Mike heard a woman's voice ask.

He was fighting to focus and could barely do anything but grunt in response.

"I think he's awake." observed the same voice.

"Mom?" his voice was hoarse and barely audible.

He felt a hand touch his face "Yes honey. I'm right here." He felt another hand touch his wrist.

His vision was returning slowly, but the bright sunlight was too much. He was squinting, and it made his already terrible headache even worse. He heard the rattling of the chains on the blinds as it quickly got darker. He could finally open his eyes. His mother was sitting in the chair beside him, a few bouquets of flowers with cards around the room. Nick was standing at the window holding the chain.

"There ya go buddy," he soothed, closing the blind all the way.

Mike laid his head back. It hurt. Everything hurt. Barely able to open his eyes, he looked around again and realized he was in a hospital room.

"What? What happened?" he asked, still struggling to talk.

"Just rest honey," his mother said bringing a small plastic cup of water to his lips. "You were in an accident."

Mike snapped upright, every muscle in his body screaming in protest. "Where's Tamika?" he demanded, in a panic.

His Mom and Nick looked at each other.

"Where is she?" Mike repeated, now getting angry.

"Michael," His mom began, putting her hands on his chest "Michael, please lay down."

"Nick? Nick where is she?" Mike asked, his face a mixture of anger, and physical and emotional pain.

Nick sat down on the bed, looked Mike in the eyes and said softly, "I'm sorry Mikey, Tamika didn't make it."

Mike's head started spinning. This isn't real, he thought. He sat back waiting to wake up from what was obviously a dream, but as seconds turned into minutes, he realized he wasn't going to wake up. Mike started straight ahead, feeling numb, wishing for the darkness to come back.

Chapter 16

Friday December24ᵗʰ, 2022, 9:30am
Hamilton Ontario

Mike pulled into his driveway. He was currently living in a small two-bedroom half of a side-by-side duplex. The rent was cheap, the bills were included, and there was really nothing tying him to the place. There was a lease, but it was in someone else's name. He gave the neighbor $100 a month to piggyback off her Wi-Fi. She was a mid-fifties woman who worked at a local grocery store. More importantly, she didn't ask questions.

Mike had initially rented a room from another ironworker named Greg, but Greg had moved out to Alberta over a year ago. The landlord knew Mike's first name, but that was it. The rent was paid monthly in cash. Aside from that they never spoke.

Mike worked, got paychecks, paid taxes. Work was sporadic at best. Nick had got him into ironworking when he was eighteen, and they both referred to it as the best part-time job they'd ever had.

Most of Mike's money came from a very simple yet reliable method: he robbed drug dealers. Not just any drug dealers though, mostly the suppliers; people who sold large quantities and were known to carried large amounts of cash. The street level dealers were dangerous, in his opinion. If they were robbed, they would fight tooth and nail to hang on to whatever they had as they were responsible for it.

In Mike's opinion, the suppliers were more likely to give it up without a fight. If they didn't, Mike killed them. It was that simple. Not a lot of fuss was ever kicked up over a dead drug supplier. There were few repercussions; most people figured the supplier either got arrested or felt the heat and skipped town. Mike was also choosy about the suppliers he chased. He didn't smoke weed, he didn't do drugs at all, but he left weed dealers alone. In his warped mind it was okay to go after people who sold fentanyl, crack, or crystal meth. Heroin wasn't really a problem in the community but if it was, he'd clip a couple of them too.

Mike walked into the compact unit. It had a small living room and kitchen on the main floor. A laundry room could be found in the unfinished basement. The upstairs held two bedrooms and a bathroom. The furniture was nice but well used. Mike wasn't sure if Greg had bought it, or if it was here when he moved in.

On his way to the kitchen, he turned on the TV. He had a 65" unit mounted to the wall right beside the front door. He grabbed the remote and hit the YouTube button. Looking over his shoulder he saw some suggestions, mostly Motown music. He hit the play button and the bass line for "Rubber Band Man" by the Detroit Spinners started.

In the kitchen he placed his lunch pail on the counter, opened it up took, out a large bottle of water and a Tupperware container that still held today's lunch. Mike had no clue what it was; the lady next door dropped it off last night. She occasionally did that. It was usually good, and she seemed happy to do it. Mike put the Tupperware and the water back in the fridge.

When the door closed, he looked at the three items stuck on the otherwise bare fridge door. The first was a picture taken ten years ago of Mike and Nick standing on an I-beam, with the Calgary Alberta skyline in the background. Nick's arm over Mike shoulder.

Also on the fridge were two memorial pamphlets given out at funerals. One was a picture of Nick, the picture taken about eight years ago, before the cancer ripped through his body, killing him in less than a year. The other was for Ron Sapiano, another ironworker that died in 2019, and a good friend of Mike's. Ron's pamphlet showed a picture of him sitting on a rock in the woods holding a beer. Mike often thought it if ever a picture encapsulated one man, that was it.

The two met when Mike was an apprentice. Ron, in his mid-fifties at the time. stood around six foot two, with an athletic build and a bald head. He had a reputation as a bit of a scrapper. Their first encounter was at an airport where they were flying out to Alberta to work on the same job site. Mike knew Ron was trying to size him up. He thought Ron was an asshole and liked him immediately.

A few years after Meeting Ron, Mike was involved in car accident when a texting driver ran a stop sign and struck him broadside. Mike received a Broken ankle and broken wrist. Two weeks later at a Union Meeting Ron stole Mike's crutches as a joke then teased Mike saying "come get'em tough guy" causing everyone around them laugh, What none of them realized was Ron also called Mike at least once a week checking in on him making sure he was OK even taking care of Mike's grocery shopping until he recovered.

They had worked together on a few small jobs over the years and always had great time, teasing, and taunting each other. Mike would call out Ron's last name in an overly exaggerated Italian accent. Ron would tease Mike about his driving abilities or lack thereof. Mike liked Ron because he never missed a beer, a joint, or a chance to party, but he also never missed a mortgage, car, or insurance payment. When Ron died suddenly of a massive heart attack, Mike was devastated. Over the years Mike had grown a bit numb to loss. This was a career, after all, where not a lot of people were blessed with longevity. A lot of guys who start at eighteen or nineteen saw the old timers who mentored start dying off within twenty years or so. Mike understood that, and had become even more guarded after losing Nick Still, losing Ron hurt.

A few months later Mike called Ron's brother with a strange request. He was wondering if he could have something - anything - off Ron's tool belt. His younger brother met with Mike and gave him one of Ron's spud wrenches that Mike still wore on his belt. During that meeting, Ron's brother told Mike the reason they got along so well was because Mike reminded Ron of himself Twenty-five years ago.

Mike walked back into the living room and flopped down on the couch, flipped through YouTube and pulled up a review of the crossbow he'd used last night to kill Rolland Friedman. The guy on the screen must have done something to the bowstring on his demonstration model. His bolts repeatedly tore right through the ballistic gel dummies he was using. Mike's bolt stopped when it hit the window. He was somewhat grateful for that. He didn't lose the arrow and was able to yank it out of Rolland. "That should confuse the cops for a little while," he thought.

Mike wasn't too worried about getting caught. He figured with a guy like Rolland, the police weren't going to waste too much energy trying to find the killer unless someone was caught literally holding a smoking gun (or crossbow in this case).

Mike did some quick math in his head. With eleven victims, the Toronto police would be looking at what, fifty? Sixty suspects? And that was just immediate family members of Rolland's victims. If you add in cousins, family friends and people who thought the same way Mike did, the Toronto Metropolitan Police could be looking at hundreds of suspects inside the city, never mind an hour away in Hamilton, where Mike lived. With that, he threw his feet up on to the couch, closed his eyes and took a long nap.

He woke up around 2:00 pm to the sound of a snowplow scrapping the road out front. He got up, made a coffee, and thought about what to do for the day. Since losing Nick, Christmas had become just another day to Mike. He had no real family. He had a sister in Ottawa, at least he thought she was still there. She was married with her own family. They hadn't had any communication since she called to inform Mike that Ed died. He hadn't seen his mother since Nick's funeral. Christmas was just another day except everything was closed.

Mike finished his coffee and decided to go for a workout. He wasn't fighting anymore, but he paid a membership at a local boxing club where he could go train a few days a week to stay in shape. The owner and coaches were nice. Mike occasionally worked with younger fighters but mostly kept to himself. He washed his coffee cup, grabbed his fight bag and headed to the gym.

When he pulled up, he was bemused to discover the place was open. Not that it mattered; he knew both the PIN for the electric lock and the alarm code, so he was able to come and go as he pleased. He was surprised to see there were people inside.

The club was big. It was a large commercial unit in a plaza, not too flashy, but the owners took pride in its appearance. The walls were white with scattered fight posters, both old and new, some framed, while others were some held up by tape and curling at the corners. There were professional posters and some blow-up pictures of current or former club members. There was also a wall dedicated to signed pictures of former and current boxers and MMA fighters.

The heavy bags were all black and hung from the ceiling joist in a perfect line down one side of the room. An eighteen-foot by eighteen-foot ring sat in one corner, and half an MMA cage rested in the other. The cage was mostly used to help MMA fighters learn how to use the sides to get back up. The floors of the gym were hardwood, but ¾ inch red foam pads had been laid out over the workout area. Bright 400-watt bulbs hung from the ceiling with domed aluminum covers.

Mike counted nine people, not including himself. Not bad for 3:00 pm on Christmas Eve, he thought as he made his way into the change room. Years ago, at Nick's suggestion, Mike had started training in Brazilian Jiu Jitsu in addition to maintaining his boxing routine. Mike had found out the hard way that boxers were like turtles: helpless once on their backs. Since more often than not, bar fights ended up on the ground, Mike took up his new practice to learn some defense.

On his first day of training, he entered the club and was greeted by Nathan, a man that Mike didn't believe could ever be intimidating. Nathan was about five foot eleven, and maybe one hundred and ninety pounds. He had a bald head and a grey beard. He was in his early fifties and was engaged in a conversation about a new video game he'd been up playing after his kids went to bed the night before. Mike thought, what the hell and I'm doing here, but hung around anyway, determined to give it a fair try.

When class started, they went through some basic techniques. At the end of the class Mike went through the new guy ritual of "rolling" with each person in the club for either two minutes or until one of them submits or "taps". When Mike faced off with Nathan, who turned out to be the head coach, he was shocked. Mike grabbed ahold of this nerdy, fifty-year-old man and though he had grabbed onto a statue. The man wouldn't budge. Before Mike could think about it, Nathan hipped tossed him, sent him flying through the air, and submitted him within seconds. Mike learned another valuable lesson in humility that day.

He continued training, eventually reaching his purple belt, although in recent months with commuting to Toronto for work, he hadn't been on the mats nearly often enough.

By 5:30 pm everyone else had left the club. Mike finished his work out, showered, and threw on street clothes. He shut down the lights and locked the door behind him, wondering what to do next. 5:30pm on Christmas Eve, he thought. Boring. He figured he'd just go home and watch YouTube, or binge watch a series on Netflix. He hoped in his truck and headed towards his house.

Along the way he passed a small plaza. The parking lot was brightly lit, but all the stored were closed and dark. It was snowing again, and still windy. Out of the corner of his eye he saw a neon "Open" sign in the window of the corner bar at the end of the plaza. Figuring they must have forgotten to turn the sign off, he didn't pay it any attention until he stopped at the light. Now looking directly into the bar, he could see there were people inside. "What the hell," he thought and pulled into the parking lot.

It was a tiny little place. Maybe thirty feet by thirty feet, not including the bathrooms off to the back. There was no pool table, only two small tables and a large L shaped bar. One of the tables was currently occupied by a young couple that might have been in their twenties. At the bar sat and an older man who was probably in his late sixties. There were no other patrons.

It dawned on Mike that this was a university bar; the type of place that held small open mic nights for standing room only crowds. The old man had probably been sitting there since Nazareth played it in 1975. Since Mike was here with no better place to be, he thought he'd have a beer. Plus, occasionally old timers were good for a conversation.

Mike had a standing set of rules when talking to others: no religion and no politics. Beyond that, a conversation with a stranger that he'd never see again would be just fine. He made his way to the bar and pulled up a stool.

The girl behind the counter had her back to him restocking the fridge. "Be right with ya," she yelled over her shoulder.

Mike sat down and took some cash out of his pocket. He placed a $20 of the counter and said "MGD when you get a second."

He looked over and the old man was smiling at him. Mike nodded and said, "How are ya?" the man nodded back and returned to staring at the barmaid's ass. Mike chanced a look as well. The old man had good taste.

He looked around the bar. Old motor oil tin signs and decorative washboards adorned the walls, along with what looked like corny cartoon adds from the 1950s, but on closer inspection were actually mock ads for fictitious raunchy products. There was Whoops Ass Cola, Donkey Punch Chewing Gum, and Camel Towing. Mike's favorite was a guy holding a hammer, his finger throbbing as if he'd just smacked it, a pin up bombshell in the background smiling, and the caption reading "Hurt your finger? Go home and soak it in cider." Clever, Mike thought.

"That'll be $6.50" a girl's voice broke through Mikes reverie as the bartender set a bottle in front of him. Mike turned around and was stuck by the lightest blue eyes dancing above a beautiful smile.

The bartender looked younger, maybe mid-twenties. She stood about five foot four, one hundred and forty pounds, but muscular. She looked like she hit the gym regularly or carried a lot of beer cases. She was wearing a short-brimmed black round military cap with short blonde hair peeking out underneath. She had on a black Blondie t-shirt with the sleeves cut off, showcasing both biceps which were completely covered with tattoos. The shirt fit loose around the neckline, revealing part of a bigger tattoo that Mike assumed went from shoulder to shoulder across her chest. She completed the look with dark blue jeans with the cuffs rolled halfway up her calves and black combat boots. She had a "don't fuck with me and I won't fuck with you" air about her, but it wasn't forced or exaggerated.

Mike was speechless at first, he looked down at the cash and pushed it towards her. She grabbed it off the counter and came back with change, a $10 bill and some coins. He grabbed the $10 and slid the rest across the bar.

"Merry Christmas," she quipped.

"Yeah, you too," Mike replied, finding his voice. "How late are you guys open?"

She shrugged "I don't know. 'Til I close I guess" she answered.

Mike nodded. "Mike." He introduced himself, sticking his hand out.

She flashed her smile again, "Sasha," she returned, shaking Mike's hand. "So, Mike. What brings you here this evening?"

"The open sign." Mike replied truthfully.

"Fighting with the wife?" she asked.

"Not married." He corrected.

"Girlfriend? Or Boyfriend?"

"Nope."

"Kids? Parents? Pets?"

"I have a house plant," Mike admitted. "It's a cactus. I haven't watered it in three years though."

She snorted a laugh.

"What about you?" he asked.

"I have a dog," she answered. "She's sleeping right now though."

The younger couple paid their tab, thanked Sasha and left. She, Mike, and the old man carried on talking for a while. The old man had introduced himself as Leonard ("but not Lenny"). Mike ordered another beer and asked Sasha to grab one for Leonard.

"Start a tab?" she asked. Mike nodded and excused himself to the bathroom.

Walking past the end of the bar he stopped as if he was looking at a poster and called Sasha over.

"What is it, hun?" she asked.

"Put Leonard's tab on me for tonight. If he has one going already, add it to mine," Mike requested.

Sasha gave him a joking look and said "You sure? That dude can drink!"

"Yeah, just tonight's though! I don't want to find out I'm on the hook for his last six years," he clarified with a smile.

"Six years? More like sixteen." She winked at him, smiling back.

Mike walked towards the bathroom. The entire hallway was painted black: the floor, walls, and ceilings. There were two bathroom doors with nothing to identify male or female. Mike assumed people pissed in whichever one was free when they got there. A stack of beer cases piled up on the left. Between the two doors was a large corkboard with a few posters and flyers: taxi companies, rooms for rent, and small business advertisements. Among them was a big black and white poster with "SASHA" written across the top and "SWITCHBLADES" across the bottom, and a black and white picture of the bartender, covered in sweat, doing what Mike assumed was screaming into a microphone. Cute, he thought.

The three of them sat at the bar talking and laughing. Around 9:30 pm Leonard said it was past his bedtime. He stood to reach for his wallet, but Sasha interjected, "On the house tonight, Leonard. Merry Christmas." He mumbled a thank you as he staggered and almost tripped over a stool.

"Leonard, you're not driving tonight, are you?" Mike asked, concerned.

Leonard straightened himself up. "Why, yes I am. Why do you ask?"

Mike looked at Sasha, a serious look of concern on his face. Sasha was showing her big bright smile explained, "He lives in the apartment's right behind here," nodding her head towards the back. "There's a hole in the fence. He's not driving".

Mike breathed a sigh of relief. He shook Leonard's hand and wished him a Merry Christmas. Sasha guided Leonard away from the bar, "Come young fella, I'll let you out the back door."

Walking out Mike heard Leonard ask, "Will you let me take you home tonight?"

Sasha replied "Oh, not tonight, hun. Ask me tomorrow"

"You said that yesterday" Leonard retorted.

"Yeah, but this is today" Sasha explained. "Ask me tomorrow."

Mike heard them laughing. He heard the lock and the big metal door open, a faint "good night" followed by the sound of the big metal door slamming shut and latching. Sasha came walking back up to the bar, pulled out two beers, opened them, and put one in front of Mike. They clinked the bottles and she let out a deep sigh.

"Long day?" Mike asked.

"Sure was," she answered. "Late one last night. Was up early today. Came in here for 3:00 pm."

"What are your plans tomorrow?" Mike questioned.

"Nothing really," she replied. "Going to hang out with my girl" she elaborated, referring to her dog. "What about you?"

Mike took a pull on his beer and said "Nothing planned. No family around here. Had an invite to a friends for dinner, but I'm thinking I rather ditch it and lay on the couch."

Flashing her smile again, Sasha offered, "I have a big couch".

Chapter 17

Sunday December 25th, 2022.
Hamilton Ontario

Mike and Sasha spent Christmas day together. Between both of their kitchens and a stop at a gas station, they were able to compile enough ingredients to make a decent breakfast. They spent the late morning and afternoon curled up watching movies on the couch together with Sasha's dog Domino, a small black and white Boston Terrier/French Bulldog mix. The dog spent all morning fighting to get in between them. She didn't know who this big guy was, but she didn't like him near her mama, and she made sure to let him know. Around 1:00 pm Sasha told Mike she had to open the bar at 5:00 pm

"On Christmas Day?" Mike asked, surprised.

"Our regulars make up two groups: lonely old alcoholics, and international students that don't celebrate Christmas." Sasha explained.

"Fair enough." replied Mike.

"Did you want to come by?" Sasha invited, smiling. Mike couldn't tell what it was, but there was something about her that drew him in.

"Sure, what time?"

"Whenever. I'm there till I leave." She hopped off the couch wearing nothing but his shirt from the night before, popped "True Romance" into the DVD player, and flopped back on the couch beside him.

Mike asked, "How long have you been working there?

"I'm just filling in for a couple weeks" she replied. "That's not my regular job."

"What's your regular job?" Mike inquired.

"Heavy equipment operator." she stated. Mike stared at her for a second trying to see if there was a punch line coming.

"Yes, really." She added without being prompted, indicating he wasn't the first to be surprised by her trade. "And what do you do?"

"Ironworker." Mike answered. She gave him a strange look, "You ever see the old black and white picture of the guys eating lunch on the beam in New York?"

"Yes."

"That," he said.

She gave him a thoughtful nod. "'K, shut up. Movie's starting."

Chapter 18

Tuesday December 27th, 2022, 7:15 pm
Hamilton Ontario

Steve had a meeting set up with one of his connections. This was it, the big one.

He had made a deal to buy two kilos of cocaine and four kilos of fentanyl. He had been working with this supplier for a few weeks now, and if all went well today, the supplier would be arrested. Steve was hoping to flip him in an attempt to move up the food chain.

Steve had to start off small but not too small. It's hard to go from $100 to $100,000 worth of narcotics in two weeks; it sends up too many red flags. Steve started by first buying bags of coke from a street level dealer at a bar. Over the course of a few weeks, he routinely bought up everything the guy had. Steve convinced the dealer to call his supplier. He worked out a deal with the supplier on the spot and started dealing with him directly. Steve was actually surprised the supplier agreed to meet with him, and more so when he agreed to let Steve deal. But money talks, and Steve was showing a lot of it.

He asked the supplier to help him get cheap cigarettes from the Six Nations Territory. They worked out a deal where Steve's "friends" from Saskatchewan came to Hamilton, picked up a U-haul truck full of cigarettes and transported them back to Saskatoon. In reality, the truck went from Hamilton straight to an evidence locker in Toronto. From that successful encounter, Steve's supplier made $40,000. Steve then arranged for another load three weeks later.

After two successful tobacco deals, Steve asked his supplier if he had a line for coke and fentanyl for the same guys in Saskatoon. The deal was made, and arrangements were put in place for tonight. It wasn't like Hollywood; they didn't meet in abandoned warehouses with guys on both sides holding sub-machine guns. The quantities Steve was looking for would fit in small duffle bag. Having just received $40,000 on two occasions for doing nothing more than parking a U-haul, the supplier was eager to do more business.

Steve, now acting as Marcus, walked up the front steps of his supplier's house. The house was a big light red-brick structure that backed on to a ravine in a new development neighbourhood. He rang the doorbell and waited.

After about a minute the supplier let him in. He was a short, stocky white guy, covered in tattoos and the scars that accompanied a hard-lived life. His name was Caleb Tulk, and according to his criminal history, he was an ideal candidate to flip. He'd been to federal prison more than once and was just now about to start getting unsupervised visits with his ten-year-old daughter. If anybody had everything to lose, it was him.

Caleb let Steve in. The house was new, Modern with light grey walls. The front door opened into a hallway with a small bathroom on the left, The hallway ended in a Large open concept Kitchen, with a family room on the right, and dining area on the left.

"Marcus, what's up bro?" Caleb greeted him, shaking his hand and giving him a one-armed hug.

"Not much, waiting to get back to work."

"When do you go back?" Caleb asked, leading him inside.

"Well, I was planning on the freedom 6/49 but my numbers didn't hit yet. So, scheduled for January second, unless I win Lotto-max later tonight."

Caleb chuckled and offered, "Beer?"

"Yeah, please." Steve followed Caleb into the kitchen.

"Grab a seat," Caleb indicated towards the couches in the large family room. Steve made himself comfortable on the couch facing the projection wall.

Caleb followed behind a moment later holding two beers. Handing one to Steve, they clinked the bottles, said "Cheers" and took a swig.

Steve took a drink of his and asked, "We good?"

Caleb looked at the small duffle bag Steve had set down in front of him, smiled and replied "Oh, yeah we're good."

He set his beer down on the coffee table and disappeared down the hallway towards the garage. Steve heard the closet door open, some rustling, then heard the door squeak shut. Caleb returned to the room smiling as he set a large Foot-Locker bag down on Steve's lap. Steve looked inside and saw five bundles wrapped in clingwrap. Caleb explained, "Bigger bundle is the coke, smaller ones are the down," then asked, "You want to try it?"

"Can't. Not mine. I'm just the prick in the middle here. I'll be seeing my guys when I leave here. They'll check it out. If there any issues, I'll let you know."

Caleb nodded. Steve drained his beer and said "Okay, I got to jet," and stood up to leave. Caleb was walking him through the kitchen towards front hallway "When you need more I can..."

There was a loud thump, like someone punching a canvas heavy bag, an impact with no slap. Caleb flew backwards and hit the floor hard. Steve was trying to figure out happened when a huge dark figure stepped into the kitchen from the hallway. Steve looked at Caleb. There was a knot starting to swell on his forehead. The dark figure was dressed in browns and greens wearing a ski mask and black gloves. The black pistol in his right hand was pointed at Steve.

"Knees. Now." The figure demanded.

"Hey, hold on." Steve started protesting, but before he could continue, the figure punched him in the face, knocking him to the floor. Steve looked up, blood running from his nose.

The dark figure said, "Face down. I don't want to kill you, but I will."

Steve could tell by the man's icy tone that it wasn't an idle threat, so he laid down.

The man walked into the family room, grabbed the small duffle bag with the cash, and continued straight through the room to the sliding patio door. Steve heard the door slide open then close, and the man was gone.

Ninety seconds later, the first of the Hamilton police cars screeched to a halt in front or Caleb's house, lights flashing. Several more, including unmarked OPP and RCMP cars followed. Two Hamilton police officers came rushing through the front door. Steve was standing at the sink holding paper towel under his nose.

"Look after him" he nodded towards Caleb who was still unconscious on the floor. The older of the two Hamilton Police officers keyed his mic and asked for the paramedics who had been standing by.

Five minutes later, Karl Sampson, Steve's superintendent, came storming up the front walkway. Karl was a large man in his early fifties, with a full head of white hair and a body that showed he had not hit the gym since landing an office job fifteen years ago. He blew past a still unconscious Caleb as well as the paramedics, who were busy assessing Caleb's injuries and fitting his oxygen mask. Karl stormed into the kitchen and shouted, "What the hell happened?"

Steve was sitting in a chair talking to another paramedic. "No idea," Steve replied. "He just appeared."

"Was he already in the house?" Karl asked.

One of the Hamilton police officers chimed in, "We're not sure. We had a van parked down the road. We're looking at the footage now."

"Well, who the fuck was he?" Karl demanded. Everyone stood around looking at each other, figuring it was better to stay quiet. "Great, just fucking great. A figment of our fucking imaginations just waltzed in here, knocked out two guys and strolled away. And nobody saw a fucking thing?" Then to Steve Karl barked, "Was your phone on?"

"Yeah, but it was in my pocket I don't think it caught anything."

"Okay, walk me through what you remember," Karl ordered, still blazing with anger.

"The deal was done. I was walking to the door. Caleb was in front of me. I was about here," Steve got up and walked to a spot about one foot in front of the blood he left on the floor.

"Caleb was walking towards the doorway looking back at me talking. The guy must have been waiting for us. As soon as Caleb walked into the hallway, I heard a thud, and he came flying back into the kitchen." Steve paused for a second then continued. "And before I could make heads or tails of anything the guy was standing in front of me."

"What did he look like" Karl asked.

"Couldn't tell. He was big. I know that I was looking up at him. He said something - I didn't quite understand it. I think he was telling me to get on the ground. I was trying to deescalate as best I could, but he hit me in the face." Steve explained, still a bit dazed.

Karl looked at the damage on Steve's face and asked, "With a baseball bat?"

"His hands, I think. He was fast. Really fast. Didn't see it coming. One second, I was standing, the next I was sitting on the floor. He told me to lay face down. Said he didn't want to kill me but would if he had to."

Karl shook his head then asked, "Then what?"

"Then he left through the back door." Steve replied.

Karl looked and saw a few police flashlights shining around. A young East Indian man in a blue jacket walked in.

"Well, we have him coming in," he began, as he set a laptop on the kitchen counter. Everybody gathered around and watched a still frame of the front of the house on a paused video, The technician pressed play, and five seconds later the bushes rustled in front on the house, almost as if coming to life. A dark figure stepped out of them, advanced to the door, and within two seconds he was in the house. The tech paused the video again. "That's it," he said.

A plain-clothes officer entered from the front door. "We found footprints at the side of the house. Looks like he came up from the ravine behind here," he explained, pointing to the wooded area behind the house. "Came around the side, in the front door, out the back, and left the yard from the same spot he entered".

"Footprints any good?" Karl asked.

He OPP shook his head. "There's shape, but there's no pattern at all. Its like he was wearing house slippers or something."

Karl scratched his head. "Who the hell was he?" he asked himself out loud.

Chapter 19

Tuesday December 27th, 2022, 8:40 pm
Hamilton Ontario

"Who the hell was he?" Mike heard, listening on a small earpiece. five days earlier Mike had let himself into Caleb's house and put a wireless Bluetooth transmitter inside a wall socket in the kitchen. The device was a small unit he'd found at the "As Seen on TV" store in the local mall. It initially boasted having a 96 hour battery. Mike didn't trust the claim, but with a few small modifications he was able to attach it directly to the socket wires, giving it constant power. Like most people, Caleb left his Wi-Fi password on the fridge. With the Wi-Fi and an app on his burner phone, Mike was able to listen in to Caleb's house anytime he wanted.

He flipped the earpiece off as he drove a silver 2004 Dodge Caravan southwest out of Hamilton towards the Ohsweken reserve on Six Nations territory. He checked the rearview mirror for a tail that wasn't there. He was going to take the county road since it was easier to know if you were being followed. While he was confident that he wasn't being followed, he reminded himself it was that type of "can't touch me" attitude that made it so easy for him to rob drug dealers. Never let your guard down.

Mike pulled over on the side of a dark road, opened the small duffle bag and quickly took the money out, giving each bundle a quick but thorough inspection, checking for tracking devices. He placed the bundles in a new bag, tossed the small duffle into the overgrown ditch, and drove off. A few minutes later he picked up his phone and called Sasha. She answered on the third ring.

"Hey!" She breathed, sounding chipper.

"Hey, yourself." he replied. "Busy?"

"Not really, just took the dog for a walk. What are you doing?" she asked.

"Just got off work. Buy you dinner?"

"Sure. What time?" she agreed.

"I'm about forty-five minutes away. That work for you?"

She smiled. "Sounds great. See ya then."

Mike continued on his way to the Six Nations territory. He came up to from a side road, found the main drag, and drove straight to a little side street. About a hundred yards down of the left was a small blue barn. Mike's friend Eric, another ironworker with a boxing history, had built it years ago and used it as a makeshift boxing club. Mike started helping him train the kids there until Eric had a mild heart attack and closed up shop. Eric had since moved to Florida. Mike struck a deal where he would put $400 a month into Eric's daughter's mailbox in exchange for rent of the barn. There was no paper trail, and Mike was certain Eric thought he lived there, so nobody ever came by.

Mike pulled the caravan behind the barn and took the plates off. The van would be going to Jocko's in the morning. Jocko was a local guy that owned a large scrap yard. Officially, he made his living as a scrap metal guy that bought and sold used cars for cheap. Off the books, he and Mike had a long-standing agreement: for cash, Jocko would give Mike the keys to a working, reliable vehicle with a set of plates, and either resell or destroy whatever vehicle Mike happened to pull up in that day. Mike would drop the van off there tomorrow, and by 10:00 am there would be nothing left.

He went into the barn. The walls were drywalled but not mudded or painted. There was a wet bar with a large mirror behind it, some heavy bags, a speed bag, and a weight bench tucked away. Behind the water heater was a gun safe that was too big to get upstairs. Mike had bolted to the floor. He spun the combination and opened the door. Inside was an assortment of firearms: three 12-gauge shotguns, one black autoloader, another camo pump, and an old CIL pump that Mike had sawed down about fourteen inches. He'd cut the stock off and had added a leather strap around the front for better control. He also had twelve pistols, semi-automatics a few revolvers and all taken off drug dealers.

Rounding out his collection was a Lee Enfield 303 riffle with a 3-9X scope, an AR-15, and a Remington 700 .308 with a 4 x 27- 50 mm scope, as well as a 12-40 x 60 mm spotter scope, usually used by a sniper's spotter to verify shots. He took the gun belt he was wearing off hung it up in the safe and closed the door.

He climbed the stairs to the loft. Upstairs there was a second, smaller gun safe. He punched in the PIN and opened the door. Inside were stacks of bills: twenties, fifties and hundreds. Beside the cash stood a couple crossbows, a compound bow, an assortment of arrows, and several knives, both decorative and tactical. The safe also held an assortment of small electronics such as miniature spy cams, listening devices, and a box with over twenty GPS trackers. Most of the trackers had a short battery life of only 24 to 48 hours, but at $30 apiece he didn't worry too much about them.

Taped on the back wall of the safe was picture of a seventeen-year-old Mike smiling at the camera, his arm around Tamika, who was starting up at him with a bright smile. The picture was taken on the waterfront in Windsor on September 28th, 2007, the day before she was killed.

Having switched the cash he stole earlier that night into a different bag and checked the bundles to make sure they weren't being tracked. He'd still have to go over them with a black light in case there was invisible markings on them, but that didn't worry him too much. They can't identify the bills if they don't know where they are. He counted it out quickly. "Shit, a hundred grand. Not bad" he mused to himself. He'd been expecting around $40,000.

Mike shut the safe door. He stood there for a minute thinking. He'd made the other guy at Celeb's out to be a cop. Mike spent several minutes trying to make sense of why he was there.

Mike had been turned on to Caleb when he overheard John Sarsens, a coworker from Six Nations, talking about how he and his brother were making a killing loading a U-haul for some coke-dealing white dude in Hamilton. Mike thought he'd check it out. It turned out to be financially beneficial, but the cop was an unexpected complication. The cop's involvement added a new level of aggravation, the most pressing being that the place might have been under surveillance. The van needed to be gone first thing in the morning. Mike fired up the wood stove and tossed in the clothes he wore that day and waited until they were completely burnt up before leaving.

Mike pulled up at Sasha's around 9:35 pm. He was running a bit later than anticipated, as he wanted to ensure there were no burning embers of clothing still smoldering before he left the barn. Sasha lived in a small one-bedroom apartment in a big yellow brick Victorian style house broken up into three units. The landlady, an older French-Canadian woman named Sophie, lived on the main unit at the front, Sasha was in the upper unit, and there was a tenant in the back named James that would glare at Mike anytime they passed each other.

Sasha's apartment was small but cozy. It had an open concept living room kitchen with a small island that looked out of place. There was a small bedroom, and a bathroom so small Mike had a hard time standing up in the shower.

He knocked on the door and heard Sasha yell, "Come in". He climbed the stairs and was greeted by Domino, her little dog, who looked more Bulldog than Boston Terrier and acted more honey badger. She held an A-frame stance, ready to fight, letting out gruff little "woo woo wooo's" at Mike as he ascended. Mike reached in his pocket and gave her a cookie. The two had forged an understanding: he'd bribe her with treats, and she'd allow him into her apartment. Sasha popped her head out from her living room to the stairwell. She was wearing black yoga pants, and a black Bad Religion t-shirt, again with the sleeves cut off.

"You really oughta lock your door" Mike said. "There's a lot of crazies around here."

Sasha looked down at her pup and pointed out "I have a guard dog". Domino was currently rolling on her chew toy, marking it with her scent, just in case Mike got any ideas. She almost rolled down the stairs. Mike gave an exaggerated nod saying he understood.

"Well?" he asked, "hungry?"

She smiled and replied with a question of her own, "Your nose work?"

He gave her an inquisitive look and she explained, "I'm cooking right now. It'll be ready in ten minutes. Beer?"

He nodded. She grabbed two brown bottles out of the fridge, opened them, and set them both on the island. Mike pulled up a stool and looked around. The décor could only be called punk/toys. She had posters up from several local bands, and a number of old Transformers and He-man toys in various erotic poses, seemingly placed at random throughout her apartment. On a speaker that doubled as an end-table, there sat a framed picture of a young blonde girl, around three years old, in the arms of a very large no-nonsense looking man. Beside it sat another picture of the same little girl, this time with a boy who looked to be a couple years older, in front of a pretty woman. Mike guessed the picture was taken some time around the mid 1990's.

"Your Mom? He asked.

She looked at the picture and nodded. "Lost her in 08," she smiled sadly. Looking at the other picture, she added, "That's my dad. Lost him a year and a half later."

"How old were you?" Mike asked, realizing he had no idea how old she was.

"Seventeen when mom died, eighteen when dad went." she replied. Mike quickly calculated the math.

"Wait, how old are you?" he asked.

She paused for a second and answered, "Um, twenty-eight, I think." She paused, then confirmed, "Yeah, born in 94. I'll be twenty-nine in August." She looked at Mike and inquired, "You?"

"I'll be thirty-three next month" Mike stated. She gave him a funny look, and he asked "What?"

She said, "I don't know, you don't look thirty-three. You somehow look older and younger at the same time. I'd believe twenty-nine or thirty-nine, but not thirty-three." Mike gave her a confused look and opted to change the topic.

"Siblings?" Mike asked.

Sasha told him she had two older siblings, a sister and brother, and one younger brother. She was in contact with them but mostly just on holidays and birthdays. They spent the next few minutes discussing the advantages and disadvantages of family estrangement when the timer on the oven dinged. Sasha spun around, grabbed oven mitts, and pulled out an aluminum foil-covered dish out of the oven.

"Let that cool down and we're golden" she said. They carried on talking about nothing of consequence. She mentioned Sophie, the landlady, who had a cat named Charlie, who was Domino's best friend. Sophie came over daily and took the dog for a walk when Sasha was at work, then kept her in her apartment to play with the cat until Sasha got home. Sasha told Mike about a few years before when work was slow and Sasha, like many people, was trying to decide between paying rent or buying food. Sophie had waived half her rent. When Sasha had broken up with her previous boyfriend Sophie appeared at the door with a big bottle of wine and two glasses.

After a few minutes Sasha decided it was time to eat. She loaded up two plates and placed one in front of Mike.

"Smells good, what is it?" he asked.

"I don't know" she replied honestly. "I just made some shit. Mostly used up what I have in the fridge. But there's a can of... something in there too." she said laughing. She grabbed two forks and sat at the stool across from Mike. They both took one bite and stopped. Not wanting to be rude, Mike froze, trying to think about what to do. Sasha met his eyes, smiled and spit it out into her napkin.

"Pizza?" she suggested.

Chapter 20

Wednesday December 28th 2022, 11:25 am

Toronto, Ontario

The following morning, Steve made the long drive into Toronto to meet with the various heads of the task force to discuss the previous night's events. Steve's head was splitting, both from the broken nose he'd sustained during the robbery, and from the bottle of Canadian Club he drank afterwards. Traffic coming into the city wasn't bad for a Saturday, but it was stop and go as soon as he left the Gardiner Expressway. While Steve enjoyed the action that came with this job, he missed the quiet roads from rural living.

He made it to a board room where everyone was already sitting waiting for him. Steve sat down and placed his coffee in front of him, steam still rising from the open lid. He was twenty-five minutes late and still stopped for a coffee. Total power move, he thought to himself.

The lead for the RCMP task force looked at him. Steve looked back at her; he still couldn't remember her name. He wondered if he should call her "mom" in the meeting and suppressed a grin.

"Thank you for joining us. I trust you got here as soon as you could?" The officer's eyes looked pointedly at the red paper coffee cup with the McDonalds logo on it.

"Traffic was a bitch" Steve explained, smiling at her.

By now most of the bruising had started under Steve's eyes. He had taken hits in the face before. Once when playing hockey, he took a puck right between the eyes. While working near Timmins, he had been involved with the odd altercation that resulted in him getting punched in the face, sometimes accidentally, sometimes deliberately. The intention behind the punch didn't matter, it hurt just the same. But this time was different; Steve had never been punched like this.

Karl, Steve's direct superintendent, sensed the frustration in the room and decided to get the meeting started. "As of right now we have Caleb Tulk in custody. He's being kept at McMaster Hospital for observation, likely to be released to our custody tonight or tomorrow. He has a severe concussion, and fracture in the frontal bone of his skull." He paused, looking up at Steve's battered face and asked, "What the hell did he hit you with?"

Steve said, "I was thinking about that on my way in. There was a store at a mall in Regina that used to sell sap gloves or heavy hitters. I think he had those on."

"Sap gloves?" asked the young East Indian man from last night. Steve saw the ID card around his neck had the name Hardeep on it.

"Think of brass knuckles," Steve began. "Yes, they do damage when you hit someone, superficial damage like cuts, bumps, bruises for example. The edges of the brass cause that. But the force, the knockout power, comes from the extra weight. Like when your dad would give you a roll of nickels to deal with the high school bully. Same effect."

Hardeep stared at Mike like he had three eyes. Obviously not a fighter, Mike thought, and tried again. "Sap gloves are like," he paused for a second and mused, "kind of like a blackjack. A heavy lead filled pouch on the end of about twelve inches of leather." Hardeep pulled out his phone typed "blackjack" into the search engine and nodded when the screen lit up with examples. Mike continued, "Some genius had the idea to combine the brass knuckles with a blackjack. Sap gloves have about a pound of lead in a leather or Kevlar pouch sewn onto the front of leather gloves. I responded to a call at a bar up north a few years back where one guy had punched another while wearing a pair. The victim's cheek was sunken in. He required corrective surgery, and lost his left eye as a result. All the fun of brass knuckles without the risk of damaging your own hands."

"OK, so we're looking for a gorilla with leather gloves" the RCMP task force lead snarked.

Steve met her stare, took a sip of his coffee, and said "So, what now? The money's gone and we have no idea where it is or who has it."

"Was it marked?" she asked.

"We tagged each bill with a direct glow marker, so it'll show up under a black light. But unless he walks into a bank with a hundred grand in cash and they call us right away, then we're shit out of luck. It won't take long to find its way into circulation." Steve paused, then elaborated, "Big bills aren't as easy to track as people think. Casinos are mostly automated now. He could go drop five grand into a slot machine, make two pulls, and cash out with clean money. Shit, if he's not working alone, they could have it all washed by the end of the week."

"Well, fuck!" she exclaimed.

Steve ignored her and directed his next question to Karl. "Caleb, is he awake?"

Karl flipped through the paperwork in front of him and said "Yes, he's awake He aware that he's under arrest. We had to film the reading of his rights though. His memory was like a goldfish when he woke up. Kept asking the same questions every thirty seconds."

Getting a bad concussion wasn't like what they showed on the screen. People didn't get laid out then jump right back up clear headed. Headaches, vomiting, dizziness, horrible light sensitivity, and terrible short term memory loss often accompanied a severe concussion. Steve thought for a few seconds and said, "Okay, so he has no idea what happened? I saw him hit the ground. He was out. He went into convulsions when the medics were dealing with him." he continued, showing no concern for Caleb.

"And?" asked "Mom".

"It means we're still in this!" Steve sat up straight and slapped the table. "He doesn't know what happened. The money was taken, but the dope was left behind. He doesn't know that. We can spin this. I can make it out that now he's $200,000 in debt to two very dangerous groups. I can use this to get closer to his connections." Steve looked at Karl. "Where are they taking him from the hospital?"

"My guess would be one of the detention centers. I'll find out. He's got to be arraigned, but they'll do that via video link" Karl explained.

"Okay, do what you can to have him brought to the police station in Hamilton and put in a holding cell instead. Then put me in there with him. Is there any way we can be arraigned together?" Steve asked.

The RCMP task force lead answered. "That's a tall order. The courts don't like to get involved, but we can have it look like you were also being brought in for questioning at the same time he is." She picked up her phone and started typing.

Hardeep asked, "Why the police station?"

Karl replied, "Because most of the pieces of shit that Steve took down over the last few years are in detention centers scattered across Canada awaiting trial." Hardeep again didn't understand. "If they see him, they'll kill him." Karl concluded.

Hardeep nodded.

Steve asked Hardeep "Did Caleb have security cameras at his house?"

"Yeah, we found four: front door, side door, one in the garage and one facing the back yard.".

"Anything of our friend coming or going?" Karl asked.

"There's a two second clip at the front door. He stepped up, used a rake, and was in in under two seconds," Hardeep summarized.

"So, he picked a lock in under two seconds?" Karl asked.

"Basically yes, but he used an electric tool. You can find them online. They're discreet and make less noise than an electric toothbrush". Hardeep advised.

"Anything in the yard? Coming or going?" asked the RCMP task force lead.

"Just the back of his head as he stepped out the patio door and disappeared into the yard" Hardeep replied, then added "Steve isn't lying, he was a big man."

"Can you delete it, all of it? The police rushing in, the EMT's, all of it?" Steve asked.

"We have his phone. The system belongs to his internet provider. We've already checked the text message notification from when there was activity. No emails. We have seized all the equipment too. It goes back twenty-one days before it deletes any clips. We got a warrant this morning to go through it and see who we can identify coming and going. So, you're good, we have everything." Hardeep assured him.

Steve drummed on the table "Okay, get me into a holding cell with Caleb. I think we can make this work."

Both Karl and the RCMP task force lead were typing away at their phones. Steve asked "Are we done here? There's a Greek place down the road calling my name."

At 6:30 pm Steve got the call from Karl. "There's a cruiser on its way to your place. They're going to bring you in. Caleb is being transferred to police headquarters in about twenty minutes".

"It's a little late, isn't it?" Steve asked, thinking if Caleb had seen a judge via video, he would be sent to the local detention center instead.

"There's two cops that are going to play the part of detectives." Karl explained. "They're tossing you guys into an empty bull pen. After about twenty minutes they're going to come for you like they're asking for an interview. You'll say you want a lawyer, and they'll leave." Karl took a drink of something and added, "Hopefully that gets Caleb thinking that they're going to leave him sitting for a few hours. He'll think the dumb cops haven't figured out you guys are supposed to be co-accused. After another hour or so, the same Dicks will come rushing in to pull you out, giving the appearance that they just put two and two together."

"Okay." Steve said.

"We have about an hour and half Steve, that's it. They're emptying out the bull pen for us, and they're not thrilled. Make it count," Karl instructed.

"Got it." Steve affirmed and hung up.

As Steve set down his phone there was a knock on the door. The two Hamilton police officers that had rushed into Caleb's house first the day before were standing there. The older one took out his handcuffs and asked, "Yeah, or no?"

Steve nodded and turned around. If anybody was watching, at least it would look real now. The drive to the downtown police station didn't take long. They entered through the garage, all three of them silent. Getting off the elevator the cuffs were removed. The older cop asked him, "Are you good?"

Steve nodded and was escorted to the bullpen. The bullpen was a large rectangular area about sixty feet long by twenty feet deep. A poured-cement bench wrapped around three sides of it. Floors and walls were painted grey. The front wall was made up of large heavy-duty plexiglass sheets, each one about four feet wide by ten feet high. As they rounded the corner, Steve was shocked to see that Caleb wasn't in there, but two large biker-looking men were. Steve looked at the cop escorting him for an explanation. The cop said, "It's fine" and opened the door.

As Steve stepped in, the cop advised, "You've got three minutes. Make it look like you've been here a while," and shut the door. Steve looked at the two men. The larger of the two nodded and asked, "Steve?"

Steve said nothing but looked at him. The man said, "Sue sent us, we're both RCMP."

"Sue?" Steve asked even more confused.

"Sue Blenkhorn" he paused, waiting for Steve to show a sign of recognition. "Operation Shooting Star?" the man explained, referencing the code name of the RCMP task force.

"Sue? Is that her name?" Steve asked, and the bigger guy laughed.

"She thought an empty bullpen would be too suspicious. She put us three in here. I'm mic'd up".

"Three?" Steve asked. The big guy nodded towards the drunk tank across the aisle. A third man, old and scruffy, looking like a homeless wino, was standing at the plexiglass door, a big wet spot down the front of his pants.

The big guy followed Steve's gaze and explained, "It's water, but it looks like he pissed himself". He turned back to Steve and said "Sue wants the mic, for our benefit, when you lawyer up. We want proof that he didn't ask at the same time". Steve nodded that he understood. "Mom" was covering all her bases. "Two minutes to show time, Steve," the big guy directed, looking at the bench sixty feet away, implying Steve needed to be over there.

"It's Marcus now," Steve corrected.

The big guy replied, "I don't give a fuck who you are" glaring at him. He had already slipped into character.

Steve went down to the far end. At the foot of the poured cement bench was a stainless-steel toilet that offered no privacy. Steve laid with his head near the wall away from the toilet and draped his arm over his eye blocking out the light. He didn't need to act exhausted; he was exhausted.

About two minutes later, he heard the door open. He looked up and saw Caleb being lead in. His face was a mess; deep dark bruises had settled under his eyes where the blood had pooled. Both eyes almost swollen shut. The door was slammed and locked, the latch echoing inside the rectangular box. Steve sat up, looking confused.

"Caleb?" he asked.

Caleb stood there shocked, trying to figure out what was going on. Both bikers were giving him cold stares, like the door opening had interrupted them and it was Caleb's fault. Caleb walked to the end of the bullpen and sat down.

"What the fuck?" Steve asked. Caleb looked at him with a suspicious glare but relaxed a little when he saw the damage on Steve's face. "Bro, what happened?" Steve asked.

"I don't know. I thought you set me up," Caleb replied.

Looking genuinely shocked, Steve said "No. I thought you robbed me!" Pausing for a second, he continued, "I remember having a beer in your rec room. Then I woke up handcuffed to a hospital bed at St Joe's," referring to St. Joseph's hospital.

Caleb was trying to make sense of everything, Steve didn't press it. Caleb had to connect his own dots.

Caleb asked, "What did they nail you for?"

"My lawyer said the dope, but he's sure they'll have to drop it." Pausing for a second, Steve asked "You?"

"The cigarettes." Caleb mumbled. "I was arrested for possession for the purpose of resale." He looked down towards the bikers. He noticed they were staring towards them.

Steve caught their stares, looked at the bigger guy and shouted, "You got a problem asshole?" The guy stared for a second then went back to his conversation. There would be hell to pay later, but at the time Steve thought it was funny. Caleb didn't see the humor. He was staring ahead at nothing, taking in what was coming his way. "That's not too bad. You didn't have them on you."

"They found the dope in the raid" Caleb sighed.

Steve said quietly, "Did you buy it? Or front it?" referring to the drugs.

"Fronted. I was supposed to settle up today," Caleb answered.

"Fuck." Steve quietly exclaimed, acting worried. "My guys too. Supposed to see them last night. They're going to be pissed."

"Marcus, these guys are going to fuck me up. Doesn't matter if I'm in here" Caleb confessed, his voice thick with worry.

"I'm in the same boat." Then, as if he'd just had a million-dollar idea, Steve offered, "I Could do a couple more cigarette runs. I'm being charged with the dope. But my lawyer says they'll kick me loose, nothing tying it to me. Plus, as banged up as we both are, They'll have to drop those charges. Hell nothing was said about the cash, That's a problem they'll be happy to sweep under the rug. I Drop our fee. Pay them back. It might take a couple months, but it's something."

Caleb's swollen face lit up for a second, then it sunk down. "No way I'm getting bail, dude."

Steve's heart was racing, he was getting everything. It was almost too easy. "I am though. I don't have a record."

Caleb looked at him, not believing him at first, Steve added "I mean, I got a mischief charge when I was like seventeen, but that's it." He waited a second and asked, "Can you get me in touch with your people."

"Marcus, I don't know about that, bro. these guys don't like new people." Caleb hesitated.

Steve shrugged "I got ya. I'm gonna do the smoke thing on my end then. Take me a couple drops, maybe a month or two to get good with them."

Caleb sat staring. Steve wasn't pushing the issue, but he was indirectly showing Caleb a way out of trouble, the financial side anyway. Right now, Caleb was more worried about his financial pressures than the legal troubles. But with being locked up with no chance at getting bail, he would need to get in touch with his people and set up a meeting with Marcus.

They both sat silently for a few minutes. The mumbles from the two guys at the end barely audible, mostly talking about so-and-so's motorcycles. The wino kept looking over at Caleb. When they met eyes, the wino asked for a cigarette. Caleb ignored him.

A few minutes later, the two cops that brought Steve in appeared in the doorway in plain clothes. The older one was mid-fifties, six feet tall and thick. It was clear he lifted, and lifted heavy. He had what used to be red hair, now grey with touches of orange. His hair was close cropped and neat, as was his moustache. He was wearing navy blue dress pants, a white golf shirt with pink and blue horizontal stripes, and his badge clipped to his brown belt. His younger partner was tall, athletic with a full head of gelled black hair, light brown khakis, a green button up shirt with the sleeves rolled up, and his badge clipped to his black leather belt.

"Marcus Atkins!" the older on yelled as he opened the door.

"What?"

"Come with us please," requested the older cop.

"Why?"

"Because we'd like to talk to you," the younger cop chirped.

"Not a chance," Steve replied.

"Come on, just a couple questions for you. Only take a minute," promised the older cop.

"Ask my lawyer, then. I have nothing to say."

Steve thought both guys deserved academy awards for their performance. The older one looked incredibly defeated, like someone had let the air out of the tires on his wagon. The younger one looked pissed, like his whole day had been spent waiting for Marcus Atkins to be brought back to the police station, only to have him lawyer up right away. He looked angry and frustrated. The uniformed officer closed the door. The younger plain clothed cop glared at Steve as he turned to follow his partner out.

Steve sat back, quietly. He figured he was running out of time but had to play it off as if he didn't care what happened to Caleb. After a couple minutes Caleb asked, "How much did you make on the smokes?"

"Same as you."

Caleb probed, "How often?"

"They'll take them every twenty days."

Caleb did the math in his head. He figured in about a month and a half, he could have the debt paid off and have some cash for his expensive lawyer. He sat thinking for a couple minutes then asked, "You know who Scott Greenspan is? The lawyer?"

Steve shook his head. Caleb explained, "That's my lawyer. When you get out, call him. He'll get you in touch with my guy in St Catharine's."

"Greenspan?" Steve repeated, clarifying.

"Yeah. His office is just over there" he nodded towards the door. "Couple blocks away from here. Just call him. Tell him who you are. I'll be seeing him soon, at least, I hope. I'll give him a phone number. He'll pass it to you. That's my guy."

Steve asked, "Okay, I'm just supposed to call him?" acting skeptical.

"Scott will call him for me too, give him a heads up that you'll be reaching out." Caleb promised, then warned, "Marcus, these guys don't fuck around. He may say we both owe him, not just me, and he may jack up the price too. Best not to argue with him."

Steve nodded.

What felt like hours later, the two detectives came rushing back in with a uniformed cop. They popped the door and ordered, "Atkins, let's go."

Steve sat up. "I said talk to my lawyer!"

The two plain clothed cops came in. The bigger one hauled Steve up by the left arm. "You're not being questioned we're moving you."

"Why? To where?" Steve resisted, trying to tug his arm loose.

"You can't be in here right now. Let's go." the younger one grabbed Steve's other arm roughly and Steve chanced a look at Caleb.

Damn, these guys are good, Steve thought as they yanked him off the bench and out of the bullpen. Steve was manhandled past two guys being processed, and out into another hallway. As soon as the door closed the two plain clothed cops and Steve all started laughing and slapping hands. "I need to get to a phone," Steve advised. They brought him into a large room with a dozen desks and left him.

Steve picked up the phone on the first desk and called his superintendent.

"Sampson," Karl answered.

"Its Parent." Steve returned.

"Well?" Karl asked impatiently.

"He bought it." Steve advised. "I'm calling his lawyer tomorrow. He'll be waiting to hear from me. Caleb is going to have him deliver a message to his connections."

"Okay, great." Karl affirmed.

"Get on the horn to Niagara Police. Caleb said the guy is in St. Catherine's." He could hear Karl rummaging through paperwork. Steve added "Caleb made it sound like these are some pretty scary guys, so any meetings I attend, they'll 100% want in their city. Make sure Niagara Police are ready to go when we call them, please. I don't want another shit show like last night"

"Anything else?"

"Yeah. Can you tell that Bitch on Wheels Blenkhorn, next time she drops two of her goons in without telling me I'll kick her ass right into the fucking lake!"

There was silence on the other line. Steve asked, "Sir?"

He heard Sue Blenkhorn reply "I'll keep that in mind Constable Parent".

Chapter 21

Wednesday February 6th, 2008.
Windsor, Ontario

Mike had celebrated his nineteenth birthday a few days ago. Not that there was much of a celebration. On Saturday, his actual birthday, he'd paced the house all day. Nick asked him to calm down, but by 6:00 pm he knew it was a pointless request. On Monday Mike was staring off into space all day. Tuesday Nick had Mike stay home from work for fear he'd make a serious mistake in his distraction and injure himself or someone else.

Today he was up at 4:00 am, showered and dressed by 4:30 am and stared at the clock until 7:45 am when they left for the courthouse. Today was the day that Kyle Sanders, the guy who was driving the SUV that killed Tamika, went to court. It had been almost seventeen months since that day. The investigation determined that Sanders had been traveling at 130 kilometers an hour in a posted 80, driving in the wrong lane, and making an illegal pass at the time of impact.

Tamika had been killed almost instantly and was buried in a cemetery in Windsor. Mike was still in the hospital at the time of the funeral was and not able to attend her service. The day after her funeral, Laurie came to visit Mike in the hospital. He couldn't look her in the eyes. She sat beside his bed while he stared out the window both were silent. After a few minutes, she stood, wiped away some tears on her face, then she wiped the tears off Mike's face. She kissed him on top of the head and walked out. Mike had not seen her or Will since.

At 8:30 am Mike and Nick made their way up the courthouse steps to a dark brown government building with a giant water fountain out front. As Mike walked up, camera crews and newspaper reporters were gathering. A high-profile rich kid facing a sexual assault charge had court that same day, and the media were turning the front steps into a circus sideshow.

Mike and Nick stepped inside the building. Nick found the court room on the list in the lobby, looked over to Mike who was standing in the near the staircase, and pointed upstairs. They walked up together.

At the top of the stairs Nick stopped and faced Mike.

"Mike, no matter what happens today. You have to stay calm." Nick advised.

Mike stared at him and nodded and started to walk. Nick stopped him. "No, that's not good enough. I need you to tell me you understand what I'm saying."

"I got it." Mike said in a flat tone that sent a chill up Nick's spine."

They made their way over to the court room. It wasn't until they were only a few feet away that Mike recognized Will and then Laurie. Mike's heart sank when he saw her. She looked like she'd aged seventeen years instead of seventeen months. Will saw Mike and nudged his mother's leg, nodding towards where he stood.

Mike stopped walking. He couldn't make his legs go forward another step. Laurie got up, dabbed her eyes, trying not to smear her makeup. She wiped her nose and calmly walked over. Nick was standing behind his nephew but took a few steps back to give them some space.

As Laurie approached, she put her tissue in her pocket then put her hands on Mikes face the same way Tamika used to. That must have been where Tamika learned it, Mike thought. It made sense; it was comforting. Laurie looked in his eyes for what felt like an eternity. Finally, she broke the silence in a soft voice.

"Michael, honey. I've missed you so much."

Mike's tears started coming. He fell into her and broke down.

When he finally let go, Will was beside him. The two hugged. "You need to come back to the club, man. Miss you there." Will invited.

"We'll see," Mike replied.

"At least come by and visit with Mom," Will continued. "We miss you brother."

"I will. Soon" Mike promised. He felt someone squeeze him on the shoulder, realized it was Nick, and understood why his attention was required: Kyle Sanders and his wife were coming up the stairs.

Kyle was in his late twenties. He stood at five foot nine and weighed two hundred pounds. He had an air about him that reeked of arrogance. He was wearing an expensive blue suit with a white shirt and pink tie. His black hair was slicked back in what Mike assumed was an $80 haircut. He was smiling and laughing with his wife.

After the accident, when Mike found out the driver's identity, he tried to find out everything he could about Kyle: who he was, where he worked, where he lived. What he found out was that Kyle was an arrogant prick. He owned an exotic pet store that his parents paid for. Through a friend of Ed's, Mike found out that Kyle was more concerned with the impact on his own lifestyle, such as whether or not he'd still be able to cross the border. He showed little remorse or even interest in the fact that he had killed a sixteen-year-old girl, destroyed Mike's life, and shattered Laurie's world. Mike tensed up.

"You said you'd be calm. Now be calm." Nick murmured, tightening his grip, reminding Mike that he could carry him out the door without breaking a sweat if he wanted to. Mike felt a seething hatred burning inside his chest. Every fiber of his being wanted to literally rip Kyle apart. Laurie put her hand on his chest.

"Michael, honey, look at me," she soothed. "Look at me."

Mike looked at her and she continued in her calming voice, "Michael, I need you to relax sweetheart. I need you to be my rock today. Can you do that for me?" His eyes darted between hers and Kyle. She repeated, more firmly, "Michael," He looked at her. "Relax. Please. I need you today." He felt like someone was squeezing his chest. But he relaxed.

Mike excused himself. "I need to go outside" He kissed Laurie on the cheek and walked back down the stairs.

Nick came outside a couple minutes later, leaned on the wall and asked, "You, okay?" Mike nodded. "Want to leave? Or stay?" Mike, breathing deep, let out a long exhale.

"Stay," he said.

Nick nodded but didn't say anything else. Nick knew when to be silent but still be present. He didn't fiddle, or look at his watch, he didn't pace, he didn't make small talk, he was just there. After about five minutes Mike took a deep breath again and said, "Okay, let's go," and they walked back up to the court room.

As they walked up the stairs, Mike could see Kyle and his wife smiling big broad smiles, and Kyle shaking his lawyer's hand excitedly. Something wasn't right. Mike looked at Laurie and Will. They didn't notice it. Kyle's lawyer ushered him down a hallway and two uniformed Windsor Police officers stepped out from the court room. Mike looked over at Nick, and from the look on his uncle's face he knew something had gone horribly wrong. He picked up his pace and hurried back to Laurie and Will.

"What happened?" he asked.

Confused, Laurie replied with a question, "What do you mean?" Mike looked past the police and tried to see down the hallway.

"Where did he go?" Mike fired, getting agitated.

"Who?" Will asked holding his mother's hand.

Nick caught up to them and directed, "Mike, relax. Breathe, buddy."

At that moment, a man in a dark black robe walked out of the court room where the police were standing. He was five foot ten with a slim build. He had dark hair parted to the right, a hooked nose and small teeth. Mike thought he looked like a ferret. "Mrs. Sellers?" he inquired. And Laurie looked over.

Mike asked, "Who's that?"

"Crown," Will explained. "The prosecution."

Laurie walked over and started talking to the crown attorney. He was explaining something, and she began to shake her head and was asking questions quietly. Then without warning she shrieked and let out a guttural cry. Both Mike and Will ran to her as she spun back to them sobbing. Both boys caught her.

"What happened?" Mike demanded, looking at the attorney. He didn't get an answer.

Nick approached the crown attorney and repeated. "What happened?" When he was ignored again, he insisted "Sir! What is going on?"

The crown attorney took a deep breath and said, "We plead Mr. Sanders down to reckless driving causing death."

"What does that mean?" Mike asked letting go of Laurie and standing upright. The attorney didn't respond.

Nick said, almost to himself, "That doesn't carry a minimum sentence." He looked at Mike and reached out to grab him, but he was a fraction of a second too late. Mike leap forward and grabbed the attorney by his robe. He was immediately pulled off by the two uniformed police. The attorney backed up and adjusted his crooked robe. The police officers holding Mike back had him pinned to a wall.

The larger of the two said to Mike, "Sir, I'm going to let you go, but you stay calm. Try that again and you'll spend the night in jail."

Nick persisted with the crown. "What did he get?"

The attorney finished adjusting his robe, ran his fingers through his tousled hair. "His license is suspended for one year from today, and he got two years' probation," he replied in a tone that suggested these people were annoying him, that the sentence was perfectly acceptable given the circumstances.

Mike almost fainted. He had no fight in him. He felt like he'd been just hit by the SUV again. "That's it?" he asked in disbelief. "But. he, he killed Tamika," he protested, staring at the attorney. The man picked up his day planner that he had dropped in the scuffle. He looked at Laurie, Will, then Michael.

"I'm sorry for your loss," he uttered, the sympathy in his words completely absent from his voice. He turned and walked back into the court room.

Mike stood leaning against the wall for support, shock and confusion swirling in his head. Laurie was sitting on a bench sobbing, with Will's arms wrapped around her. Mike looked at his uncle Nick, who wore a completely blank expression. Mike started walking, towards the stairs and out the front door. Nick caught up to him.

"Hey, hey, hold on. Where are you going?" Nick asked.

"Walking home." Mike answered.

"Mike, come on. You'll freeze out here." It was mild day for February, forecasted to reach a high of 7 degrees, but Mike was in a suit with no winter coat. "Bud, I know you're upset. If you need to be alone, I understand. Come home, get dressed, and go for a walk." Nick said.

Mike paused for a few seconds and, without saying anything, started walking back to Nick's truck. As they drove home, Mike stared out the window. After about five minutes he said. "I should have killed that motherfucker when I found his house."

Nick, looking out from the side of his eye said, "And throw your life away?"

"Would I though?" Mike snapped. "Really? That piece of shit killed Tamika and walked out of the fucking courthouse today... With an armed escort at that!"

"I know how you're feeling, buddy. I've lost people I care about to..."

"This is different!" Mike snapped even louder. "I'm sorry Nick, but you were a soldier, Ed was a cop. Uncle Rob was a firefighter. But every one of you knew the dangers when you signed on. You knew there was a chance you or someone close to you might die. No different than us working on the iron. But you have time to prepare for that. When it happens, it sucks but it's not a shock."

Mike paused to wipe away more tears. "She was the only person that ever loved me. The only person that ever saw me as more than a knuckle dragging idiot. Yeah, if she was still alive there's a chance we wouldn't be together anymore. I don't own a fucking crystal ball; I can't see into the future. But that piece of shit stole her from me!" Mike was breathing heavy, the anger pouring out of him.

"There is no doubt you guys would still be together bud, that girl loved you. I know a lot of people who met their partners as teenagers and are still together now. And you're right. I don't know how you feel. But you're not alone right now." Nick soothed, trying to calm him down.

"Our whole legal system is fucked." Mike spat.

"Our legal system is fine, Mike. Our criminal justice system needs work."

"Tomato, tom-ah-to" Mike said "Every day, I read more and more stories. Fucking child molesters and rapist getting eighteen months, or two years less a day, then serving their time with other diddlers. A few months later they're out and re-offending. New and improved predators is what they are. They get sent to rapist college to learn from other people's mistakes how not to get caught next time" Mike wiped his nose. "I read about a guy in the paper, convicted of drunk driving after crashing into a bus shelter. He's on his sixth DUI conviction, he's already had three lifetime driving bans! Why the fuck was he let out after the second one?"

"I know Mike, our criminal justice system needs to be overhauled" Nick agreed.

"Overhauled? This system has failed the victims. Did you read about that guy in Alberta last week?" Mike asked.

"No."

"Guy beat and molested his stepdaughter for years. Years! Got sentenced to eight years in prison. But he played the "fire the lawyer" game. Twice. So he ended up spending thirty-six months in a detention center. Three years. When he got sentenced, they knocked off six years. They knock off six years on an eight-year sentence because of that two-for-one bullshit. And this piece of shit has two years left. He'll be out in less than twelve months. Is that justice? Think this guy is coming out rehabilitated? No. he's going to spend the next twelve months with a bunch of animals that all get off on that sick shit, jerking off in a group while talking about what they've done to little kids. Then he'll get out and do it again. Our system doesn't need an overhaul. People need to start dealing with this shit themselves. Some good old fashion back-door justice."

Nick sat silently, the hum of the road under them. He knew Mike was angry, heartbroken, and had just been kicked while he was down. Mike wasn't thinking clearly, but still, part of Nick agreed with his nephew.

"Ya know," Mike continued. "I have no illusions about who Ed was or is. Especially on the job. But you know what sticks out?" he asked, and without waiting for an answer, he continued, "I don't know the specifics about it. But one day Ed pulls up in an alley. A guy and his teenage son have some dude backed up against a fence, ready to throttle him. I don't know if they called and Ed showed up, or if he happened to be driving by. But either way, there's Ed in an alley with dad and junior and some dirt bag. The dad is ready to pummel the dirt bag because he was trying to molest a little girl in the alley. So, you know what Ed says?" Again, without waiting for an answer, Mike continues. "Ed looks out the window, recognizes the dirt bag as a dirt bag with a long history of being a dirt bag, from a family full of dirt bags. So, Ed tells the dad, 'A child molesting report will take me about six hours to do the paperwork. An injured person report will take me twenty minutes. I'm going to go have a coffee. I'll be back in a half hour,' and drives away."

Nick had heard Ed tell the story before and knew the dirt bag from childhood. The man had been beaten so badly that day he could barely walk anymore. "Think that guy ever fucked with another kid?" Mike practically shouted. "Doubtful!" he answered his own question again. "If, and that's a big if, there was anything left of him, he was probably so mangled and gnarled that kids ran away screaming any time they saw him."

Nick knew Mike was blowing off steam and decided to let him keep going. Today was the first day in almost eighteen months that Mike had showed any feelings. Seeing any emotion in him at all was a relief, even if it was anger. It was a start.

Still looking out the window, Mike continued. "For the last year and half, all I've been hearing is 'He'll get what's coming to him, he'll get what's coming to him'. But you know what he got? His wife has to drive him across the border to Joe Louis Area so he can use his season tickets for the next twelve months." Mike wiped away more tears. "Switch places with her right now if I could just see her face while we're passing each other."

Mike was quiet for the rest of the drive home. Nick pulled in the driveway and shut the truck off. Mike was staring out the window at the neighbor's eavestrough, not moving. Nick thought Mike had something else to say so he waited. Mike took a deep breath in and sighed loudly, letting it out. He took another breath and confessed, "I never told her I loved her."

Nick looked over at him but stayed silent.

"All the times she said it to me, I only ever said, 'me too' back. I never told her I loved her." Fresh tears started streaming down Mike's face.

Nick, searching for what to say, put his hand on Mike's shoulder and said, "She knew Mike, Everybody knew." He opened his door and said, "Take your time."

Nick got out of the truck and walked up to the house, tears running down his face fighting the urge to breakdown. He felt horrible for Laurie, and even worse for Mike. Mike was going to live the rest of his life not only with the pain of losing Tamika, but also with lifetime of regret and a bad case of survivors' guilt to compound it.

Chapter 22
Friday March 15th, 2008, 7:55 pm.
Windsor, Ontario

A little over a month had passed since Kyle Sander's court date. Mike was working with Nick erecting a series of big box stores in a new commercial development in Windsor. On this night, after five days of being pestered and harassed by his coworkers, Mike was going out for drinks to celebrate Lucky's birthday.

Lucky was another ironworker. Mike had no clue what his real name was. Late last year when a grouchy safety officer for the general contracting firm wouldn't allow nicknames to be worn on hard hats, Lucky had replaced his name with the obvious alias of "Aiden Chislong", and just for fun added the name "Jack Hoffalot" to Mike's hard hat.

Lucky was five foot ten with very broad shoulders and a large head. Mike often though he looked like a life-sized Lego man. He wore his hair in a mohawk for no other reason than he was bored the day he cut it. He had a very sharp wit that often had people stop and look at him wondering if they had heard him correctly.

He spoke in a gruff voice and was known for sneaking out to the parking lot on coffee and lunch breaks for a couple beers or, "attitude adjustments," as he called them. He was the type of guy whose life seemed to be constantly in shambles but would always drop what he was doing to be a there for a friend or a brother ironworker in need. After the incident at the courthouse, Lucky made a point of reaching out to Mike and checking in with him regularly. Mike really liked Lucky. It was out of his fondness for Lucky that he reluctantly agreed to join them. That, and because he figured they would need a designated driver.

Around 8:00 pm the guys started showing up at Nick's. Their first stop was at a bar called Sammy's, known as the Thursday night spot to pick up women. As it was Friday, Sammy's was dead inside, allowing the guys to order burgers and a couple beers to prepare for the evening.

They decided their next stop would be downtown. Mike parked at a parking garage and the six men set out on foot. They tried their luck at a few local night clubs; some were too loud, others were too packed, and some were too empty. Inevitably they settled on hitting one of the local strip clubs.

By 11:30 pm the guys were all feeling good. They'd had beers, the occasional round of shots, a lot of weed, and periodically a group of two or three had snuck off to the bathroom for a line of coke. Mike was staying sober but had to admit he was having fun. There had been more than one moment of pure hilarity that night, and being out was better than sulking in his room.

As they were sitting at a table in the club, Mike and Lucky were having the standard boxing debate of Ali vs Tyson. Mike looked across the bar and saw Dion, the guy that had jumped him a few years ago. Mike's blood instantly ran cold. Lucky didn't notice the change in Mike's demeanor and kept talking, trying to make sure Mike the boxer understood why Lucky the non-boxer's opinion was the right one.

Mike's eyes were locked on Dion. He was with one other guy. They made what was an obvious drug deal at the table, trying to mask it, but making a bigger spectacle of themselves in the process. Dion got up from the table and put his coat on. Without thinking about it, Mike said, "Excuse me", and got up. He placed his hat on his seat and made his way across the room.

He walked towards the bathroom area, grabbing a bright red hooded jacket off the back of an empty chair on his way by. Stepping into the bathroom, he put the jacket on with the hood up. The jacket didn't fit him, but it would do. Stepping back out into the black-lit room, his eyes found Dion stepping out the door. Mike walked out quickly after him, trying his best to crouch with his head down to make himself look smaller.

Downtown was a tricky area to navigate. There were a lot of alleys and blind corners, but you were never far from a busy street. Mike wasn't sure what he was going to do, but he needed to find Dion, and do it quickly.

Stepping outside, he moved out of the view of the security camera. He scanned left and right and found no sign of Dion. Across the street was also empty. Dion must have gone down one of the two alleys on either side of the building. Mike figured he had a 50/50 chance and went right. Empty. Damn, he thought.

He stepped into the alley anyway, took off the red jacket, set it beside a garbage can and took off running down the alley. If he was fast enough, he could meet Dion on the street at the other side. Mike sprinted as fast as he could. He got to the corner but didn't see Dion, so he turned right and jogged to the next alley.

There was Dion, about sixty feet from the alley entrance. Mike continued his pace, head down, and continued down the alley, trying to look inconspicuous. Nothing to see here, just a man in no jacket jogging to the next bar to keep warm.

As he passed Dion, he pulled his own wallet out and said, "Hey, buddy. I think you dropped this," holding the wallet in his right hand.

Dion stopped. Mike was jogging back to him, holding something out. Dion padded his pocket and was about to say it wasn't his when he realized who it was. By now Mike was too close and moving fast. Before Dion could react, Mike hit him in the mouth as hard as he could. The run up the alley had gotten his blood flowing and given him some momentum. Dion's body went stiff, and he fell straight back, smacking the base of his skull of the ground with a loud clunk that echoed through the alley.

Mike looked around. Nobody was watching. He soccer kicked Dion in the head once, then jogged back the way he first came. As he rounded back up the other alley, he pulled the red hooded coat back on. He walked back into the strip club, into the bathroom, and removed the coat. He made his way back towards his table. As he passed the seat that he had taken the red jacket from, he stopped and said, "Excuse me?" The guy looked up and Mike continued, "I think your coat fell off your chair. It was on the floor here." The guy thanked him. Mike sat back down, put his hat back on and smiled at Nick.

"Where'd you go?" Nick questioned, noticing Mike was a little winded and sweaty.

"Nowhere. But just in case anybody asks, you had eyes on me all night. All night. Except for the less than two minutes I was just in the bathroom."

Nick looking at Mike asked, "Mike? What happened?"

"Nothing.". Now in a much better mood, Mike turned back to Lucky and said, "Where were we?" and continued with the debate.

The next morning Nick burst into Mike's room. "Get up. NOW" he demanded and walked out into the living room.

Mike sat up and looked his alarm clock. 9:03 am. He got up, threw on jogging pants and walked out. Nick was standing in the living room. "What happened last night?" Nick insisted.

"What do you mean?" Mike asked, feigning innocence.

Nick's patience was wearing thin. "Mike don't play me for a fucking fool. When you left the bar, what happened?"

Mike, cold and calm replied, "We came home."

Nick was now clearly very angry. "No, before that. Why did you tell me to say I was with you all night if anybody asked? You left the bar. I could see it. You were sweating when you sat down."

"It was hot in there. I went to the bathroom." Mike lied.

"So, it's just a fucking coincidence that you told me to say you never left my side, and someone was found dead in the fucking alley right near the bar this morning? Is that what you're telling me?"

Mike was unwavering. "I don't know what you're talking about. I went to the bathroom."

Nick was so angry he couldn't speak. He just stared at Mike. Mike looked more relaxed than Nick had ever seen him. "Then why did you say that?" he finally asked.

"Because I did a line of coke in the bathroom with Chris." Mike lied again without flinching.

"You did a line of coke?" Nick questioned, not believing him.

"Yeah, thought you'd be mad. I was the driver. I know it was stupid, but it wore off before we left. I just needed to keep going," Mike explained, still calm but looking a little remorseful.

Nick stood looking at Mike, completely unable to read him. "A line of coke?" he repeated.

"Yeah. It was stupid of me. But it's not like I killed someone." Mike said in a tone that once again gave Nick a chill up his spine. Mike walked back towards the kitchen scratching his stomach and said "I'm hungry. Want to go for breakfast?"

Mike stepped into his room to get changed. He hadn't meant to kill Dion, but he didn't care either. It stands to reason a six-foot five-inch, two hundred and twenty plus pound man punching someone while running at them would definitely knock them out every time.

Mike thought about the sound that Dion's head made when it smacked the pavement. He knew from multiple post-fight doctor visits, and even from his summers at Uncle Ken's, that it usually wasn't the punch itself that killed someone; it was the back of their head smacking the ground when they fell. The cerebellum is at the back of the brain. Cerebellum is Latin for "little brain", and it contains more nerve cells than the other two hemispheres of the brain combined. Mike had worked with a guy a few months before who slipped off the first rung of a ladder and was killed when his head hit the ground, just because of the way it hit.

Mike got dressed and came back out to the living room, Nick was still sitting on the couch looking at his laptop "Coming?" Mike asked.

Nick looked at him for a moment and said, "Yeah, give me five." and got up.

They went to a small local restaurant not far from their house. Nick noticed Mike was in an unusually good mood. Nick ordered bacon and eggs, with rye toast. Mike ordered French toast, eggs, bacon, sausage and hash browns, and order of brown toast, with an orange juice.

"Hungry fella?" Nick asked.

"Yeah. Starving." Mike said bouncing his head to the music playing lightly over the speakers. Nick couldn't put his finger on it, but Mike was different today. He didn't look like someone who had done a line of coke last night, but he definitely didn't look like someone who had committed a cold-blooded murder in an alley either.

Chapter 23

Friday December 30, 2022, 1:30 pm
Toronto, Ontario

Steve called in to speak with Karl for an update.

"Did he see his lawyer yet?" Steve asked.

"Call you back in five," Karl replied and hung up without waiting for a reply.

Steve had left the Hamilton police station around 9:30 pm Saturday night but it was suggested he not return to his apartment, just in case. Instead, he got an unmarked car and drove to Toronto, putting himself up at the Fairmont Royal York Hotel. At $350 a night over the holiday season, he didn't worry too much about the cost. He'd expense it back to the operation and thus the taxpayers.

He had looked very out of place in the lobby when he checked in. His face was a mess of dark bruises, the blue flannel jacket did nothing to hide the blood-stained t-shirt. He'd thrown on the t-shirt from the night at Caleb's when the Hamilton cops were coming to grab him and had not had a chance to change. He held a brown paper bag from the liquor store and a 12-pack of Bud Light under his arm. Needless to say, he stood out amongst the other guests.

Six beers and half a bottle of bourbon later, Steve left the hotel looking to find some coke. After a few failed attempts, he found a guy in a small basement bar before heading back to his room to get high and drink in private. He spent Sunday sleeping it off and then repeating his mistakes.

On Monday he woke up around 10:30 am, threw up in the toilet, showered, and checked out of the hotel. He spent the next few hours napping in the unmarked car in a parking garage off Queens Quay west until a parking attendant banged on his window, waking him up. Steve flashed his badge, the attendant left, and he called Karl.

As promised, less than five minutes later Karl called back and confirmed, "Yes, he met with his lawyer at 10:30 this morning. He's still sitting in the bullpen. They're shipping him to Barton Street jail this evening."

Steve replied, "Okay thank you." but Karl had hung up before he finished. He googled the lawyer's name and called the listed phone number. The receptionist answered politely and said Mr. Greenspan wasn't available. Steve gave his name as Marcus Atkins and said he needed to speak to Mr. Greenspan as soon as possible. He rung off, stepped out of the car, and stretched. He walked to a corner, took a piss, then got back in the car. He started it up, backed out of his spot, and his phone rang. "Private Number." Steve answered.

"Talk to me," he drawled.

"Mr. Atkins?" he heard a whiney nasally voice at the other end of the phone.

"Talking to him" Steve quipped.

"This is Scott Greenspan. You let a message for me?"

"Oh, hey Scott. Yeah, I got your number from a friend of mine. Caleb Tulk. He said I should call you." Steve was careful to sound a little naive.

"Ah, of course. What's your availability Mr. Atkins. Are you close?"

"I just walked out myself actually."

"Can you come by my office right away?" Greenspan asked.

Not wanting to send up red flags, Steve replied "I need to see my lawyer first. And I also need to shower and eat. I could be there around 3:00-3:30 if that works?"

"Very well" Greenspan concluded, then added "Who is your counsel Mr. Atkins?"

Steve was caught off guard and responded. "Kevin Gibson. He usually does real estate, but I was in a pinch. He's going to refer me to someone else."

"Probably a wise choice," Greenspan advised. "Okay Mr. Atkins, I'll see you later this afternoon." and hung up.

Steve called Karl back right away. The supervisor answered on the third ring. "What?" he barked, sounding annoyed.

"The lawyer called me. I'm meeting him at 3:30 pm in Hamilton." Steve advised.

"Okay, keep me posted."

"Listen, call that piece of shit Gibson. Tell him if anyone calls him. he's representing Marcus Atkins until he can refer him to a criminal defense lawyer."

Kevin Gibson was a lawyer from Toronto that had a thing for younger-looking hookers. He was initially arrested during the human trafficking sweep but worked out a deal to cooperate with authorities in exchange for them looking the other way. Steve knew what a sick fuck Gibson was, and consequently hated the idea, but he had used the lawyer to his advantage on a few occasions since then. Steve would call with a favor that was really more of a demand. With favors, you had a choice. Gibson didn't have a choice. Last time they crossed paths, Gibson asked Steve, "How much longer are you going to hold this over me?" Steve's answer was, "Until one of us is dead."

"Why am I calling him?" Karl inquired.

"Greenspan asked who my counsel was. I had to give him a name. And it's the least that piece of shit can do." Steve added. "I need to haul ass back to Hamilton and change. I'll call you after I meet with Greenspan."

"Fine," Karl replied and hung up again.

"The fuck is his problem today?" Steve wondered aloud to himself.

Steve got on the Gardiner Expressway. He flipped the lights on the unmarked car and floored it back to Hamilton, making record time. He pulled up at the Hamilton police station, entered through the garage, and spoke to a desk sergeant who looked at Steve suspiciously, likely courtesy of his bloody shirt and busted face. It didn't help that he still reeked of last night's drinking with a hint of vomit on his breath.

After a quick phone call from the sergeant, who never took his eyes off Steve, a uniformed officer came out and gave Steve a ride home. It was 2:42 pm. He dropped Steve off two blocks away, and Steve jogged to his door, fighting the urge to puke on the doorstep. He ran inside, stripped his clothes off, showered, brushed his teeth, and threw on some less filthy clothing. Within fifteen minutes he was on his way back downtown to the lawyer's office.

Steve parked in a no parking zone in front of Greenspan's office. He pulled out his work phone and called Karl again, who answered right away.

"Sampson."

"I'm about to walk into the office. My phone's on." Steve advised.

"Hold for thirty seconds." Karl instructed, then moving his mouth away from the phone asked, "Hardeep, are we good?" There was a twenty second pause before Karl informed, "You're good," and hung up.

Steve felt a little better now. He was walking into the lawyer's office completely unaware of what was waiting for him in there, but Karl and Hardeep were watching and listening live via his phone.

He walked up the steps. It was an older building, a large downtown home built in the mid-1800s and renovated multiple times over. Two oversized double doors at the top of the steps bore the names "Greenspan, Greenspan & Martinell" in gold letters on the glass. Steve pulled one open and stepped in. There was another glass commercial door in front of him that was locked. It had a sign that read, "Please ring bell for service." He pressed the button, it chimed and then a female voice came through the small speaker.

"Can I help you?"

"Marcus Atkins, I'm here to see Scott Greenspan." He heard the mic click off then waited. After a solid two minutes he pressed the button again. The girl's voice came back on and directed, "Please wait." and the mic clicked again. After another minute she came back on and said, "Please take a pair of the blue bootie covers on your right and put them one over your shoes." He looked at the box, grabbed a pair, put them on, and the door buzzed open.

He stepped into a large dark wood-paneled and brass-trimmed lobby. Everything looked original. Ugly, but original. The bitchy receptionist was sitting at a large desk twenty feet away. She was a short heavy-set girl with brown hair, bad skin, and thick glasses. Steve figured he understood why she was so unpleasant. If he saw that in the mirror first thing every morning, he'd be miserable too.

Without looking she said, "Please sit down".

He found an uncomfortable chair that fit the office décor and sat down. About ten minutes later, a short man in a dark suit with a bright red tie stepped around the corner, He was about five foot six, maybe one hundred and thirty pounds. He had frizzy brown hair that was way too thin on top. Little round, black-framed glasses perched on his nose. An exaggerated smile showed small but white teeth, almost too white. Steve thought he looked like Where's Waldo's younger, nerdier brother.

"Mr. Atkins?" the little man asked.

"Yeah, here." Steve raised his hand like he was getting attendance taken in grade ten home room.

"Come with me please." The small man turned and walked away.

Steve hopped out of his chair and followed behind. He thought of all the lawyers he had met over the years, and how even though they were lawyers they would still try to be somewhat polite and accommodating. Steve asked, "Any chance I could get some water please?"

"No, I'm sorry. We don't have any," the small man replied in his nasally voice.

They walked to the end of the hall to a big dark wood door with privacy glass taking up the top half. The name "Scott Greenspan Barrister and Solicitor" was written in the same gold lettering as the front door.

Greenspan led Steve into the office.

"Please sit," he said standing at the doorway, closing it behind them. He then walked around to his chair behind the desk. As he sat down, he confessed, "I must say Mr. Atkins, I find it strange that you're not being charged together."

Steve knew better than to try and match wits with a defense lawyer in his own office, so he just shrugged and said "I woke up yesterday hand cuffed to a hospital bed. The only lawyer I know was the guy that handled our house deal. I got out this morning."

Greenspan stared at him for a few seconds, then opened his day planner and took out a piece of folded paper. He handed it to Steve and instructed, "Don't open it here. Wait till you leave. I don't know what's on it, nor do I want to". Steve took the page and Greenspan began writing something in his planner.

"Are they expecting me?" Steve inquired.

Greenspan looked up from his book with an unimpressed expression on his face, then went back to writing. Steve let himself out. He walked past the girl at the counter and quipped, "Later sweet cheeks." He bounded down the steps to his truck. Once inside he opened the paper. The paper had the word "Stebar" scrawled on it, along with a phone number. Steve called Karl.

"I got a number," he advised.

"Okay, call them and set it up," Karl replied.

"Niagara Police ready?" Steve asked.

"Waiting for the call," Karl confirmed.

"OK." Steve hung up. He didn't like how this was going. He got the number he wanted, but the lawyer had caught him off guard with his question. Steve was about to contact people he knew only one thing about, and that was that bad people were very afraid of them. He'd already had his nose broken when the Hamilton cops fumbled that play. This one could be a lot worse, especially if they knew who he was. He dialed the number. It picked up on the second ring.

"Yeah," A deep voice answered.

"Got your number from a friend. He's tied up at the moment."

"Togo's Bar on Church Street in St Catharine's. Tuesday at 3:00 pm." The voice hung up.

Ten seconds later, Karl called Steve.

"Get back to Toronto. We need a game plan."

"Now?" Steve asked.

"No, Tuesday at 4:00 pm. Yes now!" Karl hung up.

By 4:15 pm Steve was racing back to Toronto at Karl's request. As he was approaching Burlington, his phone rang again. "Yeah," he answered seeing "Dad" on the caller ID.

"Where are you?" Karl asked.

"Just got on the QEW from 403, heading to Toronto." Steve advised.

"Go back to Hamilton, it's your lucky day." Karl instructed, sounding excited. "Phil Carson was just arrested. One of his customers O.D'd on some bad coke with fentanyl mixed in."

"OK?" Steve didn't quite follow. "Who is Phil Carson?" he asked. There was silence on the other end for a few seconds.

"The dealer that introduced you to Caleb" Karl sounded exasperated and a little annoyed. "He's looking at manslaughter. Get down there. Try flip him on Caleb."

Fifteen minutes later Steve was walking into the Hamilton Police Station through the garage again. The same sergeant was sitting behind the glass. Steve told him why he was there and waited. Almost immediately he was buzzed in and asked to take the elevator to the second floor.

As soon as he stepped off, he was greeted by an Asian man who introduced himself as Detective Jason Nguyen. He was in his late thirties, five foot ten, wearing a light blue striped dress shirt that was clearly straining against the large muscles under it, and grey dress pants. He had a full head of thick black hair and black framed Buddy Holly style glasses. He reached his hand out to shake and said, "We have him in an interview room down here." As he quickly stated walking away Steve asked, "Has he asked for a lawyer?" and raced to catch up.

"No, not yet, but we haven't talked to him at all. As soon as we picked him up, we were notified he's part of your investigation. We called up right away."

"Okay, thank you." Steve and Nguyen made it to the door. Steve asked if the camera was on. Nguyen shook his head "No".

Philip was sitting in a chair head down. He was a ginger with pale skin, his red hair peeking out from under a red sequined baseball cap with the word "Legend" across it, worn sideway over top of a red bandana. He was in his early twenties and dressed like it, wearing baggy black jeans and shirt that was three sizes too big and had a print of a tiger highlighted by glittery sequins on it. A large silver chain with a silver bitcoin medallion hung from his neck. Steve had always thought the kid was an idiot. The way the kid was dressed removed all doubt.

Steve walked in. Philip looked up and smiled. "Hey, Marcus." Then the realization hit him.

Steve knew he needed to talk quickly before Philip asked for a lawyer. "My name isn't Marcus, I'm Constable Stephen Parent with the OPP. And you're in deep shit right now."

He pulled his badge out to show Philip then quickly added. "You sold some bad shit, and someone died. You're looking at a manslaughter charge right now. That carries a maximum of life in prison." Steve chose not to mention Phillip could also be handed probation. "Now, you have two choices, and you need to decide right now, before I leave this room. This offer is good for five seconds, and five seconds only, after I finish talking.

"One: you can test your street cred in prison. I'm talking big boy prison, not a holding cell. Sweet, doughy little fucker like you. You'll be used as currency. They'll have you cleaning toilet bowls with your toothbrush and forfeiting your meals. On the plus side, that'll only last about six years until some other white rich kid going through an ethnic identity crisis fucks up and they decided to beat the shit out of him instead."

"Two: you give me Caleb Tulk right now. You agree to testify at his trial. And you're back home tonight. If you ask for a lawyer, the deal is off, and we go ahead with the manslaughter charge."

Then to show he was serious he held his hand up and started counting down, "Five.. four.. three.."

"Okay, I'll do it!" Philip almost leaped out of his chair.

Steve smiled. "Good boy," and banged on the door. Nguyen opened it. Steve quietly instructed, "Turn on the camera and get me a note pad." Nguyen nodded and disappeared.

Steve stepped out into the hallway and called Karl.

"He flipped. I've got more on Caleb. I want to talk to him today."

Karl asked, "What are you thinking?"

"We can pin this manslaughter beef on him. I'll tell him if he cooperates with us, we'll drop the manslaughter and all other charges known and unknown in the city of Hamilton, with the exception of any violent crimes that may come up. Hamilton can clear several cases this way, and by cooperating he does six months." Steve explained.

Karl silent for a few seconds, then said, "That's a lot". He was quiet for another ten seconds. "Do what you need to do."

"Get me into the jail to see him. I'll lock this down, then head up there."

"On it." Karl promised, and hung up.

Steve left the police station and headed straight to the Barton Street Jail, the local detention center. He was greeted at the main entrance by a prison guard.

"Parent?" the guard asked. Steve nodded. The man gestured for Steve to follow and started walking. They went through what seemed like a maze of several locked doors that they had to wait for someone in a control room to open. They made it to a small room, windowless except for the ten-inch by ten-inch window in the heavy steel door. Steve looked in the small glass opening and saw Caleb sitting at a table wearing orange coveralls that had been rolled down to the waist, and a thin orange t-shirt.

Steve waked in the room. Caleb went through several stages of recognition: first happy to see him, then confusion, then right into the realization that he was screwed.

Without giving him a chance to speak Steve got right down to business. "I'm Constable Steve Parent, with the OPP. I'm here to tell you that you're under arrest for manslaughter." Without giving a name for the victim he added, "You sold some bad shit, and someone died. Now you're fucked."

Not wanting Caleb to ask for a lawyer, Steve quickly continued. "You have two choices: you can go back to prison on both the dope and the manslaughter charges and kiss the thought of any relationship with your daughter goodbye, or you hand me over your guys in St Catharine's. You cooperate with us. That means you testify when the day comes. You plead to the dope; you'll do six months on it, and we drop all other charges against you, known or unknown in the city of Hamilton, including this manslaughter unless we find you were involved in any other violent crimes. You confess to everything else in your past and we clear it all. You have five seconds to answer. Give me anything other than a yes or no right now and we go ahead with the manslaughter."

Steve again held his hand up and started counting down "Five.. four.. three.. two."

"Yes." Caleb choked out, then looked up. "I'll do it." He had a look of pure hatred and disgust in his eyes as he looked at Steve.

Steve winked at him and said, "I'm impressed. You're not as dumb as I thought." He banged on the door. The guard opened it and Steve ordered, "Put this asshole on suicide watch," and walked out.

Steve got outside and called Karl.

"He go for it?" Karl asked.

"Yes. He's going to plead guilty to the drug charge. If the courts aren't too backed up, we can get him sentenced in the next couple weeks."

"Okay. Get back up here. We need to talk about Tuesday," Karl instructed.

"On my way." Steve hung up and got in his truck. It was 4:45 pm. Not bad, he thought to himself.

He arrived in Toronto fifty-five minutes later. The task force was seated in the same conference room as a few days ago. This time they were joined via video conference by several older white men, all police in various cities, all in either white or blue police uniform shirts.

Sue Blenkhorn waited for Steve to sit down and said "Okay, joining us now is Constable Steve Parent with the OPP. He's been our guy in the field. Steve has connected with someone in St Catharine's, which I believe is your area Chief Riddell?" A man in a white shirt nodded on the TV screen, the letters NRPS under his name.

"Who did he make contact with?" asked a man in another square with the letters LPS under him.

"We don't know," replied Blenkhorn. The man rolled his eyes in response.

"Is there a problem?" Steve cut in right away, not caring that the faces on TV could see him. "I've been out here busting my ass, and my face for the last few months. And you have the conceit and arrogance to roll your eyes?"

Karl interjected, "Parent, relax."

"No. Fuck that. I've been the one out putting my ass on the line. A simple buy a few nights ago turned into a giant cluster fuck. And now this dick bag is going to roll his eyes at me?" Steve spat, anger rising in his voice.

"That 'dick bag' is the deputy chief on the London Police services," Blenkhorn snapped.

"I don't give a goddamn rat's ass who he is. In case he or any of the other people on that screen have forgotten, I don't exactly have time to sift through peoples resumes and perform background checks before I meet with them." Steve said hotly.

The man with LPS under his name cut in, "I apologize. I was out of line there." He added. "We've all been feeling the pressure from every direction. The first four days of every month our police, fire and EMT are pushed to the breaking point with overdose calls. We all want this operation to be a success. Sincerely, I'm sorry."

Steve, still not feeling placated retorted, "Yeah, well, you guys all threw your support behind a fat fucking moron who slashed funding to public health, mental health and substance abuse programs. What the fuck did you think was going to happen?"

They were all silent for a few seconds and then Karl redirected, "Okay, let's get back on topic here. We have a meeting at a bar called Togo's on Church, in St Catharine's tomorrow at 3:00 pm. Chief Riddell, we will need all hands-on deck from Niagara Police."

"I have twenty of my finest ready to go." Riddell advised.

"We need every angled covered, every possible entrance and exit. I'd like surveillance to start at 3:00 am and around-the-clock for twelve hours." Blenkhorn's tone was firm.

The look on Riddell's face said it would be tough, but before he could respond Blenkhorn added, "We have another ten RCMP and twelve OPP we can add, that brings our count to forty-two. They can all work together in case anything goes wrong."

The screen dinged and a green square lit up around the name that said "Hamilton PD."

"Go ahead" said Blenkhorn.

"We have two drones. Battery life is about six hours on each. We could use it for overhead. I have four officers able to fly them, you can have the two drones and the four officers."

Chief Riddell chimed in. "We have two as well. Send two of your guys and the two drones. We'll start three-hour rotations starting at 12:00 am tonight. We can catch anybody coming or going. We'll be using traffic camera to identify license plates on the ground as well."

Blenkhorn nodded then asked. "Can we get access to utility vehicles?"

Steve jumped in "Before we get too far ahead, I don't want people in cherry pickers working on Hydro poles in the snow. This is a meeting tomorrow not a buy. Keep the surveillance in place. Keep some door crashers close on standby. But Tulk's lawyer had some unsettling questions for me. I don't want any red flags. Out of sight, out of mind."

"I have to agree with him." Karl stated. "Too many moving parts means too many areas to break down. Let's keep tomorrow simple. Aerial surveillance and we can have two mobile units ready to go if there's trouble."

Blenkhorn asked "And what do we constitute as trouble?" looking pointedly at Steve.

"My understanding is these guys aren't friendly. There will likely be threats, maybe some slapping around. But they're out a shit-ton of money, so they're not going to kill me," Steve explained, then added "I hope."

"How much money are we talking about" asked the man from London.

"$100,000," replied Blenkhorn.

"$200,000" Steve corrected. "They're out the dope they fronted and the cash for it. That's $200,000 in total."

There was silence in the room. Finally, Blenkhorn spoke. "I think Constable Parent needs to be commended on his performance thus far. We would be nowhere without his hard work." A few of the heads nodded.

"Just be careful. There are cameras everywhere," the man from Hamilton said.

"We're not the ones making national headlines for cops that are smuggling drugs and planting evidence," Steve said referring to the number of Hamilton police being arrested in recent years.

The man from Hamilton glared at the camera and asked, "Are we finished?"

The call ended at 6:10 pm. Steve, Karl, Hardeep and Sue were sitting at the table. Karl and Sue were staring at Steve. Feeling their eyes on him, he sighed, "What?"

"Was that really necessary?" Blenkhorn asked.

"Any time you want to pull me out and stick one of those fat bloated fools in there, you feel free. Until then I'm the one jumping in and out of the flames and I'm not going to be condescended to by some fat asshole that couldn't tie my shoes on his best fuckin' day." Steve said indignantly.

Karl interrupted, "That'll be all Parent. Check in tomorrow at 11:00 am. Goodnight."

Steve walked out of the office, jumped in his truck and drove to the first liquor store he saw. He bought six beers and a mickey of Canadian Club to hold him over until he got back to Hamilton.

Chapter 24
Friday December 30th, 2022, 6:15pm
Hamilton, Ontario

Mike and Sasha were sitting in her apartment. Mike was deep into a highly aggressive game of tug-o-war with Domino while Sasha prepared dinner. After her last culinary attempt, they had decided simpler was better, so she was making spaghetti. Mike was on his knees and elbows growling back at the dog who was yanking with everything she had to get the toy back from him. Both were determined to show no mercy.

"Hold on," Sasha instructed. Mike continued to growl at the dog. "Hey, quiet!" she said, louder. Mike stopped. Instantly they both heard a man yelling, and it seemed to be coming from Sophie's apartment. Without another word, Sasha flew down the stairs and out the door. Mike got up and followed, stopping for only a second to slip on his shoes. As he rounded the front of the house, the yelling got louder. He saw Sophie on her porch looking afraid and holding her chest. Sasha was screaming at James, the tenant from the back unit, to get away.

James was short, around five foot nine, and chunky. He had a look that indicated he survived off junk food and liquor. When Mike first started seeing Sasha, James would glare at him. Sasha told Mike that he'd once had a thing for her, and he'd sent some inappropriate texts on multiple occasions. When she told him she wasn't interested he became insulting and rude, even going as far as calling her a slut when she didn't reply to a late-night invite to come to his apartment.

"What's going on?" Mike asked Sophie. She didn't speak just pointed at James.

Sasha was furious. Mike heard her yell, "What the fuck is wrong with you?" walking towards James.

Mike hurried over and stepped between them. "Hey, hey. Relax." He turned to Sasha. "What happened?"

"This fucking piece of shit was screaming in her face. She was trying to get away, but he had her on the stairs." Sasha seethed, rage burning in her eyes.

Trying to get a sense of the situation, Mike redirected her. "Okay. Go check on her."

Sasha looked at Mike, then glared at James and went to speak to Sophie. James turned to leave, and Mike directed, "Stay there."

"You can't stop me from leaving." James spat defiantly.

"I can stop you from seeing tomorrow fucking morning, and I will if you take one more step," Mike said calmly. James tried to give an intimidating stare, but it missed its mark. Mike chanced a quick look over at Sasha and Sophie. Sophie was sitting on the steps with tears running down her face. Sasha was holding her hand, talking to her. After about thirty seconds, Sasha came marching back towards them furious.

"You fucking loser," she yelled. Again, Mike stepped in front of her, stopping her.

"What happened?" he asked, trying to stop her from attacking him.

"This fucking goof hasn't paid his rent in five months. She just confronted him. That was him yelling at her when she knocked on his door. She left, went back to her place and he chased her up here and started threatening her." Sasha stared loathingly right at James.

Mike looked at him, wondering what kind of man would berate an elderly woman. Sasha started again. "Feel like a big man picking on an old lady? You fucking clown!"

Mike could tell that James was the type of guy that called himself an alpha, and it was driving him crazy that a woman was speaking to him this way. Trying to de-escalate the situation, he calmly said to Sasha, "Okay. It's done. Relax."

Sasha stopped. She looked at Mike. With one last dig at James she said, "This is why you can't get a woman, Because you're a weak pathetic little worm."

Her comment hit its mark. Shit, this girl knows how to draw blood, Mike thought. He decided to save that knowledge for future reference.

When James heard Sasha's words, his face snarled. He spat out, "Fuck you, bitch" and took a step towards Sasha.

Instinctively, Mike snapped out a right hand that clipped James on the side of his jaw. His legs buckled and he dropped to one knee. He looked up at Mike with absolute shock on his face, holding his open jaw. He jumped up and screamed, "You're going to jail!" running back to his apartment, pulling his phone out.

Sasha, a little shocked by how fast it all happened, looked at Mike. "Shit, you should go. Quick."

"No," Mike replied. "If I leave, they'll arrest me. He was threatening an elderly woman and came at you. I was defending my girlfriend." Sasha stared at him, then looked back at Sophie.

A few seconds later, James emerged from the driveway, walked over to Mike's truck with his cell phone in hand. He bent down and read the license plate to the police dispatcher. What an idiot, Mike thought as he suppressed a chuckle. James, still on the phone with the police, saw Mike smiling and became livid.

With his phone in one hand, James swung at Mike with the other. Mike ducked back, and James connected with his collar bone. Mike snapped out another fast right hand, hitting James in the mouth. James dropped his phone and charged in. Mike, with twenty-five years of boxing experience, slipped to his left and hit James in the nose with another right hand.

Now bleeding from the mouth and nose James yelled out, "Dude, you're getting it!" screeching like a kid on the playground. He ran in a third time and tried to kick Mike, who fired off a left-right-left combo in rapid succession. All three shots hit their mark, and James collapsed in front of him.

Most people either don't understand or refuse to understand that fights in the street between trained fighters and "street fighters" are not fights at all. People who have spent any time in a boxing club can generally end a street fight without trying. Nothing irritates a trained fighter more than drunk people telling them "I've never trained, but I'm a street fighter." Mike heard that phrase all the time.

James landed in a twisted heap on the snow-covered grass. Splotches of red blood scattered about. He picked himself up. Mike chanced a quick look around and tagged him one more time on the forehead with a left. James fell back, rolled to his feet and staggered to his apartment. Mike had to hand it to him, the guy could take a punch. Not a lot of people could take Mike hitting them, let alone four solid hits.

Mike wondered for a minute if James was going to come back out from his apartment with a weapon like a knife or a club, but before James could do so, a police car pulled up. Mike walked to the back of his truck, dropped the tail gate down, and sat on it with his hands on his knees in plain sight. The cop was male, around thirty, close to Mike in size but still sporting a baby-faced look. He walked over and asked, "Did you call?"

Mike nodded up the driveway towards the back apartment and corrected, "He did."

"You involved?" the cop asked.

Mike nodded but didn't say anything. A second police car pulled up and younger female cop got out. The male said something to her, and she made her way towards the back.

He looked back at Mike and questioned, "What happened?"

Remembering the rage that came with "over there" answers, as Ed called them, Mike started to explain, "I was upstairs," he nodded toward the upper unit. "My girlfriend heard yelling. We came down. He was threatening the elderly lady on the porch." Mike nodded towards Sophie, keeping his hands on his knees. "My girlfriend told him to stop. He came at her. I shoved him back. He said I was going to jail, called you guys, and then tried to sucker punch me while he was on the phone with you." Mike's voice was calm.

"Where was he threatening her?" the cop inquired.

"Right there on the porch," Mike indicated.

"Was there a fight?"

"If you want to call it that. He tried to hit me. I defended myself. That was all. He came at me, I hit him to back him up. When he stopped coming, I stopped hitting."

"What's your name?" the cop asked.

"My I.D. is in my wallet, in my back pocket. Would you like me to get it out for you?"

The cop nodded. Mike got his wallet out and handed over his driver's license. The cop looked at the address. "You live in Windsor?" noting the I.D. still had Nick's address on it.

"Yes. I'm an ironworker. I'm up here for work. Windsor is slow right now," Mike said.

"Where do you stay when you're here?"

"I was at a friend's over near Limeridge Mall. I'm sorry I don't remember the name of the street. I followed him home from work the day I came up. Now I stay here," he nodded at the upper unit, then made eye contact with Sasha, hoping she got the hint.

The cop nodded and asked, "How many times did you hit him?"

Mike, still calm replied, "Two or three."

The cop started to run Mike's name, taped his earpiece, said "Excuse me," to Mike, and started off toward the back apartment.

Sasha tried to hop up on the tail gate but needed help. She sat beside Mike and smiled at him. "Girlfriend?"

Mike bumped her with his shoulder and grinned. "Don't let it go to your head, I always lie to cops." She laughed in response.

A few minutes later, the young female cop came out. She walked over to the truck and blew out a sigh. "Wow, that guy has issues."

Then, in true police form, she proceeded to ask the same questions her male counterpart had just asked, looking for any discrepancies. Mike, still sitting with his hands on his knees, repeated what he'd said earlier, word for word.

The male cop returned, looked at Mike and raised an eyebrow. "Two or three?"

Mike shrugged and suggested, "Six or seven?" The cop continued to stare at him until finally Mike explained, "I was a boxer for a long time."

The cop snorted a laugh. "I can see that."

A neighbor across the street came out saying, "I saw everything," speaking directly to the female cop. Fuck, Mike thought as he replayed the first and last punches over in his mind. He knew he could get in shit for them.

Both cops stepped over and spoke to her, Mike could her the older lady saying "The guy back there came running up yelling at Sophie. Those two came down and he attacked the big guy. The big guy punched him like," she mimicked a terrible punch. "Just like that a couple times until that asshole stopped coming. You're not putting him in jail, are you?" she asked, looking over at Mike.

The male cop returned and handed Mike back his ID. "We've told him to stay away from both Sophie and you guys. If you hear anything else, call us."

Mike replied, "If we hear anything else and we call you, it'll be to come clean him up. I'm not going to sit idly by while he berates or assaults an elderly woman."

The male cop nodded that he completely understood and whispered, "I have to say that."

Mike nodded back and said, "Make sure you tell him." Looking between both cops he asked, "Are we free to go? Dinner's ready."

Mike and Sasha walked back up the stairs. Sasha stopped at the top step. Mike was one step lower. He was still taller but now they were closer in height. She kissed him on the mouth and said, "Thank you." He smiled and shrugged. She went into the living room and asked. "How long did you box for?"

"Oh, I started when I was nine, fought until I was seventeen. I was in a motorcycle accident, so I took a break, then started again about a year and half later. Had my last fight at twenty-four. There was no future in it. Had too much going on outside the ring." He paused, then added, "I coach sometimes. But not often. I still train, but not to compete anymore."

She stared at him, curious. He'd been fighting for more than half his life, and never mentioned it. "How many fights have you had?"

"Amateur or Pro?" he asked as he sat down.

"Both, I guess?"

"Um, maybe around around fifty, fifty-five amateur fights and nineteen pro." He said casually.

Sasha was shocked at the number. "How many did you win?"

"You think I stayed this pretty by losing?" he replied with a laugh.

She chuckled too, and retorted, "You do look like you've been chasing parked cars."

"I prefer the term 'my head looks like chewed bubblegum', thank you very much."

She smiled and climbed on top of him while he sat on the couch. She took his face in her hands and kissed him again. It felt familiar. "So, girlfriend huh? Is that what I am now?"

Mike smiled back and said, "Do you want to be?" She didn't say anything, she just smiled and kissed him again.

They sat at the island and ate. A few minutes into dinner, Sasha looked out the window and saw James loading a few bags into his little red Honda. "Maybe he's moving out?" she suggested.

Mike looked over towards the window. "Hopefully."

On Tuesday morning Sasha was up early and left for work. Mike was off for the day and stayed in bed. He woke up around 8:00 am and walked Domino, who still pretended to be unsure about him but wouldn't pass up a chance to go for a walk. Sophie had been informed that James would be moving the last of his things today. When Mike got back, he checked the tire tracks in the unshoveled driveway. James's car had not returned. He put the dog inside, hopped in his truck and drove out to the barn.

The silver Dodge Caravan had been traded for a small black Chevrolet pickup. Mike headed back to Sasha's, He parked down the road, seeing James's car in the driveway. A few minutes later James reemerged from his unit carrying a couple of boxes. He made one more trip, carrying a black plastic garbage bag, and got in the car. As he pulled out of the driveway Mike followed at a distance.

After about twenty minutes, James's pulled up at a house on the outskirts of Hamilton. Mike pulled into a Mazda dealership about two hundred yards away and watched. He couldn't see much There was a blue Toyota Camry in the driveway. James got out of the car and brought the boxes inside. Good enough, Mike thought, content to know where James was living now. Mike returned to the barn, swapped trucks, and went home.

Chapter 25

Tuesday January 3rd, 2023.
Hamilton, Ontario

Steve woke up at 9:30 am only because he didn't have any curtains and the sunlight was relentless. He was hung over and miserable.

He got out of bed, threw up again, and made coffee, but even the smell of it was turning his stomach. His phone rang at 10:30 am the screen said "Dad."

"Yeah," he answered gruffly.

"Everything is ready. Surveillance started at midnight. One unit is in place already, the other gearing up now. They'll both be in place before 11:00 am," Karl advised.

"Okay," Steve grunted.

"Jesus Christ Parent, you sound like shit," Karl exclaimed, a little worried, more likely about the meeting than Steve's health.

"I'll be fine," Steve assured and hung up.

At 2:30pm he pulled off the highway in St Catharine's. St. Catharine's is the city equivalent of "always a bridesmaid, never a bride". It's the sixth largest city in Ontario with a population on over 140,000. It's 51 kilometers straight south of Toronto across Lake Ontario, but it takes 120 km to drive there. Driving 21 km to the southeast will find you in Niagara Falls Ontario. The Falls has less than 2/3 of St Catharine's population but twenty times the notoriety. Tell someone you're from St Catharine's, you're immediately saying, "It's near the Falls".

A blue-collared city, St Catharine's was the previous home to one on the largest General Motors plants in North America. But thanks to outsourcing and corporate greed, St Catharine's was left like countless cities across the continent. It was now known for being a seedy town, and if you were dumb enough to leave something in your car in plain sight, then you deserved to have it stolen. The city wasn't without its charm though, and many locals were quite fond of it.

By 2:35 pm he was parked down the road from Togo's and looking at his watch. He called Karl and inquired, "We good?"

Karl replied, "Wait one." It was quiet, and twenty seconds later he authorized, "Good to go."

Steve hopped out of his truck and started walking towards Togo's. He'd left his badge and gun at home. His Stephen Parent ID was in Karl's possession at the moment, so in theory, he had nothing to worry about. Nothing but the fact that he was walking into a hornet's nest full of very pissed off people who believed Marcus Atkins owed them $200,000 because he got robbed. Or worse, they thought Marcus Atkins stole $200,000 from them. Either position wasn't a good spot to be in.

The temperature was hovering around the freezing mark; it wasn't too bad outside. The sky was gloomy and grey. Steve walked to the front door at Togo's and checked his watch. 2:50 pm. Close enough, he thought, and walked in.

The place was dark. Even though it was grey outside, his eyes still had a hard time adjusting to the dim interior. It was a small bar with a few booths on the right wall, a couple pool tables with what was left of the green felt looking paper thin, and half a dozen mystery stains scattered across both. The left side was an assortment of mismatched chairs and tables. Steve hazarded a guess that one or two were from the original set, but after the others were used to bash people, they were replaced with whatever the owner might have had in his basement or found on Kijiji the day he needed them.

As his eye adjusted, he noticed three men in the bar. The first was sitting in a booth on the right. He was a large man in his mid-thirties with the telltale signs of steroid abuse, tall, pushing six foot two, with short cropped dyed blond hair. He was wearing a black tank top that showed off his arms. Steve thought they had to be at least twenty-two inches. He wore a big silver chain around his neck and both hands showcased an assortment of rings. His eyes were fixated on Steve.

On the left was an older man, smaller than the first but not by much. He was about an inch or two shorter, had thinned brown hair and a face that had seen several bare-knuckled fights. He was wearing a blue Polo shirt, black jeans, and steel toed boots with the steel caps showing. Steve thought the show was a bit much, but c'est la vie.

Lastly, at the bar was a short, squat man. His head and face were clean shaven. He looked at the younger guy and nodded.

"Help ya's?" he directed to Steve.

"I called last week. I was asked to come here for three?" Steve stated.

"It's not three, is it?" The older guy spoke in a menacing tone.

Steve looked at his watch and asked, "Okay, should I come back?"

The bald guy at the bar said something Steve couldn't hear. The younger guy looked impatient and said, "What are you waiting for?" and nodded to the bald guy. Steve started walking to the bar when he heard the younger one bark, "Hold it!" before jumping up and walking towards him.

Steve instantly thought of the robbery the other night. This guy fit the bill: overall same size. He looked huge now, but in dark clothing with a mask he could be the one who did it.

The big guy came over and patted Steve down. He took out Steve's wallet, opened it and looked at the ID. Next, he took Steve's phone and his keys, dropped them into a paper bag, and sat back down crinkling the bag nonstop. Steve guessed even he couldn't fuck that up. He walked up to the bar and stood next to the little bald guy. The bald guy was doing a crossword puzzle. Steve asked, "Mind if I sit.?" The man nodded and Steve sat down.

"Hi, I'm Marcus," he said sticking his hand out.

"I dun care who ya'ar" he replied with the thickest Scottish accent Steve had ever heard. "Whatda fock appened, an' where's ma monay?"

Steve was prepared for the hostility, but the accent threw him off. He began to explain, "I have no clue what happened. I went to meet with him, we had everything worked out. I woke up the next morning looking like this," he pointed to his face. The Scotsman finally looked up. Steve continued, "handcuffed to a hospital bed."

The Scotsman held his stare. Steve shut up. He knew the number one way to give yourself away or tell someone you were lying was to offer up too much information. The Scotsman looked back down at his newspaper.

He said "So how'd ye git ma numba?"

"Oh," Steve gave him a confused look, like he figured they guy must have known. "I was in the hospital overnight. They let me out sometime around 5:00 or 6:00 pm. I was brought back to the police station. Caleb got brought in about an hour later. He looked bad, face all smashed up."

"Ya dini answer ma question." The Scotsman sounded annoyed.

"Caleb told me to call his lawyer. And he'd get me in touch with you."

"Why?" the Scotsman asked, now visibly irate. "Why did ee give ye 'is lawya's numba, and why did ye call mi?" His voice was rising. The older man stood up and started walking over, looking like he was on a mission.

"Okay, hold on a minute. I thought you knew about all this." Steve held his hand up.

"'Old it, Paddy" the Scotsman said, and the older guy stopped.

Steve tried again. "Okay, let me start over. I'll tell you everything from the beginning."

The Scotsman turned to face him. Steve elaborated, "I met with Caleb. I don't know what happened at his house. I woke up the next morning in a hospital bed with my face worked in. I was told I'm being charged with possession for purposes of trafficking. I spent the whole day stressing and wondering how I'm going to make it up to the guys on my end.

"Later that day I was brought back to the police station. I was tossed in the Bullpen. I was there for I guess about an hour, then Caleb got brought in. He looked like he'd been hit by a truck. His face was smashed right up. Caleb and I are looking at each other. He thought I set him up.. I thought he'd set me up. But judging from the state we were both in, neither one of us was in on the attack. We were both dummied."

"I don't know how, why, or when the police got involved. I have no memory of it at all. Caleb and I started talking in the bullpen and I could see he was a wreck. He was scared shitless. He said he was in deep shit, and it didn't matter that he was in custody.

"My Charges were dropped, they were looking at Caleb. Far as the cops are concerned I just happened to be there when he was raided. But I was still on the hook with my guys, I was trying to think about how I could unfuck myself in this situation. I decided I'd try to work it off with the guys on my end. I've known one of them for twenty years. I have a side deal lined up getting smokes off the reserve and shipping them out to Saskatchewan. Figured I could waive my fee, maybe take me a month to work it off. I could live with that. Caleb asked if I could cut him in. I can't just drop an envelope off at the jail every three weeks with forty grand in it, so he gave me his lawyer's name and tells me his lawyer will get me in contact with you so I can pay you Caleb's share. And now here we are."

So much for not giving too much information, Steve thought.

"So ya heer to pay me ma monay?" the Scotsman asked.

"Well, not exactly," Steve clarified. "I'm here to get myself out of trouble. I've talked to my guys. It was their money that was lost. I have to waive my share on the smokes three times. That's a hundred and twenty grand out of my pocket. They're keeping it all. I got the smoke connection through Caleb. He was cut in for forty Gs a drop too. He's asking me if I'll give you 100 grand from his next three drops, then drop the other twenty off at his lawyer's."

The Scotsman turned back to his newspaper. "Ye'll drop ma the full $120,000 fer Caleb's end of the loss". He looked back at Steve and added "An anutha $80,000 of yurs afta."

Steve acted like he was about to protest before offering an explanation. No legit runner would agree to the Scotsman's terms without a fight.

"I have a run every twenty days. I have to cover my guys first, otherwise they'll stop coming here and none of us will get anything."

Paddy stepped up to him and said, "Oh, no. you'll get something."

Steve looked over at Paddy, then back to the Scotsman. "Look, I appreciate the theatrics, but put that dog on a leash please. I came here as a gentleman to correct a problem I had no control over. I don't need this goon breathing down my neck."

The Scotsman smiled "Go si' down, Paddy." He looked at Steve and inquired, "Whataya thinkin?"

Steve replied, "Between me and Caleb it was $80,000 profit every twenty days. If you'll let me, I'll give them the first eighty. After that, half of the next load. Our next date is seven days away. So, in twenty-seven days I'll be back here with forty grand. Twenty days later another eighty, and twenty days after that the final eighty. That's sixty-seven days and you're paid back in full. And nobody has to lose out on anything else."

The Scotman nodded, then asked "Whare's Caleb now?

Steve was hoping he'd ask this question. He leaned closer and disclosed, "I don't know if it's true, but I heard he was on suicide watch," and shrugged.

"Ay. Herd da same."

"Now look, I have half a mind to tell Caleb to go get fucked, give you the $80,000 you want from me, and tell him, 'Sorry brother not my problem'. But I can't do that. A deal is a deal, and that puts me in a bad spot with you. I could have just disappeared. You had no clue who I was. I could have been back out on the east coast in two days, and you'd never find me. I don't want to do that. I'm here in good faith to show you that you can trust me. I had a deal worked out with Caleb that would have made a lot of people a lot of money. If you're interested, I can still work it. We'll just cut Caleb out. But I'll need to know right away."

"My guys are looking for a new hook up. It's the fucking wild west out on the coast right now. Way too hot. The Asians are battling internally, and street gangs are shooting up hotels. There's nothing moving. I have a dedicated buyer that is looking to capitalize on an open market. He's got the money and the security to not be fucked with. He's smart and low key. You'll never meet him; he'll never know who you are. There's a lot of money to be made. But I need to set something up before he finds someone else." Steve leaned in. He had the Scotsman on the hook.

The Scotsman sat quietly. He'd heard about the wars on the west coast. Drama like that was bad for business. Police didn't care if the gangs shot each other up. It's when civilians start getting hurt that the cops started to get pissy. If this Marcus guy was right, the prairies were wide open. Someone with money and a good security backing could lay claim and make a fortune.

He thought about it for a moment and asked, "whata they afta?"

Steve said "What I had with Caleb to start. two keys of coke and four of fentanyl. Powder, not the patches. I don't know what your price was. I was getting it off Caleb for $100,000, I quoted my guys $120,000."

"How oft'n"

"If everything was good thy were going to double it on the next smoke run," Steve advised.

The Scotman sat for a minute. "Aye, I wont $90,000 for da orda. Start et naow." Then he added, "Ya kick op ya share until ya paid ma back."

Steve said. "I'll go see them now. How do I contact you?"

"Ya don. Ya call Stebar afta the next cigarette deal and come back tha next day with ma monay." The Scotsman directed.

Steve got up. He grabbed the paper bag from the bigger guy, waved at the older one, and walked out into the grey light. He moved quickly back to his truck. His phone rang immediately, and he answered it via Bluetooth. "Hey dad."

"Hi Marcus, you were supposed to call last Sunday, are you well?" Karl asked.

"Yeah. I'm good. Just been busy. I'm about to get on the highway right now. Can I call you when I get home?" Steve said.

"Sure thing. Your mother and I are stepping out for dinner at six." Karl said.

"Okay, talk soon," Steve rung off. He was worried about either bugs or tracking devices put on or in his truck and was playing is safe until he could speak with Karl securely to make sure the aerial surveillance confirmed nobody was near it. He also needed to ensure the big guy didn't do anything to his phone, keys, or wallet.

Steve was excited though. The meetup had gone well. He'd thrown Caleb under the bus. By mentioning suicide watch, he'd shown that Caleb wasn't able to be trusted. He'd also set himself up to start buying directly from the Scotsman, putting him one step closer to finding out how this garbage kept flooding the streets.

Chapter 26
Wednesday January 4, 2023.
Hamilton, Ontario

At 6:30pm Mike returned to the Mazda dealer and continued his surveillance. He saw James red Honda and the same little blue car from earlier. Mike shut the lights down, turned the heat on and watched the house. The stakeout was boring, but he amused himself with audio books. An older couple left around 7:00 pm and came back shortly after 9:00 pm. Mike figured he'd come check again the following Wednesday and see if they left again. On Friday he drove by again and saw James's car still in the same spot. It hadn't moved since he parked it there a few days before.

Friday night Mike and Sasha went to the bar where Sasha worked and watched a local band play. It wasn't Mike taste in music, but Sasha was having fun, afterward they went back to her place and noticed it was freezing inside when they walked in.

"Shit," she cursed. "Furnace went out again".

"Is it just this unit or the whole place?" asked Mike.

"The whole place, I need to go check on Sophie"

Mike waited upstairs. He heard Sasha leave then a quiet knock on the door below. Only silence followed. Mike looked out the window and saw Sasha cross the street. She knocked on door of the older woman who had come out to speak to the police during the altercation with James. The light came on and the door opened. They chatted for a minute then Sasha walked back across the street. He heard her door open and she yelled up "She's across the street at Linda's".

Mike asked, "Does this happen often?"

"Every now and then. Linda's son owns this place. His friend comes by to fix it. Apparently, the pilot light goes out? I don't know."

She went into her room and grabbed a small heater. "Just put that on low so the pipes don't freeze," Mike advised. "We'll stay at my place tonight. I'll look at the furnace in the morning."

Sasha packed up some clothes and a bag of treats for Domino. When they got to Mike's, she let the dog sniff around out front. Mike went up and opened the door. Sasha came up the steps, walked inside and stopped. The place was barren. In the living room was a couch, a coffee table, and a wall mounted TV. No pictures, not decorations, nothing personal. The walls were bare except for the black curtains. She let the dog off her leash, and the pup started her reconnaissance in the little house.

"Throw your stuff on the stairs," Mike directed, then went to the kitchen. "Beer?" he offered.

"Uh. Yeah sure," Sasha replied, looking around the place. It seemed odd. It was clean but lacked personality or warmth. She followed him into the kitchen and found a small table, two chairs, a fridge, stove, sink, and counter. No decorations or personal touches except for three pictures on the fridge. She looked at them. The first was of Mike and another guy at work. She had no idea how old it was. The other two were pamphlets from funerals. Looking closer she saw the guy in the first picture with Mike was on one of them.

"Your dad?" she asked.

"No, uncle. Took me in when I needed it. Great guy. Cancer. 2016." Mike explained.

She looked at the other. "And him?"

"Friend. Coworker. Had a lot of fun working with him. Died in 2019"

That's when it dawned on Sasha: she knew very little about him. Things most people would brag about like boxing, He only told her about after he pummelled her neighbor.

She turned and looked at him. "Where's your family? You mentioned a sister in Ottawa, but where are your parents?"

Mike stared at the wall and answered, "My mom's up in Ottawa I think. We don't talk often. My fault mostly. When my parents split, I stayed with my dad."

"How old were you?"

"Twelve or thirteen." He replied. "The old man died about twelve years ago, I think. I don't know, I didn't go to the funeral. My sister called and told me, but I didn't care. After I hung up I didn't think about it again. I got a call a few months later. A lawyer had been trying to find me. I guess we had to sell his house. Split it with my sister. I gave my share to a local boxing club I used to train at. I didn't want anything from him."

Sasha asked, "What did he do? I mean work-wise was he a steel worker too?"

"Ironworker." Mike corrected. "Steel workers make steel. Ironworkers erect iron. And no, he was a cop."

She looked at his face and she realized she knew the story without asking him. Mike had grown up in an abusive household. She changed the subject. "Well. I love what you've done with the place," she smiled, sweeping her arm towards the living room.

Mike chuckled. "Yeah, well until recently I had no idea how long I'd be staying."

"Oh?" she inquired with a raised eyebrow. "Found something to hang around for?"

"Not sure yet," he grinned. "But I'm willing to hang out and see."

She laughed at him and groaned, "Oh my God, you're so corny," then kissed him.

They grabbed their beers and went to the couch. Mike tuned on the TV, hit Youtube and James Brown popped up. He hit play and sat back. He asked, "What about you? What's keeping you here?"

She took a sip off her bottle. "Nothing now. Mom died and I hung around to take care of my younger brother. He's grown now, and doing good. He's happy. I've thought about leaving but where would I go? I can do the same thing in Alberta I'm doing here."

Mike understood her point. You got to be somewhere, might as well be here.

Sasha turned to Mike. "What about you. Did you have plans to leave?"

"No. Not really. I've kind of lived out of a suitcase since I started working. I know a lot of guys that make $200,000 a year but are essentially homeless. I knew this one guy from Calgary. Dude had to have at least a couple million bucks in the bank but lived out of a motorhome. He towed it all over, lived in the thing all year. Just him, his wife, and his dogs. Didn't matter where he was, he was home every night."

"What happened to him" She asked.

"Died in a motorhome accident." Mike replied with a smirk. She stared at him, and he laughed. "Kidding. I don't know for sure. I know his home base was in the Calgary area. Last I heard, he was still travelling to wherever the work took him." Mike took a swig of his beer then added. "I don't know. I don't have any strings anywhere. I've worked all over the country. I prefer the southern Ontario climate. I'm not much for rural areas. I like B.C. But it's expensive."

Sasha added, "And the Hippies"

"Right, the filthy hippies." Mike agreed with a grin.

In the morning, they left the dog at Mike's where it was warm and stopped by Sasha's. They found Sophie, and she let Mike into the basement to look at the furnace. It took him a few minutes to diagnose the problem. They headed to a hardware store to find a new thermal couple. Mike was walking down the aisle, more browsing than anything. Sasha was looking at paint swatches when he found her.

"Painting?" he asked.

"No, you are." she replied. He gave her a curious look and she elaborated. "Your place is cute, but it needs to be painted. The walls have been washed a thousand times, but the paint is original."

"But what if I don't want to paint?" he asked. She stared at him not blinking. Finally, he sighed. "Can I at least pick to colors?"

"No. I've seen your decorating. I'm helping you. Now accept my love or get out of the way."

Mike wasn't able to argue with that logic. And the more he thought about it, the more he agreed that a fresh coat of paint would brighten the place up. Sasha picked out a few colours, light ones mostly, while Mike loaded up with brushes, rollers, and paint trays. He met her at the paint counter where a young girl was handing Sasha the first paint can. When the girl saw Mike, she stopped what she was doing, ran around the counter and wrapped her arms around him.

"Hey, kiddo! How ya been?" he asked. Confused, Sasha heard the young girl mumble something she couldn't make out. Mike politely said, "Speak up."

Louder, the young girl repeated, "I'm good, I work here now."

"I see that. Are you done school?" he asked.

"Yes. Last June." She answered.

"Well, what's next?" Mike probed. "College?"

The young girl shrugged "I don't know what I want to take."

"Come see me at the club," he invited. "We'll talk about what you like, see what you can do?" the girl nodded her head and gave him a hug again. Then handed the rest of the paint cans to Sasha.

As they walked away, Sasha looked at Mike inquisitively. "Who was that?"

"I used to help coach an outreach program for at risk youth. She was one of the students. Sweet kid. She's autistic, very smart. Learns quickly, just a little socially awkward sometimes. Great kid though." Mike explained.

"Come by the club?" Sasha inquired.

"Boxing club. She was supposed to, a while ago, after high school. Talk about college or an apprenticeship." Mike said.

"Well. Look at you! Guidance counselor Michael!" she laughed, nudging him.

"A lot of these kids weren't dealt a very good hand in life." Mike shrugged. "Sometimes they just need someone to show them the right kind of positive attention. She learned to box, and she picked it up quickly. Something she never thought she could do. That showed her not to limit herself. It showed her the possibilities are endless."

"You're full of surprises" she smiled at him.

"Very few of them are good ones." he advised.

They returned to Sasha's place. Mike got the furnace back up and running without any difficulty. Then to his place dropped, off the paint and took Domino for a walk in a new neighborhood. The rest of the afternoon was spent painting Mike's living room and kitchen. Both ceilings were painted white, then a light cream color was added to the kitchen walls. Sasha had chosen a light grey for the living room, and a a turquoise accent wall. Mike had a James Brown and Sam Cook play list running on the TV.

"What's with the music?" she asked.

"What do you mean?"

"The Motown. Is that all you listen to?" she asked.

"No. I like everything. It's just the playlist that came on. I grew up listening to this though. Detroit was just across the river. All our TV and radio growing up came out of Detroit: the home of Motown."

"You just don't strike me as someone that listens to that kind of music," she admitted.

"Well, I wore my hair in a giant afro until last summer," Mike joked. Sasha stared at him, a little afraid he might not be kidding.

When they finished, Sasha washed the brushes off while Mike cleaned out the paint trays and put away everything until it was time to tackle the upstairs rooms. Drying off her hands, she looked around and admired, "There. Doesn't that look better?"

"Looks the same, except the colours are different" Mike observed.

"You motherfucker," she laughed, flicking the left-over water from her hands at him. "Hungry?"

"Was this all a shameless ploy to get me to buy dinner?" Mike asked, gesturing at the freshly painted walls. "'Cause if you want breakfast too, the neighbor said her roof was leaking."

Sasha rolled her eyes. "Feed me," she sighed, smiling at him. They decided to shower and go for dinner at a little local Greek restaurant not far from Mike's place. The food was decent but came back to haunt them both immediately. After dinner, Sasha asked Mike if he'd be interested in going for a beer at a bar near her place. She said a friend of hers was bartending, and that the place was usually quiet. Mike agreed. They picked up Domino and headed back to Sasha's so she could change. After checking in on Sophie, they headed out and by 9:00 pm they were walking up to the doors of a bar called The Outlander.

The Outlander was a surprisingly large bar. It opened into a spacious room with a row of booths on the right, and the long section of the L shaped bar of the left. At the end of the bar was a left turn that led to a few tables before the bar opened up again with a stage big enough for a five-piece band. Three pool tables sat just past the stage. There was already a handful of people scattered around. Music played from somewhere, although Mike didn't see a juke box anywhere.

They decided to sit at the bar. The bartender was busy filling pitchers for a few guys who had settled themselves by the pool tables. She was short, full of energy, and looked to be in her early thirties. Her multicolored hair reached her waist and overlaid her black tank top, partially obscuring the logo for a band called The Bitchfits. Completing the outfit was a leopard print skirt over thick black nylons and rainbow striped Converse Chucks. She was cute and seemed to really enjoy working an empty bar. She noticed Mike and Sasha sit down and bounced over.

"Hey gorgeous!" she greeted Sasha. "What are ya having?" Sasha ordered herself a rye and Coke, and an MGD for Mike.

The bartender looked at Mike. "Ohhh I've heard all about you," she teased, raising her eyebrows and smiling.

"Shut up." Sasha warned through a clenched grin. She turned to Mike. "This is Carrie. She's full of shit and likes to cause problems."

"Seems lovely." Mike replied, and Carrie laughed to herself. She brought their drinks back.

"I need a smoke. Wanna come out with me?" Carrie asked Sasha.

"I'll keep an eye on the bar". Mike offered, and the girls stepped out front. He looked around the bar. There was another couple at the far end that looked like the type that closed the place every night. One booth had four people sitting in; Mike could only see the tops of their heads. He heard what sounded like a pool game going on in the other section but had no clue how many people were over there. There were three TVs behind the bar, all of them set to different hockey games. Mike wasn't much of a hockey fan, but he watched to pass the time.

After a few minutes the girls came back in. Carrie threw her jacket behind the bar, did a quick once around to see who needed drinks, then then joined Mike and Sasha. Carrie was nice. She was perpetually happy and had a very quick wit coupled with an infectious laugh. She asked Mike what he did for a living. When he told her he was an ironworker, she said she had a couple of uncles were ironworkers too. They spent most of the evening chatting, occasionally interrupted by a few people coming and going.

Around 11:30 pm Carrie had asked Mike where he was from originally. When he answered, he noticed her eyes shift towards the window outside.

"Uh oh," she muttered, her big smile leaving her face.

Mike looked over his shoulder and saw two guys standing at the window looking in. They looked like brothers, both around six feet tall, Medium builds but gruby looking. They both had short dark hair. One had a beard and glasses.

"What's up?" Mike asked

"Ugh. That's my ex," Sasha explained.

"Do you want to leave?"

"Just stay. If he bothers you, I'll kick them out," Carrie advised.

Sasha looked at Mike he said, "Up to you." She nudged her stool closer to his.

Shortly thereafter, the two men walked in. Mike thought both of them looked like they had crawled out of rural Alabama; scruffy and unkept, wearing dirty clothing. The younger of the two was trying to glare at Mike. The one with glasses saw Sasha and walked over. Mike turned on his stool to face him. The guy ignored Mike and put his hand on the small of Sasha's back.

"Hey Babe. Missed ya."

The younger brother took up a spot on the other side of Mike. He was smart enough to understand what a flank was, but too stupid to realize he was seriously outgunned. Sasha shrugged away and warned, "Brad, leave me alone."

He put his hand on her shoulder again. Mike could tell Brad and his brother were drunk and itching for a fight. They had paused at the window, saw Sasha and Mike, and came up with a game plan. Mike, still sitting at his stool, said, "Hey, asshole. Are your ears painted on? She said fuck off."

Brad looked at Mike with a crooked smile and opened his mouth to say something. Before the words could come out, Mike open-hand slapped him using the heel of his right hand across the side of Brad's head. He sprung up off his bar stool, grabbed Brad by the head, and kneed him in the gut while simultaneously smashing his head into the bar. Brad crumpled to the ground.

Without waiting, Mike spun around and grabbed the brother by his winter coat. Mike kicked his feet out from under him and slammed him on the ground, knocking the wind out of him and several barstools over in the process. Still standing, Mike grabbed the brother's wrist and wrenched it around so the guy was face down on the floor with his right arm extended straight behind him. Mike stood on the back of his shoulder applying just enough force to crank the joint but not break it.

In a calm, icy tone Mike said, "I don't want to hurt you, but I will if I have to. I'm going to let you go. You're going to get up, grab that sack of shit you came in here with, and leave. Do you understand me?" He gave the arm a light wrench, the guy yelped but didn't answer. "I asked you a question." Mike said.

"Yes!" the guy yelled.

"Good, I thought I'd lost you there for a second." Mike, still calm said, "Now, when I let you up. If you act the fool, I'll break you in half. Understood?" He waited a second, then repeated, "Tell me you understand, or I'll rip your fucking arm out of the socket," adding a slight crank again.

"I UNDERSTAND, I UNDERSTAND!" the guy yelled. Mike let go and sat back on his stool. All the bar patrons by now were watching the event. The guy helped his brother up, who almost fell walking to the door. The two left. Mike watched Brad stagger through the parking lot while his younger brother tried to hold him up. He turned back to Carrie who was sitting at the bar with her mouth open.

"So anyway. I was born in Windsor."
He continued, as if nothing had happened.

Chapter 27
Saturday January 7th, 2023. 11:30 pm
Hamilton, Ontario

Steve was sitting in a bar not far from his apartment. The investigation was going to be slow until next week when he met with the Scotsman again, so he decided to do what he does every night: get drunk.

He went to his usual spot, a bar where he was always able to score some coke. Plus, on Saturdays there was a feisty little bartender that he figured he had been wearing down. He sat at his regular spot at the end of a bar, away from the door and windows. He was watching the world Junior's hockey highlights on the TV and fiddling with his phone. The guy he normally scored from wasn't at the bar, so he'd been texting other people to see what he could find.

The Bartender came by and asked, "Refill?" He nodded. She dropped a shot and a glass of beer off in front of him. She was being shitty tonight, he thought, talking with another couple at the end of the bar all night. If she didn't smarten up, he was going to have to take someone else home.

He continued scrolling through his phone, looking for someone to hook him up, when out of nowhere he heard a glass break, a loud thump and a girl scream. He shot up from his stool and looked towards the door just in time to see a very large man grab a guy and throw him down. It took a second to realize the big man had a guy on the floor and was holding his wrist and standing on him. He was speaking calmly. The bar was silent.

The guy was huge, at least six foot five and two hundred and fifty pounds. But he was fast. Incredibly fast. Steve heard him warning the man on the floor, "I don't want to hurt you, but I will if I have to..."

Steve instantly knew not only the words, but the calm, honest tone in the man's voice. It's the fucking guy that robbed us, he thought to himself. Steve considered the bruising that still coloured his face and the fact that the oversized gorilla likely still had all the money he'd stollen that night. Steve decided he deserved a little payback.

Steve heard the guy on the floor yelp. The big guy let him go and sat down while the guy scrambled up from the floor, picked his buddy up off the floor, and left. The big guy watched them leave, then turned and started talking like nothing had happened. No adrenaline. Nothing. It was as if the guy had just dispatched two people in seconds and his heart rate didn't climb above eighty-five beats per minute. Just like the other night.

Steve realized if the big guy saw him, he'd be made. He peeled $60 off his cash roll, placed it on the bar where he was sitting, put on his coat in an exaggerated fashion to cover his face. He walked past them saying, "Got to run, Carrie. Cash is on the bar," and left as quickly as he could. He hustled down to his truck, hopped in, and decided to drive around the block until the big guy came out to leave. He thought for a minute. He knew he had seen the girl the big guy was with before. At The Outlander and somewhere else. He couldn't place it. But she was friends with Carrie, he knew that.

He waited until 11:45pm, at which point his phone chimed. Someone had come through with some coke for him. He looked at the phone, then the bar, and the phone again. "Fuck it," he said and started the truck. He raced to an apartment seven minutes away, ran inside and bought two grams of coke; one for himself, the other for evidence. He raced back to his truck and hurried back to the bar, fishtailing around the corner and almost colliding with a city bus. He skidded to a stop in front of the bar.

He couldn't see inside fully from where he parked. He could still see Carrie walking around. She made several trips around the bar, but hadn't lingered at the end like she had been earlier. He was getting frustrated, and the line of coke he's snorted off the truck dashboard didn't help. He decided to chance a look. He put the truck in gear and drove past the bar. The stools were empty. The big guy was gone.

"Shit!" he exclaimed out loud. He thought about going back in and talking to Carrie, but if they'd moved seats or were playing pool and the big guy saw him, he'd be screwed. He thought about waiting for Carrie to close, but there was a chance her friends might stick around. Steve knew that Carrie didn't work again until next Saturday. With few good options, he decided his best bet was to wait until then.

Steve put the truck in reverse and decided to find another bar. As he left his parking spot, he had an idea. He'd watched the two guys that had been pummeled leave the parking lot and turn left. There wasn't much down that way. Another bar, and some industrial buildings.

He pulled up at a small plaza, with a convenience store, a laundromat and a bar called Soapy's. He slammed the truck into park and hoped out. Halfway to the door he noticed both guys outside the bar. One sitting with his head in his hands the younger pacing back and forth.

"Hey, who was that guy?" Steve asked walking up.

"A fucking dead man, that's who," spat the younger one, continuing to pace.

Steve ignored him. The kid listened to too much 2Pac and thought he was a thug. He redirected his questions to the older one who was sitting. "Did you know him?" The older one looked at him then back down. The younger one was still pacing.

With dwindling patience Steve repeated, "Hey. Buddy. Who was he?" The older one once again ignored him. Now Steve was angry. He grabbed the younger one, slammed him into the Brick wall, punched him in the face, then threw him in a snowbank. The older one looked up, mouth agape. Steve smacked him in the side of the head and said "I get annoyed asking stupid people the same question over and over. Who the fuck was he?"

The older one screamed, "I don't know!" his voice shaking. Steve slapped him again, then kicked him.

"Tell me who he was, or I'll do some real fucking damage," Steve growled.

The younger one got to his feet and stumbled over. "We don't know. Never saw him before."

"Why did he rag doll you then?" Steve asked.

"The girl he was with. That's his ex," the younger one nodded towards his brother.

"What's her name?" Steve demanded.

"Sasha," the younger one replied.

Steve punched him in the nose, hard. "Sasha what, you fucking shit stain!"

The younger one was on the ground, blood gushing out from between his fingers "Sasha Horvat," he blubbered through blood, snot, and tears.

Steve kicked the older one once more for good measure, then looked at the younger one. "Next time either of you think you're thugs, remember this night." He jumped back him his truck and drove away.

Steve woke up at 9:30 am on Sunday, not hungover for the first time in what felt like years. He called Karl right away.

"Good morning, Marcus."

"I'm alone." Steve informed.

"What do you need?' Karl asked.

"I need any information we can find on a Sasha Horvat. Hamilton, female, mid to late twenties. Not a very common name, shouldn't be too hard."

"On it". Karl advised "Anything else?"

Steve thought about telling Karl he'd found the guy that robbed him, but he refrained. If he involved Karl and the task force, he wouldn't get to challenge the attacker himself, and he certainly wouldn't be able to keep the stollen money. "No. Just need that."

"Okay, come in tomorrow morning. We need to go over this Wednesday." Karl said.

Steve hung up. He'd found the guy that robbed him, he we sure of it. But he wasn't sure what to do with that yet.

Chapter 28
Sunday January 7th, 2023, 9 am.
Hamilton, Ontario

Mike woke up and went to the boxing club for a workout. He didn't drink much but when he did, he liked to sweat it out the following day. Afterwards he drove by James's place. The car was still there, untouched, not even cleaned off from the snow two days before. He drove out to the barn, packed up a few of his guns and met with a friend that had converted his 110-acre farm into an unofficial shooting range.

Mike brought his Remington 700, his .308 And 200 rounds of ammo. He owned a few pairs of silencing ear buds, electronic ear plug that picked up voices and ambient noise but blocked out the loud band of gun fire, however firing a high-powered
rifle required earmuffs. A .308 round was about 155 decibels, or 30 decibels higher than where sound starts to cause pain. He had just installed his scope and was going to spend the day sighting it in.

He laid prone on the mat he'd set out and looked through the scope a hundred yards down range at the targets set up in front of a large berm. He lined up the cross hairs on the center, controlled his breathing and squeezed the trigger. The first round went high about four inches and left three inches. He used the top turret and adjusted the windage, moving the vertical cross hair left to right. He then adjusted the side turret, moving the elevation, or the horizontal cross hairs, up and down. Mike chambered another round and breathing slowly, he squeezed the trigger. This time the bullet hit low one inch and about a half inch to the right. Carefully, he adjusted the turrets again, chambered a third round, and hit the edge of the yellow ring, a little high and a little right. He repeated this process another twelve times until he punched the center of the ring three times in a row.

He moved back a hundred yards, lined up the cross hairs and fired again. He hit a little high this time. At two hundred yards the bullet was still climbing. Instead of adjusting the crosshairs, he left them as they were and compensated for the height difference by aiming a little lower. He hit the ring. He fired another twenty rounds from this distance.

He backed up and completed the same process at three hundred and then four hundred yards. At four hundred yards he was hitting the center ring with less frequency, four out of five were finding their home. Any that missed were either to the left or the right. At this distance the wind was playing a factor, but Mike was hitting with enough accuracy to get a head shot at that distance and that was good enough for him. After sighting in his new scope, he packed everything up and returned it to the barn.

Sasha had agreed to pick up an afternoon shift at the bar from 1:00 pm until 6:00 pm. Whoever closed the night before hadn't fully restocked the fridges, so most of her shift had been spent pulling cases from the back. She was in the bar alone when a man walked in. "Be right with ya," she yelled. She turned around and saw a scruffy looking man with big dark black circles under his eyes. She thought he looked like a very drunk racoon. Someone had broken his nose for him, that was clear, and judging by the vibe he was giving off and the way he was staring at her, she figured he probably deserved it. "What can I get ya?" she asked.

"I'll take a Bud Light," he replied before casually asking, "Hey, were you at The Outlander last night?"

She grabbed his beer, popped the cap off and placed it in front of him. "Yeah. I go there sometimes."

"Thought I saw you there. I never forget a pretty face," he smiled, hoping he was coming off as charming. He wasn't.

"$6.50," she replied. She couldn't put her finger on it. But this guy was giving her a very bad vibe.

He placed a $10 on the bar. "Keep it," he practically purred. "What was all the ruckus about?"

"Ruckus?" she asked innocently. "What do you mean?"

"Come on, that big gorilla slamming those guys around." He took a sip of his beer, trying to seem nonchalant. "You were sitting right there." He was smiling, but the look in his eyes was scary.

"I saw it. Not sure what started it," she answered cautiously.

"That big guy, he your boyfriend?"

"He's a friend." Sasha turned, trying to look busy again.

"What's his name?"

Sasha stopped. "Why are you asking?" She gave him a suspicious look that said she was tired of whatever game he was trying to play.

The smile on his face turned into a mean sneer. He pointed at his nose and eyes "Because he's the coward that did this to me. Who is he?"

"I think you need to leave," she said firmly. "Now, Or I'm calling the police."

He barked out a laugh, stood up, and started walking around towards the bar opening. "Go ahead. Call them. See how long it takes them to get here." As he made it to the opening, Sasha picked up a baseball bat from the behind the counter and without giving a warning, swung it at his head. He backed away, laughing.

"Ooh, this kitty has claws. Meow." He teased. She swung again, but this time he caught it. He yanked it out of her hands. She backed away fast, ready to jump over the bar if she needed to. He took another step and the bell above the door jingled. Leonard, the bar's most regular customer, was walking in and saw the commotion. Leonard wasn't a big man, even in his younger days he topped out at five foot nine, one hundred and sixty pounds. But he still rushed in with his hands up ready to fight.

"Leave her alone," he yelled.

Steve looked at him, looked back at Sasha, laughed a little louder and started walking out of the bar. As he passed Leonard, he did a fast step towards him trying to make him flinch. Leonard stood his ground, so Steve shoved him, knocking him down. Sasha grabbed the bat off the floor and rushed to Leonard's side. Steve walked out the door. Pausing, he looked back and said, "Tell your boyfriend I'll see him soon, Sasha," and left.

"Who was that guy?" inquired Leonard as Sasha helped him up.

"Not sure. Some creep," she replied. "Thank you for helping me."

"Will you let me take you home now?" he asked, his eyes twinkling.

"Ask me tomorrow, hun." she answered with a wry smile.

She sent Mike a text asking him to call her on the bar phone. Ten minutes later the phone rang.

"What's up?" he asked.

"There was a guy in here. He knew my name. Said he was at The Outlander last night," she began.

"Okay," Mike replied. "And?"

"His face was busted up. He said you did it to him," she finished.

Mike was silent for a few seconds. then asked, "What did he look like?"

"Bigger guy. Scruffy looking. Long greasy hair, beard."

The cop, Mike thought. This wasn't good, but it was better than it being Caleb. "Are you okay?"

"Yeah, I'm fine, Leonard saved me. He's like my Popeye," she said loud enough to hear, flashing him a smile from behind the bar.

"Okay. I'm going to pick up the dog. I'll bring her to my house. After work I want you to take a cab to the little mini mall down the road from my place. I'll meet you there. You can stay with me for a few days," he offered.

"Mike, what's going on?" Sasha sounded worried.

"I'll fill you in tonight. You're fine. Just come to my place, okay?"

"Okay. I'm done at 6:00 pm."

"I'll see you right after that." He assured and rung off.

The rest of her shift was uneventful. She only marked down one of every two beers Leonard ordered. Her relief staff came in a 5:45 pm. Sasha kissed Leonard on the cheek, thanked him again and called a cab to the bar.

The cab arrived at 5:58 pm. She hopped in and asked the driver to drop her off at the plaza Mike had indicated. The taxi was blue and driven by a middle-aged woman who clearly smoked in her car when nobody was in it. Sasha stared out the window while the driver complained about some politician who was coming to town tomorrow.

Sasha texted Mike "2 min out." Her phone rang immediately.

"Hi," Mike greeted.

"Hi. Almost there."

"Get out at the main door. Cut through the mall. And leave at the door near the video game shop. I'm right outside that door in a little black pickup," Mike instructed.

"Do you want me to get out there then?" she asked.

"No, get out at the main door and cut through the mall. I'm parked here already." he said again.

They hung up. She sat in the back seat wondering why the clandestine actions, but she figured she'd play along. The guy at the bar had a major creep vibe, so she listened to Mike.

"Drop me at the main door please," she asked the driver.

Steve was following the blue taxi in his silver Dodge pickup. He wasn't trying too hard to stay back but wasn't following too close. He watched the taxi turn at the last second into the mall parking lot. "Shit!" he cursed and cut across two lanes of traffic, causing several other drivers to honk and scream at him. The taxi pulled up at the main door and he watched Sasha get out.

"What a waste," he muttered out loud. "Fine piece of ass like that and she's wasting her time with that shaven gorilla." He sped through the parking lot, looking for a place to park. He was driving fast and looking at the front door of the mall. He didn't see the elderly couple pushing a green shopping cart and had to stand on the brake to avoid hitting them.

He brought his truck to a stop, taking up two spots. Slamming the truck into park, he jumped out and ran inside. Moving quickly, he scanned each store as he walked by but didn't see her. He rounded a corner and saw her, about a hundred yards away, leaving through the other exit.

"Fuck!" he cursed and sprinted towards the door. He shoved past a lady and her teenage daughter and burst into the parking lot. There was no sign of her. Just people coming and going and a few vehicles pulling in and pulling out of parking spots. He'd lost her.

He heard a lady say, "Excuse me."

He looked back. It was the lady he had practically run through in his pursuit. "What?" he asked impatiently.

"Uh, you slammed into me back there. I think you owe me an apology," she replied indignantly.

Steve looked at her Starbucks coffee cup and slapped it out of her hand. "Oops, sorry." he said in an exaggerated tone. He bumped into her again and walked back to his truck.

Mike and Sasha pulled out of the parking lot. Mike was checking the rearview mirror and saw the cop fly through the door and start looking around. He turned left out of the parking lot and through the first green light then asked Sasha.

"Are you okay?"

"Yes. I'm confused though. Who was that guy and why is he looking for you."

Mike sighed. "I think he's a cop."

"A cop?" Surprise filled Sasha's voice. Then, remembering his face, she yelped "A Cop! You did that to a cop?" she said her voice rising.

"I didn't know he was a cop at the time. He wasn't acting like a cop." Mike reflected.

Sasha sat quiet for a second then conceded, "He wasn't acting like one today either. He threatened me. Came behind the bar. I don't know what he was planning. Leonard tried to help me and got pushed to the ground. Are you sure that guy's a cop?"

"Yes. I'm pretty sure. He was acting the same way when I hit him. I only hit him once," Mike lied. After a minute he asked, "What did he say to you. Tell me everything."

Sasha filled Mike in on the events of the encounter: The Outlander, the creepy vibe, the sneer on his face, how he got up and threatened her. Mike listened and thought to himself, he's making it personal.

"Should we be worried?" Sasha looked concerned.

Mike liked the sound of the "we". He replied, "If he saw us at the Outlander, he must have gotten your name from Carrie. You should call her and see what, if anything, was said, I'm not too worried. He went to the bar today trying to shake you up, hoping you'd either tell him who I am, or you lead him directly to me. Whatever he's doing, he's doing it off the record. This is a personal vendetta for him. If it was official, he'd have come into the bar in his uniform or with a couple uniformed cops. He'll get tired eventually."

Sasha placed her hand on his. "And what do we do till then?"

"Well, if he found your part time job, he probably knows your address. He hasn't figured out my name yet. Carrie only knows my first name. Even if he knew it, he couldn't find my address. We'll chill out at my place for a few days. Your scary guard dog is there now," he said with half a smile.

"Okay, can I get picked up for work at your place?" Sasha asked.

"We'll figure something out. If he's doing this on his own time, then he can't run twenty-four-hour surveillance. But he'll definitely contact your employers and ask where you're working."

Sasha smiled, pulled out her phone and dialed a number. "Hey hunny how are you?" Mike could hear a muffled voice from the other end.

"Has anyone called asking what site I'm working at?" Another muffled response.

"Okay, if anyone does ask, please tell them I'm laid off till spring." Another pause.

"No. I had some trouble with Brad last night and it got a little messy. I'm fine, but he isn't. I don't want the police or someone in his family calling and causing problems." Mike heard laughing on the phone.

"Thanks, hunny," Sasha said and hung up.

"Who was that?" Mike asked.

"Carly. Her dad owns the company. We grew up together. She'll have my back. Anybody calls looking for me, they'll be sent to her. I mentioned Brad because she hates him." Sasha paused, then added "I can get picked up at your place. I'll call her back later."

Sasha called Carrie next. She answered on the second ring.

"Hey doll," Sasha greeted. "Was anybody asking about us at the bar after we left?" She listened for a few seconds before replying, "Kind of a big guy. His face was all beat up. He said he was there." She listened again and explained, "He came in while I was working today and threatened me." She listened for a few more seconds before saying, "Okay, thanks love," and rung off.

She looked at Mike and said "The guy started coming around her bar a few months ago. Buys a lot of coke. His name is Marc or Marcus. He didn't ask her about me last night. He was the one that left right after the incident. But he did beat the shit out of Brad and his brother Scott after you did last night. Sounds like he broke Scott's nose."

"That's how he found you," Mike concluded.

The rode in silence for a few minutes before Mike asked, "Hungry?

"Starving" Sasha replied. She looked around, as if just noticing her surroundings for the first time. "Whose truck is this?"

"A friend's. Mine's at his place." Mike knew it was unlikely the cop would check the camera in the parking lot if this was a personal mission, but just to be safe the truck and the plates would be dropped off in the morning, and Mike would trade the guy for something else in the yard. For now he'd park a few blocks from his house.

Chapter 29
Monday January 9, 2023, 8 am.
Hamilton, Ontario

Mike woke up Monday morning with a mission. First, he drove the little black truck out to the Six Nations territory, pulled up at Jocko's yard, and tossed him the keys as he got out. "Wreck it," he directed.

Jocko nodded at him. "S'up?"

"Had heat on me yesterday. Lost them on the highway, but they have the make, colour, and plate I'm guessing. Truck's no good. Scrap it." Mike explained.

Jocko nodded again and whistled. A young guy came outside of the office trailer. "Get rid of it," Jocko ordered, nodding at the truck. The kid ran to the big garage and reappeared thirty seconds later driving a large forklift. Without slowing down, he drove the forks straight through the passenger door. The window exploded and the metal screeched. He picked the truck up and disappeared around the side of the building again. "What are ya after now?" Jocko asked.

"Something quiet, with balls in case I need it," Mike requested.

Jocko looked around the yard. "Got an '08 Charger over there. 5.7, Hemi. Body is shit, rotten. Rear struts are fucked, and I haven't got to them yet. Just did the brakes and the tie rods on the front. About 180,000 km on'er. Need a little more than five bills though."

"What do you have put into it?" Mike asked.

"I got about four hours, maybe another $400 in parts. Was gonna fix the body. Maybe try'n get $2000."

"I'll give you a $1500 right now. Throw plates on it?" Mike asked.

Jocko nodded, spit on the ground "Plates on'er are the ones it come in with. Nothing changed yet. You could get a week, maybe two before the cops bust your ass about it."

Mike walked over and looked at it. It was an unremarkable shade of maroon. Both rear wheel wells had rusted right out. Some spray foam insulation, a light layer of Bondo, and some colour-match paint would bring it to look like exactly what it was: a shitty patch job. But it would blend in enough that a cop wouldn't give it a second look.

"Lights all work? High beams, blinkers, taillights? Everything?" Mike asked.

Jocko nodded again. "Check em 'fore ya leave though."

Jocko grabbed the keys from the trailer. Mike peeled off fifteen $100's. He checked the lights. All good.

"You know where John Sarsens lives?" Mike inquired. John was the guy Mike had overheard talking about Caleb.

"Junior or Senior?"

"Junior, I guess. Be about thirty," Mike clarified.

"Next line over," Jocko nodded over his shoulder, referring to the street. "Go to the stop sign, turn left. Turn left at the next line. He's about three or four house up. Got a Mohawk flag at the mailbox."

"Alright, thanks. I'm out." Mike handed Jocko the wad of $100's.

Jocko, looking at the bills said, "Always welcome here," and walked away.

Mike dropped the newly acquired Charger behind the barn, then made his way over to John's. The two had worked together several times, enough so that a random pop-by wouldn't be too strange.

Mike saw a red flag with the yellow sun and side profile of Mohawk warrior flying at the mailbox. He pulled into the driveway and was immediately greeted by several barking dogs, none with collars. Mike sat in the truck waiting.

After a few minutes of listening to barking at his windows, Mike saw a woman step out of the house. She wore jeans and black hoodie. Her long, dark hair was pulled back into a loose braid. She yelled at the dogs, and they scattered in all directions. Mike popped the door and stepped out.

"Hi. John kicking around?" greeted Mike.

"Who are you?" she inquired, somewhat suspicious. They didn't get a lot of unexpected white visitors.

"Mike Wolly," he introduced himself. "We worked together."

She nodded and opened the door. "Babe. Big white guy here to see ya," and went back in the house without looking back. A few seconds later John appeared in the doorway.

"What's up Mike?" John walked over with a smile.

"Hey brother. You got a second? Need to talk to you," Mike began.

"Yeah, come on in." John headed back towards the house and waited for Mike to come up the steps.

The house was small but cozy. John and his wife had built it together a few years before. It was modern and clean but lived in. They had four children between the two of them, all of which lived there.

As Mike walked in, John introduced him to the woman from the driveway. "This is my wife, Amanda." Mike nodded to her and apologized for disturbing them. She was sitting on the couch folding a basket of laundry with two more baskets already folded in front of her. She was a strikingly good-looking girl. Dark skin with light eyes and long straight black hair. She was wearing one of John's union hoodies, flashing a forced but pretty smile, Not at all happy to see a large white man standing in her living room..

"It's okay, I'm about to leave for work." she advised.

"Coffee?" John offered.

"Water, if you've got it." Mike requested. "Sorry to stop by unannounced. Figured it was better not to call or text it."

John poured himself a coffee, not bothered by Mike's statement. "What's up?"

"Heard you talking at the airport last month. The smoke runs. I got a guy in Manitoba asked me a couple month back if I could get cigarettes out here and hook him up. Didn't know anybody at the time. I reached out to him the other day. He said he was still interested. I told him it's gotta be worth it though."

John took a sip of his coffee "Yeah. I can help ya. What's he looking for?"

"I'm new to this, man. Help me out." Mike replied.

"Okay, most people buying large quantities will buy by the case. A case is $1,800. There's fifty cartons in a case. Sell 'em at $50 a carton. That's $2,500. Buy a case, flip it. He'll make $700 a case." John explained.

"He's saying he can get $80 a carton. Store brands are $140. Says he can sell the $80 cartons all day long." Mike advised.

"OK, so that's $2,200 per case in profit. He buys ten cases a month that's $22,000 dollars, cash every month." John calculated quickly.

The numbers made sense to Mike. That's why John was making so much working with Caleb. A big U-Haul could easily hold a couple hundred cases. Maybe a thousand. At the initial price John quoted that could be $700,000 a truck load. "How much do you need to make it worth your while?" Mike asked.

"With the guys I'm dealing with now, my brother and I each get $10,000 cash every three weeks. I'm meeting them tomorrow. But they offered it. If you're boy is looking, I'll charge an extra $100 per case. You should charge a couple hundred per case for yourself. I don't care if he buys one or a hundred. Its free money to me." John quipped.

"What about the heat?" Mike asked.

John laughed "That's for you white devils to worry about. I can sell them to anybody I want to. Amanda manages a smoke shop down the road. I'm telling you now though, I supply, hell I'll help load the motherfucking truck. But I don't leave the Rez, anybody buying from us, they pick it up on the Rez. That's nonnegotiable for me. If I get caught leaving the Rez with them, I can get in shit."

Mike nodded. "Okay. What do you do, meet somewhere?"

John shrugged. "Wife's smoke shop." He took a sip of his coffee and added, "Eh, Mike. If he ain't willing to pick them up here, don't do it. I know a lot of guys got jail time for driving truckloads of smokes off the Rez. Be the middleman, not the delivery man."

Mike nodded again. Without realizing it, John gave Mike a way out of the deal without sending up any red flags. "You working?" Mike asked.

"Naw, with this smoke thing going on I'm going to take the winter off. I'll see what it's like in the spring. I ain't working in the cold if I don't have to." John replied.

The two shook hands and Mike went back to his truck. He didn't care about the cigarette hustles. He'd heard the radio ads run by the government and police agencies, claiming that running cigarettes off the reserves was funding organized crime. He didn't buy it. Mike and just about everybody he knew understood it was nothing more than the government seeing a lot of dollars trading hands that they were not able to tax the shit out of to line their own pockets. He also felt they should be more concerned with taxing Walmart and Costco into paying their fair share instead of bothering hardworking First Nations people, but he wasn't going to hold his breath for that to happen either.

Mike now had a game plan. There was a cop looking for him with limited information. Mike was willing to hedge his bets that since the deal was still on for tomorrow and John never mentioned Caleb or that one of the guys was arrested, that the cop was in on the deal. This also meant that those truckloads of cigarettes weren't going anywhere but a police evidence locker. If that was the case, he'd warn John right away and let him know the buyer was a cop, giving him time to stash the money. If the police were spending that kind of money on an investigation, they'd be coming back for every cent they could find when it was done.

Chapter 30
Monday January 9th, 2023, 9:12 am.
Hamilton, Ontario

Steve woke up to the sound of his phone ringing. The time on the front illuminated a bright 9:12 am. He had sixteen missed calls. His head was splitting, there was vomit on the floor beside his bed and on his shirt. He remembered leaving the mall and going back to The Outlander to see if Carrie was working. She wasn't so he started drinking. He vaguely remembered being thrown out. And driving home. His phone rang again "dad".

"Hello," Steve croaked.

"Where the fuck are you?" Karl yelled.

"Huh?"

"Parent! Get your ass up."

Steve coughed holding the phone away from his head. "On my way," he groaned and hung up.

An hour and a half later he walked into the board room, carrying a coffee and wearing sunglasses. He flopped down in the seat across from Sue Blenkhorn and Karl. They both stared at him. Sue shook her head. "That's it. We're pulling him out."

"Oh, hey. Come on," Steve protested. "I had a late night. I'm sorry."

"What do you think this is, a college midterm?" Karl barked. "We have almost a dozen police services tied up in this and you show up two hours late and drunk!"

"I was working all goddamn weekend, last night included. I was trying to lock down a pill supplier. I was friendly with a dealer and ended up waiting at the bar until 2:00 am. The guy never showed," Steve lied.

"Who gives a fuck about pills!" Blenkhorn cut in. "We have a meeting with a supplier coming up and you're nickel-and-diming a pill pusher?"

"I'm not seeing him until Wednesday. I have the cigarette buy with those savages tomorrow. And where do you think these junkies that are dying in the streets start? It's the pills."

"Fuck the pills!" Karl yelled as he slammed his fist on the table. "Get your head out of your ass or you're done. Do you understand that?"

"Yes SIR" Steve snapped back. He took a sip of his coffee. "So what's the plan for Wednesday?"

"Let's start with tomorrow," Blenkhorn began, trying to ease the tension. As much as she didn't like Parent, if they lost him or pulled him, the entire operation would be a waste. "Where are you meeting?"

"Same place," Steve answered. "I tried asking them to meet in Hamilton. Even offered to kick up their share. They flat out refused."

"We can arrest them if they drive off the reserve. They won't risk it," Karl affirmed.

"I tried everything: more money, told them I can't get there, told them my driver got spooked last time. This guy won't budge. We pick them up on Six Nations territory and drive them off ourselves, or we don't have a deal," Steve advised.

"Okay, continue as planned. We can try and go back on them later," conceded Blenkhorn. "Now, let's talk about Wednesday. What is the plan?"

"I have to go back to Togo's on Wednesday. I don't know what time. I call them tomorrow when I have the money and they'll give me the time," Steve explained.

Karl and Sue looked at each other, Karl asked "Can we get Niagara Police on the phone right now?" Sue was already dialing.

"What's the problem?" Steve inquired.

"Once the deal is done, they may ask you to come right away, a day early. We won't have time to set up. They might be planning to catch you off guard," Karl advised. Sue was on the phone telling whoever she'd called to bump everything ahead on their end to tomorrow morning instead of Wednesday. She rung off and looked at Karl.

"Hamilton Police and their drones will start surveillance tonight, six-hour rotations until we're done Wednesday." She turned to Steve. "What time are you meeting tomorrow?"

"Noon," Steve replied.

"Okay, do we need a unit ready for that?" she asked.

"No, these guys are harmless. I wouldn't bother with this deal. But if word gets out that we didn't pick up and I still show up there with cash, it'll set off some alarms. I don't know if they're intertwined at all." Steve paused before asking, "Where are we with Caleb?"

"He plead guilty to possession for the purpose of trafficking. The crown agreed to six months on the condition that he signs an affidavit that the Scotsman was his supplier. He's been fast-tracked through. He's in court today for sentencing," Karl advised.

"So, it's a done deal? He doesn't need to testify?" Steve was surprised.

"Nope. He already signed. We'll have to add the Scotsman's name when we find it, but that's it," Karl concluded.

"How many other crimes did he cop to?" Steve inquired.

"Quite a few actually. A lot of smuggling, some dealing, fencing stolen property. There got to be about two dozen." Karl said.

Steve sighed, then stood up. "Okay, are we done?" Neither Karl nor Sue responded immediately. He started towards the door when Blenkhorn stopped him.

"Constable Parent," she began. "This is it. No more last chances. If you slip again, you're done." He chose not to reply and left the room.

Steve took the elevator to the parking garage and found his truck. He'd left in such a hurry this morning he didn't realize the front passenger side was smashed up. He stopped and looked at it for a few seconds, then remember he'd driven home so drunk that he'd dozed off and woke up when he hit a parked car. He cursed the damage and jumped in the driver's seat.

He stopped at the liquor store and jumped on the highway heading back to Hamilton. He needed a shower and wanted to find that Sasha bitch. She would lead him to her oversized boyfriend and the stollen cash. Drinking a tall can of bud-light with one hand and scrolling through his phone, he found the company she worked for and dialed the number.

"ADJ Construction," a lady's voice with an eastern European accent answered.

"Hi, this is Constable Steve Parent with the Ontario Provincial Police. I'm looking to contact one of your employees, Sasha Horvat?"

"Please wait," she replied, then put him on hold without waiting for a response. He waited a few seconds, then a polite woman's voice came back on.

"Carly speaking."

"Hi Carly. Constable Parent with the OPP. I'm looking to contact one of your employees. A Sasha Horvat."

"Oh no! Is Sasha okay?" Carly sounded concerned.

"Yes, she's fine, as far as we know. We're just looking to speak with her. Is she in the office today?"

"Office?" Carly asked, puzzled. "Sasha doesn't work in the office. Sasha's an equipment operator."

"Sasha Horvat?" It was Steve's turn to be puzzled. "The one I'm looking for is female. Works part time as a bartender. Pretty girl."

"That's her," Carly confirmed. "She's a heavy equipment operator. She's off for the season right now."

"Do you have a number for her?" inquired Steve.

"No, we don't. Most of our field level workers start checking in around the middle of March to see when we can hire them back. Nine times out of ten they check in with new phone numbers, especially at the start of the season," Carly lied.

"We'll if you needed to contact her right now. How would you do it?" Steve asked, irritation creeping into his voice.

"Mail her a letter?" Carly suggested. Steve was silent and Carly added, "If I hear from her, I'll tell her you're looking for her."

"Yeah, thanks," Steve hung up, frustrated. "Fuck!" he cursed and threw his phone down. It bounced off the seat and fell on the floor in front of the passenger seat. He cursed again and tried to lean down to pick it up. The truck swerved causing Steve to spill his beer on his lap. A big semi blew its horn as he drifted in front of it, almost getting rear ended. "Fucking bitch!" He cursed her again. "I'll get that fucking bitch, I swear it," he promised himself.

Chapter 31
Tuesday January 10th, 2023, 7 am.
Ohsweken, Ontario

Mike got up early again. He drove out to the barn, picked up the Charger, and grabbed the spotter scope from the gun safe on the ground level. He also grabbed a duffle bag with a couple small GPS trackers, a fall harness, and some heavy-duty winter clothes.

The Native territory was set up almost like a grid. The roads running east to west were Lines; First Line, Second Line and so on. The north to south roads were named after various indigenous tribes: Cayuga, Mohawk, New Credit, Ojibway. The Six Nations Territory was demographically the largest native territory in Canada with a population of around 27,000 people and was the only territory in North America with representatives of all six Haudenosaunee nations living together. They include the Cayuga, Mohawk, Onondaga, Oneida, Seneca and Tuscarora and a few Lenape. Many of the residents relied on the tobacco industry for their bread and butter. Mike often thought some of the hardest working men and woman he'd ever known came from this territory.

Mike loaded the bag into the Charger and set off for a radio tower not far away. He pulled up and idled at the gate. Using an electric rake, he popped the padlock on the chain link fence. He had done this before. He parked the car out of sight from the road and locked the gate behind him. He slipped into the bulky winter gear, pulling his large harness over top, and started climbing the ladder of the 400-foot tower.

His harness was a ADELP class, designed for working on towers. What set it apart from other fall harnesses was the large sturdy plank attached across the butt of the person wearing it. When the worker was in position, they would throw a positioning lanyard made of heavy static rope over a piece of steel attaching on either side to rings at the wearer's waist. This allowed the worker to sit on the plank and dangle off the tower. They were also used to repel down a building if needed.

He clipped a small tool bag to his belt. Inside he kept a few big burnt-out lightbulbs in case he got caught. He could say he worked for a small telecommunications company and his job today was to come out and swap a couple bulbs. Often, what started as a multimillion-dollar telecommunications company being awarded a maintenance contract was sold and resold so many times that eventually Uncle Bob's Back Yard Light Bulb Emporium would be the group that did the actual climbing.

Mike attached a rope grab, or a piece of safety equipment that clipped the ring on the chest of his harness to the steel safety cable that ran vertically up and down the ladder. The rope grab was designed to allow the wearer to climb up and down a ladder safely. If the worker lost their footing, the mechanical device would lock in place preventing the worker from falling before the fall happens. Mike clipped on and started to climb. At six foot five, two hundred and fifty pounds plus winter gear and a tool bag, it was a slow and long climb. He would climb each fifty-foot section and engage the rope grab, allowing him to lean back and rest his arms that were on fire from the climb.

At four hundred feet the wind was hard, and the air was bitter cold. Mike had dressed in layers. He was still feeling the early morning chill, but he could manage it.

Each tower had a set of angle iron knee braces in three locations with guy wires going back to the ground for stability referred to as a star buckle. Mike got to the bottom of the star buckle and threw his positioning lanyard over. He sat in his harness and got comfortable.

To help the time pass he popped in ear buds and started listening to the latest Lucas Davenport Novel by John Sandford. As the sun rose over the horizon, he could see John Sarsen's house. Using his spotting scope, he could see both cars were still in the driveway. Bundled up and trying to think warm thoughts, he sat back and waited.

About thirty minutes later, he saw what looked like movement. Using his scope, he saw both John and Amanda leaving at the same time. He followed them on their trek, even as they drove at 80km/hr. At this height and distance, it barely looked like they were moving.

He followed Amanda's car about for three kms until it arrived at a small plaza. Mike could clearly read the sign which read, "Howling Wolf Tobacco." He watched Amanda pull in.

The scope was great. If he held it steady enough, he could read the license plate on her car. He looked for John's truck and saw it again. He continued to follow it until it turned off left and he lost it behind some trees. He sat back and waited, keeping an eye on the front of the Tobacco shop.

Another twenty minutes passed, and Mike saw a big orange and white U-Haul heading towards the store. He watched it pull in.

Looking through his scope, Mike watched as John jumped out of the passenger seat. Two pickups pulled in behind them. The first was black. A guy that had to be John's brother jumped out of it. The second was an older model with the front-end passenger side smashed up.

Mike kept the scope on the second truck. He saw the driver step out. It was the undercover cop. He was wearing a black Carhart work coat, with a red flannel shirt underneath, blue jeans, and black boots. His nose and eyes were still a mess of bruising. The cop opened the big roll-up door on the back of the truck and watched as John and the other two men started loading boxes into the back.

Mike kept his lens on the cop. He knew he had seen him before, even before Caleb's house. He couldn't put his finger on it, but he was sure he had seen him somewhere. It didn't matter, Mike thought to himself. He'd have plenty of time to figure it out later. For now, he put the scope away, clipped the rope grab onto the steel cable, undid his positioning lanyard, and started his decent down the ladder.

Thankfully gravity worked in his favor on the way down, and in less than seven minutes he was on the ground stripping off the layers. At the 10-minute mark, he pulled the gate shut, locked it and sped off towards the tobacco store.

Mike coasted past the store doing 80km an hour. All three trucks were still there. He pulled in at another tobacco store across the street and waited. The sheer number of smoke shops on the territory was staggering. It seemed like every other property had a stand set up. Mike ran inside. He bought a lighter so the owner didn't complain, and hurried back to his car, He mimed being on the phone, but used the camera to snap a few pictures of the cop and his truck. He was having a hard time getting the plate number. It didn't really matter, he only needed it for his own verification, and the smashed up front end would do for now.

It didn't take long before the door on the U-Haul was rolled down. The driver pulled out and drove off. John, his brother, and the cop stood in the parking lot talking. Mike watched as the cop got in his truck and drove off away from him. Mike waited a few seconds and then followed at a distance. The truck drove to the end of the Line, turned left and started heading towards Hamilton.

Mike waited at the intersection, allowing a few cars to get between them, then carried on following. He didn't worry too much about being spotted right now. This road ran straight into Hamilton, and even if the truck turned off before then, it wouldn't look suspicious if Mike followed him. It was a busy highway and a main artery between Six Nations and Hamilton with only a few intersections. Mike would have to do something spectacular to draw attention to himself at this point in the drive.

Mike followed the truck into the city, watching as it pulled into a parking lot outside a liquor store. He parked the Charger and watched the cop get out of his truck and walk inside. Mike hopped out of the car, walked to the truck and placed a small magnetic GPS tracker under the truck bed. Once he was sure it was in place, he got back in the Charger and left.

Mike returned the Charger to the barn and picked up his truck. He drove by James's farmhouse. The car had moved but was parked in the same spot facing the opposite direction. Mike returned home. Using an old burner phone, he logged into the wi-fi and pulled up the app for the GPS tracker. He set the phone on the windowsill and started emptying out his bedroom to paint it before Sasha got off work.

Chapter 32

Tuesday January 10th, 2023, 11 am. Hamilton, Ontario

Steve walked into the liquor store, bought Twelve tall cans of Bud Light and a bottle of spiced rum. He got back in his truck and called Karl.

"Sampson," the voice on the phone barked.

"Smokes are done," Steve advised. "Let me know when I can call Stebar."

"Call you back in five" Karl said and hung up.

Steve cracked a beer and immediately drank half the can, hoping it would help with his headache. The phone rang a few minutes later. The caller ID said, "Dad."

"Go ahead," Steve answered.

"You're good" Karl replied and hung up.

Steve called the number for Stebar. The call was answered on the third ring. The same deep voice grunted, "Yeah."

"Supposed to call today," Steve said.

"Same place. 2:30 am. Tonight." The voice hung up.

Steve's phone rang right away. Karl again.

"You got that?" Steve asked.

"Yeah. We're on it. How soon can you get back here?" Karl was referring to the Toronto office.

"Hour and a half. Two hours maybe," Steve replied.

"OK. Hurry up," Karl directed and hung up.

Fifty minutes later, Steve made his way down the hallway and stopped outside the conference room door. He could hear Sue Blenkhorn and Karl talking to what he assumed was another large scattering of faces on the large TV.

"I have reservations about his abilities, if I'm being completely honest," he heard a voice from the TV say.

"Yes, he's problematic. But he's good at what he does," Karl defended.

"Call a spade a spade," Blenkhorn retorted. "He's good at what he does because he's a piece of shit. If he wasn't working for us, he'd still be hanging out in the same bars dealing with the same dirtbags."

At that moment, Hardeep the technician walked out the door in a hurry. He stopped and looked at Steve, a look of shame crossing his face. He put his head down and scurried away. Steve continued to listen.

Blenkhorn continued, "At this point we are way too far in to stop. If we pull him now, we'll never make contact again. I don't like him anymore then you do, but for now we're stuck with him."

Steve chose that moment to walk into the room. "Sounds like a real fuck up. Who are we talking about?" He gave an exaggerated grin as he plopped down in a chair. Both Sue and Karl looked guilty, like they were caught with their hands in the cookie jar. Steve chanced a look at the screen. The same old white men, looking uncomfortable. "No, please. Don't let me interrupt," he insisted. "Who are we talking about? We don't need a loose cannon like that around here. He could fuck everything up." Bitterness was creeping into his voice.

Steve waited for a second, then continued. "No? Nothing eh? Just going to sit there on your fat white asses." Steve looked directly at Blenkhorn.

The silence was deafening. Steve dropped the sarcasm. "These guys don't keep bankers' hours. They don't follow the rules you've set out. If they did, then none of us would be sitting here. I'm going to propose that all of you," Steve hadn't taken his eyes off Blenkhorn, "be ready to support me. And come in when I need it. And until then keep your goddamn opinions to yourself. The more support you give me now, the better your fat, bloated faces will look when you're all on TV sucking each other off and taking credit for doing nothing."

With his speech finished, Steve got up and walked out of the room. Karl followed him down the hallway, yelling for his attention, He finally caught up to him at the elevators.

"What the hell was that?" Karl asked furiously.

"Might ask you the same thing," Steve snapped back. "You cocksuckers left me in the inferno last year, watching kids-- they were kids-- getting abused while you all sat back doing nothing. Looking to build a bigger case so you could pat yourselves on the back. Now you're doing it again. You pulled me into this. Now you sit quietly looking at your palms while that cunt trash-talked me?"

Karl stared at him, unable to reply. Steve continued, "I'm here because I'll get you the results you want. So let me do my job. Are we busting them tomorrow or not?"

Karl looked down at his shoes, giving an answer without saying a word. It hit Mike like a punch to the gut. "Oh, for fuck sakes. You want multiple buys, don't you. Going for an organized crime charge instead?"

"We need to send a message, Steve. With trafficking, they'll be out in seven years." Karl haphazardly explained.

Steve stared at him with complete disgust. "As opposed to the eight they'll serve with organized crime attached?" he asked sarcastically.

The elevator dinged and the door opened. Steve took a breath and shook his head. "Call me when everything is in place. I'm not driving back up here. These meetings are pointless. You assholes are going to do what you want to anyway." He stepped into the elevator.

"Hey, wait a minute," Karl protested as the door closed, but Steve refused to listen. He rode the elevator in a stony silence until the doors opened up to the lobby. He left the building, got back in his truck, cracked another beer and drove back to Hamilton. He had time to kill before his meeting tonight, and he figured he'd find that bitch Sasha.

An hour later he pulled up in front of her apartment. The front walkway looked shoveled. He stepped around to the side of the house, seeing the small wooden stairs that would bring him to her door. The snow was fresh and had no footprints. She hadn't used the stairs in a couple days. He cursed her again and started back for his truck when he heard someone ask, "Can I help you?"

Steve looked over and saw an older woman standing on the porch of the front unit. "Hi. I'm looking for Sasha. Does she live here?" he inquired.

"Who are you?" the lady scrutinized his bruised face suspiciously.

"I'm Constable Stephen Parent with the Ontario Provincial Police. I just need to ask her a few questions." He walked over and pulled out his badge.

Sophie looked at the badge, then at him. "What happen to your face?"

He pointed to the front end of his truck and explained, "Car accident last week. Hit my nose on the steering wheel." He smiled sheepishly, hoping she was buying his bullshit. He needed to move things along or he was going to get nowhere with this old lady. "Is Sasha here, or do you know where I can find her?"

"I think she at her boyfriend's," Sophie advised in what Steve was detecting as a slight French accent.

"Do you know where that is? Or how I can contact her?" Steve probed. He knew from his experience working up north that the Yakuza and Mafia had nothing on old French women when it came to keeping your mouth shut when dealing with police.

"I don't know," she replied. "If I see her, I tell her you're here looking for her."

Steve was ready to leave when he saw another lady marching across the street with purpose.

"Can I help you?" she demanded.

Steve identified himself again and explained why he was there. The lady asked to see his badge. He showed her. She spent a few seconds inspecting it, then asked, "Why are you looking for Sasha, she hasn't done anything wrong."

"Ma'am I can't discuss an open investigation. Sasha may have seen something, and we need to speak to her, that's all." Steve said.

"Is this about the fight here last week?" the woman inquired.

Steve considered the night at The Outlander and shook his head no. Suddenly his head snapped up. "Wait. The fight here? There was a fight here last week?"

The lady who introduced herself as Linda explained, "Yes, the tenant in the back was threatening Sophie. Sasha and her boyfriend put a stop to it."

"Is he a large man?" Steve asked, his mind racing. "Bigger than I am?"

"Yes." Linda confirmed. "The police already told him he wasn't in trouble."

Steve's ears perked up. He thanked both woman and ran back to his truck. He called Hamilton police on his personal cell and asked for Detective Nguyen. He waited on hold. After a few minutes the call was answered. "Nguyen".

"Jason! Steve Parent, OPP."

"Hey, what can I do for you?" Nguyen asked.

"Listen. I'm working on something here. I think you can help. Last week sometime, Hamilton Police responded to a fight between neighbors on the," Steve looked out the window to confirm the address. "1100 block of Campbell Ave. I need the names and addresses of the people involved."

"How soon do you need this?" Nguyen inquired.

"ASAP," Steve replied. "This may be the missing piece to my puzzle. Call this number. It'll be on all day." Steve gave him his personal cell number and rung off. "Got ya, bitch," he said to himself, thinking about how good it would feel to beat the shit out of her asshole boyfriend and get the money back as he drove away.

Chapter 33

Tuesday January 10, 2023, 11 am.
Hamilton, Ontario

Mike had been monitoring the GPS on his burner phone. He watched the cop pull up at Sasha's apartment. It didn't surprise him. The cop had found out where Sasha worked, he would have figured out where she lived. Mike sent Sasha a text that said, "Call me please."

Ten minutes later his phone rang.

"Hey, what's up?" she asked.

"Your cell phone. Is it on a plan or pay as you go?" he inquired.

"Not sure it's in ADJ's name." she replied.

"Okay, good enough." He seemed satisfied.

"Why?"

"That cop was at your place. I was wondering if he'd be able to watch your phone. But if it's not in your name, it's all good," he explained.

"Wait, how did you know he was at my place?" she asked.

"Maybe let's not ask questions we don't really want the answers to." He half-joked.

"Okay, we need to have a serious talk tonight," she advised.

"Ugh. Fine," he sighed with a small smile. He knew he owed her some sort of explanation. "See you after work."

Mike had finished the first and second coat of paint in the bedroom. Now he needed to let it dry. He figured he'd kill time by going for a jog. The cardio was good in the cold air, and he always did his best thinking while on a run. He dressed in winter running clothes and set out on the trail down the road from his house. He jogged at a steady pace. No music, just his thoughts. The cop was still looking for him. He obviously didn't know who Mike was yet. The cop was going around in circles. Mike had enough info on the cop to make his investigation difficult, at least with Sarsens. But he could always use a little more.

Mike had made the cop, and the cop didn't know it yet. That was a big advantage. Uncle Ken had previously taught Mike the importance of capitalizing on such an advantage. And Mike was sure he had seen the cop before. He tried thinking about where, when, and how he's seen him. He pictured the cop standing in the parking lot at the cigarette store. There was something so familiar about it. Like when the answer is right on the tip of your tongue but it won't come out.

Mike jogged along. He kept picturing the cop in his black coat and red flannel shirt. He stopped in his tracks. The red flannel shirt. Mike had seen a picture of that same cop in a red flannel shirt last year when the human trafficking raids happened. He was on front page of several newspapers, escorting a young girl from a crime scene. Mike turned around and ran at a full sprint back home. He needed to find that picture.

Mike flew up the steps to his house and crashed through his door. He grabbed his cellphone, looking for anything he could find on the human trafficking story. Mike was familiar with the case. He'd killed an Asian motel owner who had worked out a plea deal that saw him not only avoid jail time but also keep his business running. Mike hated the thought of that.

The man had peddled in the rape and torture of young girls and got off clean. Sure, he got probation, but what did that mean? It meant all he had to do was lie to a university graduate who had no idea what life was like outside their own small world. It meant he could continue to abuse children, only this time be more careful about it.

Mike followed the man and his wife home one night. He broke into their house at 1:30 am while they slept. When the man got up around 2:45 am to use the bathroom, Mike crept in behind him and shot him in the back of the head with a pistol he'd taken off a drug dealer in Toronto the year before. When the man's wife ran out the room screaming, Mike punched her in the face, twice. He held her from behind and shot her in the head with the same gun. He placed the gun in her hand and was pleased a few days later to read in the newspaper that the local OPP detachment had reported a murder/suicide in their area.

After a few minutes of scrolling, Mike found what he was looking for. It was a picture of the same undercover cop with a young girl who had been rescued from a motel room about an hour and a half north of Toronto. The beard was scruffier now, and he looked less like a homeless man in the photo. But Mike was 100% sure this was the same cop.

Sasha got home from work. Mike had dinner ready. They ate, she showered, and when she came back downstairs drying her hair she sat down. "Okay, we need to talk."

"Shit, are we there already?" Mike joked half-heartedly. "It's only two weeks."

Sasha sat on the couch holding Domino, who gave a little growl and nipped an Mike's elbow. "Let's be honest. Yes it's been two weeks. I've watched you beat up three people and you have a cop after you."

"Well in fairness, it was three people but only two occasions, and both were for you. I might like to ask how many more people in your circle I'm going to have to fight," Mike retorted with a hint of a smile.

Sasha looked at him and smiled in spite of herself. "Okay. That's fair. I'll give you that. But that cop scares me. First, he shows up at the bar with his face looking pretty messed up. Then today you told me he was at my house. What happened, and how did you know that? And please don't lie. I like you. I like what we're doing. But not if you lie to me." Her eyes were pleading. Mike couldn't bear to let her down, but knew he had to be careful how much he told her.

Mike let out a big sigh. "Okay, yes, he's a cop. I don't know if he's a crooked cop, but he's definitely a piece of shit. He got out of line one night and I hit him. Once. That was it. I didn't know he was a cop until later." Mike conveniently left out that he just happened to be robbing a drug dealer when he hit the cop.

Sasha nodded. The cop had after all left The Outlander that night and beat her name out of two people. And he was a total asshole when he confronted her at work. If he'd been acting like that at another bar and Mike saw it, she could easily see the big man intervening. "How do you know he was at my place today?" She repeated.

Mike pulled out his burner phone with the map showing. A little pig icon was on the map. "That's him. At least, that's his truck". He turned the phone to her.

She looked for a second, then realizing what she was looking at, exclaimed "Woah, What the fuck? How did you-?"

"I followed him after I found out he was looking for me. It wasn't hard. He's an idiot. I put a little tracker on his truck. He was parked at your place for about ten minutes today." Mike explained.

Sasha stared at him and asked, "Who the fuck follows the police?"

"People who get harassed by them." Mike answered. "Okay, full disclosure; my dad was a cop. I know how these guys can be. He doesn't have anything on me. He isn't going to arrest me for punching him. That would open a can of worms he doesn't want opened. I have the tracker on him to see if or when he comes near me. I don't doubt he would try to plant something on me. He'll get tired of chasing me soon enough. Someone else will piss him off in a few days and he'll start bothering them." Sasha seemed to understand. Mike added. "I'm sorry this came to your doorstep. He doesn't know who I am so he thinks he can get to me through you. I really am sorry. But he'll go away soon."

She handed the phone back and asked, "How long is the tracker good for?"

"Couple days," he replied. "I have a bunch of them. They're cheap. If he's parked in the morning, I'll swap it out with another one."

"You aren't like, following me, are you?" Sasha looked a little uncomfortable.

"Not unless you try to have me arrested for something I didn't do." Mike replied.

Sasha seemed to accept his answer. She took a deep breath. "Okay, let's go put the bedroom back together.

Mike knew she couldn't stay with him forever. He also knew he needed to get this cop off his back. He decided that tomorrow morning he'd start making it happen. They put the room back together, took Domino for a walk, and called it a night.

Mike awoke at 1:30 am to the sound of the tracking app on the burner phone making a ding. He went downstairs to let Sasha sleep and watched as the cop drove towards St. Catherine's.

Chapter 34

Wednesday January 11, 2023, 1 am.
Hamilton, Ontario

Steve awoke to the sound of his alarm going off. He'd picked up the money for the buy at 2:00 pm, spent most of the evening drinking, and laid down at 8:00 pm. He got up, showered and was on the road by 1:30 am. He called Karl who answered right away, also sounding like he'd just woken up.

"Are we good?" Steve asked.

"Yes. I just spoke to Hardeep. We're live. Aerial Surveillance has been up for over twenty-four hours now. The place was busy this evening. A lot of vehicle and foot traffic. Niagara Police have hours of work ahead of them, combing over video of everyone coming and going, trying to I.D. them. We have three response units in the area, although we don't know how good that'll be. We can't see or hear anything inside. Be careful in there. Call me as soon as you're done." Karl almost sounded concerned.

Steve hung up, opened a beer, and settled in for the drive to Togo's. He pulled up a block away, took the money and a chrome 1911 .45 pistol out of the bag. He looked at the pistol and smirked at the elaborately carved detail. A shiny gun with a pearl handle was something a cop would never carry. He stuck the gun in the back of his waistband and started for the bar.

He tried the door, it was locked. He banged once. A window upstairs opened, and someone yelled down, "They're closed, asshole!" and slammed the window shut. A minute later, the big blond guy from the last meeting answered the door. He let Steve in and looked both directions down the empty street. Satisfied that |Steve was alone, he closed the door behind them.

"Need to search ya," the blond brut said, stepping up behind Steve. Steve handed over his wallet, keys and cell phone, trying to have the camera show the guy's face. "Need to pat you down too."

"I have a gun in the small of my back," Steve admitted.

"And why do you have that?" The big guy inquired, his face flashing anger.

"Because I just walked through this shithole city with $130,000 cash in my coat, you fucking jackass. In case I needed it!" Steve snapped back.

The big guy took a step forward, and Steve took one to match him. They were standing nose to nose when Steve heard Paddy interject, "That's enough." Steve held his position. The big guy dropped Steve's affairs into a paper bag with a crinkle and sat in the corner. Steve wondered how much the idiot was paid for this job.

He looked at Paddy and asked, "Where's the man?"

"What man?" Paddy answered.

Steve walked to the bar and sat down. He took the bag of money from his coat and the gun from his waistband and set them both on the bar. "We good then?" he asked.

Paddy walked behind the bar, sat on a stool, emptied the bag and quietly started counting.

"A beer would be lovely," Steve felt there was no point in being subtle.

Paddy looked up with an irritated glare, put the counted money back on the pile and started over.

Steve sat quietly looking around the bar. It was a typical shithole bar in a shithole town, he thought. He paid close attention to the area behind the bar and in the corners. He would need to double check on the way out, but he didn't see any cameras in here at all.

It took Paddy just under twenty minutes to count everything. He said nothing, disappeared into the back room, and came back out with a medium-sized Foot Locker bag. He handed it to Steve, then sat down behind the bar.

"What'll ya have then?" Paddy asked.

Steve had a beer and a shot of Jameson's. They made small talk. Paddy was actually a pretty decent guy once business was done. Steve finished his drinks and got up, the big guy still glaring as he handed Steve's belongings back and lead him out.

"Have a good night." Steve waved as the heavy steel door slammed in his face. He looked around for a second and noticed several cameras pointing towards the entrance, but there had been none inside. He got in his truck, stopped at the first McDonalds he saw that was open twenty-four hours, Got out and called Karl from his personal phone.

"Nobody was near your truck." Karl answered.

"OK, Great."

"Come to the office in the Morning." Karl instructed. |We'll go over your things."

"Have Hardeep come to Hamilton," Steve answered. "That drive is killing me."

Karl was silent for a few seconds and replied "Hardeep said he'll come now. He's here and there no traffic. He'll meet you in Hamilton at Main Street and the 403 in forty-five minutes."

"Good enough," Steve conceded.

"How did it go in there?" Karl inquired.

"The Scotsman wasn't there. It was just his two goons. Minimal conversation. Had a beer after he counted the money. There are no cameras inside, but I have an idea on how to get one in there." Steve said.

"I'm listening." Karl sounded intrigued.

"I'll take care of it. You'll want plausible deniability. But get someone onto the Niagara fire department. We'll get them called in. Our guy can install it while everyone is outside." Steve instructed.

Karl was silent again, Steve hated when he was silent. Finally, Karl asked, "When?"

"I'll get back to you. Soon though. I'm taking tomorrow and Friday off. I need to deal with my ex-wife's bullshit," Steve advised.

"Check in on Friday around noon." Karl instructed, and hung up.

Steve met Hardeep off the highway as planned. He handed over his phone, keys, and wallet. The keys and wallet were simple to check. Hardeep plugged Steve's phone into his laptop, performed a scan and handed it back. "Clean," he said.

Steve handed over the drugs. They both signed for it to preserve the chain of custody. A few minutes later Hardeep was back on the highway to Toronto while Steve drove past Sasha's again. Still no footprints. It was 4:34 am nothing was open, so he went home and slept.

Chapter 35

Wednesday January 11, 2023, 4:40 am.
Hamilton, Ontario

Mike and Sasha both woke up before the sun when her alarm went off.

"Why is that so early today?" Mike groaned.

Sasha's smiling face emerged from the blankets. "Where's his truck?"

Mike gave her a puzzled look then grabbed his burner phone. "He left around 1:30 am and went to St. Catherine's. He's…" Mike looked closer at his app, "looks like he's back in Hamilton, heading towards home, assuming that's where he's been staying."

Sasha took the phone, placed it on the bedside table and kissed Mike, pulling him on to her.

At 5:25am she came out from the shower and asked, "He parked?"

Mike checked again "Yup. Been there for about twenty minutes."

"Do you have another tracker?" She asked. He nodded, and she said "Let's go. I'll put it on his truck."

"You don't need to get involved," he cautioned.

"Fuck that guy. He threatened me and hurt Leonard. He's lucky I don't firebomb him." Sasha looked pissed, even in the pre-dawn light.

Mike stared at her making sure he'd heard her correctly. "Okay, let's go."

They grabbed a sleepy Domino and worked out a game plan. Mike told her to always assume she was being filmed. The trick is to act like you belong there.

"There's a magnet on the tracker, but you have to get it somewhere they won't see it. Wheel wells are always good, especially in the winter. Twenty minutes of driving and it's covered in slush" Mike instructed.

Their plan was in place. First, they needed to see where the truck was parked. If it was in a driveway, it could be tricky to get close, and would become more difficult depending on how deep the driveway went. This morning, they were in luck; the truck was parked on the street. Mike drove up two blocks turned onto the side street. Sasha got out with her mean little dog.

Mike said, "Wait here. I'll go back to the block before his. I'll park. When I flash my lights, you jog by. We have one shot at this."

Sasha flashed her smile. "Okie dokie."

It was a residential neighborhood with many of the houses converted into duplex and triplexes. Large trees grew up and down both sides of the street and would act as a canopy for half the year. Mike turned left again, down three blocks, Made another left, to Steve's street, He made another left turn and saw Sasha three blocks away with Domino on her leash.

The two saw Mike's truck and started running. The dog, not realizing it was supposed to be a leisurely jog, was bulldogging in her harness, trying to pull Sasha down the street. Mike watched as Sasha stopped, bent down, and tied her shoe. She then continued on her jog. She made it back to the truck and hoisted Domino in. The pup had spent all the energy in her little body by running in her harness and was panting heavily, too tired to give Mike any of her usual attitude.

"Well?"

"Wheel well," she smiled.

"I didn't even see you throw it."

Sasha winked at him and asked, "Is it working?"

Mike checked his burner and signed in. it was. The battery life showed 99%.

"Yup. Usually good for forty-eight hours. In the cold more like twenty to twenty-four, but we're good. I'll swap another one this evening. If I find him in a parking lot, I'll grab the other two." He put the truck in gear and drove off.

Chapter 36

Wednesday January 11, 2023, 9:15 am.
Hamilton, Ontario

Steve was woken up by his personal phone at 9:14 am.

"Hello?"

"Parent, It's Jason Nguyen. Good morning."

"Hey, good morning. What's up?" Steve asked groggily.

"Got some information for you." Nguyen said.

"Great! Hold on, let me grab a pen." He found a pen and a piece of paper and said "Go."

"Friday December 30th, 6:22 pm. 9-11 call came in from a tenant at 1183 Campbell. He said the neighbor's boyfriend attacked him. Two units responded spoke to," Steve heard him flipping through a page, "a James Kowalski. He claimed to be the victim. Police also spoke to a Michael Wolly. Wolly claimed the other man was threatening an elderly woman, a Sophie Ruelle. Story was corroborated by a Sasha Horvat, and a neighbor across the street named Linda Vukic. All agreed that James Kowalski was the aggressor, that Sasha Horvat and Michael Wolly intervened, and that Kowalski attacked Wolly. Both responding officers noted that James Kowalski looked as if he'd been battered. Kowalski was aggressive with the officers. Wolly was calm and respectful. There's a side note in Constable Williamson's report that states that Wolly, upon questioning, openly stated he was a boxer but maintains he only defended himself and quote, 'when he stopped coming, I stopped hitting,' end quote. Does this help you?" Nguyen asked.

"Immensely!" Steve replied. "Did they get an address for Wolly?"

"They did. Addressed is listed as," Steve heard another page flip. "Huh, 3663 Guy Street, Windsor Ontario. That make sense?" Nguyen asked.

Steve thought for a second. That would explain why Sasha was in the wind. "Make's perfect sense," Steve said. "Thank you!"

He rung off and jumped out of bed. He used the bathroom, scrolling through the early morning activity on his home monitoring system while sitting on the toilet. Nothing seemed out of the ordinary. At one point while it was still dark, a girl jogged by with a small dog. She stopped and tied her shoe. Looked like she had something on her hand that she flung towards the road where his truck was parked, then continued jogging. Steve finished his business, showered, and got dressed. He hit the liquor store then got on the highway heading towards Windsor.

Highway 401 is a long, boring, and dangerous stretch of road. Fog in the spring and fall have been attributed to cause several multi-vehicle pile-ups over the years, many resulting in death tolls into the 40's and 50's. On this morning it was cold but clean and Steve was pushing his truck hard. He was excited and anxious to get to Windsor. He pulled off the highway just after 12:30 pm, stopped at a coffee shop, and punched the address into his GPS.

At 12:43 pm he pulled up in front of 3663 Guy Street. It was a small blue house with white trim. A garage in the back had a "Harley Davidson Only" parking sign above the roll up door. Steve did a walk around to the back and looked around. There was a nice deck with a hot tub with fresh tracks going to and from the patio door. He climbed the steps and looked into the kitchen window. He walked back down the steps and was heading towards the garage when a man stepped off the porch.

"Help ya?" the man inquired. He was in his mid-sixties, around six feet tall, with a medium build. He had grey hair and a moustache and was walking with a cane.

"Looking for Mike Wolly," Steve replied.

"He ain't here. Who are you," The old man asked.

"Where is he?" Steve returned the question, his frustration showing.

"I told you, he ain't here. Who the hell are you?" the old man demanded.

"Where is he?" Steve growled.

"I ain't got time for this." The old man turned to walk away. Steve rushed over and grabbed him, spinning him around.

"You stupid old bastard, where the fuck is he?" Steve snarled.

"Get your goddamn hands off me!" The old man shoved Steve back. He was older and needed a cane, but he was surprisingly a lot stronger than Steve had anticipated. Steve staggered back a step and then came forward punching the old man in the face knocking him down. Blood coming out of his mouth. He touched his lip, then looked at his hand.

"What the hell is wrong with you?" the old man shouted.

"I'm sorry," Steve countered, almost sincerely, realizing his aggressive tactics weren't getting him anywhere. "I'm looking for Mike Wolly. I was told he lives here. I need to speak with him. It's important." He reached down to help the old man up.

Swatting his hand away, the old man picked himself up and steadied himself on his cane. He reached into his pocket and pulled out some tissues and dabbed at his lip. "This is Mike's house. He comes and goes as he damn well pleases. I rent out a room," The old man explained.

"Who are you?" Steve asked.

"None of your goddamn business, that's who. Last I heard, Mike was working in Edmonton. I ain't seen him in about a year, maybe less. He was here for a few weeks last March. Been out working since then." He dabbed the blood on his lip again.

"Who does he work for?"

"You get the hell out of here. Or I'm calling the police." The old man threatened. Steve took another step forward; the old man used his cane to push him back. Steve now furious grabbed the cane and punched the old man again. And then again, knocking him to the ground a second time. He kicked the old man while he was down.

"I'm calling the police!" Steve heard a lady yell from across the street. A short stocky man in his forties was crossing the street carrying a snow shovel. His wife on the porch had her phone to her ear. Steve hopped off the porch, jumped in his truck and backed out of the driveway without looking.

Chapter 37

Wednesday January 11, 2023, 12:30 pm. Hamilton, Ontario

Mike had been watching the tracking app on his phone. He didn't think much when he saw the cop get on the highway. When the cop passed through London it had more of his attention. When he passed through Chatham Mike made the decision to call Claude.

Claude, his old boss, had been badly injured when his work truck was hit by a semi a few years before. He lost his livelihood and was relying on disability to get by. Mike offered to let Claude live in the house he'd inherited from Nick. Claude paid the utilities and his own food, but otherwise lived there for free. Mike didn't mind the old man. He kept the house clean and in the odd times Mike did find himself back in Windsor, he always had a good visit with the old guy. Claude answered on the second ring.

"Hello."

"Hey, old timer. How ya keeping these days."

"Oh. I'm doing just fine. How are you?" Claude asked.

"Not bad. Listen, I need to give you a heads up. There may be someone coming around there looking for me. A cop. Can't miss him. His face is bruised up." Mike explained.

"Are you the reason his face is bruised?" Claude asked.

"Accessory after the fact, old man," Mike responded with a smile.

Claude laughed a bit and asked, "That why he's coming here?"

"Could be," Mike admitted.

"I'll deal with him. You have nothing to worry about."

"Thanks. How are you doing? Do you need anything?" Mike offered.

"Five foot seven, slim, blond. No morals. And big tits if you have it," Claude didn't hesitate.

"Fresh out. But I'll keep my eyes open. I'll check in later" Mike laughed and rung off.

Mike watched the cop pull off the highway, stop for a few minutes, then Mike watched him drive straight towards Claude. The cop pulled up in his driveway even. Five minutes later the truck was moving again. Mike called Claude.

"Hello, again," answered Claude.

"What happened?" Mike asked, concerned.

"How did you- Never mind" Claude contradicted, realizing that Mike always seemed to be two steps ahead of everyone else. "That son of a bitch. He punched me in the face and kicked me."

Mike was silent for a few seconds. "He did what?" His tone was calm and icy.

"I tried to walk away. He grabbed me, I pushed him off, and he punched me. I got up, he punched me again a couple times then kicked me while I was on the porch. Tammy and Christopher across the street stopped him." Claude spit blood out of his mouth. "They're both here now. Boy I tell yeah if I was five years younger, I'd have taught him something."

"I don't doubt that at all." Mike took a breath. "I'm sorry Claude. I didn't think he'd hurt you."

"He didn't hurt me. My second wife hit harder." Claude laughed.

Mike said "Yeah, well. I'll teach him something for ya. Save your money. I'll cover the bills for the next few months. It's the least I can do."

"Least you can do is find me that blonde," Claude corrected.

"I'm looking, I'm looking. I'll keep an eye on this guy. Keep your phone handy. If it looks like he's coming back, I'll call you right away," Mike instructed before adding, "And thank you."

Claude whispered "He thinks you're in Edmonton. So don't go to Edmonton."

"Noted," Mike smiled and hung up.

Mike sat in his living room and stared at the wall. This cop had threatened Sasha, assaulted Leonard and now attacked a clearly disabled senior. He needed to go, and soon.

Mike spent the rest of the day painting the upstairs hallway while keeping an eye on the tracking app. He watched the truck come back up the 401.

At 3:30 pm Mike decided to let the second coat of paint dry and used that time to run out to the barn. Opening his safe, he grabbed six more small trackers. Judging from the cop's history, it was only a matter of time before he stopped at a liquor store, which would give Mike more than enough time to grab the other trackers and replace them with a new one. He closed the safe door, bounced down the stairs and froze when he saw Sasha standing in the barn.

"What-- what are you doing here?" He sputtered. He was usually so careful coming out to the barn. He checked his mirrors and had cameras all around the property, including up and down the street and facing the back so nobody could sneak up on him. If this had been a retaliation he would have been killed before he knew he'd been found.

"What is this place?" she asked with a smile on her face but a strain in her voice. Her eyes showed confusion and a little fear.

"My friend's barn, I store some things here. How did you find me here?" he asked again.

Sasha held up her phone showing the same tracking app. "What's out here Mike?" she pleaded, looking at the gun safe behind him. "Please don't lie to me." Her voice tremored slightly.

Mike was angry that she'd followed him, but he decided he'd address that later. He knew trying to turn this around on her wasn't going to work. He also knew that if she walked out, there was a chance this barn would be no good to him anymore. And if she was really pissed, the cop could find out about it.

"It used to be a small boxing club. My friend built it. I helped him coach some local kids. He's in Florida now, so I rent it out. Sometimes I come hang out. I keep stuff I don't want in my house here," he explained, trying to answer her without giving away too much.

Her eyes kept darting between him and the gun safe. "Like what's in that safe?"

Mike followed her gaze. "Yes."

"What's upstairs?" she inquired.

"Nothing really. Another safe. Some toys." he replied carefully.

"Are you seeing someone else? Or am I a side chick?" she practically choked on the words.

Mike laughed a little, "No. God no. No, I'm not seeing anybody else. Is that what this is about?"

"Something isn't right Mike," she confessed. "I like you, A lot. I feel safe with you. But something isn't adding up. I can't put my finger on it. And I'm not letting myself get hurt again."

Mike understood where she was coming from. She was a sweet girl, but in the short time they'd been seeing each other he'd learned she had been through a lot. She'd lost her parents young, dated some abusive men. Her hard shell wasn't an act, it wasn't exaggerated. She'd developed it over years of being abused. Mike could relate.

Against all his better judgement, he invited her in. "Okay. Come on up," he said as he walked up the stairs.

Sasha followed him and saw an open loft. The upstairs was finished and painted white. There was a bed at the far end, and a small room off to the side that held a stand-up shower, sink and toilet. At the front was a small kitchenette, another smaller safe, and a collection of arrows, compound bows, and cross bows. There was a large TV mounted on the wall with a couch and loveseat sitting opposite from it. Near the safe was a 32 inch screen showing multiple security camera angles that Mike had clearly ignored while he was here today. It was an open concept and just as devoid of personal touches as his place in the city.

She looked around and asked, "Can I sit?" Mike nodded and she gently sat down. She collected herself and spoke. "I love being with you. I know it hasn't been long. But I feel myself falling for you. Probably too quickly. But what's going on here doesn't work for me. From this point on, we're together or we're not. But I need full honesty from you."

Mike sat beside her and asked "Okay, what do you want to know?"

"The Windsor address." she began. "Who lives there?"

"It was my uncle's house. He left it to me when he died. Between the day he was diagnosed with cancer and the day he died was less than a year. About nine and a half months, actually. I don't like being there. It upsets me. But I can't bring myself to sell the place. So, I rent a room out to my old boss. He keeps an eye on things. If you'd like we can go there some day. There's no wife and kids hiding there."

Sasha watched his face. "What about this place? Why this one and the place in the city."

"This is where I keep things I don't want in my home. It's also a backup place to stay, like in the case of that cop. If he found my place in the city I could stay here." The words came out of his mouth before he realized it.

"How often does that stuff happen Mike?" Sasha asked, needing to know but afraid of the answer. "How can you make me feel safe while living such a chaotic life?"

Mike was speechless. He couldn't understand how this girl he'd only known for such a short time was making him feel so defenseless. She'd found him at the barn, and he'd had a slip of the tongue all within a few minutes.

"What's in the safe?" she asked.

Mike heard the words, and his heart sank. He knew this wasn't good. He was either going to have to open it, or she'd leave. He said nothing. "Mike, what's in the safe?" she repeated. Mike continued to sit in silence. As tears filled her eye, she placed her hand on his and whispered, "I'm sorry. But I need to leave now." She got up and started walking towards the stairs.

"Wait." He called after her, standing up. "If I open it, please don't freak out."

"Is it body parts?" she asked, smiling while wiping a tear away.

"No. Just. I'll show you. But don't. Ugh. Fuck." He stammered, exasperated. He walked to the safe, punched in the code, turned the handle, and paused. After a second, he opened the door. Sasha looked in.

"HOLY SHIT!" she said. looking at the stack of money. "How? How did-- how much is there?"

"About, $250,000 dollars," Mike estimated.

The realization hit her. "Where did you get that?" she asked, eyes wide.

Mike said, "I don't like banks. Too easy to track people. Some of it from work. The rest from other places."

She looked in saw a few very expensive looking cross bows, some mean looking arrows, a plastic tray with a couple dozen little GPS trackers, and what she guessed were other electronic spy devices. Her eyes focused on a picture taped to the back showing a very young Mike with a pretty, biracial girl.

"Who is that?" she asked curiously, looking back at Mike.

Mike had a look on his face she hadn't seen before, he looked sad and angry. "Tamika," he explained. "She's why I do it."

"And what's that?" Sasha asked.

"Are you sure you want to know?" he asked staring at the picture. She nodded.

"Sometimes our criminal justice system fails the victims." He left the silence hanging in the air answering the questions. Sasha looked at the cross bow's, the arrows, the knifes, the spy gadgets and she understood what he was telling her without him saying it out loud.

"What happened to her?" she asked quietly. Mike's eyes met hers. He said nothing and closed the safe door.

He turned away. "She died." He walked back toward the couch. "If you want to leave, I understand. I won't bother you. Just, please don't tell anybody about this place. Not that cop, not your friends, nobody."

Mike figured that was it. He would need to empty this place out tonight. There was nothing in the city he needed. Maybe the pictures off the fridge, but if he packed up when Sasha left, he could be at his place in the city grab the pictures and be on the highway by 6:00pm. He wouldn't bring the safe's, but it would only take a couple minutes to empty both into duffle bags.

He liked Sasha. He'd felt comfortable with her. He didn't want what they had to end. But the cards were on the table. He'd shown his hand. He flopped down on the couch, not wanting to believe how fast this had all unraveled.

Rubbing his face with both hands, he wiped his eyes and was surprised when he regained focus and saw Sasha standing in front of him. She straddled his lap facing him, took his face in her hands and kissed him.

"You won't hurt me, will you" It was much a statement as it was a question. She searched his eyes.

"Not on purpose. But I deal with assholes like that cop sometimes." He sighed and continued, "You understand, I do things that can't be undone. There are things I can't tell you, for your own benefit. I need you to understand that."

"I can handle that. Just don't lie to me. Deal?" she asked.

"Don't ask too many questions then." He retorted with a small smile. She barked out a laugh, climbed off, and sat beside him. "Are we okay?" he asked.

She smiled and answered, "Maybe. What's in the gun safe downstairs?"

"Guns."

She nodded and said "Okay, we're good then."

Chapter 38

Wednesday January 11, 2023, 12:30 pm.
403 Eastbound, Southern Ontario

Steve was racing back up the 401. Windsor had been a complete bust, and he was pissed. He took the exit from the 401 East to the 403 and settled in for the drive when his phone rang. The caller ID showed, "Dad."

"Parent," he answered, irritation in his voice.

"Where are you?" Karl asked.

"403, on my way back into Hamilton," Steve replied.

"How far out?"

"I'll be there in about thirty minutes, why?"

Karl explained, "Philip Carson was just arrested again. Another overdose."

"They dead?" Steve inquired.

"Yeah. Happened last week. Same day as the last one."

"Okay. Is Carson at the Police station?" Steve asked.

"Yes, Nguyen called. Asked if you want a crack at him," Karl advised.

"Yes. I do. I'm heading there now. Send me the list of crimes Caleb Tulk confessed too outside the city of Hamilton as well please." Steve added and rung off.

His frustration had dropped a little. He was still searching for that bitch Sasha and her boyfriend. But in the meantime, he was going to get to nail Phillip Carson and Caleb Tulk to the wall.

His phone dinged a few seconds later with an email from Karl with an attached pdf file. Steve scrolled though while driving. There had to be thirty different cases listed, the ones outside Hamilton's city limits had been highlighted yellow.

Steve pulled into the underground garage at the police station. He was buzzed in and took the elevator to the second floor. Jason Nguyen was once again waiting at the elevator doors. They shook hands and started towards the same interview room that Phillip was in last time.

"What do you have him on?" Steve inquired.

"Possession for the purpose of trafficking. He had a gun on him this time No serial numbers. And the manslaughter. He asked for you specifically." Nguyen updated Steve.

"Camera's on?" Steve asked. Again, Nguyen shook his head no "Okay be ready."

Phillip was sitting in the same chair again, wearing ridiculous clothing. Steve barged in. "Phillip, you wanted to see me?"

Phillip started and looked up. "Yeah, uh can you help me on this one?" he stuttered.

"Maybe," Steve said. "I want all your homies. Everything you know. Anything. Drugs, guns, any of your little faggot friends pimping out their girlfriends. Who you buy from when Caleb isn't around. Who in your clique is selling, who your competition is on the street. Everything."

Phillip looked at him with shock on his face. "For real, bro?"

Steve stepped forward and slapped Phillip's hat off his head. "I ain't your fucking bro, you rat piece of shit. You want my help, it comes at a price. I got your fat piggly ass out of the fire once already. That was yesterday's price. You want out again, you pay todays price. This isn't a fucking democracy; we don't put it to a vote," Steve snarled. "You want to keep operating in the street? From now on you work for me. You tell me everything I want to know every time I ask. Or you get on the bus to Millhaven tomorrow morning. Understand, porky? Now are you going to tell me what I want to hear or are you wasting my time?"

Phillip nodded his head.

Steve stepped back and banged on the door. Nguyen opened it from the outside, and Steve asked him for a note pad and a pen. Nguyen returned two minutes later. Steve looked up and saw the camera's red light was now on.

They spent the next two hours with Phillip writing out a long statement, complete with names, addresses, even birthdates for some of his associates. It included maps of where his friends stashed drugs and guns.

When they were done, Steve stood up and said, "You'll be arraigned tomorrow morning. We'll need time to get this to the crown." Phillip was staring down at the table, the gravity of the situation settling in. "Don't feel bad, porky," Steve sneered. "Most of you shitbags rat each other out for your next case of beer or bag of weed. At least you were a piece of shit to save your own bacon." He banged on the door again. A uniformed officer opened it. Steve left and headed straight to Nguyen's desk.

"Here," he announced as he dropped the statement on his desk.

The detective looked at it. His eyes bugged out of his head as he skimmed the pages. "Holy shit," he exclaimed, flipping through the document. "This is a blueprint to everything. What are we asking the crown for in exchanged?"

Steve laughed. "Nothing." Nguyen looked at him, confused. Steve added "I didn't make a deal. I went in told him I wanted everything. He assumed I was going to help him."

Nguyen stared agape. Steve continued, "Hit him with everything, see what sticks. Either way, the fat little fucker is going to the penn. Keep things under your hat though, Barton Street leaks like a sieve. If word gets out that Carson's a rat, that list is worth nothing to you."

The detective hopped out of his seat smiling and shook Steve's hand. "Thank you. Shit I owe you one."

"No, we're even now," Steve said and started walking away. He stopped and asked, "Can you print something off for me?"

Twenty Minutes later Steve walked through the front door at the Barton Street jail. He was processed again and lead to another small room with a small window in the door. He looked in and saw Caleb sitting at the table wearing a large blue padded Velcro mumu.

"What the fuck is he wearing?" Steve snorted to the guard.

"He's on suicide watch," the guard replied with an expressionless face.

Steve walked in the room Caleb lifted his head and a look of defeat crossed his face. "Hey Caleb, nice duds. New fashion statement?" Steve teased as he sat down. "Oh, come on, I'm joking with ya. I got some good news, some really good news."

"What's that?" Caleb asked, his voice barely a whisper.

"Well. That fat fuck Phillip Carson just gave us everything. Again. That kid, I tell ya. Just the thought of coming in here, he pisses himself and stars singing like a choir girl," Steve chortled.

Steve pulled out a piece of paper and placed it in front of Caleb. "Take a look at all the yellow highlighted ones."

Caleb reached out with handcuffs on and took the page. He looked at it, trying to make sense of what it was.

Steve saw Caleb's expression and explained, "Those? Those are all charges we're slapping on you. Some good ones there. That home invasion? Right there?" Steve tapped at the page. "With your record, that's good for what, ten years?" Caleb looked up in complete disbelief.

"What is this?" he asked, incredulously. "You said all other charges, known or unknown."

Steve smiled. "In the city of Hamilton. The home invasion was in Toronto. Toronto isn't Hamilton. This one right here, selling guns?" he pointed again. "That's good for five. We have another manslaughter to add on too. Porky had a couple people die off his shit. Signed another statement, swearing he sold it in the street as he got it from you."

Caleb looked up at him speechless. Steve asked, "Who does the Scotsman get his shit from?"

"I want to see my daughter." Caleb stammered.

"Tell me what I want to know, and I'll arrange it. Who does the Scotsman get his shit from?" Steve repeated.

"I don't know. I only met him once. I always dealt with another guy."

"Paddy?" Steve asked, and Caleb's eyes lit up at the mention of the name. "That's it. You deal with Paddy?" Steve confirmed.

Caleb put his head back down. Steve got up to leave. "So, what was the good news?" Caleb asked.

"That was it. You're going away for a long, long time." Steve smiled, adding "I didn't say it was good news for you."

He banged on the door. The guard opened it and Steve walked out. "Keep him on suicide watch," he said to the guard.

"I want to see my daughter!" he heard Caleb yell. "Marcus? Come on man Let me see my daughter!"

Steve walked down the hall whistling. He was in a much better mood since leaving Windsor.

Chapter 39

Thursday January 12, 2023, 10:30 am.
Hamilton, Ontario

Steve was woken up by his phone again. He was hung over and miserable.

"Yeah," he managed.

"Parent, it's Jason Nguyen. How are ya?"

Steve's mouth tasted like road tar and sour milk. "Good. What's up?"

"Listen, that girl's name came across my desk again. Sasha Horvat?" the detective said.

Steve sat upright quickly, and the room spun. He leaned his head against the wall. "Oh yeah? How so.?"

"Same officer that took the report on the 30th was called to McMaster Hospital early morning on Sunday January 8th Around 1:30 am. He saw two brothers, Scott and Brad Holland. Both were pretty banged up. Brad, the older of the two, had a bad concussion and a broken rib. Younger one had a broken nose. Both guys said they were attacked at a bar called The Outlander late Saturday night by a big guy, now dating Brad's ex-girlfriend, Sasha Horvat. The claimed they were attacked again later that evening by an unknown male."

Steve held his breath, waiting to see if there was anything identifying about the "unknown male". Nguyen continued.

"We followed up with a Carrie Collins. She was the bartender. Carrie and two other witnesses stated that both Brad and Scott were the aggressors at the bar. Based on the description we believe the current boyfriend is Mike Wolly. He defended his girlfriend. Everyone we spoke with said the big guy could have seriously hurt both brothers and didn't, much like the James Kowalski incident. Wolly defended himself and subdued them. Carrie told the officer that she heard that a regular at the bar named Mark caught up with both brothers later that same evening and threw both of them a beating. The officer asked the brothers about it, but they refused to comment."

"Do we know anything else about this Wolly?" Steve asked trying to keep the attention on Mike. "Seems like everywhere he goes, he's 'defending' himself. The guy is a fucking gorilla. Who in their right mind is picking fights with him?"

"Actually, you took the words right out of my mouth. Michael James Wolly, born February 2nd, 1990, in Windsor Ontario. Son of the late Ed Wolly, retired sergeant Windsor Police. Talked to a friend in Windsor who said Michael was a very accomplished boxer. He's been charged with assault nine times and never convicted, which means he either has a really good fucking lawyer or he knows how to walk the line close to the edge," Nguyen concluded.

"Do we know what he does for a living?" Steve asked.

"We do." Nguyen advised. "He's an ironworker. Started in Windsor, transferred into Hamilton a few years ago."

By this point Steve was up walking around his apartment like a caged animal. "Hold on, I need a pen," he requested. A minute later he repeated, "I-ron-wor-ker," as he wrote it down. "Know where he's working now?"

"No. Haven't checked. Figured I'd see if you want this."

"I do, thanks," Steve said.

"Can I ask what the link here is?" Nguyen inquired.

"I'm not 100% sure. It's more to eliminate him than anything else." Steve lied. "This group in the falls, they have hired muscle. I was tipped off to this Wolly guy, but the more I look the less likely I think he's involved. Still need to be sure though."

"Well, You might be on to something." Nguyen added. "Two of those assault charges were Windsor Police officers. One suffered a broken jaw; the other was put through the glass at a bus shelter."

"What? How the hell did he beat that?" Steve was stunned.

"Cameras are everywhere." Nguyen explained. "There was a brawl on Ouellette Avenue in Windsor. Police rushed in. Wolly was not involved in the altercation at all but happened to be nearby at the time when police arrived. Sounds like two overzealous cops saw a big guy and tackled him. One hit Wolly with a flashlight, the other stomped on him while he was down. Wolly started fighting back. The end result was one cop with his jaw wired shut, the other put through tempered glass with eighty six stiches in his ass. Whole thing was caught on camera."

"Jesus Christ!" Steve exclaimed.

"Yeah, no shit. Cops charged him with Agg assault on a peace officer, Assault causing bodily harm on a peace officer, and two counts of resisting. Apparently Wolly's lawyer got the video from the bars in the area, then went to the press, released the videos. Much as I hate to say it, they blindsided him and he fought back. The judge scolded the cops in open court, Threatened disciplinary actions. Rumor is, Wolly was smart enough to get the fuck out of Dodge right after his case was dismissed. His address, driver's license, taxes, insurance, everything is listed as Guy Street in Windsor, but apparently, he spends his life working on the road," Nguyen advised.

"OK. I'll keep that in mind. Thanks," Steve muttered distractedly and rung off.

Steve went to the bathroom and checked his home monitoring videos. Nothing worth noting. He took a shower and googled the phone number for the Ironworkers Union Hall in Hamilton. He called, received an automated voice recording and decided to drive to the address and ask in person.

The sky was clear, but the air was cold, hovering around -10 degrees. Steve stopped at a liquor store. He grabbed his usual six beers and a small bottle of whiskey and continued on his way.

The Union Hall was a big, light grey building in the center of a large commercial and industrial area on the outskirts of Hamilton. A large, rusted steel sign with a round stainless-steel logo depicting a man standing in front of an I-beam with the word "IRONWORKERS" around the top was visible from the road.

Steve walked into a modern lobby area. Pictures of various structural projects, some recent, some as old as the 1940's, lined the walls. A large glass case inside the door showed a number of thank you cards from various charities and from family members of recently deceased members. Steve walked up to the counter. A dark-haired girl in her early thirties came to the window.

"Are you a member or travel card?" she asked Steve.

"A what?" Steve had no idea what she was asking.

"Are you a member of this local?" she asked again, politely.

"No. I'm looking for someone," Steve replied.

"Oh, okay." She smiled politely. "Who is it you're looking for."

Steve was scanning the walls "One of your workers. Mike Wolly."

The girl's face seemed a little confused. "I don't think I know him. He doesn't work in the office. Give me one minute please." She disappeared around the corner coming back a few minutes later with a large First Nations man.

"Can I help ya?" the guy offered. Steve didn't realize how big this guy was until he reached the window. He looked like he was in his thirties, with broad shoulders, He had a baby face with big a bright smile. He seemed polite.

"Yeah. Looking for an ironworker. Big guy," Steve requested.

"You'll need to be more specific." The guy smiled again.

"Uh, looking for a Mike Wolly. Do you know where these guys are working?" Steve gestured to some of the more recent pictures on the walls.

"Yeah, I'm the dispatcher," The big guy advised. "I can't give that information out though, I'm sorry. If you want to leave a message for him. I'll pass it along when I see him next."

Steve pulled out his badge. "Does this help?"

"Yes. Yes, it does. Hold on".

The big guy disappeared quickly, returning a minute later with another man. The new guy was shorter and grey haired with a matching moustache. He looked to be his fifties and a held a naturally hard expression.

"Hi, I'm Rob Perrot, one of the Business Agents. What can I help you with?" he inquired.

"Jesus Christ, how many fucking people do I have to deal with here?" Steve muttered a little too loudly to himself.

"Nobody, if you don't watch your tone." Rob replied curtly. "What can I help you with?" he repeated.

Steve left out a big sigh. "Looking for Mike Wolly, where is he?" He flashed his badge again.

Rob looked over his shoulder as the big guy came back in with a clip board and handed it to him. "Mike is," he flipped then scanned the page. "Off until Monday. We have him slated to start at Dofasco in Hamilton. Working for," he ran his finger along the page, "Martel. A mechanical contractor. Shift starts at 7:00 pm. Four-day job, twelve-hour shifts." He looked up at Steve and put the clip board down.

Steve didn't like the look of the guy. "What's his phone number?" he grunted.

"Can't give you that." Rob replied.

"Address?"

"Can't give you that either. Not without a warrant. Now if there's nothing else?" Rob looked expectantly at Steve.

Steve held his gaze, glaring. He turned and walked away without saying anything else. He jumped in his truck and fired it up. There was something about the Rob he didn't like. He grabbed the bottle of whiskey to take a swig and realized it was empty already.

Chapter 40
Monday January 16th, 2023, 7 pm.
Hamilton, Southern Ontario

Mike was sitting in the lunch trailer inside the steel mill waiting for his assignment. Steel mills were an awe-inspiring experience for those that had never been in one. They were massive in size; close to 800 acres of land or roughly the size of a small town. Within the Dofasco mill were hundreds of buildings, almost thirty kms of roadways and sixteen km of railways.

Still mill life was also unique with its own culture. Shutdowns were an odd experience in trades. They could range anywhere from one day to over one hundred. Some days workers found themselves working like crazy from start to finish. Other days they'd be sitting in a lunchroom for days on end waiting to be told they were allowed to finally go to work.

The waiting was a killer. Some guys loved it, but it drove Mike crazy. The worst, in his opinion, was when you spent ten hours waiting and were told with two hours left that your job was ready to go. By then, most guys had mentally checked out hours ago and their desire to work was long gone.

Many of the jobs saw the trades workers and contractors crawling into the dirtiest, greasiest, nastiest areas imaginable. Mike had once seen a bumper sticker that said, "What you call Hell, an ironworker calls a day at work". He initially thought it was a bit of an exaggeration until he worked his first shut down in a steel mill. Afterwards he thought whoever came up with that sticker deserved a medal.

The job wasn't all bad though. Hamilton had a reputation in the ironworking world as producing some of the most diverse tradesmen and women out there. People that could put up iron, maintain car plants, move heavy machinery, and work themselves stupid in steel mills all came from the same union hall and they could all do the work no matter where they were sent.

Mike was reading a newspaper someone from the day shift left behind when his foreman, D.B., came in. D.B. was short for Daniel Brant. Most guys onsite called him "Douche Bag" behind his back. His close friends said it to his face. He had a good sense of humor about it.

D.B. was a First Nations man around the same age as Mike. Rumors had floated around that he played in the NHL when he was younger. Not one to follow the rumor mill, Mike had asked D.B. about it one day while they were working together. "I was drafted to Pittsburgh in 2013. Didn't play any regular season games though. Got drunk a lot, eventually got cut. Came back crying to my dad. Now I work iron," D.B. admitted.

"Wolly! You got your winter gear?" DB asked, walking by Mike without slowing down.

"Yup," Mike replied.

"Good. I need you to hook up with Curtis Walters. You guys will be landing on top on the furnace," he instructed, dropping two padlocks into Mike's hand.

"Is the elevator working? Or should I bring my lunch? Mike asked. Eating at the work site was only done in extreme circumstances. Men over the years had fought and died on picket lines to give trades workers the right to eat in a proper lunchroom with wash up facilities nearby. If you brought your lunch with you then you'd better get paid extra for bringing it.

"There's a lunchroom and bathroom one level down. So, bring everything with you." D.B. responded as he walked away, already on to the next task.

Mike grabbed his lunch, insulated clothing and his tool bag, and met Cutis at the bottom of the blast furnace.

Mike had worked with Curtis a few times over the years. He wouldn't say they were friends, but they got along well enough. Cutis was shorter, around five foot ten, and just shy of two hundred pounds, sporting a physique that only comes from years spent behind penitentiary walls. He was covered in tattoos from his knuckles, up his arms, and across his chest and back. Mike had not met a lot of people in life that he would be leery about tangling with, but this guy was one of them. It wasn't the tattoos or the build. It was the aura he gave off.

A few years back a younger, big-mouthed wanna-be gangster name Reggie was annoying everybody in the lunchroom with tales of how bad he was. Curtis finally had enough and told him to shut his mouth or it would get shut it for him.

Reggie, trying to maintain his image taunted, "You sound awfully sure of yourself."

Cutis replied, "I've never been more sure of anything in my life." in a tone that made others get up and leave the lunchroom. At the end of the shift, Mike watched as Reggie and two of his friends attempted to confront Curtis in the parking lot.

One of Reggie's buddies nodded at Curtis and asked, "Is this the guy?" Curtis responded with a left hook, hitting him in the jaw and knocking the guy out cold. He did it without taking his eyes off Reggie, who in turn backed away without further comment or incident.

Curtis, like Mike, was of the mindset that empty drums make the most noise. In construction trades, there was no shortage of blowhards who felt the need to constantly tell you how awesome they were in case you might forget it. Mike figured those guys were trying to convince themselves.

Mike liked Curtis for his no-nonsense attitude. The fact that he was one of the most skilled ironworkers Mike had ever met was just a bonus. The two men worked well together. Occasionally if there were breaks in the shift they would engage in small talk, but when it was time to work, they both did it without having to worry about what the other was doing.

"What's the plan?" Mike asked Curtis, dropping his gear on the ground and placing a pad lock on the board. The board held the keys for the main control console in the blast furnace. Every worker on the project would apply a lock. One lock left on meant the door on the board could not be opened, thus preventing anything from starting up while someone was still working.

Curtis shook Mike's hand after the pad lock was installed and replied, "Pretty easy night. The brick guys are relining the top section. We have two guys on the ground hooking the load on the crane and sending it up. We'll receive it, send the scrap down when its ready."

The process was known as 'flying and landing'. Like many tasks they faced, it could be fast paced and steady, or very slow and mind-numbing, depending on how fast the brick layers were working. On night shift, it was generally not very fast.

The two took the elevator to the top of the furnace. The benefit of being at the top of the furnace was that it gave you a 360-degree view. The downside was that the 360-degree view was of Hamilton. Mike didn't mind it at night. The city lights twinkled in the darkness that hid most of the neglect and grime. On a clear night like tonight, he could see the CN Tower across the lake in Toronto.

They set their gear in the lunchroom and made their way up the last flight of steel stairs to the top section where the day shift guys were waiting. They handed a CB radio to Mike. One guy said, "Brickies aren't here yet," and the two walked towards the elevator.

Mike did a radio check to make sure it was working properly. A few minutes later, the brick layers night shift arrived. They did a quick introduction and Mike asked, "How long until you need material?"

The brick foreman did a quick walk around. "Now, if we can?"

Mike keyed his radio. "We're ready up here."

Jim, Mike's friend on the ground, crackled through the radio, "Coming at ya."

They heard the faint sound of an air horn blasting at ground level. It was the universal sign to keep workers out of the area while the crane is lifting.

The view Mike and Curtis had was great. They were three hundred feet in the air staring down the section of the crane called the boom. The operator would run the cable all the way up, a full 325 feet. Once given direction by Mike over the radio, the operator would tip the boom arm down bringing the load over top on the platform.

Once the boom was in the proper location, Mike directed him to "cable down" on the load while calmly telling him "Fifteen feet." At ten feet off the deck, Curtis grabbed a hold of the tag line, a piece of one inch manila rope tied to the bottom of the basket to better control it. Mike continued with the direction "Ten feet, five feet," until the load was about a foot off the deck. "Hold that," Mike instructed. He and Curtis each grabbed a side of the basket and rotated it into its final position.

Mike keyed his radio again. "Okay, touch it down." The basket with 2000 lbs. of bricks was gently landed.

"That's good, coming down a bit more," Mike directed. The four chains with hooks on the ends attached at each corner came down a little more and went slack, Mike and Curtis each grabbed two hooks. Mike passed his over to Curtis. Mike was the radio man. Curtis had the extra hand.

"Up easy," Mike called into the radio. The operator brought the cable up a few feet until the chains were safely above their heads. "Swing left," Mike advised. The boom arm started drifting left slowly until it was over top of an identical basket full of broken bricks.

"Hold that" Mike instructed. He and Curtis let the swing in the chains stop. "Coming down" Mike said, and the hooks lowered slowly towards the basket. "Down easy". Curtis grabbed the hooks, Mike let a little more slack come down. "Hold that". The hooks stopped.

Mike reached over. Curtis had already separated his hooks from Mike's. Mike looked up, making sure he didn't cross his chains, He was told when he was an apprentice, "Any asshole can hook on to a crane, a professional does it right with no overlaps and no twists in the chains."

Mike put the hooks on his side of the basket. He looked at Curtis who nodded, indicating his side was ready. Mike keyed the radio, "Coming up easy."

The operator inched the cable up slowly first taking the slack out of the chains then adding another one hundred pounds.

"Hold," Mike said. The operator stopped. Both men stepped back from the load in case it swung towards them when it lifted off the deck.

"Jimmy you listening?" Mike checked in to make sure the guys on the ground were ready to receive the basket. "Go for Jim," Mike heard in response. Mike replied, "Coming at ya." He heard the air horn again and told the operator, "Come up easy."

The load came up and drifted about six inches towards Mike. The operator held the load there for five seconds. Nothing shifted, so Mike continued, "Run'er up. She's all yours".

The load started rising fast as the cable rolled up. The boom arm pulled back and started swinging back to the right. It cleared the deck and stopped. Mike heard the air horn again and the operator ran the cable back to the ground fast.

That was it for now. The deck was clear, and the brickies had a full load. There would be another hour, maybe more, before they'd need anything. There was nothing to do now but wait.

Mike walked down to the lunchroom and grabbed two chairs for the deck. He and Curtis sat down and chatted a little bit.

Curtis was from Ottawa originally and had a bit of a checkered past. It had gotten to the point that Ottawa police would, in his words, "Fuck with him," every time he left the house. After a bar fight that saw him sentenced to two years in prison, his wife and daughter moved to Hamilton for a fresh start. When Curtis was released, he relocated there.

Curtis stumbled into ironworking by chance. He first found a job in a small fabrication shop as a welder. The owner liked his skills and work ethic and brought him into the field.

Curtis said his apprenticeship wasn't too hard. Most guys didn't give him a hard time like they did with younger apprentices. He did all the apprentice work: he left the lunchroom early to fuel up the machines, turned on the welders, and ran the welding cables and air lines for the journeymen. He often ran back to the tool crib thirty times a day for whatever the journeymen needed.

He was offered a spot in the apprentice competition; something most apprentices dream about, but he declined. He was happy going to work, making clean money, and going home to his wife and daughter every night. He seldom went out for beers after work with the guys and was often the quietest guy in the lunch trailer. He worked hard, he was smart, and even as a journeyman he showed an eagerness to learn that kept him working.

The two were talking about boxing vs. MMA when the bricklayer foreman came out. "I think we're ready," he signaled, as two young guys pushed a full basket of broken bricks out to the deck. They left it where the previous basket was sitting and wheeled the empty one back with them. Mike keyed his radio, "Jimmy, got your ears on?"

"Go for Jim," he heard.

"Ready for another one?" Mike asked.

"Coming at ya."

Mike heard the air horn and the process repeated, dropping off the full basket of new bricks, and lowering the basket of broken ones. Mike plopped back down in his chair. Another hour to wait. Curtis went down to the lunchroom and came back a few minutes later with a large thermos and two paper coffee cups.

"Rocket fuel?" he offered, handing Mike a cup.

"Yeah. Might as well. It'll be a long night." Mike filled the cup halfway, staring at the Toronto skyline in the distance.

"Oh, what's this now?" Curtis asked, looking in the other direction.

"What's up?"

"Looks like the cops are here," he observed. Mike got up and followed Curtis's gaze. He saw two Hamilton Police SUV's.

Curtis looked back at Mike and saw his face. "They here for you?" he asked, not a hint of humor in his voice. Mike met his eyes but said nothing.

Curtis reached into his pants pocket through the side slit in his coveralls and pulled out his keys. "Black Ford Escape in the main parking lot," he nodded towards where the bus had picked them up earlier in the evening.

Mike looked at the keys then at Curtis. "Give me your number. I'll text you from a burner and make arrangements to get it back to you."

Curtis nodded and the two ran down to the lunchroom. Curtis wrote his number on a piece of paper and smirked, "If you can get it back here before the shift ends, that'd be great. Otherwise, my wife will kill me."

"I'll try," Mike promised, sticking the keys and the phone number in his pocket. "If I get it back here, keys will be in the gas cap."

"Please try. Hard. She, Not kidding she'll kill me." Curtis replied.

Mike looked at Curtis and realized he wasn't kidding. They shook hands, Mike said, "I owe you." and took off out the door.

Mike used several staircases to get back to ground level. The inside of the steel mill had a resemblance to a M. C. Escher drawing with stairs going in all direction and often leading nowhere. After getting lost a couple times he found a door the lead him outside.

He hustled across the road to where he could see his lunch trailer. The two cop cars were parked there. Shit, he thought to himself. He needed to get out of here quickly. He walked back the way he came.

During the shutdown, there were around three hundred contractors working: ironworkers, pipefitters, boilermakers, and labourers, all working for half a dozen different companies. Mike saw a brick layers truck parked on the road and quickly walked over. He chanced a look inside. Thankfully this foreman followed the rules and left the keys in the ignition. A site policy in case of an emergency or if his truck was blocking the road and needed to be moved. Mike hopped in started the truck and drove off.

There was a lot of traffic in the area; multiple contractor vehicles driving in and out of the steel mill. Mike drove by the parking lot and saw two more Hamilton Police SUVs parked inside the gate. "Shit," he muttered to himself.

The parking lot was huge, about the size of a square city block, with a chain link fence dividing it into two sections. Each section had a separate entrance: one for contractors, the other for mill employees. Mike drove around and checked out the other parking lot. There was a hole in the fence between the lots that a person could fit through. The other parking lot was empty with the exception of a few cars.

Mike drove down the first side street and parked the truck. He stripped off his winter gear, balled it up tight under his arm and walked back toward the employee parking lot. He crept around the outer perimeter, hoping the cameras wouldn't see him. He finally crouched down in a shadow created by an overgrown shrub and waited.

After a few minutes that seemed like an eternity, Mike looked back towards the main gate of the mill and watched a slab hauler drive out. A slab hauler was a huge piece of heavy equipment designed to pick-up red-hot slabs of freshly poured steel that weighed upwards of 117,000 pounds, and carrying five or six of them at a time. It was interesting to watch them drive at night because the slabs were still glowing red. As the slab hauler drove past the gate for the contractor parking lot Mike figured that would be the best time to move. If the cops had their attention on anything else tonight it would be the slab hauler driving by.

Mike crept through the opening and stayed low. Scanning the parking lot up and down the aisles, he was looking for a small black SUV. He could see a few of them, so he crawled between vehicles looking for Curtis's. On the third line he found it, closer to the back fence then the entrance.

Staying low, he unlocked the door with the key hoping to hell the alarm didn't go off. It didn't. Barely opening the door, he reached in, and tapped the unlock button, Gently closing the door he slid back and opened the back door. He'd need to be quick. He climbed in. He wasn't too worried about the cops seeing the dome light; there was a large truck blocking the view. He sat in the back seat looking at the top of the cop cars. They hadn't moved.

Curtis ran back up the stairs at the blast furnace and watched as the cop cars pulled up at their lunch trailer. He sat back down and waited. Fifteen minutes went by, and he heard the radio burp, "Wolly, come in." It was D.B.

Curtis grabbed the radio. "He ain't here."

"Where is he?" D.B. asked.

"Said he was going to the shitter. Just left a second ago." Curtis hoped to buy Mike a few extra minutes.

"Go get him. Need him in the trailer right away" D.B. instructed.

"Ten Four." Curtis replied. He sat back and drank his coffee. He waited another fifteen minutes, and the radio burped a second time.

"Curtis Walters," He heard D.B. say again.

He waited then answered, "Go ahead."

"You find Wolly?"

"No. shithouse is empty. Must have gone down." He smiled to himself.

Curtis worked by himself for the next load. Around 11:30 pm he heard footsteps coming up the stairs. He looked and saw D.B. with two Hamilton Police officers and another guy showing the tail end of bruising under his eyes, now yellow and purple. The bruises were accented by the metal halide bulbs that lit the area up, making it look like daytime on the deck.

"Where's Wolly?" D.B. demanded.

"Haven't seen him," Curtis replied without standing, "and if you find him, tell him to get back here or send me someone else. I can't land by myself."

"Where did he go?" asked the guy with the bruised face.

"Said he was going for a shit. That was a couple hours ago." Curtis looked at him, then the other two cops. "If he saw y'all coming, my guess is he got the fuck outta here." He went back to staring at the city lights.

"Fuck!" the guy with the bruised face cursed and stormed down the stairs. The other two followed him.

D.B. looked at Curtis. "He gone?" he asked in a tone that let Curtis know the answer would stay between them. Much as D.B. didn't want to call Mike down or bring the cops up, as a foreman he had no choice. None of the guys in the field would fault him. But ironworkers were still brothers. Curtis knew D.B. wouldn't rat Mike out.

"He saw them pulling in. Fucked off when he saw 'em." Curtis confirmed. "He's long gone now."

DB nodded. "I'll send someone up to help you, I need to get these guys offsite." He walked back down the stairs to the elevator. Curtis heard D.B. key his radio and say, "Anybody out there have eyes on Mike Wolly?" more for show, and to play the part of the police-helper.

Chapter 41

Tuesday January 17th, 2023, 7:15 am
Hamilton, Southern Ontario

Cutis was riding the crew bus from the blast furnace back out to the parking lot. Everyone was buzzing about the police looking for Mike. He sat quietly, looking out the window trying to see if his car was still there. As the bus pulled in, he saw it parked where it was the night before. The bus stopped and a sea of trade workers emptied into the parking lot. Curtis was walking towards his vehicle and saw the lights flash. That's odd, he thought, but kept walking. He went around and opened the hatchback. Mike was sitting in the back seat.

"Hey dude," Mike greeted, tossing Curtis his keys. "Cops still at the gate?"

"You drive a black Chevy pickup?" Curtis asked.

"I did," Mike answered, smiling.

"Yeah, they're in the lot watching it."

"Gimme a ride out?" Mike requested.

"Buy me breakfast?"

"Deal." Mike lay down and covered himself with his winter clothes. Cutis got in the front seat and drove out of the parking lot unbothered.

A few hours later Mike was sitting at the barn. He sent Sasha a one-word text: "barn", then called the Ironworkers Union and spoke to the dispatcher.

"Ironworkers," the dispatcher answered.

"Hey, it's Mike Wolly. I need to go on the waiting list. Put me on will call", meaning Mike would contact the hall when he was ready to go back to work.

"You got it. Everything good?" The dispatcher inquired.

"Not sure. Anyone call looking for me?" Mike replied.

"Nobody *"called"* he stated, adding an inflection.

"Patch me over to Rob please?" Mike requested.

"Yup. Keep in touch buddy". The call switched over.

"Ironworkers, Rob speaking"

"Rob, Mike Wolly. Thought maybe I should reach out."

"Hey Mike. How are things? Are you okay?"

"That's why I'm calling. Anything I should know about?" Mike asked.

"A very drunk cop with two black eyes was here the other day looking for you. If that's what you mean," Rob offered.

"That's what I was wondering. I'm on will call. I'll check in once this is sorted." Mike advised.

"Mike, I don't like having to tell them anything, but I have to cooperate. You understand?"

"No issue from me Rob, I understand. Sorry I brought it to the hall," Mike apologized.

"Take good care of yourself Mike. Let us know when you're good."

Mike hung up. The cop was getting closer. He still didn't know where Mike lived and definitely didn't know about the barn, so he was okay for now. Mike called D.B. next.

"Hello?"

"It's Wolly. Sorry I had to bail," Mike said.

"All good. Coming back?"

"No, man. Call the hall get someone else working. Don't hold my spot. My truck is in the parking lot though." Mike said.

"I'll call my cousin. He has a towing service on Six Nations. $150 he'll pick it up and drive it to his yard. You can grab it there." D.B. said.

"Set it up," Mike instructed, then added, "Curtis told me you covered for me. Thanks."

"Anytime. Call me tomorrow. Truck should be good by then," D.B. advised, and disconnected.

Mike sat back and pulled up the tracking app on his burner. The icon was moving. Mike hopped in the Charger. It was almost time to swap out the GPS tracker, and driving around was better than sitting in the barn.

Steve was sitting in his truck, furious. He could not understand how this fucking gorilla was always two steps ahead of him. Every time Steve thought he had him, Mike Wolly had slipped through his fingers. He hadn't seen or heard anything from Sasha in over a week. It was like they both vanished. He was told Mike was at the top of a blast furnace. Wolly had nowhere to go and still Steve missed him. Wolly's truck was sitting in the parking lot at Dofasco, so he must have another vehicle. His insurance showed a motorcycle, a 2015 Harley Davidson Street Glide, but Steve had no idea where it was stored. He'd driven by Sasha's work, but that was an office building in the middle of a commercial area. It wasn't like she was operating a bulldozer in the back.

He pulled in at a liquor store and was walking in when his phone rang the call ID read, 'Mom".

"Parent," he answered.

"We found a loophole with the natives." advised Blenkhorn.

"What's that?" Steve inquired.

"If we can connect the dots between the natives and the Scotsman, we can hit them all with an organized crime charge," Blenkhorn explained.

"Okay, and if the dots don't connect?" he asked.

"Make them!" she instructed. "We'll set up another buy. Start dropping hints and see what they say. Even if you get them to buy some of the dope, we can connect it and take them all down. Call your guy out on the reserve. See if he can do another shipment sooner. Tell him they're flying off the shelf in Saskatchewan and your buyers need more. While you're there, offer to sell him some coke."

"I'll see what I can do." Steve took a bottle off the shelf and placed it in a plastic hand basket. He paid for his order, walked back to his truck, and hopped in. Cracking a beer, he started the engine, blasting the heat. He dug through his phone and found John Sarsens' number. He sent a text saying, "Can we do another load this week?"

After a few minutes he got a reply. "No."

He sent another message. "How about next week? My guys need more."

Another minute, and another negative reply. "No."

Steve looked at his phone confused. Sent a third message. "Can we up the next order?"

A minute passed. "No."

Steve knew something wasn't right. He sent another text. "When can we meet?"

A few seconds passed and the reply came in, "Never."

"Fuck!" Steve yelled. He started the truck and patched out of the parking lot. Thirty minutes later, he pulled up at Howling Wolf Tobacco. He jumped out of his truck, slamming the door, and barged into the shop. There were a few customers inside: two older First Nations women, and one younger guy in his mid-twenties. "All of you get the fuck out of here," Steve snarled, staring at Amanda. The younger guy looked at her, she nodded, and he left.

"What do you want, pig?" Amanda asked.

"Get your old man down here. Now," he demanded.

Amanda held eye contact. She picked up her phone and dialed. John answered on the third ring.

"Yo,"

Amanda, still looking Steve in the eye, replied "That fucking cop is standing in the shop. Said you gotta get down here."

"You good?" John asked.

"Yeah. Just hurry." Amanda replied and hung up. Looking at Steve she said, "He'll be here in a minute."

Five minutes later, Steve heard the sound of a truck pulling up. Then another. Then several more. He heard what sounded like at least ten doors slamming shut. Amanda's phone dinged. She looked at the screen and advised Steve, "He's outside," a smile crossing her pretty face.

Steve walked to the door and looked out. What he saw scared him to his core. It looked like at least twenty men, from late teens to early fifties, were standing in the parking lot. All were holding deer rifles or shot guns. Sarsens was standing front and center.

"Come on out," Sarsens yelled.

Steve looked back at Amanda, her smile wide, her eyes cold. "I ain't helping ya," she said. "Better get out there. They just want to talk. If they have to come in, they'll be pissed."

Steve looked at her, sheer panic in his eyes. She explained, "Those are our Warriors, they're peaceful people. Until you give them a reason not to be."

Steve realized he was in deep shit. Taking a deep breath, he stepped outside. In less than five minutes twenty armed people had gathered, and he guessed there were probably more on the way.

"What do you want?" John asked.

"We need to talk," Steve attempted.

"You're not welcome here." John said calmly. "You're a cop. You lied to us. We've done nothing wrong. We've broken no laws." He paused. "Yet."

Steve stared at him, unsure of his next move. John added "You need to leave. Now. And never come back." With that, all the men behind him moved, showing a clear unobstructed path to Steve's truck.

Steve asked, "Who told you I was a cop?" His question was met with silence. Steve understood. These men did not care who he worked for. He started walking. About halfway to his truck, the young guy that was in the shop stepped in front of him.

"You owe my grandmother an apology."

Steve stopped and saw the two older ladies that were in the shop. "I'm sorry" he apologized to the man.

"Not to me. To her," the young man corrected.

Steve met the older ladies' eyes and apologized to both of them. The young man moved, and Steve walked quickly towards his truck. He jumped in, started it and sped out of the parking lot as fast as the truck would go.

Chapter 42
Wednesday January 18th 5:30pm.
Hamilton, Ontario

Mike's truck had been towed back to The Six Nations territory like DB promised. Mike stopped by the yard where it was being held. He spoke to the owner and offered him another $300 to go over the truck make sure there were no tracking devices on it. He then offered him an extra $500 for each one he found, knowing there was at least one that Sasha had placed on it.

From there, Mike drove to the farmhouse. He was sitting in the Charger down the road waiting for the old couple to leave. He'd checked in a few Wednesdays in a row and the couple always lefts around 7:00 pm. Mike received a text from Sasha.

"Where are you?"

"Back around 9:00," was his reply. She let it go.

Mike was listening to another audio book to occupy himself; engine running and lights off. At 6:54 pm he watched the old couple leave. He waited ten minutes, then shut the car off. Pulling his dark brown mask over his head, he made his way over to the farmhouse. He crept around slowly, peering in the windows, keeping his foot tracks inside the tire marks. From a window at the back of the house, he saw James sitting on a couch watching Wheel of Fortune.

Mike slipped back to the front of the house. Using the electric rake, he slowly opened the door. He stepped quietly through the house, staying close to the walls. Old farmhouses tended to creek and squeak; if he moved slow and close to the edges it was generally quiet.

He made it to the kitchen doorway and waited. James was still on the couch in the living room. Mike looked around and decided he needed to lure James out. This guy had to go. James was the type of man that wouldn't hesitate to attack an elderly woman. There were no circumstances in Mike's mind where that type of behavior was acceptable.

Mike backed down the hallway to the small room that held a dining room table and chairs. The room was dark. Mike reached out into the hallway and knocked a painting off the wall. It hit the ground with a loud bang.

"What the fuck?" he heard James say as he got up off the couch. He listened as James walked through the kitchen into the hallway. James saw the painting and bent down to pick it up.

Mike stepped out into hallway with his hands crossed over holding a piece of rope. He wrapped it around James' neck and uncrossed his hands, turning the rope into a garrote, He stuck his knee in James' back, holding him upright while choking him. Another thing movies always got wrong was killing someone via strangulation. People could lose consciousness in as little as ten seconds, but death took four to five minutes of steady pressure, sometime longer.

Mike leaned back, pulling the rope like the reins of a runaway horse, his knee driving between James' shoulders like a fulcrum. Unable to fight back, James blacked out in seconds.

Mike held the garrote tight by pushing his knee out. He hummed the song "American Pie" by Don McLean, eight minutes would be more than enough time. When he finished the song the second time, he let go.

Mike did a quick search around the house and found that James had been sleeping in the basement. He carried him downstairs, tied one end of the rope around James' neck, and tied a knot in the other end.

Leaning James against the wall, he stuck the knot in the closet and shut the door. James was half standing. Mike yanked down James' shorts and placed James so that his dick was in his hand. Using Incognito mode on James' phone, Mike pulled up a porn site, scrolled to a random page and started a video. He then placed the phone on a chair in front of James.

Mike went back upstairs, rehung the painting, and cleaned up the floor where James had pissed and where Mike had left boot prints. He bagged up the towels, stepped onto the porch, and re-locked the front door. Quietly, he made his way back to the Charger.

Mike drove back to the barn. An ADJ work truck was there, he parked off to the side. Sasha and her mean little dog were inside. Mike came up to the loft where she was watching the TV.

"Hey, where were ya?" she asked with a smile.

Mike met her eyes and said nothing.

"Is this one of those occasions I shouldn't ask questions?" she guessed.

Mike held her stare but continued his silence for a few more seconds. Finally, he said, "If anyone asks, we were together all night." Sasha nodded.

Mike fired up the wood stove, stripped off his clothing, and jumped into the shower. Seven minutes later he came out of the bathroom wearing dark brown work pants and a black long sleeve shirt. The fire he'd started was hot and burning furiously. He threw all the clothes he had on earlier into the flames and made sure they burned completely.

He sat down next to Sasha on the couch and asked with a sigh, "How was your day?"

She smiled and replied, "Uneventful. Yours?"

He smiled and leaned in to put his arm around her. "I needed to tie up a couple loose ends, that all."

She ran her fingers through his damp hair and asked, "Anything on that cop?"

"Working on it. That's my next stop tonight."

Mike took out a phone and looked at the tracking app. The cop was in St Catharine's.

"I have to go," Mike said abruptly. He gave Sasha a piece of paper with a phone number on it. "That's Claude. He lives at my uncle's place in Windsor. If I don't come back, I want you to call him tomorrow. He'll give you a four-digit PIN." Sasha took the paper and looked with confusion at Mike.

"That's the combo for the safe," he explained. "Keep it, all of it."

Mike got off the couch and gathered a few necessities. As he headed for the stairs, Sasha jumped up.

"Wait!" she yelled. He stopped and she ran over "I don't care what you do tonight, but please get back to me safe, okay?"

"I'll try," he promised and turned to leave.

"Mike!" she shouted, grabbing his shoulder. "Please? I love you." She said, eyes brimming with tears.

Mike hadn't heard those words directed towards him in what felt like forever. "Me t--". He stopped himself and started over. "I love you too." He kissed her, then left.

Chapter 43

Wednesday January 18th, 2023, 7:30 pm
St Catharine's, Ontario

Steve dialed Karl's number.

"Sampson."

"We have anybody on St Catharine's fire department yet?" Steve asked.

"Yes. We have a guy. He's OPP. The St Catharine's FD is going to let us drop him in. They don't like this cloak and dagger shit though," Karl explained.

"Send me his info. We can do this tonight." Steve hung up.

Thirty seconds later his phone chimed with a contact card. He opened it up and dialed the number.

"This is Decker," the voice on the other end said.

"Decker, Steve Parent. I hear you're our ticket in with the fire department."

"I guess so. What do you need?"

"Need to meet with you. We have a surveillance camera we need installed in Togo's on Church," Steve advised.

"How are we getting in there?"

"I'll explain when I see you. Where can we meet? I'd like to do this tonight," Steve said.

There was a long pause and Decker replied "There's a McDonald's at Welland Road near Bunting. Be there in thirty minutes." He hung up.

Thirty-five minutes later, Steve met with Tom Decker. Decker was a big man, around six foot four, two hundred and seventy pounds. He was in his late fifties but still in great shape He was a retired OPP, and currently worked on a volunteer fire department near Niagara Falls.

The two shook hands and Steve said "Okay, there's going to be a call at Togo's for a fire. Everyone will be evacuated. When you guys go in, there's a vent above the front door. Install this facing into the bar." He handed Decker a small, black case. "There's a battery pack with it. Plug in, point, and shoot. Battery is good for about a week."

Decker cut in, "Whoa. Fire?"

"It's fine, nothing to worry about. Just a diversion. The bar owner is in on it," Steve lied. "All you need to do is bring a multi-head screwdriver, pop the vent, and put this in there. We can zoom in and out and rotate the lens on our end."

Decker opened the case and looked. The whole unit was no bigger than a modern cell phone.

"How soon can you be ready?" Steve inquired.

"I'll head to the fire hall now," Decker advised.

"Okay, give me an hour to button up my end, then the call will come in," Steve said. They shook hands and Steve went back to his truck.

A few minutes later he pulled up at the intersection of Queenston and Oakdale, an area known for homelessness. He spotted a younger guy in his early twenties. Tall and rail thin, his face showed years of abuse, first physical as a child and now substance. He was pushing a broken baby stroller full of scrap metal. Steve pulled over and walked up to him.

"Hey Buddy. Wanna talk to ya."

The young man looked scared and backed up a step. "Wh-what do you want."

"Got a proposition for ya," Steve offered, smiling.

The young guy said nothing.

"Here's the deal. I need something done. You're going to do it, and I'll give you $100. If you don't do it, I'll throw your ass in jail," Steve proposed.

"I'm not gay," the young man protested.

"What? No. Stupid I need you to do something for me," Steve corrected. "You know the bar Togo's on Church?" The young man nodded. "I need you to go in. Order a beer. Pay for it. Then go into the bathroom, light a cigarette, fold it up in this match book, and toss it in the garbage. Finish your beer and leave. $100 in it for you."

The young guy knew about Togo's. Everyone in the area knew about Togo's. It was a place you didn't want to fuck around in. But the prospect of a $100 dollars to a homeless drug addict was something he couldn't turn down. "$100?" he asked. "Let's see the money."

Steve pulled out two red $50 bills. He gave him one. "Half now. The other half when you're done." He peeled off another $10. "For the beer. I'll be parked right here".

The young man walked towards Togo's. Steve waited. After about twenty minutes he saw the young man return, walking fast. He approached Steve's window.

"Okay, it's done," he advised, holding his hand out.

"Just wait," Steve insisted. Less than a minute later his phone chimed. It was Decker. "Call came in. heading there now."

Steve peeled off the other $50 and gave it to the young guy. He put his truck in gear and started back towards Hamilton.

Thirty minutes later his phone rang. The call ID read "Dad".

"Parent" Steve answered.

"Have you lost your fucking mind?" Karl screamed.

"What?" Steve asked in an exaggerated tone.

"You set the fucking bar on fire? Are you fucking crazy?"

"I didn't set the bar on fire. I wasn't even in there. I had someone cause a small distraction, that's all. Nobody was hurt." Steve promised, then pointed out. "You got your camera in there now, don't you?"

"Jesus Christ on a cracker, Parent. There is a disabled woman in one of the apartments upstairs. They had to carry her down. She's suffering from smoke inhalation. The bartender has second and third degree burns on her hand!" Karl was furious.

"Yeah, and if they search the video footage outside, they'll see a junkie leaving right before the fire. I told you I could get us in there. I also told you not to ask how," Steve retorted.

There was silence on the phone. Steve thought he'd finally done it: Karl was too pissed to yell. Karl finally spoke through gritted teeth. "Get your ass up here, 9:00 am tomorrow." He hung up.

Steve smiled to himself and drove back to Hamilton. What's the worst that can happen? They gonna fire me, he thought to himself. He was coming up on twenty years in March and planned on applying for early retirement sighting mental health and PTSD as his reason.

In reality, there were a few reasons he wanted to retire early. For one thing, he honestly felt like this job had chewed him up and spit him out. The other reason was if he retired on disability, all three of his ex-wives would get nothing. And that was just fine with him. Getting the stolen money back from Mike was the financial security he needed to finally walk away from a career of being told to watch criminals continue to make victims of innocent people.

Steve stopped at a liquor store, grabbed some beer and a bottle of bourbon. His plan was to go home, have a few drinks and stop by The Outlander. It was Wednesday, and he could generally find coke and someone to go home with mid-week.

He turned onto his street and was coasting slowly with a beer in his hand when he was T-boned at the intersection before his apartment. It wasn't bad, but it knocked him around.

Within seconds his door was wrenched open and the big blond guy from Togo's was standing there. He punched Steve in the face several times. Paddy rushed over. The two dragged him out of his truck. "Leave his stuff," Paddy ordered.

They yanked Steve off the ground and threw him in the back of a black Chevy minivan. The blond guy jumped in the back with Steve. Paddy hopped in the driver seat, and they took off. The whole ordeal lasted less than ten seconds.

Mike had been parked down the street from the cop's apartment. He was planning to place a new GPS tracker on the cop's truck when he watched it get hit at the small intersection. Then the driver of the other vehicle assault and abduct the cop.

"Huh, didn't see that coming." Mike said out loud, more than a little surprised. He put the Charger in drive and started following the minivan.

They made their way through Hamilton and onto the QEW heading towards Niagara Falls. Mike figured he was good to stay half a kilometer back. It was about seventy kms to St. Catherine's, and Mike was 100% sure that's where they were going.

The van approached the exit for the 406 highway into St. Catherine's. Traffic would be lighter here. Mike would need to be extra diligent to keep from being spotted.

The van took the exit. Mike followed, staying back a couple hundred meters. The van continued along the winding highway, passing the St Catharine's exits, through Thorold, before finally exiting in Welland.

Mike tried his best to stay back but when the van took the offramp, there was a red light at the end, and Mike was the only other vehicle. Mike had two choices: follow the van that was turning right, or turn left, then try to pull a U-turn and race back, hoping they didn't notice. The van was stopped at the light. A sign mounted under the traffic light showed a red light with a right arrow inside a red circle with a slash through it, telling drivers right turns were illegal. Mike opted to go left and pull the U-turn. The charger had a shit body, but the engine ran smooth, and it had a lot of power when he needed it. The light changed and both cars turned.

Chapter 44

Wednesday January 18th, 2023, 10:58 pm
Toronto, Ontario, and St Catharine's, ON

Karl Sampson was lying in bed, still furious over the fire. He'd asked Steve Parent to come to Toronto in the morning. He wasn't sure what they were going to do, but they needed to wrangle Steve in quickly. The phone beside his bed rang, startling him. It was 11 pm, too late for a social call. Unknown caller showed on the ID.

"Sampson," he answered.

"We have a problem," Blenkhorn advised.

Karl sat up, thinking the hammer was about to fall on him for the fire in Togo's. "What's up."

"The Hamilton Police chief just called me. Parent's truck was found smashed up at an intersection near his apartment. Neither vehicle occupant was found at the scene. There is blood on the ground outside of Steve's truck. His keys, wallet and cell phones were left inside," Blenkhorn informed.

"What the? Okay, I'm heading to our office now," Karl sputtered, standing up. "I'll call tech. See what, if anything, they have." Karl rung off, threw on a pair of jeans, an OPP pullover and some mis-matched socks. Two minutes after hanging up, he was in his car heading to the office.

Karl called Hardeep while driving and woke him up at home.

"Hello?"

"Get up. Get to the office. Parent is missing we need to access his phone." Karl instructed in haste. Karl always liked Hardeep. He was smart, well-educated, and usually on the ball. Karl seldom had to repeat himself with Hardeep.

"Coming." Hardeep hung up.

By 11:30 pm Karl Sampson and Sue Blenkhorn were sitting in the conference room, each calling the individual police chiefs or deputy chiefs they had been dealing with through the investigation, asking them to log on for an emergency online meeting.

Hardeep hurried into the room. He was wearing jogging pants and a University of Toronto t-shirt under a black OPP parka. He had his laptop open and sat it down on the table.

"9:48 pm, Parent was driving. The video from his phone is dark. He must have had facing down, but…" Hardeep hit play.

The screen was dark, then suddenly it was light and hard to see. Nothing was in focus, just blurring, moving lights. The screen came to rest. It took Karl a second to realize the screen was showing a view at 90 degrees; the phone was on its side.

Karl could see the right side of Steve's head. Steve was clearly dazed. The car door opened and a large man with short blond hair punched Steve in the face and pulled him out of the truck. they could hear more punches landing but couldn't see anything. A voice barked, "Leave his stuff." There was some more scuffling followed by the sound of a sliding door rolling shut. The video went silent.

"There's nothing else until eight minutes later when Hamilton Police appear on the screen," Hardeep advised.

Karl was silent. Sue was staring at the paused screen. "Fuck me," was all she said.

Mike made the left turn, drove across the overpass, then pulled a skidding U-turn as soon as he was clear. He stomped on the accelerator and sped back over the bridge seeing the taillights of the van.

Mike sped up to close the distance. They were on Woodlawn Road, and he lost sight of them as they went around a bend. Mike floored the Charger to try and catch up. He came out of the bend just in time to see the van turn left onto Niagara Street.

Mike didn't let off the gas. The light ahead was green but changed to yellow as Mike neared the intersection. This wasn't terrible, Mike thought as he sailed through the changing light. If the driver of the van was watching and saw Mike whip through the turn, it would look like he was trying to beat the red light.

Mike turned left onto Niagara Street. The van was about sixty yards ahead. Mike followed them, keeping his distance. As the van neared Thorold Road, the light turned yellow, then red. The van stopped. Mike turned right into the plaza with a fast-food restaurant at the end. The drive thru was empty. He got in line. Keeping an eye on the car, he pulled up to the order speaker. He waited, then drove ahead without ordering. He drove out of the parking lot on Thorold Road in time to see the light turn green. He watched the van passed through the intersection. Mike turned right from Thorold back onto Niagara Street and continued following. There were two cars between them, but Mike could see them clearly.

Karl, Sue, and Hardeep were sitting in the board room with the TV full of disheveled looking men, all roused out of bed. Hardeep hit play on the video and each head was able to see the clip on their own screens. The clip lasted just under ten seconds. When it stopped, each man's face was somber. The man with NRPS under his name spoke up, "Wait, can you freeze the frame with the attacker's face?"

Hardeep clicked his computer a couple time's and a grainy still frame popped up on the screen.

"That's Cameron Taylor," the NRPS deputy identified.

"Who's is Cameron Taylor?" Karl inquired.

"He's a low-level goon. Sold weed and ecstasy in high school. Got popped a few times. In his mid-twenties, he found steroids. Got a job working at a few bars as security. Fancies himself a muscle man. We've watched him a few times. Beats people up for money, that kind of thing." The NRPS deputy replied, then added, "He hangs around Togo's, actually."

Karl and Hardeep looked at each other. Without being asked Hardeep pulled up the footage from the camera they had installed earlier in the night. There was nothing showing on the live feed. The bar was closed since the fire. Hardeep backed the video up to when it first started recording. Ten minutes after the fire department left two men walked into the frame from the back room. One was Cameron Taylor. They grabbed a bag from under the bar and left the way they came.

"Back that up again, please," the NRPS deputy requested.

Hardeep went back and pulled up another still image this one a little clearer.

"Oh, fuck," cursed the NRPS officer.

"Who is that?" Karl asked.

"Thomas Paterson. They call him Paddy. He's bad fucking news," the NRPS deputy informed the group. He grabbed his phone and dialed a number. "We need to locate Paddy Paterson. As soon as fucking possible." He looked back into the camera and commented, "Paddy is a monster. Old-school bare-knuckled fighter. Meaner than a burlap sack full of rattlesnakes."

"Is he the Scotsman?" Blenkhorn asked.

"No. He's Canadian born, and no way is he smart enough. If this Scotsman you're talking about needed muscle in St Catharine's, he'd definitely hire Paddy though." He paused for a second and added, "Taylor too. If he has both these guys working for him, then Parent is in a lot of trouble."

Karl and Sue both nodded, and Sue said, "We're on our way."

Mike followed the van down Niagara Street until it crossed Main Street where Niagara Street becomes Division Street. Shortly after the intersection, the road bends to the left and crosses over a bridge. As Mike came out of the bend, he saw the van turn right onto King Street. Too late to follow it, Mike went through the intersection. There was a small plaza on the other side of the road. He turned right into it, drove around the building. He came to a side street called Avenue Place that would have brought him back on to King Street except it was a one-way, going in the opposite direction. He crossed the street into the next parking lot, sped through and came out on Young Street. He turned right, and reconnected with King st. He saw the van a couple blocks up ahead and followed it again at a distance.

About a kilometer later, the van turned into a parking lot. Mike got closer and saw it was an old boarded-up nightclub. He drove past the parking lot, but the van was nowhere to be seen. He parked up the street, keeping the driveway in his mirror. He didn't have to wait long; less than five minutes later the van pulled out with the blond guy that beat up the cop driving. Mike used the same tactics as earlier to follow him.

Steve was pulled out of the van and brought into the back of an old building. He had no idea where he was. He hadn't lost consciousness, but he was woozy and disoriented. He guessed they were somewhere near St Catharine's, but he wasn't sure. He was sitting on a stage, tied to a chair, with Paddy sitting about fifteen feet away holding a black handgun.

"What the fuck is this?" Steve asked. His nose had been broken again, his head was pounding, and he could taste the dirt and salt from the blond guy's boot on his lips.

Paddy stared back not saying a word.

Cameron parked the van in a public park a few blocks away from the old bar. He took a few minutes and wiped it down, then got out. He locked the door and walked towards his truck that had been left in the same lot earlier. As he got closer, he heard a slight whistle. He turned to look back and was punched in the face, seeing nothing but a white flash.

Cameron hit the ground. "What the fuck?" he murmured, looking around through blurry eyes. It was dark and his eyes were watering. He saw what looked like the trees moving and realized there was a large man standing in front of him.

"How many people are at the bar?" the man asked.

"What?" Cameron asked, disoriented.

Mike kicked Cameron in the chest, knocking the wind out of him. "I don't want to kill you. I will if I have to. How many people are with the cop at the bar?" he asked again.

Cameron rolled over, onto his hands and knees gasping for air. He waved one hand behind him, almost asking the man to wait a second. He caught his breath and replied with a question of his own. "Who the fuck are you?"

Mike backed up a step. "How many people are at the bar. Tell me, and I'll let you go. It's that simple. If I have to beat it out of you I will," Mike said calmly. "If we go that route, I'll kill you."

Cameron had had regained his breath. His nose hurt, but it wasn't the first time he'd been hit. He rolled forward in a big clumsy summersault and bounced up onto his feet. He looked back at Mike. "Fuck you." He took a step forward.

Mike put his hands up. If the guy wanted a fight, it was his choice. Cameron came forward. Mike set his stance and slid his right foot forward, closing the distance. With a pair of heavy hitters on, he stuck a stiff jab into Cameron's nose again. Pain shot through Cameron's skull.

Cameron backed up two steps shook his head. He was angry now. He also failed to recognize the disadvantages of fighting in a dark area. His opponent was wearing dark clothing, including a mask. Cameron could barely see his eyes let alone his head or his hands. It was like trying to fight a shadow. Cameron himself was wearing a light blue down-filled jacket with bare hands, making him much more visible to his opponent. Letting his anger get the better of him, he rushed forward. Mike side stepped to his right, while throwing a solid right hand that connected with the left side of Cameron's jaw. Cameron fell face first.

"You done?" Mike asked. Cameron, dazed and bloodied, stood back up and looked around trying to focus.

"Guess not," Mike answered his own question. Cameron darted towards Mike. Mike slid forward again, this time landing a clean right upper cut on Cameron's chin, causing his head to snap up. Mike pivoted on his left foot as Cameron's momentum carried him forward. Mike threw a left that crashed into Cameron's right temple. Cameron fell in an awkward heap headfirst, his head, then both shoulders hitting the ground at the same time. Mike grabbed him by his coat and dragged him to a cement parking barrier. He sat Cameron on the ground against it. He put his knee in Cameron's chest and pulled out a hunting knife and held it point up under Cameron's chin.

"I'm gonna kill you right now you don't tell me what I want to know," Mike said truthfully. He slapped Cameron's face lightly. "How many people are there?" He pressed the point of the knife upward, the tip cutting into Cameron's skin.

"Okay, okay, okay," Cameron conceded. "Paddy is there with him now. We're watching him till morning, making sure nobody is coming for him. Then Jack is coming."

"Who is Jack?" Mike asked.

Cameron stated back at Mike in confusion and a hint of amusement. "Jackie Stewart? You don't know who Jackie Stewart is?"

"Enlighten me."

"Fuck, buddy. You're in way over your head right now." Cameron laughed.

"What time is he coming?" Mike continued.

Cameron said nothing. Mike pushed the blade up again. Cameron gasped and quickly replied "7:00 am. He said if things are quiet, he'll be there at 7:00 am. He wants to watch the highways. Make sure the cops aren't rolling in with numbers."

Mike was still holding his knee on Cameron's chest. "Was that so hard?"

Mike then drove the knife up and towards the back of Cameron's skull, burying the blade to the handle. Cameron gargled and flopped. Mike pulled the blade all the way out, wiped it on Cameron's jacket, then walked back to the Charger.

Chapter 45

Thursday January 19th, 2023, 12:20 am
St Catharine's, ON

Karl and Sue raced toward Niagara Falls in a black unmarked SUV. Karl was at the wheel, pushing the big V8 engine hard. At one point he looked down and saw the digital speedometer reading 175 km per hour. He backed off to 160. Sue Blenkhorn was texting on her phone.

"How far out are we?" she asked Karl.

Karl looked at the GPS. "Thirteen minutes," he replied and gave the SUV more gas.

She dialed the number for the Niagara Falls Police chief. "We're fifteen minutes out. How many guys do you have ready?

"I have twenty here suited up. We're watching both Paddy and Taylor's homes. No movement. We have warrants ready to go." The voice said.

"Sit on them for now. We need to assume Parent is still alive. Start breaking down doors on empty houses and some asshole will post it on Facebook. Right now they don't know we've identified them. Let's use that to our advantage." Blenkhorn instructed.

"I have everyone on the streets looking for them. If either is spotted, they'll be brought in." The voice reassured.

"Perfect. See you soon." Sue hung up, sat back, and continued staring out the windshield. "Are you okay?" she asked Karl.

"No," he replied honestly, drifting across three lanes and stepping on the gas again. She didn't blame him. This was not good.

Mike made his way back to the boarded-up bar. There was a medical complex across the street that made a great vantage point. He scanned the old building with a FLIR thermal scope, looking for cameras or other people. He saw neither. He made his way around the back of the bar. Creeping through the shadows, he saw a dumpster sitting next to the building that would give him access to a second story window. Mike crept back toward his Charger. He had a plan now.

Karl and Sue pulled up at Niagara Police headquarters. They were greeted at the front desk by a uniformed officer who escorted them directly to a conference room where the Police and Deputy police chief were already seated.

"Anything?" Sue asked, walking in.

The chief was wearing a blue polo shirt. His grey hair was haphazardly combed, and his face was tired. "We found Cameron Taylor."

"Why do I get the feeling that's not good news?" Karl could feel the vibe in the room. It was uneasy.

"Because it isn't. He was killed sometime this evening," the chief explained. "And who ever did it sent a message."

"Which is?" Blenkhorn inquired.

"Was he working with you?" The deputy chief interjected.

Sue looked at Karl. "I assure you he was not." Karl promised, speaking for both of them.

"Well, someone beat the shit out of him, then damn near cut his fucking head off," the deputy announced, clearly frustrated.

Karl and Sue sat silent while the deputy continued. "He was found in a public park. Two vehicles in the lot: a Red F-150 that belonged to him, and a black Chevy minivan. Plates on the van were registered to a white Hyundai Sonata that had been reported stolen. There was blood in the back of the van. His wallet was emptied, phone is missing. We're waiting for more information."

"Who found him?" Blenkhorn asked.

"Some couple. Apparently, they're both married to other people. Pulled up for a late-night rendezvous and found Taylor sitting against a parking block, soaked in blood. First officer on scene said it was bad, really bad," the deputy answered.

"Maybe someone is cutting the dead weight?" suggested Karl. "They kidnapped a fucking cop for Christ's sake. If you're paying someone to do that, you either really trust them, or you plan on killing them right after to shut them up."

"Three men will only keep a secret if two are dead," the chief quoted.

Blenkhorn asked. "So, we still don't know where Parent is, who has him, or if he's still alive even?"

"Correct," the chief replied.

Mike stayed out of any obvious lines of sight and made it back to the Charger. He quietly popped the truck and grabbed a black bag before gently closing the trunk. Making his way back toward the bar, he took out a M-100 and a small utility knife out of the bag. The M-100 was a firecracker that packed the same punch as a quarter stick of dynamite and was thunderously loud. He lit a cigarette and took a couple big puffs to get the amber burning bright. Using the small screwdriver of the utility knife, he poked a small hole about three quarters of the way down the shaft of the cigarette and fed the wick through.

He walked down the sidewalk, looking like an average pedestrian, and tossed the M-100 into the street in front of the bar. He casually kept walking. He made it to the next building, ducked down the alley, and made his way back towards the boarded-up bar. He crouched in the shadows of the building next door and waited.

After about three minutes the amber hit the wick. The fuse lit and was soon accompanied by a colossal *BOOM* that shook the windows across the street.

Simple distractions were always the best, Mike thought to himself. Whoever was in that boarded up bar would have rushed to a door or window to look outside.

When the blast went off, Mike counted to seven and ran across the parking lot, leaped up on the dumpster, and hopped onto the small roof with the second story window. He pressed himself against the vinyl-sided wall and waited. He counted to one hundred and twenty. He heard nothing, no noise. He took out a small telescopic wand with a one-inch round mirror on the end. He used it to look around the window's perimeter for cameras or an alarm. He saw nothing. He moved in front of the window and started working to open it quietly.

Paddy continued to sit in the same chair, waiting. He was starting to get antsy. Cameron should be getting back soon. He pulled out his phone to check the time and heard what sounded like a bomb going off outside. He looked at the cop, pointed his gun at the cop's face and ordered, "Shut up. Don't make a fucking sound."

He walked backwards towards the front door, keeping his eyes on the cop. There was a loose board covering the window in the door. He pulled at it and took a quick look down the street. He saw nothing. No people, no traffic. Paddy quickly checked on the cop who hadn't moved. Going back to the door he looked in the other direction. Nothing there either. He waited at the door, checking back and forth while watching the cop, trying to convince himself that his mind was playing tricks on him and that the blast he heard was nothing more than a car backfiring. He walked back to the chair, keeping his gun pointed at the cop. He pulled out his phone again and sent a text to Cameron. "Where are you?"

Mike quietly slid the window up, popped his head inside and looked at the floor. His first priority was making sure the floor was there and that it was stable. His second priority was to determine the best way to walk on it without being detected; broken glass and debris could make a lot of noise. He slipped in, slid the window shut, and waited. He heard nothing.

He breathed a small sigh of relief, which came out as a visible puff in front of his face. He realized it wasn't much warmer inside then it was outside. The heat was off. Which meant the place had no power.

Mike started to cautiously move down the hallway and was just reaching the top of the stairs when he felt the phone in his pocket vibrate. It had belonged to the blond guy. Mike checked the text. It was just a phone number with the words, "where are you?" Mike texted back, "Had to stop for a shit, be back soon." and hit send. Three seconds later he heard a phone ding, followed by a voice saying say "Oh for fuck sakes." He didn't hear anybody else, but the phone and the person checking it were close. Mike would have to move carefully.

Mike found a quiet corner beside the top of the stairs and settled in. It was just after 1:00 am. The blond guy had said things were happening at 7:00 am. He needed to keep his opponents a little off-balance and out of their comfort zone, much like he did in his boxing days. At 1:15 am he saw the screen on the phone light up with another text. It was from the same number. "What the fuck?"

Mike smiled; the guy was getting angry. Mike replied, "It's cold in there. I stopped for a coffee. Want one?" and hit send. Three seconds later he heard the ding from the phone downstairs. He looked at his screen and saw the dots bouncing on the bottom of the message. "No, get your ass back here", came the reply. Mike couldn't resist poking the bear and replied, "Cop want anything?"

He heard the phone ding and the voice below say, "Are you fucking kidding me?"

Mike sent another text. "LOL. Be rite there", deliberately misspelling the word.

Mike waited, patiently listening. He could hear the man start pacing. Another twenty minutes went by. The screen lit one more time. "Where are you?" it asked again. Mike wanted to keep the charade going. He replied. "Can't do this. I'm out", and hit send. Three seconds later he heard the ding followed by the man's voice shouting "FUCK!" He heard what sounded like a temper tantrum. The guy was kicking chairs and throwing tables. Perfect time to move. While the man was smashing everything in sight, Mike moved down the stairs to the same level and hung back in the shadows.

Chapter 46

Thursday January 19th, 2023, 1:45 am
St Catharine's, ON

Paddy saw the message from Cameron and lost it. He kicked the chair he had been sitting on, picked up a small table and smashed it. He was going to kill that fucking Cameron when this was done. He stopped, took a breath, and attempted to regain his composure.

He heard the cop say, "Listen, dude. Just let me go, okay? You leave. I'll wait thirty minutes and call in. You'll be long gone by then."

Paddy marched over to the cop, pushed his chair over sideways, and pressed his gun into the side of the cop's head, pinning him to the floor. "Open your mouth one more fucking time, I'll shoot you in the face right here!"

He stomped back, pulled out his phone, and dialed a number. The phone rang and rang before going to an automated message. He hung up and kept pacing. He sent a text and continued pacing, looking out the window, then back to watching the cop. A few minutes later his phone rang.

"Yeah," he said breathlessly, answering it.

The Scotsman was on the other line "What?" he inquired.

"That fucking Cameron bailed on us. He left to get rid of the van. Hasn't come back. I messaged him. He said he couldn't do it. He was out." Paddy had, fury and panic creeping into his voice.

There was silence for a few seconds before the Scotsman finally quietly commanded, "y'aknow what, do it"." and hung up.

Paddy put his phone away, walked back toward the cop and raised his gun.

Steve saw him coming and closed his eyes, waiting for the bang. His face was splashed with something warm. He struggled to understand what was going on. He heard a strange guttural sound. He opened his eyes and saw Paddy with both hands at his throat, blood coming out of his mouth and running down the front of his coat. It sounded like he was gargling mouth wash.

Paddy fell on the floor, gurgled for another second, and then went quiet as he stopped moving in the rapidly growing pool of blood.

Steve was still laying on his side, trying to figure out what had happened. His face was covered with Paddy's blood. He hadn't heard a bang. Nobody had come rushing in. It seemed like there wasn't anyone else in the room besides himself and a dead Paddy on the floor. But that was impossible. He struggled to sit up, a futile gesture. Suddenly he saw the silhouette of a man moving out of the shadows.

Mike had been watching Paddy pace the room. A phone call had come in. Mike heard Paddy tell the caller that their partner had bailed. He saw him hang up, march towards the cop, and draw his gun.

Mike had been watching all of this through the scope of his crossbow. When Paddy started to raise his gun, Mike squeezed the trigger and released the bolt. It was tipped with a one-and-a-half-inch diameter arrowhead with three razor sharp blades, all tapering to point, designed for killing large game like moose, elk, or a grizzly. The bolt sailed out of the crossbow and hit Paddy dead center on the right side of his neck, two inches below the ear. The arrow passed clean through, slicing the internal and external carotid arteries, severing the windpipe, and shattering the vertebrae.

Paddy dropped his gun, blood erupting from his mouth and neck. He gurgled, fell over and bled out in less than seven seconds. Mike calmly walked over, picked up Paddy's gun, placed it in his waist band, then picked up the bolt he'd shot Paddy with.

"Shit," he cursed softly. "Fucked up my tip." Mike examined the slight dent in one blade on the arrowhead. He jumped up on the stage where Steve was lying on his side still tied to the chair. Mike grabbed him by the shoulder and yanked him back upright.

"Wolly?" Steve asked, struggling to put the pieces together.

"Yup," Mike replied, unscrewing the tip and placing it in a small plastic protective case.

"How did you know I was here?" Steve asked.

"Followed you," Mike answered, jumping off the stage and nudging Paddy with his boot. "You're clumsy, and you leave a trail like a snail." Mike finished nudging Paddy, satisfied he was dead.

"So, what now?" Steve asked hesitantly.

"I'm leaving," Mike advised. "It's up to you whether I call and get you rescued or leave you for the rats."

Steve was silent, waiting for Mike to state his terms.

Mike continued, "By I'm leaving. I mean, I'm going away. From all this. Away from Hamilton, away from Ontario, away from Canada. Now, are you going to let me go? Or do I leave you for the rats?"

Steve sat, quietly contemplating his options. After a minute he asked, "Why did you kill them? If you're just going to leave me here."

"What is this, twenty fucking questions? Do I need to map this out for you? You tell your boss that this fuck," he nudged Paddy again with his boot, "killed the blond guy, and their boss killed Paddy." Mike instructed. "If you're worried about how you lived, I can shoot you in the shoulder. You can say he had bad aim, I don't fucking care. I'm leaving. And I don't want you, or any of your friends ever darkening my door again. That's the deal. Your life for my freedom."

Steve nodded. He realized he really didn't like being the one forced into making a life altering decision with no chance to think about it. But this was literally life and death. "The blond guy is dead?" Steve asked.

Mike sighed, "I'm outta here." He started walking towards the door.

"Okay wait, wait. Yes, we have a deal," Steve shouted.

Mike stopped and said "I'm going to leave. I parked down the road. As soon as I'm in my car, moving, I'll call for someone to come get you."

He waited a few seconds and warned, "If you don't honor this deal, I kill you in your own home while you're sitting on the shitter."

"Okay then," Steve almost chuckled.

"No, tell me you understand what I'm saying," Mike insisted.

Steve heard the tone in his voice. After watching how easily Mike had killed a man not two minutes before he solemnly stated, "I understand."

"That goes for me, Sasha, and the old man in Windsor." Mike clarified. "Deal?"

"We have a deal," Steve promised.

"Who do I need to contact for you?" Mike asked. "You have people worried, I'm guessing. Who should I call?"

"Uh, Karl Sampson. He's, my boss. He'll be the one worried the most." Steve said, hoping it was true. He gave Mike a number. Mike stared walking towards the door and Steve asked, "What happened?"

"With?" Mike asked.

"Why do you do this? Wiping out drug dealers. What happened to you?"

Mike looked back and said, "Honor our agreement. I'll send you Paddy's boss's name." and walked out the door.

Chapter 47

Thursday January 19th, 2023, 2:05 am
St Catharine's, ON

Karl and Sue were still sitting in the conference room. The uncertainty was driving Karl nuts. They had no leads. Sue wanted to hold off on searching Cameron's house. He understood why, but he didn't like it. He stood up to walk the hallways when his phone rang caller ID saying, "Unknown Number."

"Sampson," he answered quickly.

"Steve Parent is in a boarded up old bar in Welland on King Street across from a medical complex," a voice said.

"Who is this?" Karl shouted, but the line had already gone dead. Sue was staring at him, a curious look on her face. "Parent's at a bar on King Street in Welland," Karl barked.

"Which one?" The deputy chief asked.

"An old abandoned one on King Street, across from a medical complex?" Karl repeated, unsure if it would mean anything to anyone.

"The old Gentleman's Club!" the chief shouted. They all got up and started leaping into action.

At 2:22 am Steve thought he saw a light go by the front door. He heard a something slam. Someone yelled, "Niagara Police! Anybody in here?"

"Yes! In here!" Steve yelled back "Steve Parent OPP. I'm tied to a chair." There was a loud crash, and Steve saw two Niagara Police officers with flashlights out and guns drawn. "I'm on the stage, my hands are tied down!" he shouted again, making sure they heard him.

"Anybody else in here?" one officer hollered.

"Just me and the dead guy on the floor," Steve yelled back.

Mike dialed the number Steve gave him. he heard, "Sampson" on the other end. He told them where Steve Parent was, hung up, and dropped the phone out the window as he continued driving towards St Catharine's off the 406.

He took Paddy's phone out. Pulled up the recent calls and hit dial. The call was answered right away "Yeah?"

"Done," Mike advised, holding the phone away close to the blowing vent hoping it would mask his voice a bit.

"Good," the voice said.

"I need to see a doctor," Mike gasped. "I'm hurt" "Wha?"

"McDonalds. Glendale and 406. In Thorold." Mike took shallow breaths, hoping that would help mask his voice more. "Hurry".

"Hang on Paddy," the voice said. Mike hung up.

At 6:30 am, Mike pulled up at the barn. The ADJ truck was still there. He walked in and Sasha came running down the stairs. She stopped and looked at him, noticing the blood all over his clothes.

"Not mine," he assured, seeing the worry on her face. He stripped down on the spot and hopped in the shower. When he came out, Sasha had the wood stove burning and was tossing last night's clothes into the flames. She ran over and hugged him.

"Is it done?" She asked.

"Almost," he promised. "The hard part is over." He walked over, pulled the blackout curtains closed and laid on the bed.

"What can I do to help?" she asked, but he didn't answer. She walked over and saw he was already asleep. She crawled in beside him and dozed off.

Steve was taken to an emergency room. His nose was broken again, and he would be sore for a few days, but overall he was okay. Karl and Sue came rushing in.

"What the hell happened in there? Sue asked.

"I'm fine, thank you for asking," Steve replied in snarky tone.

Karl asked "Are you okay? Physically or otherwise?"

"I'm okay," Steve answered.

"Okay, great. So, what the hell happened in there?" Sue repeated.

"Internal cleansing?" Steve offered. I heard them talking. They killed the blond guy. I didn't see it though. I don't know what happened at the bar. They'd smacked me around. I came to when Niagara Police showed up."

Sue gave him a suspicious look. "So, you saw nothing?" she asked.

"Nothing," Steve confirmed to her, then to Karl he asked "Can we do this tomorrow? I've been in a car accident, kidnapped and battered. I'm a little tired right now."

Karl nodded. "I'm glad you're okay. I'll call you this evening. We'll set up an interview for Friday." He patted Steve on the shoulder. "Get some rest."

"Hey. Hold on a second," Sue protested.

Karl led her out of the room. "We'll talk to him later."

Mike woke up around 12:30 pm. Sasha was sleeping beside him. He figured she must have been up all night worried. He got out of bed and made coffee. Sasha stirred.

"Morning handsome," she smiled.

"Did you sleep okay?" Mike asked. She nodded her head yawning.

Mike brought her a coffee and sat with her on the bed. "When this is done, do you want to get out of here? Go somewhere else?"

Her face registered confusion, then a smile. "You mean like move away? Or vacation?"

"Long vacation. With the option to become permanent," Mike explained.

"Where?" she asked.

"Vancouver Island? I visited Tofino a few years ago. I'd like to go check it out again. Stay for a while. Would you come with me?"

"I'd need to give two weeks' notice at work," she said, not wanting to leave her employer shorthanded.

"Just tell them, 'In about fourteen days, you're going to notice I ain't been here for two weeks,'" Mike grinned.

She thought for a second and smiled. "I guess. I don't think Carly would have a hard time replacing me." She was quiet for another second. "Tofino huh? My older brother is in Victoria."

"Or the east coast. I've always wanted to ride out there. Point is, right now there isn't really anything keeping us here. And with the way things are going, hiding in this barn is getting old," Mike said without going into detail.

"It's not all bad." she admitted, cuddling up to him. "When do we go?"

"I have a few loose ends I need to tie up. I don't want us to be on the run. When we go, I need it to be a fresh start."

Sasha looked in his eyes, a big smile crossing her face. "Yes. Let's do it," she agreed.

"I need to go to Windsor today. Pick up a few things. I'll be back first thing tomorrow. We can leave as soon as I'm back. Is that okay?"

"Sure. What do you need me to do?" she asked.

"Is there anything you want from your apartment?"

"Some photo albums. And the rest of my clothes," she answered after she thought for a moment.

Mike opened the safe, counted off ten thousand dollars and said "Give this to Sophie. Both her units will be empty. This should help."

"Mike, you don't have to."

"It's fine. Give it to her, please. I'm going to be heading out shortly. Can you pack up both safes? There is a black hockey bag behind the bar downstairs." She nodded.

He refilled her coffee cup and requested, "Upstairs safe in one bag, downstairs in the other. Keep them separate please."

Mike got dressed, took another stack of cash from the smaller safe, kissed Sasha and said, "I'll be back in the morning." He made his way down the stairs, then she heard him open the safe. He yelled up to her "Don't freak out!" and left.

Steve woke up in his bedroom around 2:30 pm. He was sore and needed a drink. He staggered to the bathroom, then out to his kitchen for a coffee. He started the coffee maker, went to the fridge for the milk and saw an envelope on the freezer door. He looked around the apartment, but nothing else looked out of place.

He pulled the envelope out from under the magnet. Written in sharpie, in big black letter he saw the words "Remember our deal!" He opened the envelope saw only a picture of the Scotsman. Steve flipped the photo over. On the back was written, "Jack Stewart. 129 James Street St. Catherine's Upstairs."

Steve searched for his cell phones but remembered they would both be at the office. He grabbed the landline and Called Karl

"Sampson."

"It's Parent! I know who and where the Scotsman is!" He filled Karl in on the name and the address. Karl was relaying the information to someone else in the room while talking to Steve.

"Okay, we'll go get him." Karl said.

"No. Fuck that. I'm going," Steve insisted. "After last night. I'm putting the cuffs on him myself."

"Are you sure you're up for it?" Karl inquired.

"Fuck yeah, I am."

"Okay, we'll have someone pick you up in twenty minutes." Karl rung off.

Shortly after 4:00 pm Steve, Karl, and Sue were standing a in a restaurant down the road from 129 James Street. They had been talking to the police chief over the phone.

"We've had three unmarked units watching the place. Front and back since 2:40 pm. We had the drone over top since 2:55 pm. Nobody has come or gone." He advised.

"Okay, are we good to go?" Karl asked.

On the way over, Karl had managed to get the green light to use his own Tactical Response Unit to break down the door. After having his man kidnapped, there was no argument from Niagara Police or the RCMP. The Niagara Police Tactical Unit was also geared up and on standby.

"Warrant is signed. Tell me when. We have units ready to breach at Cameron Taylor's and Thomas Paterson's. We want to hit their houses at the same time." The chief said.

Karl looked at his watch. It was 4:04 pm. "Six minutes. At 4:10 pm we go," he instructed.

129 James Street was a narrow old brick building. A cement plaque centered over the main door had the year 1883 A.D. chiseled into it. The main level had a glass face with a double door leading into an upscale coffee shop.

Next to the coffee shop was a heavy steel door, painted a high gloss black, with antique rivets. Karl had spoken with the building's owner and asked him to unlock the ground level door. When he refused, Karl informed him that the OPP would use a battering ram if he did not unlock it, destroying the very expensive, vintage looking door in the process. The man reluctantly pulled a key off a ring and handed it over.

As the building owner started to leave, Karl shouted, "Stop him!" Two uniformed Niagara Police stood blocking the doorway. "Take a seat," Karl said to the owner. "Can't have you calling anybody and warning them."

At 4:09 pm the OPP Tactical Unit was in place along the side of the building, the point man looking at his watch. When the digital display read 16:10, he turned the corner, unlocked the door and instructed, "Go, Go, Go!"

The first two tactical men to get in the door were carrying a large black metal tube with handles welded on and white lettering that read, "May I come in?" down the side. The first man reached the top of the stairs.

"OPP! SEARCH WARRANT!" he yelled, and without waiting, used the large ram to smash in the old wooden door, splintering it into pieces. The rest of the unit was right there carrying sub machine guns and AR-15 tactical rifles. They poured into the small office space with a fluidity that comes from hundreds of hours of training.

"Clear."

"Clear."

"Clear." Three different voiced confirmed.

Karl and Steven were waiting outside. They heard the "All Clear" over the radio and made their way up. Steve stepped into the Large office space and froze.

The room looked like a bomb had gone off inside, but the damage had been done before the raid. Directly inside the room on the floor to his right was a large man, Steve couldn't identify much more about him. He'd been shot in the back of the head and half his face was missing. Across the room in the far right corner, another man was sitting in a chair, four bullet holes in the chest and two in the face, a black pistol at his feet. The Scotsman was lying on the floor in the center of the twenty five-foot by twenty five-foot room, his face a bloody mess. Steve noticed the fingers on his left hand were all bent and distorted, and his teeth were laying strewn throughout the room.

"Jesus," Steve observed, taking in the scene, and the Scotsman in particular. "Someone made him try to pick up his own teeth with broken fingers." One of the tactical officers snorted a laugh.

Steve stepped over the Scotsman's body looked around room. The left wall had a four-foot by four-foot wall-mounted safe, the kind usually hidden by a painting. On the floor beneath it lay a fallen painting that had some blood on it.

Steve looked inside the safe. There were three gun impressions that were empty, and a few wrapped packages. Steve assumed they were drugs. Half the safe was empty. Steve figured it once also held cash. He used the tip of his finger and swung the door closed, on the outside was a red bloody print about the size of the Scotsman's face.

"What the hell happened in here." Karl asked, looking in disbelief.

"Someone came through that door and shot this guy in the back of the head," Steve nodded to the body laying just inside the door. "Next he killed that guy," he waved an arm at the body in the other corner, "while he was trying to get his piece out."

Stever turned to the twisted, mangled body of the Scotsman, "Then he beat this asshole to death."

Karl's phone rang. "Sampson," he answered. He listened for a moment, then asked "Both homes?" He listened for another few beats before saying, "Okay Have someone go over both." and rung off.

He looked at Steve and said, "Both Paddy and Cameron's houses were robbed. No idea what was taken. Whoever killed them was probably looking for whatever was taken from that safe."

Steve continued looking around the room. He took an inventory of what was on the desk. He was shocked to see a clipping of himself, the photo of him escorting the young girl out of the motel.

"Who did this?" Karl asked, more to himself than anybody else. Steve was tempted to name Mike but thought better of it. After all, the guy had killed five people, and broken into three homes, one of them Steve's. And he had managed to do the latter in broad daylight without Steve's camera's picking it up. Mike had done all of it in the last twenty-four hours. Steve figured his safest bet was to honor the deal. He was never going to see that money.

Chapter 48

Thursday January 19th, 2023, 6:30 pm
Windsor, ON

At 6:30 pm Mike pulled up at Nick's old house on Guy Street in Windsor. Walking up the front steps the door opened, and Claude stepped out.

"Hey, young fella," Claude greeted Mike with a big smile, the light shade of bruising slowing fading from the attack.

"Hey old timer," Mike replied. The two hugged as he got closer and went inside. The little house looked the same as the first day Mike came to live there. The TV was newer and bigger, and there were two photos on the wall: a high school graduation picture of Mike, and another picture showing Mike in a robe and Nick in khakis and a polo shirt, taken on the day of Mike's graduation. These were the only noticeable differences.

"Staying?" Claude asked.

"Just tonight," Mike said.

When Claude moved in, he took Mike's old room. Mike had moved what little he kept at the place into Nicks room. Aside from a small box in the corner, the room was untouched. Mike went into the room. The same picture of Mike and Nick with the Calgary skyline in the background was framed and on Nick's dresser. Mike dropped his bag on the bed and went back to the living room.

"I've got a proposition for ya," Mike began. "Your van still running good?" he inquired, referring to the van Claude had bought the year before his accident. It was a 2010 GMC retrofitted as a luxury camper, similar to Ed's old green one, but newer.

"Yup, tiptop," Claude confirmed.

Mike took out an envelope and dropped it on the table. "Fifty G's and my truck as a trade. Interested?" he asked.

Claude's face lit up. "Hell, yes I am!" he exclaimed with a big smile.

"Need to keep the van in your name for a while though. I'll pay the insurance," he proposed.

"Yeah, whatever," Claude agreed distractedly, flipping through the stack of bills.

"I need to use the truck for an hour though." Mike said. Claude nodded.

Mike pulled up in front of the little house with the brick porch. He hadn't been here since the afternoon Tamika was killed. He sat in the car for a few minutes thinking back to all the times he'd walked eagerly up the steps. Now, with the same feeling he'd had before every boxing match, he mostly felt nervous. He walked up the front steps, knocked on the door and waited.

He watched the curtain move and heard the locked fumbling. The door flew open.

"Michael?" Laurie exclaimed. "Michael!" He figured his sheer size was what gave him away. She pushed the screen door open. "Come in. Come in." Mike smiled at how she kept repeating herself. He stepped inside.

She closed the door and placed her hands on either side of his face, the same way Tamika had. Mike hadn't seen Laurie or Will since the day at the courthouse. Tears welled in her eyes. "Oh My God, I've been so worried about you," she admitted. "I think about you all the time. Praying that you're ok." She pulled him in and hugged him, the long-forgotten feeling of safety when he walked in this door hit him again.

"I'm okay. I mean, I've been okay." Mike fumbled for words.

"Please come in, sit down," she insisted, taking his hand and leading him to the dining room. "I was making tea. Would you like one?"

"Sure," he accepted.

Mike sat at the table and looked around. The house was the same. Some of the same pictures on the walls. A few new ones: Laurie smiling with two small kids at Disney World, more camping photos, and some beach pictures. Laurie was almost sixteen years older than the last time Mike saw her, but she looked good. She had started taking care of herself. He saw a recent picture of Will, with his high school girlfriend Katelyn and two young kids. A girl around ten, and a boy around seven.

"I saw Nick's Obituary" Laurie said from the kitchen. "I didn't see it until the day after the service, or I would have gone."

"That's okay. It was a small service. I didn't go to the after party," Mike said.

Laurie came in and set a tea in front of him. "It's so good to see you," she glowed.

"How's Will?" Mike asked.

"He's great. He and Katelyn got married. He's the HR manager for Kitchen's Construction. She's the office manager for a law firm downtown," Laurie informed him, looking at the picture. "Those are my grandbabies. William Junior and Tamika Jane," she said smiling. "What about you?" She placed her hand on his. "How have you been?"

Mike smiled. He'd forgotten what a beautiful heart Laurie had, and instantly felt guilty for losing touch. "I've been okay. Started working with Nick after high school. Been traveling all over, working. Met some great people. I just kind of kept moving."

"No wife, kids?" she asked.

"No. Well, no kids. No wife, but someone special."

Mike cleared his throat and pulled an envelope out of his pocket and handed it to her. She gave him a puzzled look and opened it. "I put it in the envelope in case you weren't here," Mike explained. There was a handwritten letter. She started to unfold it, but Mike stopped her. "Read it when I'm gone, please." She nodded. A picture slipped out of the envelope. Laurie picked it up, and her smile brightened. "That was taken the day before she...." Mike paused unable to finish the sentence.

Laurie's eyes started watering again and she smiled looking at it. "You two were such a perfect little couple," she murmured.

"I think," he stuttered. "I think I need to let this go now. Can you keep their memory alive?" Mike pleaded, referring to the young, innocent couple in the picture.

Laurie smiled back at him and said, "I understand sweetie. And yes, I will."

They finished their tea, Laurie caught Mike up on her retirement, and Will's family. At the door she gave Mike a hug, placed her hands on his face again and said, "As long as I'm here you'll have a home." She kissed his cheek. And he left.

Chapter 49
Friday January 20th, 2023, 8:45 am
Six Nations territory, ON

Mike pulled up at the barn. No other vehicles were there. He stepped inside and heard Sasha and her vicious guard dog stir. Mike looked at the bar. A large black duffle bag and blue backpack were on top. Two suitcases and a box were on the floor in front of them. Sasha bounced down the stairs, her beautiful smile showing.

"Everything Okay?" she asked.

"Yes ma'am," he confirmed. "Ready to roll?"

"This is so exciting!" she exclaimed. They grabbed her suitcases and stepped outside. Sasha stopped when she saw the big silver van. "What's this?" she asked.

"This? This is home until we get to Tofino," Mike explained. "Of course, we'll stop at hotels too." He smiled.

They tossed her luggage and boxes in the side door, then went back for the black duffle bags. Mike took the heavy one with the guns. Sasha took the smaller blue one. He opened the back door on the van, pulled the bench seat up and placed the gun bag inside. Sasha placed the smaller one in and saw a medium sized black bag already there. "What's that?" she asked quizzically.

Mike unzipped it, showing a large stack of bills. "Nest egg," he replied, zipping it closed and shutting the door.

"How much is in there?" she asked.

"Counting what we had in the safe," he said letting the "we" hang in the air. "A little over 2.3 million."

"Won't someone come looking for it?"

"No," he answered. "Nobody knew about it, and if they did, the crooks will think the cops stole it, cops will think some crooks stole it. And neither side will confront the other. The only thing we need to worry about is getting pulled over with it."

They both climbed into the van. Domino, standing on her hind legs, with her front paws on the center console looking out the windshield. She was on guard duty. "Ready?" Mike asked Sasha.

Sasha's smile was big, beautiful, and bright. "Yes sir." she replied. Mike put the van in gear and pulled away.

Steve walked back into the conference room in Toronto at noon. He was thirty minutes late and holding a coffee again. He sat down in the chair. The TV screen once more was a mash up of old white men staring at web cams.

"Thank you for joining us," Blenkhorn droned in her usual shitty tone.

"Traffic was a bitch," Steve lied, taking a sip.

Karl went through the motions, thanking Niagara Police for their fast response, providing a quick update on Steve's condition as if he wasn't in the room. They discussed the five dead bodies left around Welland and St Catharine's, congratulating themselves on the Scotsman's operation being taken down.

"It doesn't matter," Steve interrupted. They all fell silent. "He's gone, sure. But there are five guys ready to take his place. Whoever he had supplying him already has his replacement, or replacements, lined up. It's not over. It's just starting. The lower-level guys are going to start killing each other off, trying to take over. I don't know why you're sitting here smiling like we've accomplished something. We're about to have turf wars popping up all over Canada."

Ignoring Steve's statement, Sue Blenkhorn asked, "Are we able to tie in the cigarette dealers on Six Nations?"

Karl looked in his paperwork and answered, "We got a warrant for John Sarsen's cell phone history. There was no link between him and anybody involved except Caleb Tulk, and we're not sure how long they knew each other. All of their text messages have been recovered. It's 100% cigarette related, no drugs, ever."

Karl flipped another page and said "At 12:54 pm on January 11th, Sarsens received a text message with a link to an article regarding Parents' human trafficking bust, and the words 'Marcus is a cop'. Sarsens replied, 'who is this?', but that was it. We tried to trace the number. It came back to a ghost number, generated by a text app. No way to tell who sent it or from where. There was an email associated with the app but it's obviously a fake and made for that reason."

"What do we know about Sarsens?" Blenkhorn inquired.

"Leave him alone," Steve interjected. "He's a family man, and according to the Six Nations laws, he Didn't do anything wrong. We're going to waste more time and money harassing him for nothing."

Again, Steve was completely ignored. Karl replied, "His wife manages a Cigarette shop. John is an ironworker."

Steve snapped to attention in his seat. The words "ironworker" and "January 11th" echoing through his head. That was it, that was the missing piece to the puzzle. John Sarsens and Mike Wolly knew each other!

"Son of a bitch!" Steve exclaimed out loud. Steve thought about it. In the bar after he killed Paddy, Wolly had said, "Followed you, You're clumsy. You leave a trail like a snail." Sarsens received the article, the same article the Scotsman had on his desk. On January 11th, Steve had punched the old man in Windsor. So Wolly had set him up. He planned the whole fucking thing. He blew Steve's cover with Sarsens and the Scotsman at the same time! He knew Steve would either be killed or need to be saved. Either way, Wolly would get Steve off his back. And by saving him, Wolly had managed to not only get away clean, but he was also able to rob Cameron, Paddy, and the Scotsman for who knows how much money while doing it.

"The balls on that sneaky son of a bitch," Steve muttered out loud as he sat back and smiled.

The meeting ended after another thirty minutes. Steve got up to leave when Karl tapped him on the shoulder "Wait one." Blenkhorn and Hardeep left the room. Karl produced a piece of paper and handed it to Steve.

"What's this?" Steve asked.

"Your next assignment." Karl replied. "You're going to rehab for the next ninety days. Effective immediately" Steve read over the paper. Karl added. "I'll drive you there in the morning," then walked out of the conference room.

The end.

Author's Note

I want to start by saying I've never really considered myself a writer. I had a story to tell, a message to put out there, and this book is the result of that. My opinion is one shared by many: that our criminal justice system in Canada has failed victims. What we truly have is a criminal legal system, where justice is often kicked to the side in favor of procedure, technicalities, and bureaucracy. This belief heavily influenced the themes and conflicts in this story.

What I am is a blue-collar man. Since the age of 16, I've worked with my hands and my back. While most kids were delivering papers, I was laying bricks. Some parts of Mike's character draw directly from my reality. I grew up boxing and have been fortunate enough to share the gym and train with some of the greatest boxers in the world. I'm an Ironworker—a career that has given me the chance to travel, work on some of the most iconic construction projects, and, more importantly, meet some of the greatest men and women society has to offer.

I grew up in a household where my father ruled with an iron fist. The similarities between Ed and my father are real but obviously exaggerated for the story. My reality growing up, however, included listening to my dad and many of his friends—most of whom worked in law enforcement—sitting around the table, drinking and laughing about the things they had done on the job.

Those stories were sometimes humorous, but looking back, I can see that, often, they were laughing about abusing their authority and stripping away the rights of the people they were sworn to protect. Those moments shaped my understanding of power, accountability, and the complexities of those who wear a badge.

I also want to address something that may stand out to readers: the use of racial slurs and harsh language in this story. These words aren't included to be disrespectful, shocking, or glamorous. They're there to reflect authenticity—to show the reality of the world I, and many of us, grew up in. The language might be uncomfortable, but it's honest, and it's part of the environment that shaped the characters and their struggles.

What I write is real to me—and a reality for many. Life isn't always pleasant, just, or easy. Some readers may see this book as amateur. That's understandable—it was written by a man who's swung an 8lb sledgehammer for 30 of his 46 years.

This story comes from a place of harsh reality, struggle, and survival. If it resonates with even one person out there who feels unseen or unheard, then I've done what I set out to do.

I hope you enjoyed this story. It's not polished, it's not perfect, but it's honest, and it comes straight from the heart of a man who's been through a few rounds himself.

Thank you for taking the time to step into this world.